At All Costs

John Gilstrap is the bestselling author of Nathan's Run

Also by John Gilstrap

Nathan's Run

At All Costs

John Gilstrap

MICHAEL JOSEPH
LONDON

MICHAEL JOSEPH

Published by the Penguin Group
Penguin Books Ltd, 27 Wrights Lane, London W8 5TZ, England
Penguin Putnam Inc., 375 Hudson Street, New York, New York 10014, USA
Penguin Books Australia Ltd, Ringwood, Victoria, Australia
Penguin Books Canada Ltd, 10 Alcorn Avenue, Toronto, Ontario, Canada M4V 3B2
Penguin Books (NZ) Ltd, 182–190 Wairau Road, Auckland 10, New Zealand

Penguin Books Ltd, Registered Offices: Harmondsworth, Middlesex, England

First published in the United States of America by Warner Books 1998
Published in Great Britain by Michael Joseph 1998
1 3 5 7 9 10 8 6 4 2

Printed in Great Britain by Clays Ltd, St Ives plc

A CIP catalogue record for this book is available from the British Library

ISBN 0–718–14339–6

This one's for Mom, who would have been so proud.

ACKNOWLEDGMENTS

Family means everything. Without the daily love, support, and encouragement from Joy and Chris, nothing would be worth anything. I love you guys with all my heart.

I owe a thousand thanks to my good friend Bruce Navarro for introducing me to Rem Dickenson, who knows more about Congress and the Capitol than any four other people on earth. Yes, Rem, I know I changed a lot of things, but that's why they call it fiction.

My debt of gratitude to Brie Combs continues to grow without bounds. Brutal and brilliant, with a perfect ear for language, she's the only person in the world who gets to see first drafts.

My editor, Rick Horgan, saw the heart of this story long before I did. At a time when "working" editors are an endangered species, I'm truly fortunate to have the best in the business.

Agents and friends don't come any better than Molly Friedrich. She's a wizard at what she does in this cutthroat trade, yet she still has a heart the size of Montana. It can't be easy. I'm truly grateful.

AUTHOR'S NOTE

This book is a work of fiction. With the exception of incidental references to public figures, the names, characters, places, and incidents are imaginary. Any resemblance to actual events, locales, companies (existing or defunct), or persons (living or dead) is purely coincidental. For example, the fictional town of Newark, Arkansas, does not exist, and neither do the Ulysses S. Grant Army Ammunition Plant nor the Newark Industrial Park. Because explosives processing facilities may resemble one another, however, readers might think they "recognize" the Grant Plant as a real facility. Anyone so inclined would be wrong.

CHAPTER ONE

The previous body shop manager at Marcus Ford—"The Best Deals in Dixie"—was fired for wearing a coffee-stained shirt to work. That the stain hadn't occurred until *after* he'd been on the job for two hours didn't matter. Old man Marcus had an image for his employees, by God, and they'd better live up to it.

Jake Brighton had no idea how many of the stories about Marcus's tirades were true, but in his current position as spear-catcher *du jour*, the tales weighed heavily on his mind as he sat stranded in shift-change traffic from the Zebra Plant. It just didn't seem right that a town the size of Phoenix, South Carolina, should have a rush hour. He checked his watch one more time and sighed. Eight o'clock, straight up.

Damn.

According to the sign on the door, Marcus Ford's body shop opened for business at 7:00 A.M., six days a week. As manager, Jake made it a point to be at his desk by six-thirty, to greet the tradesmen as they started trickling in around six forty-five.

Jake knew from his interview five months ago that Clint Marcus couldn't abide tardiness, but he was reasonably sure the seventy-year-old widower would look the other way just this once. Two months ago Jake had given a leg up on the waiting list to Lucas Banks, an obscenely wealthy local attorney whose family vacation had been threatened by a fender-bender. According to the letter of praise sent to Marcus, "Jake Brighton and his team are the best in the business, and you can count on me as a devoted customer forever."

The letter had stretched Marcus's scowl into a rare smile. "It's about time we got a decent man in this slot," he'd said at yesterday's weekly employee meeting. "Keep this up, Jake, and you'll have one hell of a future here." High praise, indeed, from a man known to roast managers for sport.

The sound of the applause still rang in Jake's ears. Sure, Jake knew that his coworkers' enthusiasm was as mandatory as the attendance, but he'd seen genuine pride in their faces, and the feeling it brought to his gut was the kind that made all the bullshit seem worthwhile. Even though he was the one singled out for credit, he'd made it clear during his impromptu speech that the letter wasn't about him but the team he'd assembled. It was truer than it was false.

His spirits had been floating so high last night that he took off a half hour early to celebrate with his family.

Ah, well. The best laid plans of mice and men . . .

Titles aside, the one who really ran the shop was Mae Hooper, Jake's spherical, seventy-six-year-old office manager, who'd managed to outlive two husbands and three of her five children. The bet was two-to-one among the body men that full-time exposure to Mae's nagging had simply sucked away her family's will to live. After twenty-two years at Marcus Ford, though, the woman had forgotten more about the body shop business than Jake would ever learn, and he knew better than to cross her.

Finally, he arrived. By parking his Subaru on the street, alongside the chain-link fence, he left the few spaces out front for customers. Old man Marcus didn't like seeing what he termed "Jap crap" parked in his lot, anyway.

As Jake climbed out of his car into the fifty-degree morning air, he offered up a little prayer that his wheels would still be waiting for him at the end of the day. In this western corner of Phoenix, a vehicle left out on the street was always vulnerable, but as long as he had it inside before sunset, he thought he'd be okay. Any later, though, and the odds plummeted. Just three weeks ago the Exxon station on the corner had been robbed in broad daylight by three gang-bangers in ski masks. No one was hurt, but the bad guys were still on the loose, and as far as Jake was concerned, any crook brazen enough to point shotguns at people in the middle of the day wouldn't think twice about boosting a car.

So much for the tranquillity of small-town America.

Jake stepped inside quickly and shoved the door closed, the slap of sleigh bells against the glass announcing his arrival. It was autumn now, and the body men had already warned him that Mae Hooper hated drafts. It was one thing if a customer was a bit slow with the door—they escaped with a pointed reminder—but a coworker committing the same offense received a withering rebuke. To compensate for the inevitable lapses, Mae kept the thermostat in the lobby cranked to seventy-five, with a ceramic heater at her feet, year-round, set on broil.

The temperature shock took Jake's breath away, and he quickly stripped off his jacket. "Jeez, Mrs. Hooper," he said. "Can't we get some heat in here?"

Mae missed the irony entirely. She simply gave a sympathetic shrug and produced a cup of coffee for her boss. "Here you go, Jake. Cream and three sugars." Those eight words had been her morning greeting every day for nearly five months now.

After hanging his jacket, he gratefully accepted the cup. "Thanks. Hey, the lobby looks great."

Somewhere between the time when he left last night and returned this morning, Halloween had arrived at the shop. A display of cornstalks and pumpkins stood where an end table used to be, and a paper string of interlocking ghosts and witches drooped along the front of Mae's receptionist station. The place looked great; homey, even. Jake was beginning to think that maybe the renovation work they'd just completed hadn't been a waste of money, after all.

Mae gave him one of her condescending, grandmotherly smiles. "Well, somebody has to take care of this place."

For years, Clint Marcus had resisted the trend among shops to make themselves look more like doctors' and lawyers' offices. According to the experts, you had to appeal to the tastes of women these days. Torn sofas and dusty end tables just didn't cut it anymore.

Marcus finally fell in line, but not until his competitors had started face-lifting their own shops and siphoning away his customers. He'd gutted the place. New, bright-white Sheetrock replaced the dingy old paneling, and he authorized new office space for both the manager and Mae, even fulfilling her request to have a sliding window between the two. That way, she could nag without leaving her seat. The old man had even installed a little play area to keep the kids entertained while mom and dad conducted business. When it was all done, the place looked great. Now, with the addition of Halloween decorations, it was downright cheery.

"When did you do all of this?"

Mae combed through a file, pretending to search for something. "I was busy decorating while you were busy being late."

He smiled. "Well, it's appreciated. You've got quite the touch."

She waved him away with a little huffing noise and quickly changed the subject. "So how was last night? Was Carolyn surprised to see you?"

Jake scoffed and rolled his eyes. "*Relieved* is more like it," he said. "Travis got into another fight yesterday. At school. Seems some kids were razzing him in the cafeteria, and he took it personally."

"Was it that 'trailer park' crap again?" At one level, Mae was everybody's mother, and she'd been tracking Travis's rocky adjustment to the eighth grade very closely.

"What else? According to Travis, the kids from 'Snob Hill' just won't let up on him. Yesterday the Lampier kid unloaded on him in front of some girls. When they started giggling, Travis stood up and punched him in the face." His features lightened as he shared a bit of Travis's pride. "By all accounts, it was a one-punch fight."

"Well, what was he *supposed* to do?" Mae protested, making a face. "Just stand there and be a wimp?"

"Well, according to the principal, Mr. *Menefee*"—Jake said the man's name as if it smelled bad—"wimpy is in these days. Getting along is more important than being right."

"And that's exactly what's wrong with this country!" She shook her head in disgust.

Jake suppressed a smile. Mae had a knack for turning every little injustice into evidence of civilization's collapse. "Well, it didn't end there," he went on. "While Travis was on his way home, the Lampier kid's older brother got the drop on him and beat him up pretty good."

Mae gasped.

"Nothing broken, fortunately, but he's pretty sore. This morning he didn't want to go back to school out of protest. Seems he doesn't think anyone will discipline the Hill kids who beat him up. He came around, though, when Carolyn finally remembered that this is field trip day."

"I don't blame him for being upset," Mae agreed, ignoring her ringing telephone. "It's just not fair anymore. You know, when I was a little girl—"

Jake interrupted by pointing to the phone. "You gonna answer that?" He hated to be rude, but he'd already heard all he cared to about Mae's childhood. She took the hint, and as she reached for the receiver, he disappeared around the corner into his office.

No sooner had he sat down than Mae's face appeared in the window, smiling a snaggle-toothed grin. "Dr. Whittaker's on line one for you. You know, the Mercedes?"

Jake made a show of grimacing. "Already? I just talked to him last night."

She laughed. "Surely, you don't think this is the *first* time he's called this morning. I think he wants to bargain some more."

Two weeks ago the good doctor had run his Mercedes into a concrete drainage ditch at better than thirty-five miles an hour, busting everything forward of the fire wall. Now he was furious that his car wasn't ready yet. He was a cardiologist, don't you know—way too important to be without his preferred transportation.

Jake reached for the blinking extension, but movement outside drew his attention to the front windows. People seemed to be gathering, even as they tried to stay out of sight. One of them had a gun.

Shit!

The lobby doors exploded open, releasing a flood of heavily armed men into the reception area. Jake instinctively jumped to his feet and yanked open the top right-hand drawer of his desk, snatching out his snub-nosed .44.

"Federal officers, don't move!"

The words boomed like a cannon. Jake jumped as his stomach fell. He moved to drop the revolver back into the drawer but hesitated. Then it was too late.

"Gun!"

He watched in horror as a dozen submachine guns swung around to bear down on him.

Mae shrieked as men in blue windbreakers pushed her to the floor and assumed shooting positions, aiming their stubby weapons through the Plexiglas window at her boss. Jake just stood there, unmoving, with his chrome-plated magnum pointing at the ceiling.

"Put it down!" the lead gunman commanded.

The voice startled Jake almost as much as the command itself. Somewhere under that helmet and SWAT gear was a woman.

Two of the cop's cohorts darted out to flank their target and get a better angle. "Put the gun down! Now! Let me see those hands! *Now!*"

He didn't know what to do. His stomach cramped with fear. If he tried to shoot, they'd drop him in an instant. Ultimately, his hands decided for him. As he gently laid the weapon on his desk, he wondered how they'd found out.

"That's it," the leader encouraged him. "Right. On the desk, just like that. Now keep your hands where I can see them, and come to the door."

Jake faced his palms forward at elbow height, his fingers splayed wide, as he sidestepped from behind his desk and toward his office door. Slow, deliberate movements were his single best insurance policy against a catastrophic trigger-pull.

"There you go," the cop urged. "Just keep moving. Right. Just like that. Good man. Just like that."

The instant Jake crossed the threshold, he was gang-tackled by three SWAT team types: the two he'd seen flanking their boss, and a third who'd escaped his notice altogether. They took him down hard, first to his knees, then face-first into the carpet, driving the breath from his lungs. From the other room, Mae screamed again. Someone put a knee on his face to keep him from moving, while the others bent his arms until the backs of his wrists touched behind him.

Jake didn't fight. Arrest was a given at this point. The only true variable now was the number of bruises he'd sustain in the process. He felt the ring of the handcuffs against his skin and winced in anticipation of the pain he knew was next. They didn't let him down, ratcheting the bracelets tight.

"Stay put," somebody told him.

No problem, Jake thought. As he lay on the brand-new maroon carpet—not yet four months old—the acid stench of the fibers irritated his nose. He fought back the urge to sneeze and tried to make the pieces fit in his mind.

We've been so careful.

A pair of black combat boots appeared in front of his face, obliterating any other view. "You Jake Brighton?"

Jake strained to look up at the lady cop who'd threatened to shoot him only a minute before. "Yeah. Who are you?"

"I'm Special Agent Rivers with the FBI. We're here to search your premises for illegal contraband." She'd stooped down to display the warrant, but Jake stared right through it.

His mind reeled. *What the hell . . .*

"And *you* are under arrest for assaulting federal officers."

Oh, this wasn't right at all. He craned his neck to get a better look at his captor, then abandoned the effort. "You mind if I sit up?"

A hand around Jake's bicep helped to bring him to his feet and over to a visitors' chair in the waiting room. Jake couldn't believe the number of cops who continued to swarm into his shop. There had to be fifty of them, split evenly between FBI and DEA, with a few locals thrown in. The place seethed with activity. Beyond the heavy fire door at the other end of the waiting room, he could hear the feds rousting the body men and painters out in the shop.

Maybe the situation wasn't as bad as he'd initially thought. DEA meant drugs.

Rivers started to walk away, but Jake called after her, "What the hell's going on here?"

Her lips bent into a humorless smile as she lifted her Kevlar helmet off her strawberry-blond hair. "This is what you call a drug raid."

Mae gasped, clasping both sides of her face with sausagelike fingers. "Oh, my goodness! Drugs! Here?" From the look on her face, she'd rather have believed that Eleanor Roosevelt was a prostitute. "That's not possible! You tell her, Jake! That's just not possible!"

He smiled uncomfortably. Mae had lived here in Phoenix since 1920, and despite her overall dyspeptic attitude, she still saw green grass under the sooty streets and happy families among the homeless bums on the corner.

"You think *I'm* involved in drugs?" Jake asked, bewildered.

"*Are* you? I think a lot of people who work for you are." Rivers picked up the warrant and riffled through the pages. "I've got a Martinez, a Willis, a MacGonegal, and a Hummer. You know them?"

He nodded. His whole goddamn paint department. He should have guessed. "Selling or using?"

"Both."

Shit. The paint crew was the one part of his team he'd regarded as a sore point. There wasn't a man among them he hadn't threatened to fire in the past five months. You name the offense: short attention spans, sloppy work, irregular hours. Classic druggie behavior. How could he have missed it?

Mae still didn't get it. "Well, why is Jake under arrest?"

"Because he tried to shoot me," Rivers answered coolly—gleefully almost.

Mae rolled her eyes. "If he'd tried to shoot you, you'd be dead now."

Jake closed his eyes and sighed. "Um, Mrs. Hooper—"

"I'm serious," the old woman persisted. "I haven't shot a gun in fifty years, but at this range, even *I* couldn't miss."

Rivers glared at her. "Maybe your boss didn't like what would happen *after* he shot me." She nodded at a grim-faced, machine-gun-bearing DEA agent standing a few feet away.

"Oh, come on, Rivers," Jake objected. "Take a look at this neighborhood, will you? Wouldn't you be a bit on edge if a thousand people rushed into your office with automatic weapons?" Without even thinking, he'd stumbled upon his defense.

Rivers measured him with a glare. "We identified ourselves."

"And that's why I *didn't* shoot." He winced a little, cursing himself for pushing too hard.

She chewed on her cheek and regarded him one more time. "I'd like to believe that, but you know what? You hung on to that weapon just a little longer than I liked." She started to say something more, then stopped. She had more pressing matters to attend to. "Now, you just keep your butt planted while we do what we need to do. We'll be transporting you and the others shortly."

Alone there on the well-padded chair, amid the raucous noise of the body shop being turned upside down, Jake avoided eye contact, humiliated yet terrified. The decorations in the corner seemed to mock him: a monument to his naive belief that a man could truly move beyond his past. Obviously, the cops didn't yet understand, but that was just a matter of time, wasn't it? Jaywalking or murder—once they processed his fingerprints, it'd be over.

Calm down, he told himself. *Panic will kill you faster than anything else.*

His thoughts turned to his family, and as they did, fear gripped his stomach hard. Was there still time to get word to Carolyn? And Travis. God, how was he ever going to explain this to Travis?

"Mrs. Hooper, would you get my wife on the line, please?" He was surprised by the calmness in his voice.

"I can't," she said. Mae always squeaked when she was agitated, and right now her voice was shrill enough to shatter glass. "These bozos have cut off the phones." She tossed her hands in the air, nudging her reading glasses even further down her pudgy nose. "You know, I could have told you those boys were trouble. From the very first day, they've never given you an honest day's work."

Oblivious to Mae's yammering, Jake inventoried all that he was about to lose. God *damn*. He closed his eyes and sighed. *I thought we'd made it.*

As Rivers and her cohorts executed their search warrant with all the zeal of a demolition crew, he tried to anticipate the next step, wishing every second as he leaned forward to keep pressure off his hands that his captors had been gentler with the cuffs. He could count each beat of his heart by pinpoint throbs in the tips of his fingers.

Clearly, they didn't recognize him yet. Amazing what a few years, a few pounds, and a full beard could do for you. He figured he had three hours—five at the most. No way would it take them any longer than that. When they finally got around to fingerprinting him, the fuse on his future would grow dangerously short.

He wondered if he and Carolyn still owned the top slots on the Ten Most Wanted list.

CHAPTER TWO

Crazy Pumpkin Days at Perkins' Discount Department Store ran 120 hours straight, from Tuesday through Saturday, bringing wild-eyed bargain hunters into Phoenix from three states. They gathered at the front doors in a formless crowd, beginning around eight, waiting for the opportunity to trample store manager Phyllis Bly the instant she turned the dead bolt.

As Carolyn watched the tidal wave of humanity flood the aisles at precisely nine o'clock, she realized she was in hell. Like so many locusts, they swarmed every department. Within a half hour, clothes littered the floors and display racks as frantic shoppers unwrapped shirts and pants and shoes and sporting goods equipment, only to find that they didn't fit, they didn't look right, or they didn't perform to expectations. With one mess made, they'd move on to make another.

After nearly two hours in the arena, Carolyn felt like she'd been playing linebacker. As a contingent, salaried employee, Carolyn spent her days moving from department to department, filling in for whoever might be missing in action. Because she hadn't been with the store long enough to qualify for commissions, five percent of everything she sold was split among the tenured union employees in her department, making her presence a pain on a slow day and a boon on a busy one.

This morning she manned the Boys' Department, where countless moms dragged their truant children around by their ears, hoping to fit them into one last bargain before the Christmas shopping season began. At the moment, she was leaning against the wall outside of the fitting room, trying to make herself comfortable as an enormous Italian woman negotiated with her eight-year-old over the purchase of a two-piece suit.

The poor little kid looked ridiculous in the triple-knit navy-blue monstrosity. "Do you think it fits okay?" the woman asked, mistaking Carolyn for an ally.

"Well, that depends." Carolyn didn't bother to suppress her smile. "Do you expect him to gain fifteen pounds before the weekend?" The suit was the last of its kind on sale for $39.95, and the family had a wedding to go to on Saturday. On a different day, Carolyn might have considered lying just to make the sale, but a morning of full-contact competitive shopping had soured her mood. Besides, he looked like he'd been eaten by a polyester gorilla. She just couldn't do it to him.

The mother scowled. "It doesn't look *that* bad, does it?"

Clearly, there was only one right answer, but Carolyn held her ground. "Ma'am, I wish I could say something positive, but I think it looks way too big."

The kid saw his chance. "See? C'mon, Mom," he whined. "I look like a dork in this. I don't wanna go to the stinkin' wedding, anyway."

The mother shot a lethal glare at Carolyn but ultimately caved in. "Okay, then, try on the gray one."

"Mom!"

"Michael, just do what you're told," she commanded. "And don't back-talk me."

The kid stomped his foot once, then yanked the charcoal-gray suit from the rack and dragged it and himself into the dressing room. "I *hate* weddings," he fumed as he disappeared.

The woman folded her arms and glared down her nose at Carolyn. "It wouldn't hurt if you could be a little helpful," she snorted.

Carolyn smiled as politely as she could. "I'm sorry, ma'am, but it would have been child abuse to send him outside in that suit. You asked for my opinion and I gave it. If that's—"

"Is there a problem here?" Phyllis Bly had materialized out of nowhere.

"I don't think so," Carolyn said defensively.

"Let's just say that your help is not being very helpful," Michael's mother tattled.

"I'm sorry to hear that," Phyllis said. As a manager, she seemed constantly at war with her employees, and the look she shot at Carolyn told her there'd be hell to pay later. "Well, I'll be happy to take over."

"I beg your pardon?" Carolyn was stunned—not that Phyllis was angered, but that she was actually going to work the floor.

"You have a phone call," Phyllis explained. "It's your husband, and he says it's important." Upon taking over control of the Phoenix store, one of Phyllis's first efficiency improvements was to disconnect the register phones from the central switchboard. That way, all incoming calls went to the Customer Service Department, and all outgoing calls could be relegated to the three pay phones in the employees' lounge.

Carolyn's stomach constricted at the news. Jake *never* called her at work. She assumed it must be Travis. *I knew we should have taken him to the emergency room for his head.* "Uh-oh," she groaned. "I'll be back."

"Don't make this a habit," Phyllis called after her, as if one in a row was a trend.

Carolyn controlled the urge to shove people out of her way as she fought through the hordes of shoppers. Customer Service sat all the way in the back of the store, in the opposite corner from the Boys' Department. Three minutes felt like ten by the time she got buzzed in behind the counter and reached over one of the customer service reps for a telephone. She ignored the dirty look as she stabbed the blinking light. "Jake?"

"Carolyn!" His tone was urgent; borderline frantic. "Where have you been? I've been hanging here for—"

"Is Travis okay?"

"Huh? Oh, yeah. He's fine, I guess. Listen—"

"Oh, thank God." Relief washed over her like a refreshing dip in the pool. Then annoyance rushed in to fill the vacuum. "Why are you calling me, then? Phyllis already—"

"Carolyn, *listen* to me. I've been arrested."

She distinctly heard the edge in her husband's voice—a tone from a distant past. His words were like a cutlass, lacerating her soul and leaving her instantly light-headed. She sat heavily on the desk. "Oh, my God," she gasped. They were the only words she could think of. Long-suppressed terrors flooded her brain as a wave of panic rose high and broke over her soul.

"Carolyn, *listen* to me, dammit!" Jake's voice was a whispered shout, and she realized that he'd been trying to get her attention. She could barely hear past the blood rushing in her ears. "You can't panic on me, honey," he whispered. His tone softened as he regained her attention. "Are you there?"

She nodded, oblivious to the tears that she blinked onto her cheeks. "Yes," she croaked. "Oh, my God, Jake, what's going to happen to Travis?" The thought of her little boy being raised by strangers was too much. How would he ever survive if his parents went to prison?

The realization that people were listening hit her with a jolt, bringing her to her feet and prompting a nervous glance toward the line of CSRs, who quickly looked away. What had she said aloud, and what had she simply thought? What could they know? Suddenly, she was horribly aware of the fish-eyed security camera overhead, and she turned her back on it.

"I'm at the police station now," Jake stated as calmly as he could. "They've got me on some bullshit assault charge, but I think Lucas Banks is talking them into letting me go."

There was something in the measured pace of Jake's words that ended the disastrous scenarios whirling through Carolyn's head. He was trying to tell her something without telling her, but she'd missed it in her burst of panic. She wrestled with her mind to bring order to the random flurry of useless thoughts. They'd planned for this moment, practiced even, though not in a long while. Everything was in her head somewhere, but she was having trouble making it come back.

"I—I'm sorry, Jake," she said, steadily gaining control. "Say that again."

Now she could hear the smile in his voice. He knew now that she'd know what to do. "I said, I'm here on assault charges, but I think they'll be letting me go."

An endless list of questions fought to paralyze Carolyn's brain, but she pushed them aside. Only one thing mattered now. "Are you being *charged* with anything?" Now, *that* question turned some heads.

"Yes. But only with the assault. They've already fingerprinted me, but Lucas Banks said they should be letting me go soon. Own recognizance, if he gets his way."

It didn't make sense, but she knew that Jake would not misspeak under these circumstances. She had no idea who Lucas Banks was, or why he'd be helping Jake, but none of that mattered much right now. It was time to fight or flee.

"So you should be home?" she asked. Suddenly, she was precisely aware of every word she uttered.

"Why don't you just go on with your usual day, and I'll catch up with you."

"Usual?" Clearly, Jake couldn't talk, but she still had to be sure.

"Yeah, usual. You know, what you've always planned to do today."

Got it, she didn't say. "And you?"

"Do what you've got to do," he urged. "And if I get hung up here and can't meet you, then you might have to pick up some slack for me. You'll know."

And that was it. The nightmare had begun. She felt ill, and for just a short moment, she wondered if she might throw up right there on the CSR's burnt-orange suit. With nothing left to be said, she paused before hanging up. "Jake?" she said softly.

"Yeah, I know," he said. "I love you, too."

*   *   *

Everyone stared. Not just the customer service reps—and God knew they had a right—but everybody in the store. She'd see them looking away just as she turned to lock eyes with them. Somehow they all knew. Was that even possible?

Of course not. You're just being paranoid.

She felt the panic welling up from somewhere deep in her gut, and she did her best to will it away. Suddenly, her mind was blank. There were a thousand things to do, but she couldn't remember a single one of them.

One step at a time, she told herself. *Step one: get the hell out of here.*

Where was her purse? In her rush to answer the phone, she'd left it in the drawer under the cash register. She considered leaving it there, until she remembered that it held her car keys.

Their plan started to come back to her. First she'd go get Travis out of school, then . . .

"Oh, my God!" She said it at a whisper, but loudly enough to draw the attention of a shopper at the cosmetics counter.

"Are you okay, dear?" the woman said.

The field trip! Carolyn just looked at her, then quickened her pace. *Oh, God . . . Oh, God . . .*

There was a way to do this; there had to be. Nothing was going per plan—*nothing*. But that was okay as long as no one panicked. She'd just have to change the order of things a bit. There was plenty of time to think. Plenty of time. Okay, so how come she couldn't make her brain work?

"Where have you been?" Phyllis snapped as Carolyn returned to her workstation. "I hope you told your husband that this is a place of business, not some—what are you doing?"

Carolyn hip-nudged Phyllis from in front of the cash register and removed her purse from the drawer.

"It's not your break time!" Phyllis said, drawing looks from shoppers. "You get back here right now!"

Carolyn never said a word. Her mind was elsewhere, reliving the terrors of her past, wondering how this could have happened again.

An assault charge? Isn't that what Jake had said? Who on earth did he assault? She chastised herself for not paying closer attention.

The escape plan was built around a single theme: family first, at all costs; everyone and everything else second. Carolyn's first mission, then, was to retrieve her son from school. Even without Jake, she and Travis could make a go of it. Jake was resourceful—brilliant, even—at these things. If they couldn't make the initial rendezvous, he would figure out a way to catch up. But Travis was still a boy. He had no idea what awaited him. He'd have to be taken care of, guarded and protected.

Damn that field trip.

With family accounted for, the next priority was to obtain the tools for survival. Life would be harder where they were going. She shivered at the memories of their previous life in hiding as they learned how to disappear; taking refuge in safe houses owned by her Uncle Harry's "business associates."

They'd learned a lot about survival in those days. A little ferret of a man who called himself Lanford "Lanny" Skiles taught them the art of disappearing. A street-smart forger-embezzler with bulbous eyes, Lanny had worked for days to change everything about them—all the intangibles. New speech patterns, new tastes in food, new dreams, new fears, were all drilled into them to the point where reality became blurred.

Thus, Jake and Carolyn Donovan ultimately became Jake and Carolyn Brighton, leaving the first names the same because, experience demonstrated, responding to them is too ingrained a habit. Early on, Jake suggested leaving the country, but Lanny said no. *Hell* no, in fact. You needed a passport to leave the country, which in turn required a birth certificate. Photos would be more carefully scrutinized, and the FBI would be reinforced by State Department investigators. Each additional step—each new involvement by law enforcement agencies—represented one more chance to screw up.

"Absolutely not," the ferret had insisted. "You and Miss Muffet here"—he gestured toward Carolyn—"are better off sticking to a country where you know the ropes. But that doesn't mean goin' back to your old stomping grounds. You better make damn sure to stay clear of anyplace you visited prior to going on the run. And don't even think of calling the 'people who knew you when.' Do that and you're toast."

Carolyn was the one who noticed that Lanny never said the word "Donovan" in their presence. If differentiation was needed between their old and new identities, he'd always say "back when you were in the world."

Some attributes, however, remained unchangeable in the short term, and they became the weakest links in their new identities. Height, weight, and fingerprints, for example, were not forgeable, though over time, age took care of two out of three. People on the wrong side of the law had tried for years to alter their fingerprints, but never with any meaningful success. About the best you could hope for was a lot of pain and a collection of scar tissue that would draw more attention than the original prints themselves.

The art of disappearing hinged entirely on one's ability to be so normal as to deny people the desire to ask probing questions. "You've got to live like Mr. and Mrs. John Fuckin' Doe," Lanny had told them a thousand times. "No one ever questions a white shirt with a blue suit, but get all snazzed up and you may as well be wearing a sandwich board: LOOK AT ME." No bow ties, no flashy dresses, no expensive anything—not that they could have afforded much, anyway.

And, of course, no kids.

Well, they'd drawn the line on that one. Truth be known, Travis was an accident. Once conceived, however, they saw him as their gift from God. In a world of deception and pain, he was their one source of genuine pleasure and pride. Carolyn shuddered at what he was going to think of them when he heard the truth.

But these were thoughts for another time, she told herself as she slid in behind the steering wheel of her Celica. At the moment, she needed to focus on necessities: tools and weapons and food and clothing. All of these things were packed in the staging area, ready to go. The question that plagued her now was whether there'd be time to collect them. There were supplies back at the trailer, all packed in duffel bags and stored in a locked closet, but she didn't dare go back to the only address the police would know. Those things were gone forever now; special things. In blatant violation of the rule against mingling identities, she'd sneaked a couple of old photos into those bags, along with one of Travis's favorite teddy bears from way back when. It hurt to leave them behind.

Every second that ticked by was a liability, and they were prepared to survive with nothing but their family and the clothes on their backs. Everything else was gravy.

Well, everything but money. Cash was the one ingredient that made everything else work. Jake always talked big, swearing that if push came to shove, they could always get money, but Carolyn knew as well as her husband that he could never threaten some clerk's life just for the cash in the kitty. Even in their most desperate times, he'd never done that. The "plan" required Carolyn to make a trip to the bank— the single weakest link in the chain. Banks were funny places, highly secure, and populated by people who were paid to be paranoid. Every place you went in a bank, your picture was taken, and there was no way of knowing how closely those pictures were scrutinized, or by whom. Today, however, she'd have to risk it.

The drive took a half hour; a full ten minutes longer than she'd anticipated. She nosed the Celica into a space outside of the Safeway, on the other end of the parking lot. Although the lot in front of the bank was virtually empty, the potential for a quick getaway seemed less important than the benefits of blending in with the other midday shoppers. The last thing she wanted was for the bank security guy to be able to say, "Yeah, I saw that lady get into a silver Celica." It was safer to be seen disappearing down the sidewalk.

She killed the engine, and instantly, her heart started pounding hard enough for her to hear. This truly was it. Everything they'd struggled so hard to hide was moments away from discovery.

"Stay cool," she told herself aloud. She took a deep breath, held it, then let it go. "You can do this." Straightening her shoulders, she checked her hair in the mirror, then climbed out of the car.

She tried to look as normal as possible as she walked along the covered sidewalk, down the full length of the nondescript little strip mall. In her tight-fitting Levi's and her short, jet-black hair and matching onyx eyes, she knew she was attractive, even at thirty-six, and her quick, light stride showed it. A couple of college-age guys approached her head-on, and as they passed, she could feel their heads pivot to watch her going-away side. Ordinarily, those glances felt nice, but today they reminded her that this was a day to be invisible, and she worked harder at being anonymous.

She'd made it nearly all the way to the bank door when she froze. *I've got nothing to carry the money in.* The original plan had called for her to bring an ugly, oversize purse from home, but it lay stuffed into the same closet as the duffel bags. What was she supposed to do now? The little fashion bag slung over her shoulder this morning was barely large enough for her wallet and keys. Even her sunglasses didn't fit inside.

The persistent flutter in her stomach grew larger by the second. *You'd better come up with something fast.* She took a few moments to inspect her surroundings, then . . .

The Safeway!

She turned abruptly and headed back the other way, drawing yet another look from the college boys, who by now had to believe that she was on the prowl. She smiled politely but otherwise ignored them as she walked through the automatic doors and into the cavernous grocery store.

"Excuse me," she said, approaching the first cashier.

A haggard woman with mostly gray hair and an unhealthy pallor turned to face her. With no one in her line, she looked vaguely relieved to have someone to talk to. "Hi!"

The cheerfulness of the greeting caught Carolyn off guard. "Um, hi." She tried to match the lighthearted lilt but fell way short. "Listen, I'm wondering if you could do me a favor."

"I'll certainly try."

Carolyn did her best to smile and keep eye contact, but she couldn't stop her eyes from darting all around. She felt . . . exposed. "Well, I'm not sure if you're allowed to do this," she began, conscious of an unnatural waver in her voice. "I'm wondering if I could have a shopping bag?"

If the clerk suspected anything out of the ordinary, she showed none of it. "Of course," she said as she reached for a shelf some-where below the register. "Plastic or paper?"

Carolyn grinned. "Paper, please."

The Johnston's Corner branch of Phoenix Bank and Trust was nothing special—just a community bank, serving the needs of sub-urban families and the service businesses that supported them. Jake had felt that a smaller bank would have fewer rules and regulations to deal with. In homage to its clientele, the place was devoid of pretense; no big chandeliers, marble floors, or gilded teller cages. Phoenix Bank and Trust was a working-class establishment, cater-ing to customers for whom tile floors, fluorescent lights, and wood-paneled teller stations were just fine.

The lobby was packed, as it usually was around lunchtime, and Carolyn waited as patiently as she could, seated in one of the imitation-leather guest chairs in the tiny lobby. Elusive bank logic prohibited tellers from helping customers with their safe-deposit boxes. Such was the domain of the manager and assistant managers whose elevated status was marked by tiny desks in a car-peted corner, separated from each other by shoulder-height glass partitions. Of these various anointed ones, all were serving other customers; mostly young couples with the sheepish look of peo-ple trying to qualify for loans they weren't sure they could afford.

As Carolyn waited, the chairs around her filled with still more customers, each awaiting his or her own audience with the senior staff. Conversation flowed easily among these people, allowing her to relax just a bit. No one seemed to suspect anything. In the ten minutes that Carolyn sat waiting, she checked her watch at least twenty times.

Every second is a liability. She was oblivious to the constant, nervous tapping of her heel against the floor. *What can possibly be taking this long?*

As if on cue, all the meetings concluded at once, and the desk-dwellers motioned for the next wave. It didn't seem fair to Carolyn that the lady who'd been waiting for only a minute or two got to speak with someone at the same time she did.

A hunky young guy—maybe twenty-five, with eyes that matched his blue Oxford button-down—extended his hand to Carolyn. "Hi," he said, flashing an expensive smile. "My name's Jeff. How can I help you?"

His voice was so smooth and his smile so genuine that Carolyn wondered just how many pretty young hearts had melted under the heat of his greeting. Fifteen years ago she might have been one of them, but today she was in a hurry, and the tone of her voice said so.

"I need to get into my safe-deposit box," she said, handing him her key ring.

Jeff's smile changed from personal to businesslike but never disappeared completely. "Yes, ma'am." He left for a few seconds, then returned with the other key and a signature card. "Here," Jeff said. "I need you to sign this."

After Carolyn scrawled her name on the card, Jeff compared it to the sample signature above it. "First visit in five months," he observed.

Carolyn launched a glare that rendered Jeff instantly repentant. "I'm very sorry, Mrs. Brighton. That's none of my business."

Carolyn said nothing, but her look told him that she couldn't have agreed more. Together, they walked into the vault, and Jeff used a set of rolling stairs to reach the Brightons' box. The lock seemed stiff, resisting his efforts to turn it. Finally, he pulled the door open and slid out a long black metal container. He handed it down to her. Carolyn could tell that he wanted to comment on its weight, but he wisely kept his thoughts to himself.

"You want a viewing room, I trust?" Jeff was sucking up to her now as he climbed backward down the steps.

Carolyn smiled patiently. "Yes, please."

Jeff led the way to one of two six-foot-by-four-foot cubicles and opened the door for his customer. "Take your time," he told her.

"Thank you."

Inside, Carolyn locked the door, and after a quick scan overhead for security cameras, she opened the box and smiled. There it was:

$62,000 cash. She'd forgotten what that much money looked like, all broken into hundreds. She pulled the Safeway bag from under her jacket, and as she stuffed the banded bills inside, she tried not to think about how much interest the money could have earned over the years, had they invested it properly. Yet another reality of life on the run.

Not that there'd been much choice. IRS regulations required banks to report large cash transactions, so that was out of the question. So were other standard investment vehicles. The key to this particular fund was instant and total liquidity. If and when the day came that the Brightons needed their cash, they would want it right by-God now; there'd be no time for a phone call to some broker. They could have kept it in the house, she supposed—in fact, for a while, they'd done just that, but not here in Phoenix. Farm Meadows was such a frequent target for burglars that many of Carolyn's neighbors had stopped locking their trailers during the day, just to save the wear and tear on their doors and windows. Then there was the risk of a fire. All things considered, the safe-deposit box made the most sense.

Carolyn wondered if the bag would be big enough to hold it all. The space seemed to be filling up faster than the box was emptying. It was heavier than she'd expected, too.

What's this? As she reached back to get the last of the bills, she found a pistol: a little .380, just slightly bigger than her hand. She didn't remember this from the memorized plan, but leave it to Jake to think of everything. She dropped the magazine out of the grip and took a look. Sure enough, loaded to the top. Like there was ever a doubt. She eased back the slide and found one more in the chamber. Jake was a planner, all right. He must have envisioned some scenario where she'd have to use more than words to get to the staging area, and he wanted her to be prepared. For the hundredth time over the years, she wondered if she'd have the guts to fire a gun, then she shooed away the thought and concentrated on her next move.

Every cubic inch of space in the bag was now occupied by a hundred-dollar bill, but at least she'd fit it all in, with just enough room left over to fold the top closed. Slipping the .380 into her jacket pocket, she hefted the bag under her left arm and, with her right arm clutching the deposit box, opened the door to retrieve her keys from Jeff.

"Carolyn!" a lady's voice boomed. It was Mary Barnett, her next-door neighbor, sounding for all the world like they hadn't seen each other in years. "How wonderful to see you!" Virtually deaf, Mrs. Barnett—"Mrs. Bullet Boobs" to the boys—was incapable of quiet speech.

Oh, God. "Hi, Mary. How are you?" She waved to get Jeff's attention. He acknowledged her with a nod but appeared to be stuck on the phone.

"Happy and hearty as can be," Mary bellowed. With her girth and baggy yellow dress, she looked like a have-a-nice-day balloon. "The question is, how is little Travis? He looked awful last night."

This I don't need.

If Mrs. Barnett had dedicated one-fifth the effort she invested in other people's business to a *real* business of her own, she'd have been a millionaire. "Oh, he's fine," Carolyn said, her spirit dancing as she saw Jeff hang up his phone.

"I didn't see you go to a doctor." Mrs. Barnett's comment was leaden with disapproval.

Carolyn ignored her, concentrating instead on Jeff's return. "Here you go," she said, handing him the box.

He walked back into the vault and returned in twenty seconds with her keys. "Thank you, Mrs. Brighton," he said earnestly.

Mrs. Barnett followed Carolyn to the door, chatting the whole way. "That's some bag you've got there. Didn't rob the place, did you?" She tittered at her little joke, until Carolyn froze her with a startled glare. "Oh, dear, Carolyn," she apologized. "I've offended you."

Carolyn smiled just a hair too slowly and shook her head. "Oh, no, not at all," she said. "I'm just a little tired, I guess."

Mrs. Barnett returned the smile, but absent her typical humor. "I'm sure. I understand."

Dammit, Carolyn cursed herself. The problem with busybodies was their keen sense of human nature. Clearly, Mrs. Barnett knew something was wrong. Put another nail in the coffin.

Hurrying, but not running, back to her Celica, Carolyn checked her watch: 12:48. *Damn. Every second . . .*

CHAPTER THREE

Phoenix Police Chief Peter Sherwood had way too much on his administrative plate to suffer any more of this catfight. If Lucas Banks said that this Brighton guy was a straight shooter, then he was a straight shooter. He'd seen enough of Lucas's courtroom antics to know when he was in his defense-lawyer mode, and this wasn't it. Sometimes it wasn't about winning and losing. Sometimes it was about justice. And as far as Sherwood could see, Lucas had a point.

Under different circumstances, he'd have cut Brighton loose by now. Unfortunately, this case belonged to the FBI, and the lady cop they'd assigned to running it was playing her role as Queen Bitch to the hilt. What was it about that agency that made them so damn difficult to deal with? God knew that DEA and Secret Service boys had huge egos, but at least they pretended to show respect for the eagles on Sherwood's collar. The FBI, on the other hand, seemed to think that everyone they encountered was either an idiot or a criminal.

This Rivers lady was a case unto herself. Barely a first grader when Sherwood was busting his first felon, she was an arrogant bitch, with what looked to be a God complex. At maybe forty years old, this well-moussed *Charlie's Angels* wanna-be thought she had the world pegged, and Sherwood wanted desperately to eat her and her attitude alive. In deference to Lucas and his client, however, he found himself playing peacemaker.

"We've been over this twice already, Irene," Lucas said evenly. It was a struggle, but he forced himself to remain in his faux-leather guest chair, legs crossed, while he strangled paper clips from the dish on Sherwood's desk. "Brighton is not a threat to you or anybody else. He's got a business here. And a family. What do you want from him?"

Rivers slumped in the other guest chair. "You're right," she said. "We *have* been over this twice—three times now, in fact. And he's a friend of yours. I heard you every time. Problem is, Counselor, that you keep forgetting the part where he drew a gun on me."

"Bullshit!" That was it. Without even thinking, Lucas launched forward in his chair and bounced a dead paper clip off the polished desktop, causing Sherwood to dodge the ricochet. He knew that shouting was a mistake, but the genie was out of the bottle now. "He didn't draw a gun on you! He drew a gun on a bunch of strangers with automatic weapons! You said yourself that he never even brought it to bear, for Christ's sake! What the hell would *you* do if you saw a swarm of terrorists flooding your office?"

Rivers shook her head. "I'm not a terrorist. I'm a federal officer." Her elbows were planted on the upholstered arms of the guest chair. As she spoke, she steepled her fingers and studied them. "Plus, I didn't like what I saw behind his eyes. I know he didn't shoot, but he sure as hell thought about it."

"Oh, for God's sake. Now you're a mind reader!"

The time had come for Sherwood to intervene, before Lucas *really* pissed her off. "Come on, Irene. I've known Lucas since we were kids. If he says the guy's okay, you can believe him. Don't get me wrong, he'll cut off your balls in a courtroom . . ." He stopped himself. There definitely was some eye contact now. "Well, you know what I mean. He's a lawyer. But this isn't a courtroom. You haven't formally filed charges yet, right?"

Her eyes narrowed. Clearly, she didn't appreciate the tag-team approach. "Why is this guy so important to you?" In sales, they would have called the question a buying signal.

Sherwood's eyebrows scaled his forehead, as if to say, "Damn good question." He left that one for his lawyer friend.

Lucas shrugged. "He did me a favor. He really worked with us to get our car fixed up before vacation, so I owe him one."

She tossed her hands in the air. "Oh, well, there you go," she mocked. "He takes a ding out of your car, and I should look the other way on a felony? What the hell kind of deal is that?"

"What felony?" Lucas insisted again. "Jesus Christ, Irene, how can I say it more simply? He didn't know you were a cop. He saw the guns, and he responded. Why is this so unreasonable to you?" Sensing a crack in Irene's resolve, he lowered his voice and sat back down in his chair. "Look. You came for a drug bust, and you got a drug bust. Let's call it a successful day for justice and let my client off the hook."

Irene inhaled deeply through her nose and held it for a few seconds before she let it go. When she looked up at Sherwood, and then at Lucas, they knew the good guys had won.

"This is a mistake," she said, seemingly to herself. "I just know in my bones that this is a mistake."

Sherwood let the words hang for a moment, not sure if it was his turn to speak. "No, it's not," he reassured her. "It's a solid decision." He stopped there, not wanting to push any harder.

She sighed one more time, then rose to her feet. "You win, boys," she said, extending her hand. "It's a mistake, but I'll do it. Won't be the first."

Lucas rose with her and grasped her hand. "Agent Rivers, I appreciate this. Trust me, you're doing the right thing."

She smiled, the first show of warmth in twenty minutes. "I hope so, Counselor," she said. "For all our sakes."

Jake shifted his position as best he could with his right wrist shackled to the leg of his wooden chair. He'd have paid twenty bucks to be able to sling his arm over the seat back; fifty to stand and stretch.

Many years had passed since he last visited a police station, thanks to a DUI problem when he was eighteen, but from what he could tell, Phoenix police headquarters had been designed and decorated by the same team who'd put together its much larger counterpart in Cook County, Illinois. The place was a jumble of desks and chairs that seemed more scattered than arranged, making it impossible for anyone to walk a straight line from one side of the squad room to the other. Every horizontal surface was littered with papers and files—including the floor. As uniformed officers and plainclothes detectives came and went, those same files and papers were kicked, walked on, or otherwise ignored. A stickler for neatness in his own shop, Jake wondered how people in this dimly lit, nicotine-stained hellhole ever got anything done.

The clock on the wall behind him buzzed noisily each time the minute hand moved, and as he struggled to find a spot for his butt that would ease the stress on his back, his eyes were drawn to the clock for the one hundred thirty-fourth time since he'd been deposited there. It was going on three hours since they'd taken his fingerprints and allowed him to make his phone call. He was cutting this way too close.

He wondered how long Carolyn would wait for him before she headed off on her own with Travis. Part of him hoped she was already gone, but he knew better. They'd been through a lot together. She wouldn't leave him behind until the very last minute, any more than he'd have left her.

Still, it was getting late. One-fifteen. In the absolute worst case they'd rehearsed, she should have taken care of everything by now, even working by herself. That left her waiting with Travis in the staging area, biding time till her patience gave out.

One way or another, Jake figured this would all be a done deal within the next sixty minutes. Surely, the cops had zapped his prints off to be identified by the FBI. When the results came in, he was done. Christ, he'd be lucky if they didn't just shoot him there on the spot. That was the negative side. In the plus column, Lucas

Banks seemed genuinely pissed that the feds had arrested him in the first place, and truly committed to getting him off. If Jake had ever doubted the value of excellent customer service, he was a devoted believer today. The lawyer's promise to get him out was a genuine source of hope.

So the clock ticked on. If only to pass the time, Jake replayed his conversation with Carolyn in his head, trying to remember if he'd given anything useful to the cops. He assumed that the conversation was taped; but even if it wasn't, it may as well have been. The cops stood close enough to share his shoes. Carolyn fully understood what was at risk here, and he was confident she knew precisely what to do. Each time he replayed the words, he relaxed a little more, confident they'd given nothing away.

The sound of an opening door drew his attention toward the chief's office, where he'd seen them all disappear so long ago. From the grim expression on Rivers's face, Jake couldn't tell whether his ordeal was over or just beginning. When Lucas emerged, though, and fired off a wink and a smile, Jake knew he was a free man.

He felt himself flush in a burst of excitement and anxiety that left him a bit dizzy. Not wanting to look *too* happy, he suppressed the triumphant grin that fought to assert itself and donned a concerned frown instead.

"Don't look so glum, Jake," Lucas said. "You're free to go."

Jake released just a bit of the smile, then looked toward Irene, who ignored him altogether as she produced a tiny key and removed the handcuffs, first from the chair and then from Jake's wrist. As she folded the cuffs at their chain and dropped them into the pocket of her blazer, she extended a reproachful forefinger at her ex-prisoner. "Don't you *ever* point a gun at me again, do you understand?"

Jake brought his eyebrows together and pretended to be scared. "Yes, ma'am." *Street clothes shrink you by half, lady.* "And thanks for understanding."

She measured Jake for a moment longer, then ended the encounter with a brief nod, before turning on her heel and heading for the coffee room.

He turned to the lawyer and shook his hand warmly. "Lucas, I can't tell you how grateful I am." As he spoke, he felt a twinge of remorse for what his newfound friend was about to go through. "You really saved my life, buddy."

Lucas smiled broadly and clapped Jake on the shoulder. "No, Jake," he corrected, "Agent Rivers over there is the one who didn't shoot you. All I saved was your reputation." They shared a chuckle. "I wish I could offer you a ride home, but I've got some paperwork over at the courthouse."

Jake waived the offer. "God, no," he said. "I'll just walk uptown and get a cab."

Chief Sherwood entered the conversation and placed a hand on Jake's shoulder. "Sorry for all the confusion, Mr. Brighton," he said, extending his hand. "Peter Sherwood, chief of police. This guy fought like hell for you. I'm tempted to wreck my car just to do business at your shop."

They all laughed. "We try to do our best," Jake said, sloughing off the compliment. The clock buzzed again, and here he was, small-talking with the goddamn police chief! "Listen," he said, as if unexpectedly struck with an idea, "I've really got to run. As much fun as I've had here today, I've got to get going."

"Why don't I get an officer to drive you home," Sherwood offered. "Or back to your shop."

Jake smiled but shook his head. "No, that's okay. I'll catch a cab."

"The hell you will," Sherwood huffed. "The least I can do is give you a ride, for Christ's sake." He called to one of the uniformed officers. "Jason! I need you to give Mr. Brighton here a ride."

Jake's stomach knotted tight. "No, really," he insisted, hoping his voice wouldn't crack. "You have bad guys to catch. I don't want to be a bother."

Sherwood made a show of walking away, not listening anymore. Jake was stuck. The nearest place to catch a cab would be out in front of the Sears store uptown, and that was nearly a mile away. No one would willingly walk that distance if they didn't have to.

Unless, of course, they had something to hide. He needed to be very careful here.

Young Jason—Officer Slavka, by his name tag—approached cheerfully, twirling his key ring on his finger. "Would you like to follow me, sir?"

Not on a bet, Jake didn't say. As he trailed the young officer out the squad room door and down the front steps, he waved one last time to Lucas Banks.

With speed zones and traffic lights, the shop was a half hour away. No way could Jake risk that kind of exposure—in a police cruiser, no less! By contrast, the staging area lay just on the other side of the business district, maybe a ten-minute drive from the police station on a bad traffic day.

Excuse me, Officer, but would you mind dropping me off at a place where I can stage a more convenient getaway?

The absurdity of it all made him smile, even as his eyes stayed focused on the cruiser's two-way radio. When the balloon went up, he figured that's how the announcement would be made. How the hell was he going to bluff his way out of this one?

For years, he and Carolyn had planned for this moment as a distant, improbable "if." *If* something happened, and they had to run, this is what they'd do. They'd developed endless checklists of ifs, each of which carried its own solution. By careful planning, they'd taken some of the edge off their fear.

Now, he realized, by obliterating that edge, they'd inadvertently opened the door to complacency. It had been months since he'd serviced the escape van; nearly a year since he'd been to the safe house. For all he knew, both had burned up or been stolen. In the context of a plan governed by ifs, he'd been able to justify these lapses, rationalizing that he could always catch up.

Now, though, the ifs had blossomed into whens, and the weaknesses of their plan were startlingly clear. By rights, the feds should have nailed him already. But for a random act of inattention by some midlevel clerk on the other end of a modem, they'd have identified Jake for who he was an hour ago. How pitifully ironic.

All the planning, all the contingencies, all the clandestine trips and purchases, came down to stupid luck, in a game where the odds were hopelessly stacked against him.

And here he was joyriding in a damn cop car!

Think, Jake. Think.

As Jason navigated the traffic circle at Maple Avenue and Tobacco Trail, Jake saw the five-story hospital in the distance, and a plan materialized out of nowhere.

CHAPTER FOUR

For roughly ten months out of the year, from noon till two, Monday through Friday, the center of power in Washington, D.C., shifted from the halls of the Capitol and the Executive Office Building to a handful of elite dining establishments. When meeting with charity organizers, industry leaders, or sports heroes, the natural choices for lunch were the Washington landmarks: Maison Blanche, Old Ebbitt Grill, and the Hay-Adams Hotel. In these places, where the press mingled freely with their prey, the rules of engagement were clear. Anything said to anyone—from one's entrée to a request for directions to the men's room—was always on the record.

Those public watering holes provided extended research opportunities for gossip columnists—a place to be seen—but matters of substance were rarely discussed there. The real business of politics required privacy: a place where security was more important than the quality of the food, and the maître d' knew who could be allowed to sit in sight of whom. Eddie Bartholomew ran such a place, the Smithville Restaurant, on Connecticut Avenue near Woodley Park. Everyone who was anyone had passed through

Eddie's place over the years, on their way toward greatness or obscurity. Yet, when pressed for a name, Eddie could never remember a single one. Maple paneling covered the walls of the Smithville, with gorgeous Constable landscapes occupying the spaces reserved in the high-profile restaurants for autographed glossies of the owner shaking hands with his celebrity guests.

In the whole world, only 278 people could make a reservation at the Smithville, each of whom ponied up $5,000 a year for the right, with the understanding that even they might occasionally be denied. It wouldn't do, for example, for the Democratic White House chief of staff to be seen dining with his mistress at the same time the Republican Speaker of the House was entertaining his special male friends.

Eddie paid big bucks to have his place swept daily for listening devices, and everyone—*everyone*—submitted to screening by a metal detector. Guests with bodyguards had to make a choice at the front door: either their security detail checked their weapons at the desk, or their master would dine alone. Eddie had learned long ago that firearms brought trouble.

Reporters and cops were persona non grata; they simply never got reservations. A couple of years ago, in fact, a reporter from the *Post* had tried to force his way past the desk to get a glimpse of the diners. The maître d' stopped him, of course, but the reporter somehow broke both ankles and his wrist on his way down the front stairs.

Currently, Eddie found himself in a tough spot. Clayton Albricht, chairman of the Senate Judiciary Committee, had been a very good customer for a very long time, and he knew the rules. In spite of this, the senator had invited Peter Frankel, deputy director of the FBI, to be his guest. When the news reached the kitchen that one of the top cops in the country was planning to dine in, several of Eddie's staff took the day off. The owner tried to explain to the paranoid cooks and dishwashers what Albricht had explained on the telephone—that Frankel's business was unofficial—but they refused to listen. Worse, following his own protocol when dealing with controversial guests of members, Eddie had informed everyone else who'd made a reservation that the heat would be there, and nearly a dozen had either canceled or postponed till after two.

Left with little choice, Eddie rationalized that Albricht's years of faithful patronage probably earned him a break, just this once. Whatever the senator's business was, though, Eddie hoped that it warranted all the inconvenience. Certainly, it would be the last time he'd permit such an intrusion.

If Clayton Albricht ever got around to dying—instead of just looking perpetually like he was on the brink—the parade of mourners would doubtless be led by a squadron of political cartoonists. The senator was a living caricature. With his drawn, pallid skin, his prominent hooked nose, and a widow's peak that rivaled Dracula's, he'd been depicted as every kind of bird imaginable, from eagle to vulture to canary. He was a staunch proponent of individual rights and responsibilities, and his five terms had been defined by his consistent and reliable vote against every handout program ever devised.

Painted by his opposition and the press as an anti-Semitic, gay-bashing misogynist, intent on watching children starve in the arms of their homeless grandparents, Albricht had long ago developed skin made of Kevlar and asbestos. He ignored the taunts of his enemies and focused on the needs of the only people who counted—the residents of Illinois. To them, he stood for the basic midwestern values of Christianity, patriotism, and fairness. That he could transfer billions of federal dollars into the pockets of his constituents was merely icing on the cake.

All politicians had enemies, but Albricht's conservative leanings had earned him more than most. Having watched the senator consistently confound their plans, the special interests he opposed had tried every trick imaginable to knock him from his perch. All part of the game, he supposed.

Of all the persecutions he'd endured, none were more bothersome or disruptive than the three special prosecutor investigations. Like farmyard dogs pursuing a wounded kitten, those bastards had torn his life apart, looking for any petty crime or indiscretion which the gentlemen on the other side of the aisle could leverage to eject him from power. In the end, they were oh-for-three.

Never especially vindictive, Senator Albricht had never mustered the depth of character required to forgive those sons of bitches. Bending the Constitution to their own needs, his opposition had tried to hurt him and his family, for no better reason than to punish him for his beliefs. Of all the investigators, however, one stood out as the most aggressive, vitriolic, and unfair. On loan to the special prosecutor's office from the FBI, this investigator had an agenda of his own and was every bit as committed to his own career as any of the spineless bastards he worked for.

His name was Peter Frankel, and he'd pounced on his assignment like a hungry wolf on raw meat. When the contents of the Albrichts' house, their cars, and their underwear drawers proved benign, he'd changed tack and started leaking stories to the press: that Albricht's daughter had been arrested for drugs; that his son was gay and HIV-positive. The tactic was as clear as it was cruel: to flush out the strong by hurting the weak.

Survivors by nature, the Albrichts got through it all with nary a punch thrown; but in the end, Frankel emerged as the big winner. He'd proved himself to be a committed team player and was ultimately rewarded with the title of deputy director—the highest nonpolitical job on the pyramid.

And now the president—himself a know-nothing poll-watcher from the Deep South—had seen fit to nominate Frankel for the director's job effective January 1, when the incumbent would retire to breed horses somewhere. At last, Frankel was close enough to touch the brass ring.

And only one man stood in his way.

As chairman of the Senate Judiciary Committee, Clayton Albricht intended to kill Frankel's nomination in as public and as humiliating a way as he could. With the hearings still five weeks away, it was too early to know specifically how his vendetta would be played out, but men like Frankel collected enemies like a boy collects baseball cards. By the time Albricht was done, every single one of them would get an opportunity to testify in open session. Revenge was a dish to be savored. And what better place to begin the smorgasbord than at the Smithville?

"How was your meal?" the senator asked as Eddie removed their plates.

Frankel patted his obscenely trim stomach. "The meal was wonderful," he said. "Truthfully, though, I found the company a bit unsettling, Senator. Now that we're between courses, I presume you're getting to the point of this little *ex parte* feast?" Frankel had a face made for television; ruggedly smooth until he smiled. That's when the dimples came out, perfectly aligned on either side of his grin. He was a walking recruitment manual for the FBI. Somehow the television cameras filtered out the lifelessness of his eyes—the raw ambition—that so intimidated people in person. Frankel knew damn well that his luncheon partner held the reins to his future, yet he still hadn't flinched.

"I assume you know, Peter, that you don't have a chance next month. When I'm done with you, the public will be screaming for your indictment." Albricht had already suffered through all the pleasantries he could stand for one day. The time had come for direct attack.

The dimples didn't move as Frankel lifted a curious eyebrow. "My, my, Senator. Sounds like you may have lost your objectivity. Perhaps I should have my attorney recommend recusal."

Albricht ignored the bait. Senate hearings were not trials, and he was not a judge; merely an advocate for the People, who ultimately would determine Frankel's worthiness to run the world's most powerful law enforcement agency.

"I brought you here for one reason," Albricht explained. "I wanted to give you a chance to step away from your nomination; to save your career and to save the president the embarrassment we both know your hearing will bring."

Frankel laughed at that one, long and hard. "And here I thought you just had an ax to grind!" he whooped. "So tell me, Clay. When did you start worrying about the political fortunes of the president? Last I heard, you were saying some pretty awful things about him."

Albricht's eyes narrowed. He'd never expected Frankel to cave in—in fact, he'd have been disappointed if he had. But he expected *something*. A momentary look of fear, maybe? Hatred? Some emotional twitch to mimic the antipathy Albricht carried in his own heart? Instead, he just got more of the laughter; the unspoken "Fuck you."

As the smile faded, Frankel replaced it with a patronizing sneer. He opened his mouth to say something, but the chirping of his cell phone interrupted him. Keeping eye contact with the senator the whole time, Frankel removed the checkbook-size phone from the pocket of his suit coat and punched a button. "Frankel."

He has something, Albricht mused as he eavesdropped on Frankel's side of the conversation. The thought made the Alfredo sauce curdle in his stomach.

"Who caught them? . . . Where? . . . No shit. Well, have that number ready for me when I get back. I want to call Agent Rivers personally." He beamed like a lottery winner as he pushed the disconnect button and slipped the phone back into his pocket.

Rising abruptly from the table, Frankel clapped Albricht on the shoulder. "Well, Clay, it looks like we'll *both* be on the news tonight," he said.

Albricht remained stoic, a perfect poker face. Somewhere along the line, he'd lost control of this meeting. And he hadn't a clue what Frankel was talking about.

The deputy director of the FBI left without so much as a handshake, pausing halfway across the room. "You know," he said glibly, "after all your years in the Senate, I'd have expected you to be less naive." He chuckled at a joke that only he had heard, then left the dining room, on his way to collect his firearm.

CHAPTER FIVE

Bullshit!"

Chief Sherwood couldn't believe what he was hearing. "They've made a mistake."

Agent Rivers's face glowed crimson and her hands trembled with rage. "It's no mistake, Sherwood! A perfect match on his prints. Your friend's client is Jake Donovan. *The* Jake Donovan. God *damn* it!" Irene moved her arms randomly, as if searching for something to throw. "Number one on the Ten Most Fucking Wanted list, and I let him go. *Fuck!*"

Sherwood felt numb; and, frankly, a little shocked by the profanity that spewed from this petite yet apoplectic young lady. As royal fuckups went, this one was certainly the blue-ribbon winner. Surely, it was a mistake. There it was, though, right there at the bottom of the sheet: "Wanted for murder."

As Irene ranted and danced around Sherwood's office, trying to comprehend the instant implosion of her career, the chief stopped listening, concentrating instead on the dog-eared Wanted poster. Sure enough, the resemblance was there if you looked hard enough. Especially around the eyes.

In the picture, Jake Donovan was a kid. While the man he'd spoken to only minutes before had a full, graying beard and soft features, this picture showed a clean-cut young man in his twenties, with a strong chin, a fighter's nose, and piercing blue eyes. Sherwood used the edge of his hand to cover up everything but the eyes and the hairline, and magically, Jake Brighton appeared.

"Well, I'll be damned," Sherwood mumbled.

"Damned my ass!" Irene exploded. "We'll be fucking crucified!"

Sherwood regarded Irene with the expression of a disappointed father. The oh-so-sure-of-herself savior of the law enforcement world now looked suspiciously like she might cry. If she hadn't been such an asshole, Sherwood might have felt sorry for her. Someone knocked on his office door.

"What's this 'we' shit, Irene? Donovan was never *my* prisoner." He stood up and opened the door to reveal a clerk standing nervously on the other side. Barely out of his teens, the young man clearly knew he was interrupting. "Sorry, Chief, but Agent Rivers has a phone call."

"Tell whoever it is that I'm in a meeting," Irene snapped without looking. "I'll call them back when I get a chance."

The kid seemed to shrink as he stood there. "Um, I tried that, ma'am, but he said I should tell you it's Peter Frankel. He said you'd take the call."

Color drained from Irene's face, like someone had pulled a plug. "Oh, shit," she groaned.

Sherwood cringed on her behalf, wondering if he should help Irene into a chair. Instead, he offered his own. "You can take it at my desk, if you'd like," he said. "I'll have the dispatcher check to see if Donovan's still with my patrolman."

She looked confused for a second, then nodded. "Thank you."

Sherwood smiled. Peter Frankel's reputation in the law enforcement community was not one of love and understanding. The call rang through just as he closed the door. Right now he wouldn't have traded places with Irene for a million dollars.

*   *   *

The story was believable enough, Jake thought. Rather than having this cop go to the trouble of taking him all the way out to the boonies, why not just drop him off at the hospital? "My mother's there getting some outpatient surgery done," he'd explained. "It'd be a hell of a surprise for her, and she'd probably love to have the company."

The cop bought it all the way, oblivious to the tremor in Jake's hands and the slight crack in his voice. And why wouldn't he buy it? If nothing else, it got him off the hook for a long drive to nowhere. And who wouldn't be a bit jumpy after spending the last few hours under arrest. That'd unnerve anyone.

The outpatient clinic shared an entrance with the emergency room. Officer Slavka pulled right up to the entrance, his badge and light bar buying a few extra yards that would have been off limits to civilian vehicles.

"Here you go, Mr. Brighton," Jason announced. "Door-to-door service."

Jake shook hands with the patrolman, then climbed out of the car. "Thanks for the ride," he said.

"I hope your mother's okay."

Jake smiled nervously, searching the cop's tone for signs of sarcasm. "Thank you," he said again. "I'm sure she will be."

He walked purposefully through the door labeled "Admissions," just like he belonged there, and continued all the way to the receptionist's desk before pausing at a water fountain to see if he'd been followed. He took a long drink—long enough to convince himself that he was alone—then started working his way nonchalantly toward the front door.

Outside again, and free at least for the moment, he fought the urge to run. He was in the open again, and if he wasn't mistaken, there were tons more cop cars out on the street today than usual.

Keep it together, he told himself. *Three more blocks and you're home free.*

He turned left at the corner of Jefferson Street and William & Mary Avenue, and there it was: the staging area. If Carolyn hadn't left yet—and he was certain, now, that she hadn't—in five minutes they'd all be a family again, and then the most immediate crisis would be over. Once they were together, they'd be infinitely mobile; and with mobility came freedom.

The sign for U-Lockit Storage rose a good fifteen feet over the sidewalk. The light inside the plastic sign hadn't worked for as long as Jake had been using the place; much like the automatic wooden arm which was supposed to keep unauthorized visitors out. Apparently, one visitor—authorized or otherwise—had taken on the challenge, splintering the wood all over the driveway.

Units 626 and 627 lay all the way in the back of the complex, well out of the way from all but a few similar concrete storage bays. Of all the bills the Brightons paid each month, U-Lockit invariably earned top priority. As long as the account stayed current, he figured no one would feel compelled to look inside and see just how hugely noncompliant they'd been with the rental covenants.

Jake slowed his pace as he approached their units and stopped completely before turning the last corner. He saw nothing; heard no sounds; but the massive, pin-tumbler lock was missing from the right-hand door. That meant either that Carolyn was inside or that she'd already left him.

No, she was there, all right. She knew better than to leave without locking the place back up. Checking cautiously over both shoulders, he hurried down the last fifty feet of roadway. As he reached for the handle to lift the door, he stopped abruptly, remembering the firepower stored inside. Everybody was a bit tense right now. Startling Carolyn could be a very big mistake.

Stepping away from the door, with his back pressed against the concrete fire wall that separated their two units, he rapped lightly with his knuckle. "Carolyn, it's me!" He shouted louder than he wanted to, but it was important for her to know that he wasn't a stranger.

"Jake?"

He heard the recognition in her voice; she was just making sure. "Yeah, it's me. I'm opening the door, okay?"

She answered by opening it for him. As the overhead door rumbled loudly to waist height, he bent low and scooted inside.

CHAPTER SIX

Jason Slavka had already cleared the traffic circle and was just a couple of blocks from the station when he heard his call sign requested over the air. He pulled the mike from its clip on the center console and he keyed the transmit button. "Two-Four David."

"Two-Four David, what's your status?"

Damn, he thought. *Time for an ethics check.* He'd hoped to sneak back into the station without changing his status on the board; that way no one would dispatch him on any calls, and he'd be able to finish the pile of paperwork on his desk.

Ah, screw it. "I'm ten-eight, en route back to headquarters," he said. The answer virtually volunteered him for another call.

"Um, Two-Four David . . ." He could hear commotion in the background as someone distracted the dispatcher with questions. "Stand by, Two-Four David."

Jason chuckled and shook his head. "Stand by?" he asked the radio, talking to it off the air, as if addressing a person. "You called me, remember?"

The speaker popped again a few seconds later. "Ah, Two-Four David, what's the ten-twenty of your passenger?"

"I dropped him off at the hospital. His mother's having an operation of some sort."

This time the commotion in the background was louder—much louder, in fact—and Jason distinctly heard the word "shit!" boomed by somebody. If he didn't know better, he'd have sworn it was Chief Sherwood's voice. "Okay, Two-Four David." The dispatcher's voice sounded like an island of calm in a sea of bedlam. "Stand by to copy."

"Oh, God, Jake, you're safe!" Carolyn threw her arms around his neck and hugged him tightly enough to hurt. "I've been worried sick about you." Inside, the place was black, lighted by a single kerosene lantern on the floor. But the work had all been done.

Once the adrenaline kicked in, she'd become oblivious to everything but her mission. She'd flown through the storage bays, collecting their prepacked duffel bags and second-guessing herself at every turn.

She'd finished early—nearly an hour ago—and that's when the panic had really started to sink in. If family came first, then how come she had everything else done, yet no one to talk to?

Loneliness was a horrible thing—if only for a few minutes at a time—and loneliness in the dark was worst of all. In the dim light of the kerosene lamp, her fears had taken on a physical dimension. She sensed that if she'd tried, she could have reached out and felt her fears with her hands, and the more she'd told herself that she was being silly, the larger and darker the fears had become.

She'd found the pint of Jack Daniel's without really even looking for it, buried deep in the middle of her duffel. She dimly remembered hiding it there a long time ago—a time when the bottle was her first priority. She told herself that all she needed was a swig—a single pull—to bring everything under control. Well, maybe two. It burned wonderfully as it sought that place in her soul where the body manufactured courage. As the level fell below the top of the label, though, she was jolted by vivid memories of a different monster, and she'd returned the bottle to the spot where it belonged, in the fold of her denim jacket, about a quarter of the way down from the top of the bag.

From the movement of her shoulders, Jake knew she was crying. She smelled of fear and dust and sweat. And, *dammit*, of booze. His vision blurred as he held her and kissed the top of her head. "I'm so sorry," he whispered.

The embrace felt magical; hypnotic almost. They'd been through so much together over the years—so much trembling and crying and running—that sometimes Jake wondered if the world could possibly spin without her. The drinking drove him nuts, and the screaming in the night terrified him almost as much as it did her, but she was the only person in the world who knew who he truly was. Even his own son didn't know—couldn't know.

The realization hit Jake like a hammer. He pushed Carolyn just far enough away to see her eyes. "Where's Travis?"

He sat all the way in the back of the school bus, in the corner, right where the teachers and chaperons expected the Farm Meadows kids to sit. He felt ridiculous with his purple eye, and the cheap imitation Oakleys he wore to camouflage the bruise really didn't hide a thing.

Travis had already been reminded three times—once getting on the bus at the school and then twice more once they arrived at the stupid plantation house—that one more fight would get him thrown out of school. Like that would just friggin' break his heart.

He was sick of school as it was; tired of always being the new kid—every asshole's most convenient punching bag. His dad had told him that this move might really be the last one; that this job might be the one to stick. And wouldn't you know it? After moving every damn year that he could remember, from one dump to another, this butthole of a town was the place his parents decided to sink some roots. Wonderful. If you asked him, the whole state of South Carolina sucked.

To distract himself from his misery, he thought of Eric Lampier, wondering if Pussy Boy was able to breathe through his nose yet. Poor baby couldn't even haul his butt into school this morning. Travis's smile triggered a stab of pain in his eye.

Yeah, it was worth it.

The "fight," such as it was, lasted all of three seconds. After enduring a good two minutes of trash talk in the cafeteria from Eric and his Snob Hill pals, Travis reached his limit when Eric referred to him and his friends as "trailer park shitheads." He simply stood up, smashed Eric's nose like a cherry tomato, then sat back down to finish his Tater Tots. A one-punch fight.

The fountain of blood and snot ignited an explosion of screams, mostly from the Snob Hill girls, with Eric howling right along with them. God, what a mess. It took maybe two minutes for word to travel to the Gestapo. You'd have thought somebody had a gun, the way they swarmed in there. No one even questioned who was the guilty party. While the nurse slobbered all over Eric, the principal, Mr. Menefee, dragged Travis off toward his office. As they reached the hallway, some panicked grown-up shouted for an ambulance. Was that not the most ridiculous thing you've ever heard? An ambulance for a damn broken nose!

"I've had it with you kids!" Menefee growled. That's the way it always was. In the minds of faculty, everything a Farm Meadows kid did somehow implicated all other Farm Meadows kids as silent accomplices.

That trailer park kids were unwelcome around there was the worst-kept secret in the world. Best Travis could figure out, J. E. B. Stuart Junior High had been the exclusive domain of the Snob Hill squeaky-cleans until a couple of years ago, when some redistricting bullshit mingled "Farm Meadows trash" with the "Hill youngsters." He didn't pretend to understand all the politics—frankly, he didn't care—but one thing was sure: the teachers and the school administration wanted things back the way they used to be.

For the life of him, though, Travis couldn't see why people complained so much. From his perspective, having Farm Meadows kids in the school made the business of discipline a no-brainer for everybody. If there was blood on the tile someplace, punish a trailer park kid. It didn't really matter that it might be the wrong kid, because everybody from Farm Meadows was guilty of something. Every time a Hill kid smoked, cussed, picked his nose, or jerked off, it was because a Farm Meadows kid had talked him into it. Travis thought it was hysterical. Like there was some conspiracy among him and his friends to lure rich kids away from their brick palaces to come live in shit-heap trailers.

At J. E. B. Stuart Junior High, a rich kid got to do or say whatever he wanted. Such were his constitutional rights. For Travis and his pals, though, the Constitution seemed to end at the point where they told the rich kids to fuck off. And to touch one of them—particularly with a fist—was more than the system could bear.

Mr. Menefee—*Der Führer* to Travis and his friends, thanks to German class—was as pissed as Travis had ever seen him. That's the word he used, too. *Pissed.* Travis wondered if he was still going to be "pissed" when he talked to Eric Lampier's lawyer-daddy. Somehow he didn't think so. Perturbed, maybe? Acrimonious (a brand-new word to Travis)? Certainly, he'd be something more elevated than pissed.

Menefee had had it with Travis's antics. He refused to tolerate violent behavior in his school, goddammit, and no, he didn't give a shit who started it. They should be ashamed of themselves. When Travis mentioned that there was no "they"—that this was strictly between Eric and him—Menefee seemed unimpressed.

"Are you going to yell at Eric, too," Travis had asked, "for swearing at me and my friends?" For an instant, Travis thought the man might punch him. Instead, he told Travis to mind his own damned business—another expression that was sure to be edited from the Lampier version.

"This is it, Brighton," Menefee concluded, his face beet red and his hands trembling. "One more time and I'll toss you out of here forever!"

Big fucking deal, Travis didn't say. In the end, he escaped with academic probation—whatever the hell that was—and a stern warning to review the Code of Behavior. Yet to be decided was the issue of whether or not the Lampier family would press charges—a concern rendered moot later that afternoon while Travis was winding his way through the woods toward Mike Howe's place to watch some X-rated videos his friend had found in a closet.

Terry Lampier—Eric's older brother—and two of his high school buddies just materialized out of nowhere, blocking his way. Instantly, Travis knew he was in deep trouble, and he took off in the opposite direction, running as fast as he could. But the jocks had him beat at all levels: height, weight, and speed. They caught up with him after maybe a dozen steps, clotheslining him and bouncing him off the hard-packed dirt path. The details were a little fuzzy after that, but he remembered putting up a valiant defense, all things considered, until an early shot to his balls drove all the fight right out of him. He didn't even remember what nailed him in the eye. All he knew was, one minute it felt like his guts had exploded, and the next, he was ten feet off the path, under a bunch of bushes.

As he pulled himself to his feet, he'd marveled that everything still worked. He wondered if maybe they thought they'd killed him and then stashed his body out in the woods. Either way, he was grateful to be in as good shape as he was. They could have killed him for real.

By the time Travis had made his way back to his trailer, the sun had started to dip, taking the temperature down along with it. With the whole back and side ripped out of his T-shirt, he felt cold. He felt dizzy for a while, too, and thought that he might have to sit down, but the feeling passed just as he turned onto his street.

Bullet Boobs Barnett was out in her garden as he approached, pretending to mind flowers when in fact minding everyone else's business. She took one look at Travis and freaked. "Oh, my God, boy, are you all right?"

From the look on her face, Travis figured he must have looked a lot worse than he felt. "I'm fine," he said. "I fell down. I just want to get home."

Mrs. Barnett arose from her knees with some effort and waddled toward the boy, pausing to step carefully over the six-inch white wire fence that defined her flower beds. "Fell down," she scoffed. "I don't believe that for a minute. Here, let me take a look at you."

Travis never stopped walking. "Really, Mrs. Barnett," he said without looking back, "I'm fine. My mom should be home now."

"You tell her you need to see a doctor!"

He acknowledged her with a wave over his shoulder, then tried to hike his tattered shirt back into place.

I'm doomed, he moaned silently. If he got that kind of reaction out of Bullet Boobs, God only knew how bad his mom was going to freak out. He didn't have to wait long to see. Apparently, Mrs. Barnett couldn't contain herself long enough for him to break the news himself. As he turned the last corner, both his mom *and* his dad came running down the street to meet him.

"Oh, my God!" his mom yelled. "Travis!"

The boy instinctively checked over his shoulder to see if anyone was watching as his folks descended on him.

"My God, what happened?"

His dad answered for him. "He's been in a fight." His voice oozed disapproval.

"Who did this to you?" his mother demanded.

"Not here, Carolyn," his dad cautioned. "Let's get him home first."

Thus beginneth the lectures, Travis remembered. They came one after another. First, there was the need to get along in their new community, followed immediately by the one about how the choices he made today could affect the rest of his life. When he tried to defend himself, describing the insults he'd had to endure from Eric Lampier, his mom jumped right in with the two-wrongs-don't-make-a-right pitch. In the end, though, he got a reprieve when his folks turned on each other over the question of whether or not they should take him to see a doctor. His mom was worried that he might have some hidden brain injury, while his dad maintained that they couldn't afford to take him unless it was a true emergency.

It was kind of weird. Travis had never thought of them being so poor that they couldn't afford to protect him from brain injury. Terrified as he was of doctors and the needles they wielded, he decided not to feel insulted. Instead, he just slipped down the short hall to his room and left them to fight it out among themselves.

Now, as the bus swung around the circle in front of the school, he sighed. In three more years, he'd be done with this crap. One thing South Carolina had going for it was their emancipation laws. He'd actually done the research. In three more years, he'd be sixteen, and then he'd be able to quit school forever.

Jake kicked at the floor. "Shit." He checked his watch without seeing the time. "When's he due back?"

"Around two."

This time he moved his watch around in the dim light until he could read the face. "That's fifteen minutes. How are we doing here?"

"I think we're about set." Carolyn picked up the lantern and led him to the back of the storage bay.

Of the two adjacent storage areas, the one on the right housed a strictly forbidden plain white Chevy van. In the five months they'd been in Phoenix, the van hadn't moved an inch. He hadn't even cranked the starter. In the eight years they'd owned the vehicle, it had been moved fewer than two dozen times, and then only at night, accumulating just under eighteen thousand miles on the odometer. It'd start, he told himself. It *had* to start.

The first order of business after renting these spaces had been to cut a doorway between them, thus allowing materials stored in the left-hand bay to be loaded and unloaded from the van without having to go outside.

Clearly, Carolyn had worked like a dog to pack it all up. All the weapons were on board, along with assorted building materials—two-by-fours and plywood, mostly—and a couple of weeks' worth of canned food, all stacked neatly on the shelves he'd installed and secured with bungees. On the other side of the makeshift doorway, Jake could see the back end of the Celica, all locked up and out of sight.

"You done good, honey," he said in his teasing hillbilly accent.

She shrugged a little and shook her head. "I just don't believe we're doing this. How could it happen?"

He sighed. "Random bad luck," he said. "It's so amazing. You plan and plan, and in the end, it's a bunch of dumb dopers who pull the rug out from under you." As he spoke, he busied himself by lifting the big Glock-17 from the rubber-matted floor of the van, where Carolyn had left it for him, holster and all. Unzipping his jacket, he unthreaded his belt from the loops on the right-hand side of his Levi's, then attached the holster high, so the muzzle was invisible below the waistband, the grip tucked securely under his arm. "Is the money already on board?"

Her silence drew Jake's eyes around. She just stood there, her hands at her sides, staring off at a spot in the dark. "Honey?"

She blinked once, then only her eyes moved. "I don't think I can do this again," she whispered.

He flapped his jacket back over the gun and walked two steps closer, taking her shoulders in his hands. As she tried to break eye contact, he wouldn't let her, moving his body to stay in her field of view. "Carolyn, honey, listen to me. We can't weaken now. Do you hear? We've known all along that this moment might come—hell, that it probably *would* come—and now it has. I wish it was some other way, but it's not. We're out of options now."

She closed her eyes tightly and sighed again. "Maybe we should just turn ourselves in this time. Let the courts handle it."

The words from his wife frightened Jake at a level much deeper than anything he'd felt in the shop or in the police station or out along the road. For any of this to work, they needed to be a team—and a strong team at that. "Carolyn, look at me. Please."

She opened her eyes. They were dry. She knew he was right.

All the same, he needed to make sure. "You know that if we're caught, there won't be any trial, right? This has gone too long and too far for whoever's in charge to let that happen. If they catch us, we're dead. It's that simple."

She nodded. She knew it, all right.

"Think of Travis," he pushed, selling to the sold. "They won't know what we told him. He won't be safe, either."

She thought about that one for a long time. "Maybe we should leave without him," she said, measuring her words.

He cocked his head. "You're not serious."

"Maybe he'd be safer without us."

He stared at her for a long time. "Do you really believe that?"

She didn't know what she believed anymore. She felt adrift in a sea of emotion, and Travis was the root of all of it: fear, remorse, guilt, pity. The years since he'd been born had been their best. And now here they were, rewarding his innocence and his love with deadly lies and mortal danger. These were things he'd never understand; never forgive.

The day she brought his beautiful face into this world, she'd entered into a contract which she believed with all her heart was governed by the will of God. In return for Travis's smile and his pranks and his love; in return for the sleepless nights of worry over unexplained fevers and colic and messy diapers; in return for unqualified, unquestioning love, the one thing she owed him more than anything else was simply to be there to hold him. In the best of times or in the worst, her job was to be always down the hall when he cried out in the night, or to be always the first on the scene with a Band-Aid for his knee, a tissue for his tears.

But he wasn't little anymore. He put on his own Band-Aids and shrugged away from her hugs and her kisses. Maybe that made him strong enough to endure on his own.

As if to prove herself wrong, the specter of her own adolescence bloomed large in her memory. She remembered all too clearly the hurt and the doubt and the insecurity, and she remembered how sometimes a willing ear or a special dinner would have mattered every bit as much as a hug or a Band-Aid. No one had been there for her. How could she not be there for him?

The contract, she realized, went on forever—for better or for worse, until the last day of her life. In the end, then, the answer was simple.

"No," she said at length, "I don't believe that at all. Let's go get him."

Jake watched her for a moment more before he shared her smile.

He brought her to him one more time and kissed her. "God, I love you."

She slugged him lightly in the ribs. "Talk's cheap. Just prove that you can get us out of here."

He went to work. Even in the darkness, he seemed to know where everything was. Leaning halfway into the van, he pulled a blue gym bag out from under the left-hand row of shelves. "Here, let me see your wallet," he said.

She took the lantern around to the front to retrieve her wallet from inside the little fashion purse and was back in no time. "Here."

"Thanks." He took the wallet in his right hand as he battled the bag's zipper with his left. "Can you bring the light around a little?"

He shifted his butt to make room for her, then produced a fistful of identification and credit cards from the bag. He handed over a North Carolina driver's license and warned, "Take everything out of your wallet and out of your pockets that has anything to do with Jake and Carolyn Brighton."

"What do I do with them?"

"I don't care. Leave it on the floor here. We are now Jerry and Carrie Durflinger."

"*Durflinger?* You're kidding, right?"

His eyebrow danced. "Sorry about that," he said, smiling. "I couldn't find any Smiths who fit the profile." He cleaned out his own wallet, except for the money, and dumped the contents on the floor. "Got everything?"

She took a deep breath, then shrugged. "I guess. Do the license plates match these IDs?"

Jake responded with a look. Of course they did.

They closed up the back of the van, and while he climbed into the driver's seat, she stood by the overhead door. Even in the yellow light of the lantern, he could see his wife's hand on her chest, her fingers crossed. He closed his eyes and offered up a silent prayer, then cheered when the engine jumped to life.

"*Yes!*"

Flashing a thumbs-up, Carolyn lifted the overhead door. Jake pulled out far enough to clear the back bumper, then waited while she pulled the door back down and locked it. As she climbed into the cab, she struggled with the money bag to make room for her feet.

"I'm ready," she said.

"Let's go, then."

As he edged the van out into traffic, he felt like he should be saying something—making some pithy remark that would somehow make all of this better. Try as he might, though, the words just weren't there. In their place was a sense of dread. Of all the stupid decisions he'd made in his life, he sensed somehow that this was the worst; of all the adventures, this was the last.

As if to emphasize the hopelessness of their plight, he had to wait for two police cars to scream past him, sirens blaring, before he could pull out onto the road.

CHAPTER SEVEN

Irene stared at the handset for a long time after resting it back on its cradle. Never in her forty-two years on the planet had anyone ever brutalized her like that on the telephone. Not even counting the two years in college when she'd moonlighted in telephone sales.

Frankel had called initially to praise her for bringing Jake Donovan to justice after so many years. He told her during the jovial first seconds of their conversation that he considered her diligence a personal favor, in light of his impending confirmation hearings.

That initial praise hurt more than any of the curses that followed. That Frankel had been the original case agent was common knowledge throughout the Bureau; that he'd progressed beyond it was nothing short of miraculous. And here, on the eve of his appointment as director, Irene had blown a once-in-a-lifetime chance to encase her career in gold. If only she'd listened to her instincts.

God *damn* Sherwood and his cronies!

Okay, that wasn't fair. Despite his smugness and annoying condescension, all Sherwood had done was state his opinion. She could forgive that. Somehow, though, that sense of charity wouldn't stretch as far as Lucas Banks. At least Sherwood was a cop. Banks, on the other hand, would do well to steer clear of Irene for the next few lifetimes. She made a mental note to speak to the U.S. Attorney about filing obstruction of justice charges against him just for the hell of it.

Of all the invectives launched by Frankel over the telephone, the one that stung the most was "incompetent." She'd been around for way too many years to make mistakes like this. Certainly, her career was dead in the water, and with it, her dreams to scale the lofty heights of the pyramid. Dishonor was dealt with slowly and painfully in the Bureau, earning errant agents either a lifetime assignment crashing doors in the world's worst ghettos or watching grass grow at some distant Indian reservation.

She could always quit, she supposed—but in the longer view, that wasn't really an option. She had her daughters to think about. Until Pam and Paula were out of college and married, hers was the only paycheck to pay the bills.

When Sherwood failed to return with news of an arrest, she'd figured Donovan was gone. So now the chase was on. As she reached for the door handle leading from Sherwood's office to the squad room, she paused for a moment, straightening her shoulders and pulling herself together. At least for the time being, she was still in charge of this case, and she was intent on looking the part.

The squad room was deserted. Half-full cups of coffee sat in the middle of incomplete paperwork. Chairs were skewed, and somehow the place looked even rattier than it had before. Obviously, Sherwood had scrambled the whole department to chase Donovan down, and God bless him for the effort.

For the time being, the Phoenix P.D. would be the only eyes and ears she had. The DEA boys from this morning were already on their way back home, and they had no jurisdiction, anyway. That pretty much left her with her thumb up her ass waiting for reinforcements from the Charleston field office, at which point the chase would take on a whole new dimension. Meanwhile, she needed to find Sherwood and his senior staff. She was, after all, their leader.

She found the chief and his three lieutenants holed up in the command center—really little more than a conference room with a dozen phone lines and maps covering three walls. A giant green chalkboard dominated the fourth wall, extending from corner to corner, floor to ceiling. Currently, the board was empty.

That will change soon enough, she thought.

"Good afternoon, gentlemen," she said officiously, striding up to the front of the room. Southern born and bred, the four men stood without thinking, but she waved them back into their seats. "You've all heard about my little adventure this morning," she opened, "and I'm sure you'll have ample opportunity to bust my chops over the next few hours or—God forbid—days." She figured the best way to regain some semblance of authority was to admit responsibility up front and to move on. "For the time being, though, somebody catch me up with what we know."

Sherwood took the lead, but not before draining his coffee and adding the cup to the boneyard of dead Styrofoam scattered across the Formica-topped conference table. "I'm afraid you already know what we know, Irene," he said with a shrug. "He bamboozled us. The officer who was supposed to be ferrying him back to his house got sidetracked by a story about his mother having surgery at the hospital. We've got officers there, of course, but I don't expect to find anything. He's a clever guy."

"You've got people at his house, I presume," she offered, drawing a patronizing glare from the chief.

"Of course," he said, his tolerance a bit frayed. "And at his office, too, though I can't imagine he'd be stupid enough to go back there."

She nodded. They were long shots, but criminals were known to make incredibly foolish mistakes. "What about roadblocks?" As she spoke, she leafed through the Wanted posters for the Donovans, trying to reconcile the printed details with the ones she'd memorized.

One of the lieutenants answered for Sherwood. "Unfortunately, we don't have the manpower to be offensive and defensive at the same time. The state police are willing to help, but they're just as flat-footed as we are right now. Give me two hours, and I can make this city vaporproof. Until then, we've got to hope for mistakes."

She dropped the posters on the table and looked up. "Well, the Donovans aren't known for making too many of those," she said. "Do you people realize who we're dealing with? These two killed sixteen people back in 1983. People they knew. *Friends* of theirs. Just mowed them down like so many bowling pins. As I recall, they were environmental lunatics, trying to prove a point about the evils of chemical warfare, so naturally, they blew up a chemical weapons plant and contaminated a couple hundred square miles of Arkansas."

"They left a note, didn't they?" Sherwood asked, trying to dislodge the details from his own memory.

She nodded. It was all coming back to her. This had been a case study at the academy for years. "Yes. They called it their manifesto, typed up neatly and left in the hotel room of a coworker who was too sick to go to work that day. In fact, they went all the way back to the motel just to blow his ass away, too. These are some sick, sick puppies, gentlemen."

With an amazing knack for vaporizing before our eyes. "We don't even have a decent photo of the guy," Irene growled. The picture in the Wanted poster bore only a vague, family resemblance to Jake Brighton, and it'd be another half hour before his new mug shot was on the street.

"Look at the bright side," one of the lieutenants offered. "At least he's as off balance as we are. I don't care how careful a planner this asshole is, there's no way he could have been prepared for what went down this morning."

"Good point," she agreed. "So, if we're gonna get him the easy way, we're going to have to do it soon. We can't possibly guess what his escape plan is, but let's not lose sight of the fact that he left here naked, for all intents and purposes. No car, no money—at least none to speak of. Where is he going to go to get those things?"

"We know he called his wife," a lieutenant said. "Probably told her to bring them."

"Do we *know* it was his wife, or are we *assuming* it's his wife?" Sherwood asked.

The lieutenant blushed. "Well, he *said* it was his wife."

Everyone laughed, but Irene spoke the words: "And he *said* his name was Brighton. I don't suppose you recorded the conversation, did you?"

"What?" Sherwood gasped playfully, bringing both hands to his face. "And violate the Fifth Amendment rights of our visiting felons?"

Shit. "I didn't think so."

"Too many lawyers are consulted on that phone," Sherwood explained, serious once again. "Judge told us 'no way' on the recordings."

"Okay," Irene said, mentally checking off one more possibility. "What do we know about the lovely Mrs. Donovan?"

"We know she killed a shitload of people," one of the lieutenants grumbled as a third one—Roper, according to his name tag—answered a ringing phone.

"Why, thank you, Lieutenant. How helpful. Do we know if she stuck with our boy long enough to become Mrs. Brighton?"

"Well, you know what they say," Sherwood offered with a big grin. "Nothing cements a relationship like a good killing spree."

"Got something!" Roper announced, dropping the telephone receiver onto its cradle. "We ran the name Brighton through the computer, filtering out everything outside of Phoenix—start small, right? And get bigger. Anyway, we got a single hit. A Travis Brighton is registered in the eighth grade at J. E. B. Stuart Junior High. Same home address as Jake's—Farm Meadows Mobile Home Park."

Irene smacked the table with both palms. "That's it!" she proclaimed. "That's our best shot. Stake out the kid, capture the parents."

Sherwood started issuing orders, even as his staff was carrying them out on their own. "Get all units out to the school," he commanded. "Everybody but the people already committed to Brighton's house and the body shop. Call the school. Have them put the kid under wraps somehow." As everyone sprung into action, Sherwood brought it all to a stop with a wolf whistle, freezing people in their tracks. "Remember, everyone! This one requires a bit of diplomacy. We've got a known murderer snatching his kid from a school. This one has 'bloodbath' written all over it, okay? Tell everybody to be very goddamn careful."

The image of automatic-weapons fire and bleeding children raced through Irene's head and gave her a chill. "How long till you have units on the scene, Chief?"

He placed his hands on his hips and took a deep breath as he glanced at the map and ran calculations. "Ten minutes, I'd guess. Maybe twelve. Kinda far off the beaten path."

She checked her watch and sighed. Somehow it seemed like forever.

CHAPTER EIGHT

They were less than a mile from the school now.

As he piloted the van ever closer to danger, Jake realized with a shiver just how high the stakes had become. It wasn't fair.

Some wild, weird conspiracy that he'd never fully comprehended had cost him his entire life; his future as well as his past. Over the years, the panic attacks had grown less common—those sudden rushes of paranoia when someone would look at him strangely, or those horrifying moments in the grocery store when someone would say, "Don't I know you from somewhere?"—but their accumulated burden had robbed him of his faith in people. Slowly but steadily, the concept of fairness had eroded to the point where his expectations were painfully simple to meet. Life was about survival; about making sure that at the end of the day you still had what was important. Today even that cynical goal seemed unattainable.

He wondered sometimes what might have happened if he hadn't run; if he'd let the justice system run its course. At the time, it had seemed so much easier to disappear. So much safer. Now he realized how foolish they'd been. In the eyes of the world, the very act of running away served as proof of their guilt.

They'd gotten into this, Carolyn and he, at a time in their lives when they still believed that it would all work out somehow. They believed then that bad things didn't happen to good people and that given their lifelong efforts to be decent citizens, they'd somehow stumble onto a happy ending. Looking back, his naïveté infuriated him.

Over the years, he'd reached a fragile inner peace with his pessimism that still eluded Carolyn. He feared she'd never stop looking for the silver lining—never fully comprehend that they were destined to die young. The real tragedy in all of this was Travis. What could a boy possibly have done, even in a previous life, that would warrant parents who would so destroy his childhood? And who were they to expose him to . . .

No, don't go there, he commanded himself. *He's your son. You're his father. You have every right. Every responsibility.*

All that mattered was family. Everything else was gravy. Jake would lie, he would steal, he would *kill* to protect them, just as whoever had set them up would do whatever it took to protect their sordid secret. And the FBI was happy to help. The Donovans represented one of the greatest embarrassments in Bureau history, and Jake could only imagine how its agents' thirst for revenge had blossomed over the years. All in the name of justice, of course. What a crock.

To the government, justice was a weapon, used to gain power over other people. Politicians and their pawns cared only about publicity and career advancement. Bring in the bad guy, get a bigger staff. If ordinary citizens like Jake or Carolyn or true innocents like Travis had to die to make that happen, well, so what?

"Jake, are you okay, honey?" Carolyn looked like she'd been trying to get his attention.

"Huh? Yeah, I'm okay." He forced a wholly unconvincing smile.

"Do you think they know yet?"

He checked his watch: 2:20. "Oh, yeah, they know. I'm sure that's why those cop cars were racing all over town. They're trying to track me down. They'll have everything covered by now—our house, the shop, everything."

She gasped and swung around in her seat, grabbing his arm. "They'll be at the school, too!"

His expression remained rock-solid. "Could be."

She recognized the look for what it was and gasped again. "Oh, God, Jake, you can't just go shooting up a school! What are you going to do?"

He looked at her across the center console. His face was calm, resolute. "I'm going to pick up my son and take him with me."

"And if the police are there?"

He shrugged and returned his eyes to the road. "If the police are there, then it's likely to get intense."

"But Jake . . ."

He slammed the steering wheel with his palm and shouted, "Goddammit, Carolyn, what are my choices? Those sons of bitches aren't getting my kid! They've taken our lives, they're not getting his! I didn't start this fight. Now, I leave the school with Travis, or I don't leave the school at all! I don't know how to state it more clearly."

She stared at him for a long time, but he refused to look back at her. She wanted to be angry with him, but deep in her soul she knew he was right. If there were any bad guys here, it was the cops—the ones in Arkansas who refused to look past their noses for real evidence on whoever did the shooting that day.

The Jake she'd married all these years ago was not the bitter, cynical man who sat next to her now, avoiding her eyes and flexing the muscles of his jaw. This was a man created by betrayal and committed to having what was rightfully his, at all costs.

Family first, everything else second.

And he was absolutely right: they were out of choices. She willed away the dreadful sense of doom and struggled to find some flicker of optimism. This was a time for strength, not weakness.

The silence inside the van grew heavier as they approached J. E. B. Stuart Junior High. Carolyn was tempted to turn on the radio just for white noise, but didn't, fearful that they'd tune in a report on themselves. The FBI would have them classified as murderers, she was sure; that's what all the Wanted posters said. Now, as Jake pulled the van to a stop along the curb at the crest of the steep hill immediately behind the school, she felt sick with the knowledge that he truly was willing and ready to kill if he had to—to live down to what was expected of him.

"Why are you stopping here?" she asked. "Just pull into the circle up front and let's get this over with."

He shook his head. "No, the cops will be looking for us in either the Subaru or the Celica. I don't want anyone to be able to tell them about the van." After throwing the transmission lever into park, he turned sidesaddle to face her. "Here's how I see it, okay?" He spoke softly now, his voice controlled and businesslike. "I want you to wait here with the motor running. If I'm not back in fifteen minutes, leave without me."

She tried to interrupt, but he cut her off. "If you hear shots, count to thirty and leave. Travis and I will find our way to the safe house somehow. I plan to just walk out of there, like it's any other day, but if we come hauling ass up that hill, scoot over into the driver's seat and get ready to book."

"Are you finished?" She spoke through pursed lips—it was her angry look.

He thought about it for a moment, then nodded. "Yeah, I'm finished."

"Well, let me tell you how it's *actually* going to happen," she fired back. "I'm waiting here for you. *Period.* Two hours, shots fired, I don't care. I'm waiting. We're together forever, Jake." Her eyes filled again, and this time she let them.

How long had it been since they'd felt this close? He smiled as he reached over and cupped the line of her jaw in his palm. To argue would be a waste of time, and he knew it. "I love you, y'know."

Her mouth remained set, yet she smiled with her eyes as she covered his hand with her own. "Just love me enough to get back here."

"I promise."

Everything that needed saying was said. He slipped out of the van and closed the door. He pulled his jacket tight against the chilly breeze, pressing his elbow against the Glock, just to make sure it was still there. God, what a beautiful day! He figured it for sixty degrees; way too pleasant for the business at hand.

He walked quickly down the steep concrete steps toward the school—the ones that were off limits to kids, according to a flyer sent home last week. Seems a little girl tripped, and now they were too dangerous for everyone.

Once at the bottom, he cut across the deserted playground, then paused for a few seconds to look back up at the van, before finally disappearing around the corner.

J. E. B. Stuart Junior High School—named, like all things in the Deep South, for one of the Confederacy's heroes—was a sprawling, one-story structure, not yet five years old. Constructed of a hideous brown brick, the school was built for energy efficiency, allowing only one window per classroom, which could not be opened, except in an emergency. With an active PTA and an upper-bracket population, Stuart fared better than most South Carolina schools in the standardized tests that measured whether it was getting the job done.

As he approached the school, Jake realized for the first time that their escape plan had never addressed Travis's schooling. Yet another hole.

Shit.

As a tutor, he felt confident enough that he could hold his own against the academic challenges of the eighth grade, but there still remained the question of textbooks and curricula. How could they have overlooked something so obvious?

How ironic, he grumped, that after years of planning and simulations, walking through a million what-if scenarios, the first major weaknesses were becoming obvious even before the plan was fully executed. *Damn.*

His eyes scanned continuously as he approached the front doors, searching for signs of anything out of the ordinary. If the police had staked out the school, they'd done a fine job of staying out of sight. Again, he pressed his elbow against the Glock.

Please, God, forgive me for what I might do. A contingent prayer, hedging his bets with God. The sheer audacity of it made him smile.

Two sets of double doors brought him into the lobby of the school, colorfully decorated for Fall Festival, with splashy banners hanging from the suspended ceiling. They couldn't celebrate Halloween in the school anymore because some religious zealot with too much time on her hands had discovered that Halloween was a pagan holiday and as such violated the constitutional separation of church and state.

Amazing.

Behind him and to the right, colorful ribbon bows had been placed behind the pictures of three children, arranged under a tasteful sign in Old English calligraphy that read "In Memoriam." The sight saddened him. In Jake's day, kids didn't die.

The school's main office lay just ahead and slightly to the right. Through the glass walls, he noted a group of five staffers clustered around the end of the four-foot counter just inside the door, one man and four women. They appeared animated, concerned. The man, in particular—whom Jake recognized as Principal Menefee—seemed especially bothered, a deep scowl creasing his forehead. The subject under discussion was clearly a burdensome one, and Jake was willing to bet he knew exactly what it was.

He made eye contact with one of the women through the window as he reached for the doorknob. Her mouth dropped open, and her face drained of color as she tapped Menefee's shoulder. He watched the man's face harden and felt his own stomach flip. The principal's expression was one of resolve, not fear, and it occurred to Jake that Menefee might turn out to be a problem. He paused just long enough to unzip his coat before pushing the door open and stepping inside.

Conversation ceased instantly, and he realized in that moment how tired he'd grown of uncomfortable silences. "Hi, folks," he said as cheerily as he could. "I'm here to pick up my son."

No one said a word. All four women turned their eyes to their boss, who himself seemed unprepared to respond. "I—I'm afraid we, uh, we can't, um, do that for you," the principal stammered.

Jack smiled patiently. Obviously, the guy knew about the morning's events, and he was stalling for time, probably to protect Travis from what he saw as a threat to his safety. In his heart, Jake admired the balls it took for Menefee to stand up to him.

"Actually," Jake said as softly as he could, "that wasn't a request. It was a statement. I'm here to pick up my son." When no one moved, he added, "Now." As he spoke, he placed his right elbow on the counter, pulling his jacket away from his side. Whether he moved enough to expose the Glock, he didn't know, but certainly, Menefee interpreted the movement for the threat that it was. "I think you'll find him in English class about now."

Menefee turned to one of the ladies. "Mrs. Harris, would you please page Mrs. Friedrich's room and tell her that Travis Brighton's father is here to pick him up?"

Mrs. Harris started to move, but Jake made her freeze with his words. "Actually, Mrs. Harris, I'd like you just to tell Mrs. Friedrich to send Travis up to the front office. You can leave out the part about me being here. That'll be a surprise." Then, as an afterthought, "If you don't mind, tell him to bring his books and his jacket with him, too."

Mrs. Harris nodded obediently and scooted quickly to the P.A. console. As she did, another woman, this one wearing a white nurse's smock, ducked quickly into another room.

"Stay here, please!" Jake called after her. He darted over to the doorway she'd just entered. It was the same woman who'd looked so frightened through the window. Now she stood frozen in the middle of the nurse's office, twitching her eyes as if expecting to get hit. A little girl with a blond ponytail—she looked less like a student than a student's little sister—sat on the edge of a cot along the back wall. Although clearly scared to death, the girl posed no immediate threat, and Jake ignored her. "Please," he urged again. "Let's just talk together out here in the lobby until Travis arrives."

The nurse raised her hands as she walked, making Jake smile. "You can keep those down, ma'am. I'm really not here to hurt anyone. I'd just like everyone to stay together."

"Did you really kill people, Mr. Brighton?" asked the ponytail girl out of nowhere.

The suddenness of the question caught him off guard. He regarded the girl cautiously, looking for something he didn't find. She seemed just genuinely curious. "No, honey," he said. "I've never hurt a soul." He moved a little closer, then bent down to look her straight in the eye. "And that's the absolute truth."

Seemingly satisfied, the little girl smiled. "Good," she said.

He patted her head, taking care not to rumple the hairdo, then turned his attention back to the adults in the office. "Have you made your announcement yet, Mrs. Harris?"

"N-no," she said. "I—I thought you wanted to hear me do it."

"That's very thoughtful." He made a special effort to show a smile. "Okay, then, let's get to it. I'm listening now."

Mrs. Harris punched a button on the console. "Mrs. Friedrich?" she asked.

The open mike on the other end sounded hollow, distant. "Yes?"

Mrs. Harris glanced back at Jake before continuing. "Would you send Travis Brighton to the office, please?"

In the background, the open mike picked up a group "Ooooo" from the class. A trip to the principal's office was never good news. "Class! Hush!" At Mrs. Friedrich's command, her room fell silent. "Okay," she said to the microphone. "Anything else?" Clearly, she was waiting for a reason.

"Make sure he brings his books and his jacket with him." Mrs. Harris looked back at Jake and seemed pleased by the smile she got in return.

"Which books?" Mrs. Friedrich asked.

Mrs. Harris deferred to Jake, who merely shrugged.

"All of them," Mrs. Harris said.

"*All* of them?"

Mrs. Harris fired another look to Jake, who made a rolling motion with his fingers, urging her to move things along. She turned back to the microphone, clearly at a loss for what to say, then gave up and turned the system off.

Her solution struck Jake as funny. "Nicely done, Mrs. Harris." She seemed proud of herself.

"Why get your son wrapped up in all this, Brighton?" Menefee asked. His tone had the hard edge of a father scolding his son.

Jake's smile disappeared. He glared at the man for a long time, deciding whether or not to answer. Finally, he said, "Don't look at me like I'm some sort of child molester, Menefee. In case you haven't realized it yet, this is a time for you to be very, very careful."

Menefee shook his head and stood a little taller, as if finding a lost vein of courage. "I don't look at you as a child molester, Brighton," he corrected. "I look at you as a murderer, because that's what you are."

The ladies gasped as one. Mrs. Harris brought a hand to her chest—as though she might be having a heart attack—and shot Menefee a surprised, angry scowl. All of them edged away from their boss, reminding Jake of that scene in every cowboy flick where the street clears before the big gun battle.

Jake never shifted his stare from Menefee's eyes, yet he registered precisely what everyone in the room was doing, where they were going. He sensed that things were about to come unraveled. Menefee was a fool to draw verbal battle lines. What could he possibly hope to gain by picking a fight with an armed man? When Jake spoke, he carefully selected every word. "If I were a murderer, you'd be dead now, Menefee. As it is, I haven't even threatened you."

"You bring a gun into my school . . ."

Jake silenced him with an abrupt movement of his left hand, making Menefee flinch. Under different circumstances, Jake might have laughed at the reaction, but not this time. He leveled his forefinger at the principal, six inches from the end of the man's nose. "It's time for you to shut up now," he said. "I've done nothing wrong. The details are none of your business, but rest assured that, to date, I have never killed a soul." He paused, shifting his eyes individually to each of the people standing there in the office. One by one, all but the little girl broke eye contact the instant he landed on them. "Also rest assured that I will do whatever I have to do to protect my family from harm. Is that clear, Menefee?"

The principal's eyes shifted from the tip of Jake's finger to the gun on his hip and back again. He swallowed hard, then nodded.

Jake lowered his finger slowly. "Good. Now, why don't you take a seat over there."

Menefee hesitated for an instant, as though unsure what to do.

"Please," Jake said, motioning with his hand toward one of the three metal secretarial desks behind the counter. "And don't touch anything, okay? Especially not the phone. Really, my business here is almost done."

CHAPTER NINE

Eleven minutes had passed, and Carolyn was freezing. She slid the temperature control further toward red, realizing that it just wasn't that cold outside. Nerves, she figured. Her body temperature always plummeted when she got nervous. Her feet felt like they might blister from the hot air blasting down on them, yet she still couldn't stop shivering.

This was taking too long. How big a deal could it be to go inside, pick up Travis, and come back outside? Five minutes? Maybe ten? Now they were closing in on twelve, and still her men were nowhere to be found. She hated herself for not going in with him. She should have insisted. At least then, whatever happened would happen to them together. The thought of being separated from the action—good or bad—was unbearable.

Twice she started to climb out of the van to check up on them, but both times she stopped herself. If things turned bad, they'd need her to be right where she was. Her mind projected a nightmare scenario, with Jake dragging Travis in a dead-out sprint up the hill, with cops close on their heels, only to find the van empty.

How many times had Jake said it? The key to success is sticking to the plan.

In her heart, though, the plan was doomed to failure. How could it possibly work? There were a million variables, with billions of combinations. This whole business with Travis and his field trip, for example. Who'd have thought? Or the drug bust that morning in the shop? Nothing was as they'd planned it. Hell, the original version of the plan didn't even take Travis into account—he wasn't even conceived yet.

In the old days, Carolyn and Jake were obsessed by the plan. They worked on it every night, investing thousands of dollars into the equipment and the tools and the safe house in the mountains. God, the safe house! How long had it been since she'd even seen it? Eleven years? Twelve, maybe? Travis was just a little guy, she knew that, and even then it was a rattrap; an easy place to avoid. Balanced right on the edge of civilization, the safe house—really an old travel trailer to which Jake had assigned the lofty name Donovan's Den—sat in the middle of a five-acre tract in the hills of West Virginia. Jake had read about it in the legal notices of the Beckley newspaper and bought it from the bank for $15,000 cash, the day before the trustee sale. According to the real estate records, the property now belonged to one Francis Wheeler, of High Point, North Carolina. Sometimes Carolyn wondered how Jake kept all of the aliases straight in his head.

Early on, the aliases had been an obsession of his. You couldn't have too many names. Every week or so, for more than a year, he went to the library and perused death notices from a dozen key papers. Once he had a name, he'd simply call the Division of Motor Vehicles under the guise of checking a driving record for an insurance company. With a little bullshit and a lot of bluff, he'd wrangle the driver's Social Security number out of the clerk, and once armed with that magical nine-digit identification, the rest was easy. Using a series of post office boxes—a new one every month—they'd get new driver's licenses. Each new application carried its own risk, of course, but if something went disastrously wrong, everything would be traceable to a defunct P.O. box, last owned by a dead man.

The Brighton persona had lasted much longer than it was ever supposed to. Credit Travis for that. Once the baby was born, the business of changing names became infinitely more difficult. And by the time he was old enough to talk, name changes were out of the question. How would they have explained it? Some secrets, they agreed, should never be shared with a little boy. So they became the Brighton family for good, switching back to the name on Travis's birth certificate.

The rest was just a matter of being careful. By obeying all laws, paying their taxes on time, and in all other ways just blending in with their surroundings, they'd been able to pull it off. In retrospect, Carolyn saw now that they'd become far too comfortable. They'd let their guard down.

Now it was all caving in on them, and she wasn't at all sure that she was up to it anymore. She was thirty-six now, Jake thirty-eight. They were too old to be pulling up stakes and starting over. And what of Travis? What were they going to tell him? How was it, she wondered, that the only issues they'd never discussed thoroughly—the only ones not a full part of the plan—were those that directly involved their son? It was as though they were afraid to open that particular door, for fear of what they might find lurking behind it.

How could Travis ever forgive them for their lies? How could he not hate them when he found out? This was no run-of-the-mill Santa Claus lie, after all. Their son's entire life was built on a collapsing foundation of sand. Every record ever made of the boy showed his name as Travis Brighton, whose mother was Carolyn Davies Mallone, and whose father was Jacob Aubrey Brighton. Yet those people—the ones who had been born with those names and lived with those Social Security numbers—were both dead; killed in separate automobile accidents back in 1982.

What did it mean for Travis, she wondered, that his parents, as he knew them, didn't even exist? Would he have to change his name if they were caught? Could they afford not to change his name even if they weren't caught? Thousands of questions flooded her mind as she sat there shivering in the warm car, trying to make sense of it all. In a rush of dreadful pessimism, she realized with absolute clarity that they had no idea what the hell they were doing. The secret to survival was not the plan, after all; but rather the ability to adapt to random slaps and shoves that life handed you as you went along, trying your best to do your best. Planning was merely a way to bide your time and rationalize that somehow you'd be able to solve your problems.

She shivered again and found herself thinking about that bottle of Jack Black nestled in her duffel bag. *That'll warm me up.* Her mouth watered at the thought of white-hot brown liquid coursing its way down her throat . . .

No! she commanded herself, so forcefully that she wondered if she'd said it aloud. *This is not the time.*

She didn't even see the cop car until it had passed her, moving quickly down the street toward the school.

Oh God, please, no.

Her heart hammered behind her breastbone as the blue-on-white cruiser approached the driveway, then slowed for an instant as it swung the turn.

"Shit!" She said it aloud this time and climbed over the center console to slide behind the steering wheel. "Oh, God. Come on, guys," she moaned through clenched teeth, scanning her obstructed view for some sign of her family. They were nowhere to be seen. "Dammit."

Reaching down between her knees with her left hand, Carolyn pulled the lever she found and clumsily adjusted her seat behind the wheel. Her first try was too close, then the second slid back too far. Two or three oscillations later, the seat was about right. She stepped on the brake, reached for the gearshift lever with her right hand, then stopped.

Somehow the shiny little .380 from the bank had materialized in her palm.

"Two days in a row," Travis grumbled as he shrugged into his jacket and stuffed his books into his backpack. He slammed his locker shut. "This is getting to be a regular friggin' habit." This time he didn't even know what he'd done, yet obviously it was expulsion time. Why else would he have to bring all his books?

Should have kissed Menefee's fat ass when I saw him in the hall this morning, he thought. Well, no great loss. He hated this school, anyway.

How the hell was he going to break *this* news to his dad? Yes indeedy, there was going to be some serious shouting in Farm Meadows tonight. He wondered absently if his mom would hold him while his dad screamed him to death, or if Dad would just handle the dirty deed on his own.

As he turned the corner from G-Hall into the administrative wing, he searched his brain for what he might have done wrong today. Surely, they wouldn't expel him for letting Eric Lampier's brother stomp the shit out of him after school. Then again, maybe they would. If he had to tell the story about his eye one more time to one more stone-faced teacher, he was going to barf. Mrs. Benoli, the guidance counselor, must have asked him a dozen times whether his mother or father had hit him. Almost seemed like she wanted him to say one of them had.

He didn't, of course. He said he couldn't remember the last time his dad had hit him. Not exactly the truth, but a spanking for biting Tommy Mution in kindergarten hardly equated to the kind of abuse the old crone was fishing for.

Travis nearly dumped in his drawers as he swung the last corner and saw his old man waiting for him in the office. Yep, some serious shit was going down.

"Hi, Dad," he said sheepishly as he pushed open the door to the office. "Hi, Mr. Menefee." Ordinarily, Travis wasn't much of a suck-up, but right now it didn't seem like a bad idea.

"Hi, Trav," Jake said, forcing a smile. Something was going on in there—Travis could almost taste the tension in the air. "Have you got your stuff?"

Travis shrugged. "Yeah. Where are we going?"

Jake put his arm around his son's shoulder but continued to look at Menefee. "On a little trip," he said.

"Don't get him involved, Brighton," Menefee urged again, daring to rise from his chair. Travis recognized the threat in his voice.

"Stay out of it, Menefee," Jake warned. He brought his finger to bear one more time.

Travis watched the exchange like a tennis match, moving his head from one man to the other. Mrs. Harris looked like she might cry. "What's going on?" he asked. "Is Mom okay?"

Jake glanced quickly down at his son. "She's fine," he said, way short of sounding convincing. "Menefee, you do what's good for you, hear? Just stay out of this."

"You won't get twenty miles," Menefee persisted.

"That's enough out of you now," Jake repeated, backing out the door. Then, to Travis, "Come on, son, let's go."

Travis looked terribly ill at ease. "What's he talking about, we won't get twenty miles?"

Jake hurried the boy along. "Let's just get going."

Once free of the office, Travis followed his dad's lead and walked quickly but cautiously toward the main entrance, just as a police car slid into the spot reserved for buses. "Whoa!" Travis exclaimed. "They're in a hurry."

Jake whirled to face the main doors, in time to see the blue and white cruiser slide into place. "Shit!"

"What's wrong?"

Jake grabbed the boy by his denim jacket and made a hard left, heading down A-Hall toward the door at the other end. "C'mon, Trav, quickly now." He drew the Glock.

"Holy shit, Dad! What are—"

"Hush," Jake snapped, pulling harder on the jacket.

Instinctively, Travis wriggled out of Jake's grasp. "What's the gun for?"

"Move!"

The desperate tone and frantic look were new to Travis. He'd never seen his father so distraught. Whatever was happening, it was far more serious than anything that had ever happened to them before. Terrified, he found himself running down the hallway, distantly aware of the fact that running was against the rules.

His dad had a gun! And he looked ready to use it. Hell, he looked *anxious* to use it. *What the hell is going on?*

As they charged together down the glossy, linoleum-tiled hallway, Travis had to take two strides for every one of Jake's. They reached the end and exploded out into the sunlight, taking a hard left and sprinting toward the hill which led to the street.

"Are we running from the police?" Travis gasped as he struggled alongside Jake to climb the grassy slope.

If only you knew, Jake thought. "I'll explain in the car."

Jake scaled the steep slope with long strides, his feet slipping on the damp grass. He fell hard, face-first, but lost only a second or two before he was back scrambling up the hill. Two steps forward, one step back.

Travis slowed after two falls, but Jake grabbed a fistful of his backpack and yanked hard. "Run, goddammit!" he hissed.

As they cleared the top of the hill, Jake nearly cheered when he saw the van, still running, still where he left it, still on an empty street.

Back on flat ground, Travis continued to run, but Jake yanked him to a stop. "No, walk now. And get in the van."

"Whose car is this?"

"It's ours. Now get inside." Jake quick-walked his son to the rear double doors and pulled them open.

"Where do I sit?" It was a cargo van, for crying out loud! No chairs, no windows, just two lines of parallel shelving running down each side in the back. All the way to the front, Travis could see his mom behind the wheel, looking even more terrified than his dad.

"Just pick a spot and get in," Jake told him, pulling him forward by his arm.

Again, Travis wriggled free. "No," he said. "I'm not going anywhere." None of this was right. These people weren't his parents. They looked the same, but these were not his parents. He felt as if he were living some science fiction movie, where alien invaders take the form of other people. Fear gripped his insides, and he refused to move. Not until someone told him what the hell was going on.

"Travis, there's no time for this. Now get in."

"You're scaring me!" Travis shouted, loud enough to draw attention if anyone was listening.

"Get in the goddamn van!" Jake grabbed his son in a bear hug.

"Put me down!"

Carolyn was ready to panic, her eyes never moving from the spot at the head of the street where the cops would rematerialize any minute. "Oh, God, Travis," she pleaded. "Don't yell!"

In a flash, Jake realized the futility of the struggle, and he let the boy go. "Listen to me, Travis," he explained urgently. "I know this scares you, and that none of it makes sense, but you have *got* to get into the van, and we have *got* to get moving. The police think we've done something that we've never done, and they are just a block away from us right now."

"Jake, hurry!" Carolyn was coming unglued.

He ignored her. "I promise I'll explain it all as soon as we're down the road a bit. But right now you've just got to trust me. If you don't get in the van right now, your mom and I will be killed. It's that simple."

Travis's mind reeled. Whatever happened to detention slips and lectures from Mr. Menefee? Those were problems he could comprehend. Whatever happened to just getting the shit kicked out of you by Terry Lampier?

"Please, Travis!" his mom begged. She was frantic.

This was wrong. He should just run away—toward the cops, not away from them. His brain screamed these things at him, even as he climbed inside the van and allowed himself to be swallowed up in darkness as the doors closed.

"Oh, honey, please hurry," Carolyn begged as Jake opened the passenger-side door. She pulled away from the curb the instant her husband's butt landed heavily in the seat. After completing a sweeping U-turn that brought the front wheels of the van over the top of the curb across the street, she aimed the van toward the Confederate Trail and on toward safety.

"Watch your speed," Jake warned. "Shoot for two miles over the limit."

"Somebody tell me what's going on!" Travis insisted.

In the side-view mirror, Carolyn saw a cop car turn the corner at the top of the hill. "Shit," she spat. "Here they come."

Jake whirled in his seat and saw the flashing blue lights in the distance. "Damn." He struggled out of his seat and crouched behind Carolyn's headrest to get a look at what she saw in the mirror. "Okay, listen to me," he said quickly. "We can bluff our way out of this."

"How?" Panic had turned Carolyn's voice reedy.

"By being friendly," Jake soothed. "Listen, they're not looking for a van, they're looking for a Subaru or a Celica. They're not looking for you, they're looking for me."

"They're looking for both of us."

Jake shrugged, noting the edge of competitiveness in her voice. "Well, both of us weren't in the school just now. Hey, it's the best hunch I've got. Who knows? Maybe they won't even pull us over."

Crouched low, Jake duck-walked back to his son, who looked absolutely terrified. "God, Dad, what's happening?"

Jake looked at Travis for a long moment, wracking his brain for a simple answer. "We're escaping," he said simply. "And as frightening and unfair as it might seem, you're a part of it." If Travis appreciated the candor, his face didn't show it. Jake reached up to one of the shelves and pulled down two green wool Army blankets. "Here," he said. "Get under this, and don't make a sound."

Travis eyed him warily. "Why?"

Jake scooted in closer, until he was nearly nose-to-nose with his son, and grew suddenly very intense. "Travis, listen to me, okay? Things are pretty desperate right now. You can't keep asking me to explain everything as it happens. Just do it for me. We need to stay invisible."

Travis's sky-blue eyes grew wide and wet. Poor kid was scared to death and didn't even know why. But he nodded and slipped the blanket over his head.

"They're pulling me over," Carolyn announced from up front.

Jake dropped to his hands and knees and crawled to the rear corner opposite the one occupied by Travis. With the Glock still out and ready, he covered himself up to his chin with the blanket, noting the sound of the tires crunching gravel as they pulled to a stop on the shoulder. "Remember, Travis," he whispered, "not a sound."

The green blob nodded.

"And you remember, Carolyn," he whispered loudly, "you're Carrie Durflinger now." As an afterthought, Jake reached up and locked the back door.

*   *   *

Carolyn inhaled deeply through her nose, held the air, then let it go silently through pursed lips. This newest strategy wasn't part of the plan, but she supposed it made sense. After Jake's visit to the school, the police would be looking primarily for him, right? And they'd be looking for him in a different car. This little exercise merely bet their lives on the assumption that the cops wouldn't make the connection. She started shivering again. The stakes were way too high.

Her first and most immediate problem, she realized, was the .380 in her own hand. Certainly, she didn't want it out in plain sight, but there wasn't time to put it away. She compromised by slipping it under her right thigh, thoroughly unconvinced that she'd be able to use it even if she had to.

As she pulled the van to a stop, the police cruiser stopped with her, pulling in close to her rear bumper. She could see the flash of two badges through the cops' windshield. For the longest time, they just sat there, lights flashing their frenetic displays, but no one moving.

"Nothing's happening," Carolyn said without moving her lips.

"Did they stop?" Jake asked softly.

"Uh-huh."

"Okay, then, they're just running the plates. They should check out, so relax."

"Yeah, right." Her stomach was alive with butterflies—no, make that condors, a flock of them. The biggest birds on the planet.

"You'll know what they know by the way they get out of the car. If their guns are drawn, we're screwed."

Travis yanked down his blanket. "Guns?" He hadn't even considered the thought of a shoot-out. His eyes focused on the Glock in Jake's hand. "Dad?" There was genuine terror in the boy's eyes now.

Jake held up a finger to silence him. "Shh. Remember what I told you. I promise I'll explain it all to you. Later. For now, I need you to stay under that blanket." He made a point to smile.

Trembling now, and crying a little, Travis did as he was told.

"They're getting out now," Carolyn said. "No guns, though. Suppose they want to search the inside?"

"They won't. No probable cause." *Unless they recognize you.*

"But what if they do?"

Jake didn't have a clue. "Then we'll wing it."

The cops got out of their car together. The one from the passenger side stationed himself at the rear bumper of the van, not three feet away from Jake. But for a thin layer of sheet metal, they could have shaken hands. Meanwhile, the driver strolled cautiously toward Carolyn's window. As he neared, she cranked it down a few inches.

"Afternoon, ma'am," the cop said.

Carolyn had to crane her neck back and to the left to see him at all. "Hello, Officer. Did I do something wrong?"

The cop was all business; not a trace of humor. "Can I see your driver's license, please?" The silver name tag over his pocket read "Pernell."

It took a huge effort for Carolyn to keep her hands steady as she fumbled through her purse for her new ID. *Carrie Durflinger,* she told herself. As she handed the laminated card with her picture over to the cop, she quickly scanned the address block and jammed it into her short-term memory. *274 Oak Lane, High Point, North Carolina.*

Pernell looked at it for just a few seconds, then stuffed it casually into his belt. "Have you seen this man?" he asked, displaying a fuzzy photocopy of Jake's ancient arrest picture, full-face and profile.

The last time Carolyn had seen the picture, a similarly outdated picture of her former self had resided right next to Jake on the sheet of paper. Carolyn made a show of studying the picture carefully. He looked so young back then; no salt yet in his pepper-colored hair, freshly shaved cheeks.

"No, I don't think so," Carolyn said at length, inwardly proud of her acting skills. "Who is it?"

The cop took the picture back and stuffed it into the inside pocket of his jacket. "He goes by the name of Brighton. He's wanted for murder."

Carolyn dropped her jaw. "Murder! Oh, my God! In our little town?"

The cop gave a yeah-ain't-it-awful smirk and shook his head. "You think you know people, right?" he said. "Ms. Durflinger, I'm gonna ask you to stay here for just a minute more, okay?"

Carolyn's heart dropped. *What did he see? What did I say?*

"Well, I'm in a bit of a hurry," she said, checking her watch.

The cop nodded. Clearly, he didn't give a hoot about her schedule. "It'll just be a minute."

"Jesus, Carolyn," Jake whispered from behind. "You're from North Carolina. This isn't your little town!"

Oh, shit! How could she be so stupid? Her stomach cramped harder still. She tensed against the pain but maintained a perfect poker face. The other cop was staring straight at her reflection in the door-mounted mirror. If she so much as twitched, he'd see it.

"Too late to worry now," Jake grumbled.

Carolyn ignored him. *Let's see you do this if you think you're so damn good at it.*

Pernell walked back to his partner. Carolyn watched as they chatted calmly, in the manner of consulting physicians: Pernell with his back to Carolyn, the partner facing her. She didn't like the other guy. His eyes were unfriendly, and as he listened, he appeared to stare straight through her. From body language alone, Carolyn surmised that Pernell was the subordinate. The boss cop asked a couple of questions, and Pernell answered each with a subtle shake of his head.

"What's happening?" Travis pleaded from beneath the blanket.

Jake reached out and touched the boy's shoulder. "Shhhh. We'll be fine."

Finally, the meeting broke up. As Pernell strolled back to the van, the boss returned to the cruiser.

"Sorry to have bothered you, Ms. Durflinger," Pernell said, handing her driver's license back through the window. After Carolyn took the card back, the officer smiled and tapped the door twice, a gesture of finality. "Have a good day."

The nerves kicked in as soon as Pernell started back to his car. Carolyn's hands trembled out of control, making it difficult for her to crank her window shut. Then a wave of anxiety swept over her, left to right, top to bottom. Within seconds, she was trembling all over: hands, knees, legs, shoulders, jaws. A crippling wave of nausea followed, along with an overwhelming need to go to the bathroom. They'd come so close, and now she was going to wreck it all in a flood of tears and vomit.

"I'm going to be sick," she tried to say, but the words came out as a garbled croak.

"No, you're not!" Jake commanded. "You don't have the luxury of getting sick. You're going to swallow down whatever you have to and pull away just like there's nothing wrong." The sternness of Jake's tone caused Travis's head to pop out again from under the blanket. He looked more frightened than ever. Jake saw the look and softened. "You've got the reins now, honey," he went on. "It's you, me, and Travis. That's all that matters. We can get away or we can get caught. Those are the only choices. And it's all up to you. You did a great job a minute ago. Don't blow it now."

Jake's words wounded Carolyn, and he knew it. She hated to be scolded like a child; in front of Travis, it was even worse. No words of praise for the wonderful deception; just warnings of dire consequences if she caved in to the flood of emotions which had just swallowed her up.

". . . just get control, Carolyn." Jake was still coaching her.

"I've got it, *okay?*" she snapped. Like flipping a switch, the emotions evaporated. Her hands and knees stilled, and her heart slowed to a survivable pace. The nausea was gone.

She slipped the van's transmission into drive and pulled away from the shoulder. She glanced back in the side-view mirror at Officer Pernell, who seemed busy with paperwork on his lap. As the image grew smaller with distance, Carolyn found herself hoping he'd never find out how badly he just screwed up.

Behind her, Jake let out a war whoop that nearly made her wreck the van. "We made it, babe! You were brilliant!"

CHAPTER TEN

By four-thirty, the full authority and resources of the United States government were behind the search for the Donovans, and, much to her surprise, Irene still had full tactical command. As a practical matter, all that really meant was that she'd been named as the official scapegoat. If she truly had lost her prey, only one career would be trashed.

Actually, two. Irene had known Paul Boersky since their days together in Minneapolis—her first assignment out of the academy, and his second. Together, they'd racked up quite an impressive list of arrests over the years, putting them both on faster tracks than their respective classmates. Irene had passed her old partner on the career ladder just fourteen months ago, thanks to the political realities of the nineties. These days, when it came time for promotions, all ties went to minority candidates—in this case, to a woman—and if you asked her, it was about damn time.

If Paul harbored any ill will toward his assignment to second chair, he never showed it. In fact, Irene's willingness to let subordinates shine on the job had served him well. No doubt his next assignment would be as supervisory agent in charge of a field office somewhere.

Well, no doubt until today, anyway. Fact was, if this Donovan thing went bad, everyone associated with it would be painted with a very ugly brush. At headquarters, they called it high incentive to perform.

Presently, Paul, Irene, and a dozen other cops and FBI agents were dismantling Farm Meadows Mobile Home Park, looking for some clue as to where the Donovans might have gone. So far, they'd found nothing; but the Phoenix P.D. was enjoying remarkable success in collaring four fugitives wanted on felony warrants. Irene overheard a cop liken the scampering felons to roaches scattering in the light. Personally, she preferred her own analogy of lifting a rock. Either way, Chief Sherwood had dodged one hell of a bullet.

There had to be a way to track them down. She refused to believe that the earth could simply open up and digest three human beings. Everything people did left a trail of some sort. Everyone, it would seem, except the Donovans.

Paul sighed loudly and leaned against the makeshift porch attached to the Donovans' trailer. "I know you don't want to hear this," he said sheepishly, "but it appears they plain just got away. The closets are still full of clothes, there's dishes in the sink and wet clothes in the washing machine. When they left, they left. Poof."

She helped herself to an AstroTurfed step. "And we missed them at the school," she sighed.

"Two hours ago," he confirmed. "We're getting a pretty good handle on how they spent their day, too. The neighbor down the street—a Mary Barnett—says she saw Carolyn in the bank this morning, looking, as she said, 'very suspicious.'"

"What does that mean?"

He shrugged. "I don't know. Probably means that Mrs. Barnett doesn't have enough to do. I've got a guy at the bank just the same, talking to folks down there."

She nodded. "Anything else?"

"Uh-huh. Let me show you." He led the way inside the Donovans' trailer, past the kitchen and the living room, and into the master bedroom. Not much for the trailer park scene herself, she had to admit that the place looked better than most. "Look here," he said, pointing to the bed. "Three duffel bags, packed with clothes and toiletries."

She arched an eyebrow. "Three bags? As in Mama Bear, Papa Bear, and Baby Bear?"

"Exactly," he confirmed. "Three bags packed with essentials, yet the drawers and closets are all full."

She scowled. "Now, you tell me how you can look at a closet and tell me it's full. You have some special power, do you, that lets you look at someone's closet and tell what's *not* there?" She chuckled and shook her head.

He scowled. He didn't like being the target of her derision, and he wasn't at all sure why she'd suddenly decided to take up residence on his back. "Think about it," he urged. "Wouldn't you think that someone throwing stuff together at the last minute would leave a mess? You'd have shit hanging out of drawers and stuff half-pulled off hangers. But look at this place." He made a wide, sweeping motion with his arm. "I mean, it's not *House and Garden*, but the place is certainly organized."

She turned her eyes back to the duffel bags. "Maybe they were going on a trip."

"The bags were padlocked into a closet."

"So?"

"So I think they've been planning for this. Look, this bag here even has pictures and baby memorabilia. No one takes stuff like that on vacation. The Donovans were ready to go at a moment's notice, which means they've got a plan. They know what they're going to do, where they're going to go, and how they're going to get there."

"But we interrupted their plan," she offered. "So maybe they're off balance."

He shrugged. "Well, okay. Maybe. But remember, these are just the essentials. Nothing here to make or break a getaway."

She considered that for a long moment. "Which means they've got more essentials someplace else."

He nodded. "I would if I were them."

She regarded him with a long look. "You think maybe you're giving them too much credit? Just because they've vanished once doesn't necessarily mean they're geared up to do it again."

"In fact, they have." Paul seemed a little embarrassed to be stating the obvious.

She sighed and rubbed her temples. Frankel's tirade hadn't yet stopped echoing in her brain. "What else do you have?"

He looked down. "Well, you know, it's still early in the investigation . . ."

"Don't go into excuses mode on me," she warned.

He paged through his notebook one more time, looking for a ray of hope, but ultimately flipped it closed. "Honestly? Beyond the interesting trivia, we don't have anything useful yet. I mean, we've got all the physical evidence in the world that the Brightons are really the Donovans, but so what? We knew that before we got here. What we really want to know is where they've gone, and there we don't have a clue. Not yet, anyway." The words hung heavily in the air. His boss looked like she might start to growl. "I wish I could tell you something you want to hear," he concluded, "but I can't."

She set her jaw. "Do you have any idea how tired I am of people telling me what they *can't* do?" She found herself repeating Frankel's words, nearly verbatim. "I can hire a sixth grader to tell me what we can't do. Careers, on the other hand, are built on the ability to find answers." She strode back toward the kitchen, with Paul close behind. They helped themselves to seats at the table.

Stung by her reprimand, Paul would wait till next week before he broke the silence. After all these years, he deserved better than this, and his expression showed it.

"One more time," she prodded. "Tell me what we *do* know."

He took a deep breath and swallowed his anger. "Okay. What we know: They're very careful people. They were ready to run and presumably have been for quite some time. We've found all the trappings of family life. You know, books, magazines, toiletries, toys for the kid. At first glance, their reading tastes tend to run toward romances and thrillers, and there's a collection of Goosebumps books in the kid's room my son would kill for. The only thing of even marginal interest is some of the magazines we've found. Lots of outdoors stuff—sportsmen's rags. To me, that's significant, if only because outdoor survival skills make it easier for them to disappear."

Irene scowled as she listened. "What about correspondence? Are there letters and such with return addresses we can trace?"

He opened the notebook again. Actually, he knew there were no notes relevant to the question, but it was a convenient way to stall for time. "We really haven't found much of substance there, either," he said. "Some unpaid bills and junk mail, mostly. We'll have a better answer in a couple of hours, once we get everything logged and examined." He sighed and raised his palms. "It's just early, Irene. I don't know what to tell you."

A new shadow appeared in the doorway. "Excuse me . . ."

The timid voice belonged to Special Agent Mike Jamison, who stood at the front door, waiting to be recognized. If people truly looked like their pets, then Jamison should have owned a horse farm. God, what a face. In J. Edgar's day, when FBI agents were required to look the part, Jamison's overbite would never have made it as far as the academy. Even today, despite an allegedly more progressive Bureau, the young agent's looks remained a threat to his livelihood. Timid and quiet, Jamison was widely accepted as a loser. Within five years, Irene figured, he'd be permanently consigned to Bureau Hell, raiding Indian stills somewhere in North Dakota.

Paul was first to acknowledge the newcomer. "Yeah, Mike, what's up?" As Jamison's immediate supervisor, Paul always looked embarrassed in his presence.

"Forget the Toyota Celica," Jamison announced, as though reciting information he'd practiced and memorized. "We just got a call from Phoenix P.D. Seems that two of their cops let the Donovans go a couple of hours ago, half a block from the school."

Irene's jaw dropped, and she closed her eyes. "Tell me you're joking."

Jamison shrugged. "I wish I was. The cops involved never saw Jake, and no one had bothered to fax the picture of Carolyn. Guess everybody was in a hurry."

"Oh, God," she moaned. "Is there anything—a single detail, somewhere—that Sherwood and his gang haven't fucked up today?"

Paul suppressed a smile and stayed focused on Jamison's report. "What about the Celica?" he prodded.

"Well, the folks stopped by Phoenix P.D. were in a white van," Jamison explained. "We've got a plate number. North Carolina, registered in the name of Durflinger."

"And let me guess," Irene growled, her eyes still closed. "The Durflingers are dead, right?"

Jamison looked deflated, his thunder stolen. "How did you know?"

"Because that's how you get a new name," Paul said, his voice heavy with disdain. It was the oldest trick in the book.

"I don't believe this," Irene moaned. "Shit. Well, put it out on the Net, pronto. Every state east of the Mississippi."

"Sherwood's already done that," Jamison offered.

Irene glared. "Yeah, well, Sherwood's done a lot today. Let's just back him up, okay?"

Jamison nodded but didn't move.

Paul's patience evaporated all at once. "Mike, if you've got more, spit it out."

Jamison cleared his throat and took a moment to search his memory. He seemed anxious to get it all right this time. "Apparently, some guy at a bank outside of town saw the news about the Donovans on TV. He just telephoned to tell Phoenix P.D. that he saw Carolyn Donovan in the bank this morning."

"Ah, the bank again . . ." Irene was growing tired of old news.

"The guy said she needed to get into a safe-deposit box," Jamison concluded.

"And?" Jesus Christ, it was like pulling teeth getting this guy to talk!

Jamison shrugged. "And he opened it for her."

"No shit, Mike," Boersky snapped. "What did she get out of the box?"

Agent Jamison looked a little panicky, like he'd forgotten to do something. "I don't know. The guy can't say for sure. He said that she entered the little room empty-handed and came out with a paper bag full of stuff. No one saw what she put into it."

Irene and Paul exchanged glances. "Cash?" she wondered.

Paul nodded. "That would be my guess."

Irene dismissed Jamison by turning away from him. "You said you've got somebody down there already?"

"Either there or on the way."

Irene waited until Jamison was gone before she talked about him. "He's totally hopeless, isn't he?"

Paul nodded and sucked on a cheek. "Yep, and he's allowed to carry a firearm in public. Makes you wonder sometimes, doesn't it?" He stood. "Great at gathering information, he just can't get out of his own way. Should have been a technician instead of an agent."

Irene's mind had already moved on to other things. "And you, Agent Boersky," she said, pointing. "I want you to get on the horn with the U.S. Attorney's Office and get me a court order to get into that safe-deposit box."

Paul looked at her like she was nuts. "Why? You think she went there to put something *in?*"

"Actually, no," she said with a frown, intentionally putting him back on edge. "I think the box is empty. Now I want you to prove it for me." She arose from her chair and headed for the door. "Besides, you look like you need something to do."

Travis sat in a folding lawn chair between the rows of shelves in the back of the van. They drove on in silence for a long time, Travis convinced that his parents had reneged on their deal to clue him in on what was going on. As the sun dipped below the mountain ridges ahead, he marveled at the different shades of orange and red and blue streaking the sky. The ridges looked like they were on fire; bright lights against a dark background. With the darkness, though, came a whole new world of fear.

He'd never seen his folks like this, so tense. He'd probably spent a million hours over the years watching them from this angle as they drove all over the place, but tonight they looked different, and the transition scared the hell out of him. His dad's jaw was set sort of funny, and the muscles in front of his ears worked all the time. And there was the new look in his eyes—same as the one when the cop came up to the window. And his mom! Jeeze, she looked ready to explode.

These long silences were frightening, too; second only to those intense, whispered conversations they'd have between themselves, where Travis could only catch bits and pieces. If there was anything good to say, they'd have said it by now.

Finally, he couldn't take it any longer. "Hey, Dad?" His voice sounded uneasy; like he wasn't sure whether to ask his question.

"Yes, Travis?"

"Would you really have shot that policeman?"

"Travis, not now," Carolyn snapped.

Jake raised his hand. "No," he said. "I think we need to discuss this."

"But Jake . . ." There was a pleading tone in Carolyn's voice.

"Carolyn, he's got to know. I wish he didn't, but now he has to."

Instantly, Travis was sorry he'd asked. Out of nowhere, he remembered a story that Jay Kowalski had told him about the day Mr. Kowalski announced to the family that he had cancer. It was a lot like this, but without the car and the guns. Jay said that his mom and dad fought for a long time about whether the kids should be told, and finally, when his father prevailed in the argument and told them everything, Jay's life was never the same. His dad was dead within a year. Travis didn't want his dad to die.

Jake began with a deep breath, the way he always did when he was about to Teach a Lesson. "Trav, there are things about your mom and me that you need to know . . ."

CHAPTER ELEVEN

Newark, Arkansas. August 1983

Building 234 lay nestled between Buildings 1719 and 2680, near the center of what used to be the Ulysses S. Grant Army Ammunition Plant. At one time, the numbering system must have meant something to someone, but now the signs were just random markings on countless low-rise red brick buildings. If the exterior of Building 234 was boring, then the interior was downright ugly. The glare of the fluorescent lighting, reflected off baby-shit brown walls, cast a yellow tint, making everyone inside look chronically ill.

As usual, Jake and Carolyn were running late, although this time it truly wasn't their fault. Not that having an excuse would buy them any sympathy. Today was opening day for the biggest job in Enviro-Kleen's history, and everything had to go perfectly. As they dashed down the hallway toward the packed conference room, Jake tried not to think about the trouble they might be in. Worrying was Carolyn's job, anyway.

"Hey, it's the newlyweds!" Glenn Parker announced gleefully as the Donovans tried to sneak in. Clearly, they'd yet to get to the serious portion of the meeting. "I was just telling everyone what a superman you were last night, Jakester. Those thin walls are better than a porno flick, man."

Carolyn blushed crimson as the room erupted in laughter and applause. Jake grinned wide and bowed. "I'll leave the curtain open for you tonight, buddy. Pictures to go with the sound."

With her jet-black hair, huge brown eyes, and pleasing shape, Carolyn was the only female on a crew of thirty-seven horny, single young men. That she undoubtedly played a major role in their fantasies as they sought relief alone in the darkness of their motel rooms didn't bother her a bit. Truth be known, it was kind of a turn-on.

"Don't have any trouble walking this morning, do you, Carolyn?" Parker persisted, drawing another big laugh.

"If you can still use your hand, then I can still walk." That one brought the house down.

Nick Thomas, site safety officer on the Newark project, and the man in charge of this last meeting before the operation went hot, struggled to regain control of the room. "Okay, okay, okay," he said, pressing the air with his palms. "Could we get back on topic, please? Jake, Carolyn, take a seat. Where's Tony Bernard?"

The folding metal seats in the conference room appeared to predate the building itself, and the two remaining at the back of the room were the worst of the lot. Guaranteed butt-busters. Jake tried sitting for about two seconds, then opted to stand.

"Tony's sick," he announced, rubbing the place on his lower back where the chair had dug in. "That's why we're late. We were trying to roust him out of his room, but he's heaving his guts out. Trust me, you don't want him here."

The concern on Nick's face was immediate and obvious. They'd rehearsed this operation a hundred times and had calculated the work-rest cycles based on a full contingent of entry workers. He turned to Sean Foley, the project manager, who'd been scowling from the corner behind Nick.

"We go, anyway," Foley grunted. An MBA marketing type, the boss had little time for the entry workers' cowboy mentality to begin with. He'd be damned if he was going to pull the plug on a multimillion-dollar contract just because somebody got sick without permission. The room fell silent.

Nick took the cue as his opportunity to continue. He flipped on the overhead projector, and the pull-down screen was filled with a line drawing labeled "Magazine B-2740."

"Okay, troops, this is our home for the next twenty-eight weeks. Assuming that this place is identical to its five hundred brothers and sisters here at the Newark Mass Destruction Emporium, we've got interior dimensions of one hundred feet across and seventy-five feet deep." As he spoke, he moved a rubber-tipped pointer to highlight items of interest on the screen. "These little squares you see on the drawing are the reinforced concrete pillars. And in case I'm going too fast for the Aggies in the crowd, pillars are things that hold the roof up."

A chorus of whoops arose from the crowd as two Texas A&M graduates extended birds high into the air. A graduate of Oklahoma State, Nick never missed an opportunity to pull their chain. As the laughter died down, he placed a color photograph on the machine.

"As you can see here, the place is built like a bunker: an igloo design with reinforced concrete all around and five feet of earth piled on the top and sides. God only knows how much dirt there is in the back. A lot. There's only one way in or out of this place, folks, and that's through these blast doors in the front."

None of this information was new to anyone in the room, and Nick knew it. Every detail of the Newark cleanup had been rehearsed in an identical magazine, far away from the exclusion zone. But this was show time, and a person couldn't be too prepared. Of the thirty-odd people gathered in the conference room, only eighteen would even leave the command center once the operation started; and of them, only six would actually enter the magazine. No one knew for sure what they would find, but by all indications, it was going to be ugly.

At one time or another, Magazine B-2740 had housed everything from high explosives to the full spectrum of chemical warfare agents. As for the present, speculation abounded, but all anyone knew for sure was that the place "had a lot of shit in it" (the words of the EPA inspector who saw a container of mustard gas near the entrance a year ago and panicked). Being more specific was Enviro-Kleen's job.

The worst concerns for everyone were the nerve agents VX and GB, both of which they expected to find in large quantity. Toxic at an exposure of 1/100,000 of one part per million, the stuff scared the hell out of Jake. Translated to layman's terms—Aggie terms, according to Nick—that ridiculously low number was the equivalent of one drop of nerve agent dissolved in the total quantity of air breathed by an average adult over a twenty-seven-year period.

"Just remember," Nick concluded, "a little dab'll do ya." Suddenly, his demeanor switched from safety guy to professor. He pivoted on the balls of his feet and pointed at Adam Pomeroy, the newest addition to the Enviro-Kleen team. "Mr. Pomeroy!"

Adam's head jerked up from the doodles he'd been drawing on his spiral notebook. At twenty-three, he looked sixteen and had already been voted most likely to contract a venereal disease. "Huh?"

"Tell me the mechanism of injury for VX agent, please."

Adam looked like he was back in school, raking the ceiling with his eyes as he searched for the answer. When he got it, he smiled. "It's a cholinesterase inhibitor," he said proudly.

"And what does that mean?"

The smile went out like a snuffed candle. "Um . . ."

"Mr. Parker."

Glenn smiled. He'd been in this business for eight years now and rarely got caught short. "It means that impulses can't pass from one nerve cell to the other."

"Excellent. Jake, what do you do in the event of an exposure?"

Jake rolled his eyes. "Oh, come on, Nick."

Carolyn nudged him with her elbow. "*You* come on, Jake," she said harshly. "This is serious stuff."

A rumbling "Ooo" passed through the crowd.

"You swell up and die," Jake answered finally.

"*Bzz,*" Nick said, mimicking a game show host. "Wrong. Thanks for playing, though. Carolyn?"

"Atropine, self-injected in the thigh." Precaution being her middle name, she'd actually practiced the procedure, using sterile saline. It wasn't nearly as difficult as she'd feared.

"Very good. Mustard gas. What happens when you're exposed to that?" This one was for anyone to answer. Jake raised his hand. "Jake."

"You swell up and die."

"Yes! That one you got right."

There was more laughter, but with a nervous edge to it; like everyone knew that show time had arrived. Nick turned serious again. "Please be careful, people."

Magazine B-2740 rose out of the Arkansas forest like some ancient native shrine, its smooth, reinforced concrete face rising twenty feet over the crumbled access road. As he struggled into his suit, just at the line where the support zone met the decontamination zone, Jake couldn't help but wonder what future archaeologists would think of this place a thousand years from now. What conclusions would they draw about the giant cave dwellers who called this neighborhood their home?

Dressing for a Level A entry like this required a group effort. The air packs came first, worn on top of two layers of clothing: the shorts and T-shirts they wore to work, under the obligatory royal-blue Enviro-Kleen uniform. Latex inner gloves came next. The final step was the entry suit itself, with its built-in five-ply gloves and booties. Leather work gloves finished off the ensemble, along with calf-high neoprene work boots, size huge, with splash deflectors to keep scary shit from getting inside and rotting either the suit or its occupant.

With his own air pack in place now, Jake fitted the holster for his portable radio around his waist and cinched it tight, threading the hands-free microphone through the straps of his air pack and into his right ear. After he clipped the customized transmit button to the right-hand shoulder strap, he mashed the mushroom-shaped button with his gloved palm. He looked like a Roman legionnaire saluting his emperor.

"Entry One to Ops. You there?"

"I got you, Entry One."

Jake shot his hand down to the volume control, cringing as Drew Price's voice pierced his brain.

"A bit loud there, honey?" Carolyn laughed on the air.

Jake stuck his tongue out at her. "Hey, Ops, give me a short test count, will you?"

He could hear the smile in Drew's voice as he replied, "Test for Jake. One, two, three, four, five. Five, four, three, two, one. That okay?"

Jake touched his chest again. "Peachy. Thanks."

While the rest of the teams went through their radio check protocols, Jake and Carolyn fitted their masks to their faces and tightened the straps.

"You look like an anteater," Carolyn's voice said in his earpiece.

"Well, we can't all be as beautiful as you, sweetheart," he replied.

"Can it, guys." Foley was on the air now. Mr. Personality. "From this point on, it's all business, understand?"

"Got it," Carolyn said sheepishly.

Jake flipped him off—well out of sight, of course.

The Donovans and their fellow moon-suiters moved to the final dressing stage, where secondary decon personnel stood waiting to seal them into their "protective ensembles." They called themselves the Silverados, thanks to the aluminized fire-resistant outer layers of their suits, which had been specially manufactured for this job. According to theory, the outer layer would buy the owner of the suit an extra ten to fifteen seconds in the event of a fire. Jake thought it was hysterical. They were dealing with explosives, for God's sake. If it burns, you die. Any questions?

The Silverados stood with their arms extended out to their sides, and their feet stuffed into their booties, as the decon toads helped them wriggle into their heavy armor, guiding their arms and hands into their corresponding holes.

Jake felt a quick rush of panic as the big hood was lifted over his head and the vaporproof zipper was pulled closed. It had happened to him before, and just like last time, he was able to swallow the feeling before it became a problem.

A body bag with a window.

His brain launched a shiver. Once zipped inside, there was no escape from that suit without help; the zipper was simply not accessible. Always a borderline claustrophobic, he'd had nightmares about being stranded inside as he sucked his air pack empty, then slowly suffocated. The thought was absurd, but he nonetheless kept a six-inch Buck knife in the pocket of his coveralls.

Literally sealed off from the outside world now, Jake could hear nothing but the sound of his own breathing: an eerie hiss that sounded remarkably like Darth Vader. He turned to survey the status of the rest of his team and caught a glimpse of his own reflection on the suit's visor. Just his eyes, actually, and they looked huge. Last came the syringes of atropine—the only known antidote for what they might find. These were duct-taped to the outside of their suits, on the opposite shoulder from each Silverado's dominant hand.

Jake pressed the transmit button through his suit. "Entry One to Entry Team. Let's do one more radio check."

"Entry Three's good to go." As the only female on the team, Carolyn really didn't need the numerical identifier, but protocol was protocol.

"Entry Two."

"Four."

"Five."

"Six."

Jake watched in turn as each person acknowledged him, making sure that all of them knew their own number.

"You copy them all, Ops?" This was the last step before moving ahead down the road.

"I got six," Drew Price replied.

"And six is the magic number," Jake acknowledged. "Okay, people, let's get to it."

The plan called for Jake's three-man team, Entry Alpha, to enter the magazine and move to the right, while Entry Bravo, the other three-man team, worked around to the left. Ideally, they'd meet in the middle, then work up the center aisle to the front. Jake shared a quick glance with Carolyn, and they touched gloves as their team's industrial hygienist—none other than smart-mouth Glenn Parker—fumbled with the lock. Designed to Department of Defense specifications, the assembly was huge. Resembling a standard padlock, only five times bigger, it dangled out of sight, hidden up inside a steel cowl. According to the locksmith who was called in to fabricate a key, the tumbler design was an oldie but a goodie— for all practical purposes, unpickable. Under normal circumstances, opening the lock would be a cumbersome task. Triple-gloved, with no sense of touch, it was a major undertaking.

Like every other operation, this one had been rehearsed a dozen times on identical magazines, and Parker had gotten as proficient as anyone. The radios were silent and tensions were high as he reached his hands under the cowl. Instantly, a swarm of wasps appeared, scrambling from their invaded nest, and all six Silverados screamed like little girls, instinctively dashing for cover.

The panic lasted for only a second or two—until they realized that even a bionic bee would bust a stinger on these outfits—but it was long enough to ignite a panic from the ops center.

"Entry teams! What's wrong?" Drew yelled into his mike.

The fear gone, but his adrenaline through the roof, Jake laughed. "Um, sorry, Ops. We had a bit of an insect problem down here. Everybody's okay. We're fine."

"You people are on vox, goddammit," Foley spat. Jake could just imagine him pushing poor Drew out of the way to get to the microphone. "Who's on vox?"

The ear mikes they used had an option for voice-activated transmission—vox—for use in one-on-one communications, but the procedure for the Newark site forbade its use. Too many people talking at once just created confusion. "Am I on vox?" Jake asked himself, but the words fell dead inside his suit.

Then he heard "Test, te—" The speaker abruptly shut up. Jake saw number four—Carlos Ortega—snaking his arm out of his sleeve to access the radio holster on his belt.

"Who was that?" Foley barked. "Who didn't follow procedure?"

Jake quickly waved Carlos off. No sense answering a question like that. "Um, Ops? We got it taken care of. Everyone's off vox now. We're proceeding with the entry."

"I want to know who it was!"

Everybody looked at Jake, who grabbed his crotch and extended a gloved bird. He motioned to the lock and Parker went back to work.

Jake marveled yet again at the total isolation the moon suits provided against the real world. There was Parker, not ten feet away, rattling metal against metal, yet the operation produced virtually no sound. The only reality for Jake was the weight of his gear, the fluttering sensation in his stomach, and the heat. God, the heat. With his arms dangling at his sides, he could already feel the accumulated puddles of sweat at his fingertips.

Finally, Parker's head nodded triumphantly, and he stood, displaying the lock as a trophy. "Okay," Jake announced on the air. "The lock's off. We're making entry now."

Drew was back on the mike now. "Okay, Entry. Here's hoping for an empty room."

Yeah, right.

Jake thought for a moment that this must be what it's like to open an ancient mummy's tomb: walking into the unknown, unaware of whatever curses might be awaiting you. Parker pulled hard to get the door to move, but once started, it moved easily, propelled by its own momentum. A sharp blade of light cut across the inky blackness of the magazine's interior. So much for an empty room, Jake mumbled. The place looked like somebody's attic, stacked with a million boxes of varying types, sizes, and construction. Generally speaking, the contents of wooden boxes were considered scarier than their counterparts wrapped in cardboard, but there were so many of each that such distinctions brought little comfort.

"Well, Ops, so much for a short-term contract. This place is packed."

"Okay, Entry. Keep us informed."

No one moved until the two industrial hygienists said it was safe to do so. In this business, the patient man was the one who lived long enough to retire. People pretended not to care about all the safety shit during the lectures, but not one of the Silverados inside Magazine B-2740 questioned for a moment that a mistake might put them in an early grave.

"I show zeros across the board," Parker announced.

"Me, too," said Adam Pomeroy, Parker's counterpart on Team Bravo.

"Tallyho," Jake said. Only Carolyn could hear the hesitation in his voice, and she looked over to him one more time. He looked away.

The seam of light died quickly as they stepped deeper into the concrete cavern. Curiously, the blackness seemed most opaque right at the line separating light from dark.

"Entry One to Operations, we're inside."

"Okay, Entry One. Any first impressions?"

The place was huge, extending far beyond the range of their hand lights, and it looked as full as it could possibly be. The wooden box that had spooked the EPA guy sat right where it was supposed to be, just inside the doors, near the center—virtually the first spot to be illuminated when the blast doors opened. *U.S. Army—Danger Poison*, it read, just above the telltale skull-and-cross-bones symbol. Then, immediately below, *Chemical Agent—Mustard Gas.*

But that was just the beginning. Beyond that one container, stretching on in all directions, was shelf after shelf of God knows what. Assuming that wooden containers with stenciled writing meant military hardware, and assuming that military hardware meant things that made craters, then this place was one huge bomb. Then there were the fifty-five-gallon storage drums, and the cardboard boxes, and the glass jars. . . . It just went on and on and on.

Jake palmed his mike button. "First impressions? Yeah. We underbid this contract by about a million dollars."

"Two million," Carolyn added. In the darkness, everyone became faceless in the moon suits, but still, she knew her husband was smiling.

With Parker leading the way, Jake's Alpha team moved deeper into the shadows, and with each step, their world became progressively smaller, limited only to that which could be touched by the beams of their hand lights. The shelves stretched high toward the concrete ceiling, and on initial inspection, everything looked the same; every angle identical to the other. Jake found himself continually glancing back toward the shimmering white wall of sunlight behind them. As long as he could see the light, he told himself, he wouldn't get lost. That visual anchor, though, was shrinking in size and getting further away by the second.

"Talk to me, Parker," Jake said.

"Still zeros. Shouldn't you guys be doing something more productive than following me?"

It was a damn good point; in fact, it was the operational plan. The I.H.s bore the task of assessing the chemical hazards of the facility, and that required them to traverse the whole place, corner-to-corner. Jake and Carolyn and the other technicians should have already started writing down their inventory. Somehow, though, the sheer scale of the project drew them deeper into the magazine.

"Hey, guys, we've got something here." It was Adam Pomeroy, and his voice was shaky.

Jake pivoted all the way around, 360 degrees, but he couldn't see a thing. "Where are you? What have you got?"

Adam waved his hand light over his head, and Jake caught a glimpse through the shelving. He had no idea that they'd become so far separated. "I'm right here," Adam said. "And I found a skeleton."

"Come again?" Jake said incredulously. "Did you say *skeleton?*" He walked as he spoke, trying to wind his way through the maze of crap.

"You got it," Adam confirmed.

"Keep waving that light so I can find you."

"I see him," Carolyn said, leading the way toward the front of the magazine.

Jake put his hand on her shoulder, bringing her to a stop. He thought he heard something odd. A popping noise. Backfires maybe, from the breathing air compressor? Shit, that couldn't be good news. "Do you hear that?" he asked on the air to anyone who wanted to answer.

"Almost sounds like gunfire," said somebody from Bravo.

Jake looked over in their direction. *Damned if it doesn't.*

In a microsecond, their world erupted into brilliant white light. Jake felt a pulse of wind and instantly became disoriented. There was a sense of flying through the air and then the reality of impacting something hard. There should have been noise, and there should have been pain, but there was neither. Only searing heat as something caught fire over where Bravo used to be. Thoroughly disoriented, he couldn't tell if he was lying on the floor, or if he'd been thrown against a wall. Up and down had no meaning in all the confusion.

A second flash rocked the inside of the magazine, and this time the noise was deafening. Yellow flames joined the white for just an instant, before the heavy black smoke enveloped everything and the heat became invisible.

He had to get out. This was the nightmare; the scenario that could never happen. In that instant, he knew that he was dead.

"Jake!"

He whirled to his right, expecting to see Carolyn, but found himself greeted by more blackness.

"Jake! Where are you!"

His earpiece! Christ, she could be anywhere, but her voice would always be inches away. He found the transmit button and mashed it. "Jesus, what was that?"

"Thank God, Jake. Where are you?"

"I don't have a clue. Where are you?"

A third grenade screamed over Jake's head, missing him by inches as it sought and found the right rear corner of the magazine. This time the explosion had a physical dimension. He felt the heat pulse pick him up and deposit him butt-first into a stack of shelving, which quickly collapsed under his weight. In the brilliance of the flash, he saw Carolyn's silver outline against the roiling billows of smoke as she was deposited within feet of him.

"Carolyn! Are you okay?"

His only answer came from somewhere in the back of the magazine, well beyond the thick black veil of smoke. An ungodly shriek rose from those depths; a howl, really, whose volume increased geometrically until it finally drowned out all other sound. Then it fell silent.

"Carolyn!" he screamed. "Carolyn, where are you?" He could barely hear himself, and he wondered if he'd been deafened.

Out of nowhere, a pair of hands landed heavily on his shoulders, and he felt his suit pull tight at the crotch as someone dragged him across the floor. He struggled first to his knees and then to his feet, cheering aloud as he caught a glimpse of the big "3" on the silver suit in front of him. Carolyn was alive!

Still disoriented, Jake stumbled after her, on the assumption that she knew where the hell she was going. The fire behind grew larger by the instant, made bigger still by secondary explosions, as munitions cooked off. Suddenly he wasn't stumbling anymore. He was running, and pushing Carolyn along in the process.

Flames and smoke billowed through the door frame as they dove face-first onto the grass-stubbled roadbed. Slapping his hand against his transmit button, Jake yelled, "Run! Run! Run!" But he still couldn't hear himself.

Together, they scrambled to their feet and dashed for the decon line, but Carolyn stopped short, causing Jake to stumble one more time. This time he caught himself before he fell. Then he saw it. Carnage. Bodies everywhere, in twisted heaps on the ground.

What the fuck . . .

Carolyn heard the shots, then saw the shooter: a faceless monster, blended perfectly with the trees but for the muzzle flashes and the bucking of the rifle at the end of his arm. He seemed so close. She wondered how they could still be alive, and in the instant the thought flashed into her head, she saw a spray of Plexiglas explode from the facepiece of Jake's suit. She screamed and caught him before he could fall to the ground.

"Oh, God! Oh, my God, Jake!"

But Jake didn't fall. Instead, he grabbed her by the arm and scrambled for cover on the far side of the magazine. He climbed the steep mound first, then practically threw her the rest of the way.

Then they ran. And ran. The woods crashed by in random flashes of green and yellow and white as they charged through the forest, away from the monster with the rifle, away from the looming smoke cloud, toward nothing in particular. They needed distance, and they needed it right now.

With each step, the heavy air tank on Carolyn's back shifted wildly between her shoulder blades, wearing away her skin under the fabric of her coveralls. Suddenly, her feet felt unsure, clumsy. A loop of vine reached up from the forest floor and snagged her by the ankle, pulling her down heavily into a pile of leaves at the base of a fallen tree.

Rest, she thought. *I just need to rest here for a minute. Get my breath* . . .

But then Jake's hands were on her again, and she was on her feet, being dragged toward God knows where. Yanking herself free from his grasp, she punched the transmit button between her breasts.

"I can't keep running," she said. Her lungs burned from the effort, her head reeled. The inside of her suit had become a sauna— hotter than she'd ever been. "We've got to take a rest." Jake wouldn't answer her, so she tried it again, thumping the button and this time yelling, "Slow down, goddammit!"

". . . slow down. Later." Jake's voice seemed distant in her earpiece, and she'd walked on his transmission, talking at the same time he was trying to talk.

She felt like she was still running, but the passing foliage had slowed down to the pace of a barely brisk walk. "I can't hear you!" she shouted. Like yelling somehow made the signal stronger. Now he wasn't answering her at all. Was he hurt? Jesus, he was shot in the face! Of course he was hurt. "Jake!"

CHAPTER TWELVE

Jake couldn't hear anything but himself. *Why won't she answer me, god-dammit?*

He could barely see through the spiderweb of broken Plexiglas in front of his face, but that didn't slow him down a step. He'd never run this hard; never felt so frightened. Yet Carolyn kept slowing down. Then she wouldn't answer up on the goddamn radio. He saw her hitting the transmit button once, but his earpiece remained silent.

His earpiece! That was it. It must have jarred itself loose as he was being tossed around. He considered stopping to correct the problem but dismissed the notion as crazy. He had a hole in his fucking suit! The bullshit lectures from Nick Thomas flooded back into his brain as he tried to remember the details.

Time, distance, and shielding. He remembered that: the three factors that controlled exposure to toxic chemicals. Limit the time, increase the distance, and shield yourself from the hazard. Well, shit! He'd been standing in a fucking smoke cloud for who knows how long with a hole in his goddamn suit. Fuck!

The negative thoughts opened the door for terror, and the panic that it brought. What had Nick said during the last pep talk? Oh yeah. *A little dab'll do ya.* Big laugh, lots of grab-ass. Now this stuff was going to kill him!

So he kept running, dragging Carolyn by whatever body part he could find. They'd be out of air soon, he knew. They had forty-five minutes' working time under normal conditions. Certainly, the designers had never run numbers that assumed their customers would be blown up and shot at before running like deer through the woods. How much air was left? Thirty minutes? Less? How long had it been already? No telling. It felt like a week.

At least his air pack was still working; he was breathing clean air. That was his greatest concern. Out of nowhere, Nick's voice popped into his head again and contradicted him. *Three routes of entry.* That's what he said, wasn't it? Inhalation was the worst, but that left absorption and ingestion. *Chemical agents are designed to be toxic by absorption through the skin.*

And I've got a hole in my goddamn suit!

Jake's worries about panic started to materialize as the real thing once he realized how light-headed he felt. *Oh, God, I'm going to pass out!* He fought with growing desperation for control of his mind, trying to remember the signs and symptoms of overexposure, but the details just weren't there.

If it looks like a duck and it walks like a duck . . .

That was one of Nick's favorite expressions. Sure, it was hot as hell out there, and he was more frightened than he'd ever been in his life, and he was probably dehydrated down to zero, but was that the reason he felt sick, or was it this big fucking hole in his suit?

Jake yelled—literally yelled—as the low-pressure warning vibrated his facepiece.

"Oh, shit! Oh, fuck! God *damn* it!" This was it. Five minutes to live—no, make that three, the way he was gulping lungfuls of air. He stopped dead in his tracks, unaware that he continued to hold a fistful of Carolyn's suit, and he fought to clear his head. It was his nightmare come true: stranded inside a suit with no one to help.

He sat down heavily in the leaves—fell down, really—and snaked his arm out of his sleeve to find his ear mike, dangling against the sweat-soaked belly of his coveralls. His fingers did all the seeing for him, locating the mike, then winding its way up toward his ear. Over the din of his alarm and the heaving of his breath, he could hear the buzzing of Carolyn's panicked cries.

". . . wrong?"

Jake used his finger to trigger the transmit button. "I'm sick, Carolyn," he gasped. "I'm fucked. Buzzer's buzzing. I'm dead."

"Bullshit."

The tone of Carolyn's reply surprised him. She sounded argumentative; not the least bit grieving. He felt her tugging on the sleeve of his suit, then saw a bundle of duct tape in her fist.

"What are you doing?" he asked. Then he saw. The atropine. "Wait!" he yelled. "Maybe it's just the heat!"

Carolyn had never been a nurse; never wanted to be, as far as he knew, and it was a damn good thing. She jammed the needle into his leg like she was squashing a bug. He wondered if she lodged it in his thighbone. The pain changed from sharp to burning as she mashed the plunger, and then the head rush came. He fell backward for an instant; then it passed.

The shot of pain cleared his head. The buzzer was slowing now. Time was short. He had to get out of the suit. Now. Right now.

Body bag with a window.

The zipper was a little thing, nestled somewhere behind his head and sealed under a Velcro flap; designed specifically not to be readily opened. That way, you couldn't accidentally snag it on something and ruin your day. Jake fumbled for a minute looking for it.

"Use your knife," Carolyn's voice instructed, seemingly from inside his head. He looked up in time to see her give herself an injection, noting just how gentle she was with her own thigh.

The knife. Yes, of course, the knife. How was she staying so damned calm? It was a stretch snaking his hand down to his pocket, but the instant his latex-clad fingers found their mark, he was rewarded with the feel of locking-blade Buck. Opening a knife was a two-handed operation, though, requiring him to pull his other arm out of its sleeve as well.

Working strictly by feel, he wrestled the blade out of its slot, just as the buzzing of his facepiece stopped. He'd never drawn a tank down this far before, but popular theory stated that once the vibrator stopped, only thirty seconds of air remained.

Shit!

Gripping the blade in his fist, he thrust it through the suit just below his chin. The five plies fought him every inch of the way, but he worked like a madman, ripping the suit to the crotch, then changing his grip to take the cut down to his knee.

And his air tank died. In midbreath, the air just went away, as surely as if someone had pinched off his nose and mouth. His lungs screamed and his gut muscles tugged for air, but it just wasn't there. In those seconds, he forgot all about his suit as panic seized him. He dropped the knife onto the ground and clawed with both hands at his facepiece. His struggles had drawn the pressure in the mask down so far that it made a quiet burping sound as he pulled it away.

"Thank God," he said aloud, bending at the waist and resting his hands on his knees. He could breathe again.

"Get out of your suit," Carolyn commanded. "You're dirty, Jake."

The suit. God, it was filthy, contaminated with whatever had burned up in there. Jake stopped breathing again—this time by choice—and shrugged and stepped his way free of the moon suit. He stumbled away from it in his stocking feet, quickly scrambling a good ten yards before stopping to look back.

He propped himself against a tree and he breathed. The hot August air felt cool by comparison, and the simple act of drawing breath in and out of his lungs seemed blissfully unregulated. And he was alive.

"How do you feel?" Carolyn asked. She was still in her suit, still talking to him over the radio, and in the background Jake could hear through his earpiece that her buzzer was sounding, too.

"You're using me as a guinea pig!" he shouted, palming his transmit button. He laughed. "You shithead! You were waiting to see if the air was going to kill me!"

Like a bird emerging from some bizarre silver egg, Carolyn cut her way out. Clearly, she'd practiced this before, if only in her mind, and her motions seemed smoother than his; graceful, even, as if her knife were somehow sharper and the effort somehow easier. After emerging from the moon suit, she stepped free of the boots, then walked downrange a good distance before methodically removing the tank from her back, then the mask from her face. Last things off were her gloves, which she meticulously turned inside out as she snapped them off, thus preventing cross-contamination.

When she was done, she looked through the trees to Jake, who stared back at her for a long moment, before they started to move toward each other.

"We're alive," Carolyn said. Her tone carried none of the happiness that the words should bear.

Jake wanted to say something clever—something to lighten the moment—but a sudden rush of emotion staggered him. Shadowy, surreal memories of fires and explosions and friends' bodies swirled in his head, and he found himself suddenly overcome. He still had Carolyn. That much made sense, even if nothing else did. And as she said, they were still alive. As they hugged each other in the silence of the woods, he had a nagging fear that the ordeal wasn't over yet.

They walked for nearly four hours before stumbling upon the cabin along the river. It was a one-room affair, done in Early Hobo, with an old Army cot in one corner, a chemical toilet in the other, and a propane camp stove in the middle. The door hung from one hinge, and it appeared that no one had visited for weeks.

"Charming place," Carolyn mumbled.

Jake smiled. "Yeah, a real fixer-upper. I don't suppose you see a phone anywhere, do you?"

She put her hands on her hips and rolled her eyes. "Yeah, sure. I think it's over there in the butler's pantry." She strolled toward a broken window.

He sighed. "We need to get to the cops."

"Well, as soon as . . . Hey! They've got a boat!"

Jake hurried to peer through the window, over Carolyn's shoulder. "Where?"

Carolyn led the way back out the front door and down toward a makeshift dock. About halfway, next to a disorganized stack of firewood, lay a well-abused aluminum canoe, turned upside down in the leaves. "Think it'll float?" she asked.

"You can't just go steal a guy's canoe! Christ, they probably hang you for that out here."

She made a face. "You have a better idea? I'm done walking barefoot through the woods, thank you very much, and I'm not inclined to stay here in this shack."

Jake looked around, as if someone was watching. "Jeeze, Carolyn, I've never stolen anything before."

"Oh, yeah, like I'm John Dillinger, right? It's not like we have a lot of alternatives here."

He took a deep breath and held it, scanning the horizon for inspiration. Finally, he shrugged. "Oh, what the hell. In for a dime, in for a dollar, right?"

He rolled the canoe onto its keel and dragged it down toward the dock, while Carolyn carried the paddle that had been stashed underneath. "Not overexerting, are you, dear?" Jake grunted, struggling not to smash his toes under the boat.

She smiled. "No, I'm fine, honey. I'll have the paddle ready for you down at the dock."

Once he got the boat past the firewood, it actually slid pretty easily across the sloping grass and into the water. Standing submerged up to his hips, Jake helped Carolyn down into the canoe before climbing in himself, taking the rear position.

They paddled for an hour, past endless stretches of forest. "Think we've gone five miles yet?" Jake asked, his first words in a long while.

"I think we've gone a thousand miles," Carolyn said, groaning. She lay on her back on the bottom of the canoe, her arm slung over her eyes to block the sun. Jake's question was really a test to see if she was awake. "Why do you ask?"

"Well, since the contingency plan calls for evacuation within a five-mile radius, I just wanted to make sure we're safe."

She lifted her arm a fraction of an inch to sneak a peek. "You're so full of shit, Jake Donovan. You never read the contingency plan."

He shrugged with a smile. "No, but you read it to me."

"Next time I'll show you the pictures," she said, once again retreating under her arm.

The river narrowed considerably in the next twenty minutes, and as the banks grew closer together, so did the distance separating the homes that lined the riverbank. "I think we're reentering civilization," Jake announced, prompting Carolyn to sit up.

The houses on either side had lost their hunting-cabin feel, and while the yards continued to double as junk heaps—dumping grounds for old stoves, refrigerators, and the like—people obviously lived here. Set precariously close to the water's edge, the houses looked dank and pitiful among the towering trees which cast them in perpetual darkness, sheltered from the invading rays of the blistering summer sun.

As Carolyn took it all in, she tried to imagine what it would be like to fight a perpetual battle against mildew. She shuddered at the thought of what these un-air-conditioned shanties must smell like.

"How can people live like this?" she asked, mostly to herself. Her mind conjured up images of filthy children playing in squalor as they awaited their next malnutritious meal.

Jake slipped his Budweiser T-shirt back over his head and shrugged. "Oh, I don't know," he said charitably.

She smirked lovingly at his never-ending optimism. "Nobility of the poor, right?"

"Well, there's certainly no shame in it." Jake sounded a little defensive. "For all we know, these people work three jobs to afford what little they've got."

"Whatever," she scoffed.

He recognized her tone as the one that dismissed his outlook on such things as naive and ill informed. It was a quirk in his wife's personality that he'd never been able to understand. She'd set a standard for herself that no mere mortal could possibly at-tain, and even as they wallowed together in that stage of their lives where an evening out for pizza and beer had to be carefully budgeted, she showed a disturbing, almost cruel intolerance for people who were "poor." Every time Jake tried to point out that their income hovered perilously close to the poverty line, she'd insist that he was missing the point. It was their *potential* that made the difference, she'd say. As college graduates, with degrees in a worthwhile, technical field, they had limitless potential. The fact that Jake's father had spent a career in the coal mines, working night shift until the day he died, and that his mom had cleaned houses to make ends meet didn't seem to impress Carolyn in the slightest. She was funny that way. Jake figured it all had something to do with her childhood; something that twisted her outlook on the world. In all other ways a charitable, giving wife, Carolyn could be brutal where money was the issue.

Jake let it pass. "Where do you think we are?"

Carolyn craned her neck, as if she'd be able to recognize this stretch of river by sight. "No idea," she said at length. "Downstream from where we were before." She smiled, lighting up the whole boat. All the snottiness and intolerance in the world couldn't cheapen the pure beauty of that smile, Jake thought.

A few minutes passed before the horizon changed again, revealing a line of dilapidated shops, which, like the surrounding residences, were built right up against the edge of the river. The tallest of the structures also looked to be the oldest, built of stone at its lowest level, with two additional stories stacked on top, sporting faded wood siding and a once-red, hand-painted sign, "Bobby's Bait and Tackle."

"Hey, look," Jake said, pointing. "Let's go see if Bobby's has a phone we can use." He steered the canoe toward shore, running it aground against the gravel parking lot, where it joined the waterline. He got out first, holding the boat steady as Carolyn joined him. Together, they pulled the canoe safely ashore and chicken-walked through the gravel, unconsciously flapping their elbows as they guided their bare feet across the sharp-edged rocks. Thirty yards later the gravel gave way to smooth concrete, and they paused to let the pain subside.

"Welcome to Buford," Carolyn said.

Jake cocked his head. "How do you know that?"

She giggled and pointed across the street. "Buford Hardware." Then, pointing two blocks down the street, "Buford Motel."

"Your powers of deduction are truly awesome," he teased. "How do you know that some guy named Buford doesn't own a hardware store and a motel?"

She shot him her know-it-all smirk. "People named Buford don't own businesses."

The town was bigger than Jake had expected. Stretching on for several blocks in three directions, it sported an interesting mix of old business district construction, with its tall false fronts and wrought-iron fencing, interspersed with the pastel and glass architecture of the sixties. The mining town where Jake grew up had been a lot smaller than this, and it bragged ten thousand residents. Using that as a benchmark, he pegged Buford—if indeed that's what it was called—to be good for about twenty. All the more remarkable, given the fact that not a soul was in sight.

"Where is everybody?" Carolyn asked, speaking Jake's thoughts.

"Kinda spooky, isn't it?" Bobby's Bait and Tackle, like every other building in sight, was locked tight, with the lights off. "Didn't I see a *Twilight Zone* that started like this?"

Carolyn shivered inadvertently, and then she got it. "They must have been evacuated!" she proclaimed. "The fire down at the plant must have run them off."

Jake scowled. "Jeeze, you think so? This far away?"

"Well, we really don't know how far away we are. Five miles is a long way."

"And this is a big town," he finished for her. "What a nightmare getting all these people moving." He placed his hands on his hips and looked up and down the street. "Do you see a pay phone?"

With none in sight, they started moving toward the Buford Motel. Surely, they'd have one there. They walked quickly, gripped by an odd paranoia. The total absence of people, at a time when

the streets rightfully should have been packed, felt strangely post-
apocalyptic. Jake half expected to see Mad Max appear with his
band of refugees.

Could it be that the contamination had actually extended this
far? Five miles was the default evacuation distance for hazmat dis-
asters, and as such carried a safety factor of at least five, meaning
that the evacuation zone encompassed five times the distance that
was truly in danger. Was it possible, in this case, that wind directions or thermal inversions, or any number of other physical or
meteorological anomalies, had actually put them in harm's way?

They discussed these things as they wandered across the street,
but Jake was the one who put it in the proper perspective: "Too late
to start worrying about it now. If this is a danger zone, then we've
been exposed all day."

Clearly, he and Carolyn had dodged the bullet for the most acute
hazards of whatever they might have been exposed to. Now they'd
just have to wait another twenty or thirty years to see what chronic
effects might lie ahead. Cancer maybe. Or blindness. God, there
were countless possibilities! Signs and symptoms could take
decades to show themselves. In any case, that particular horse was
out of the barn.

And that's what made this such a scary business. Some of the
most hazardous chemicals on earth were colorless, odorless, and
tasteless, with toxic effects that took years to manifest themselves.
How could a person know if the tumor that materialized after his
sixty-fifth birthday was just another tumor, like the last three that
the oncologist had treated, or if it was the result of some ancient
chemical exposure?

The parking lot of the Buford Motel was deserted, just like
everything else in town. A single story in height, the complex
looked like every other motel constructed in the 1960s. A couple
of dozen rooms stretched out at parking lot level, anchored on the
near end by a small, glass-walled office. Being this close to a bed
and an air conditioner made Jake realize just how exhausted he was.
Suddenly, each step took just a little more effort than his legs were
willing to give.

"Not bad, all things considered," he commented. Someone here had quite a green thumb. A sea of phlox and pansies surrounded the small swimming pool, itself an obvious afterthought, planted as it was smack in the middle of the parking lot. Geraniums grew in uniform clusters in colorful window boxes outside of every room.

"You suppose they rent for whole nights, or just for a few hours at a time?" Carolyn quipped.

Jake shook his head. "You're such a snot." He was careful to keep a smile in his voice.

She chuckled. "Well, I can afford to be snotty when I'm so fashionably dressed." He hadn't thought about it until that very minute, but they looked like hell. Sweaty, sunburned, barefoot, and filthy, they truly were quite a sight.

"I need a nap," he said, reaching for the tinted glass door to the office. Surprisingly enough, the door pulled open easily.

Like the building itself, the furniture was old yet clean. Sort of Early American, with some Colonial and Danish Modern thrown in for flavor.

"How nice," Carolyn mumbled sarcastically.

"Shh," Jake snapped. "Hello?" he called to the room. "Anybody here?"

"Maybe we shouldn't be here," she whispered. "I feel like a burglar."

"Well, hi there!" The two of them jumped a foot as the clerk materialized from behind the counter. Pushing seventy, with a genuine smile brightening his stubbly face, the guy looked way too old to be greeting visitors at the counter. "Sorry, folks. Didn't mean to startle you. Name's Terrell. Can I help you?"

The visitors laughed as the moment passed. "Oh, that's okay," Jake told him. "Guess we're a little jumpy. Kind of a spooky place today."

Terrell's smile remained unchanged, but his eyes darkened as he took in his visitors' appearance. "Y'all okay? You look sorta . . . Well, everythin' okay?"

Carolyn opened her mouth to answer, but Jake touched her back lightly. "We're fine, thanks," he said. "But we've had a bit of an accident. Mind if we use your phone to call the police?"

Suddenly, Terrell's smile disappeared, replaced with a deep, concerned scowl. He hurried out from behind his counter. "Goodness, folks," he said, motioning them toward some chairs. "You hurt?"

Jake waved him off with a smile. "Oh, no thanks, nothing like that. Just had a bit of a problem with our boat, is all. Sure could use a cop." He could feel Carolyn's eyes boring into him for his transparent lie, but he ignored her.

"You're sure you're okay?" Terrell seemed ready to drive them to the hospital in his own car.

"Perfectly fine," Jake assured him.

Terrell regarded them for a moment longer, then pointed to the seats. "Please, sit down." They did. "You're welcome to use the phone, but unless there's somebody dead in the road, or the Russians are invading Little Rock, you'd best save the quarter. Every cop within a hundred miles is up at Newark helping with the evacuation. Threatened to arrest me, as a matter of fact, if I didn't leave, but gave it up once they got word they had to evacuate the jail." Terrell laughed hard, triggering a cough.

Smoker, Jake thought. *Menthols.* "Evacuation?"

The look Carolyn shot him spoke volumes. *What the hell are you doing?* Again, Jake ignored her.

"You ain't heard?" Terrell gasped. It was as if they'd just admitted they didn't know what a Razorback was. "There was a big explosion and fire out near Newark. Got nerve gas, nuclear weapons, all kinds of stuff, and it all leaked into the environment. Every place within fifteen miles has been evacuated."

Jake did a great job of feigning surprise. "No kidding! Are we in danger, then?"

Terrell scoffed and strolled back toward his counter. "I don't believe in none of that stuff. I figured if the Good Lord wanted me with him today, I'd be havin' a heart attack in the evacuation shelter, know what I mean?" He disappeared around the corner but kept talking the whole time. "Way I figure it, this is a perfect time for punks to come around lootin'. They come around here, though, and I got one hell of a surprise for 'em." He produced a sawed-off twelve-gauge, with a combat grip where a stock should have been. "Now, tell me, wouldn't you think twice about taking my stuff if you were staring down one of these?"

Carolyn gasped. Jake felt his stomach cramp. *So much for Grandpa Hospitality.*

At the sight of them, Terrell turned immediately apologetic and put the gun back behind the counter. "I'm sorry. There I went and scared you folks a second time."

This time the Donovans' laughter sounded a bit forced. "No, no," Jake said. "That's okay. Guess that should make me feel safe."

The grin returned to Terrell's face.

"So how long before they lift the evacuation?" Carolyn asked.

"Can't say as I know," Terrell answered, shifting his eyes. "I can't imagine it'll go on much after tomorrow. Can y'all wait that long for the police?"

Jake looked to Carolyn and made a face. "I gotta tell you," he said at length. "What I really need is some sleep. Maybe we could rent one of your rooms and call the police from there?"

Terrell's eyes brightened even more. "Well, I can sure as shootin' accommodate you there. You can have your pick of the rooms." He pulled a registration card out of a box and a pen out of his pocket. "Just fill out this information here."

Jake filled in all of the blanks on the card, fighting off a final wave of exhaustion. His brain felt numb. When he was done, he handed the card back to Terrell. "You take Visa?"

"Oh, we take 'em all." Terrell laughed, clearly delighted there'd be at least one customer today.

Three minutes later the Donovans were making their way across the parking lot toward room 15, which, according to Terrell, had the best view of the pool.

"You want to tell me what that was all about?" Carolyn asked.

Jake shrugged; kind of a shiver, really. "I don't know, I just got a funny feeling. This place is so inbred, for all I know, that sniper on the hill might be Terrell's brother. Just didn't seem like a good idea to share the story yet. I want to tell it directly to a cop."

They arrived at their room, and Jake opened the door. Same decorator as the office.

Carolyn collapsed dramatically onto the bed. "So are you going to call right away?"

"In a minute," he said.

CHAPTER THIRTEEN

Jake awakened to the sound of distant sirens.

Disoriented at first, he stretched his back and scanned the darkened room. "Shit," he moaned. "I fell asleep." He checked his watch. *For three hours.*

He'd fallen into the sagging, overstuffed lounge chair just for a minute, he thought. To give his back and shoulders a rest. He didn't even remember closing his eyes.

The sirens reminded him that he'd forgotten to do something. Then, like a curtain being parted, the events of the day raced back into his consciousness.

Somebody had tried to kill him! The bullet came within an inch, for Chrissakes! As his mind replayed the impact of that bullet, the sheer force of it, even as it missed him, a lump formed in his stomach, and his hands began to tremble. Trapped in the netherworld between sleep and reality, he felt the blast of heat all over again, blistering hot against his shoulders and his back, despite the protection of his suit. And he saw the bodies of his friends, scattered like logs across the old roadbed. Even in his memory, they didn't look real; they didn't look dead. He could only presume that the man on the hill had shot them, just as he had tried to shoot Carolyn and him, but the horror of it all was somehow muted by the absence of blood and the facelessness of the bodies.

"Got to call," he whispered. *Got to find out what happened.* Taking care not to make any noise, he pulled hard against the arms of the chair and sat up straight. Raking a hand through his hair, he twisted first to his left and then to his right, releasing a ripple of pops from his spine. Only twenty-four years old, and tonight he felt every bit of seventy.

In the darkness of the room, the sparse furnishings were visible only as shades of black against a charcoal-gray background. Fumbling blindly along the nightstand, Jake placed his hand on the telephone but paused as his attention turned once again to the sound of the sirens. They seemed to be growing louder. He stood and hobbled over to the front window, where he used two fingers to part the heavy, rubber-lined blackout curtains.

A gentle but steady rain fell in the empty parking lot, giving everything a glassy, reflective look, which in the darkness of the night took years off the age of everything. The wail of the first siren reached a crescendo, then stopped abruptly as a police car sped into view and slid to a stop in front of the motel office.

"What the hell is this?"

Carolyn stirred at the sound of his voice. "What's going on?" she groaned sleepily.

"I don't know yet." He watched with a growing sense of dread as the trooper climbed out of his car with his hand on his pistol and moved cautiously to the door of the office. The cop pulled hard against the lock, then pounded heavily with his fist on the glass panel. "I think our friend Terrell might be in a bit of trouble." In the distance, more sirens approached.

Her curiosity piqued, Carolyn joined her husband at the window and watched as a light came on in the office, casting a greenish hue through the tinted glass. Soon Terrell's lanky form appeared through the glass. He opened the door wearily, then seemed suddenly animated as he listened to whatever the trooper was telling him. He nodded a couple of times, then shook his head a couple more.

Finally, Terrell pointed directly at Jake and Carolyn. They both jumped. "Holy shit," Jake gasped.

"What?"

"This doesn't look good." The trooper moved quickly as he said something into the microphone clipped to his shoulder, then climbed back into his cruiser. He never took his eyes off their motel room.

"What?!"

Jake could hear the edge of panic in Carolyn's voice—the same emotion he felt building in the pit of his own stomach. "We've got to get out of here."

"What are you *talking* about?" she insisted. She was crying now, gripped with fear.

He turned two quick circles in the dark, trying to figure a way out of the room without being seen.

"Jake!" she nearly shouted.

"Shh!" he commanded. "The bathroom window! Come on!" He dragged her by the hand toward the back of the room, even as the police car's high beams pierced the thin seam in the curtain and cast a laser-width spear of light against the far wall.

"What are we doing? I'm not going anywhere," she insisted, following along as she spoke.

"Look," he snapped. "People tried to kill us today, and now that cop looks mad as hell. Looks to me like staying here could get us shot."

The window in the bathroom was of standard height and size, but made of smoky white glass. Yet another siren peaked in volume and fell silent. *Shit,* Jake thought. *There's two of them now.* And still more in the distance. The window lock turned easily, but he had to pound upward with the heels of both hands to get it to slide open.

"Jake, this is stupid!"

He made a stirrup with his hands. "Here. You go first."

"Go where?"

"Out, goddammit!" he hissed. "I don't know where. Just out."

Carolyn opened her mouth to argue but then complied. No sooner had she placed her bare foot in his hands than he nearly launched her through the opening. She came out too fast, tumbling headfirst into the wide alley behind the motel. She got her hands out in time, though, preventing damage to everything but her pride.

Jake arrived feetfirst, just as the blue and red lights of a police car began to sweep the trees at the far end of the complex to their right. "Shit! They're coming around to the back, too!"

They needed cover; something to hide behind. With the cop car approaching, they'd never make it to the tree line without being seen. The Dumpster! Jake grabbed Carolyn's hand again and pulled her quickly behind him as he dashed twenty yards or so and ducked behind the maroon trash receptacle. The warm rain had reinvigorated the stench of old garbage and rotting food, and he found himself instinctively breathing through his mouth.

"Why are we hiding from the police?" Carolyn shouted at a whisper. "We've done nothing wrong!"

"I don't know. I just have a bad feeling." It was as honest an answer as he knew to give.

The second cop car approached more cautiously, killing his lights as he closed in on the back of their room. Once in place and stopped, the cop opened his door carefully and rolled quickly out of the car, taking his twelve-gauge with him. He scampered over to the passenger-side door, where he could use the vehicle as cover.

The Donovans exchanged panicked glances in the dark.

"Are they trying to *arrest* us?" Carolyn whispered.

Jake answered with a shrug that was invisible in the darkness. "Jesus, look at him. He's scared shitless."

They both jumped as the cop's radio squelched and an electronic voice pierced the muted thrumming of the rain. "All units be advised, we have positive ID from the manager. These are definitely our shooters."

The cop muttered something unintelligible into his microphone, then racked a round into the chamber of his shotgun and leveled it at the window they'd just climbed through.

"Oh, my God," Carolyn breathed.

"He can't wait to pull that trigger," Jake said, not believing what he was seeing. This trooper wanted them bad, and he didn't much care whether they were breathing or not. Jake pulled Carolyn away from the Dumpster and headed for the tree line. "We gotta get outa here. They're liable to have dogs and all kinds of bullshit out here soon."

This time she needed no pulling or prodding to get her to run. A second car pulled up to the rear of the building just as they reached the first line of cover. The police were shouting now, apparently no longer worried about a stealthy approach, and that was the Donovans' cue to run like hell, while noise didn't matter.

"We going back to the boat?" Carolyn asked.

"I sure as hell hope so."

They'd floated in the dark nearly all night before Carolyn got the idea to contact her uncle in Chicago. A men's clothing retailer turned real estate mogul, Harry Sinclair had more money than God, and if there was anyone in the world with the connections to lift them out of this mess, it would be him. They still didn't know why they'd gone from near victims to Public Enemies #1 and #2 in the space of just a few hours, but it was clear as crystal that they needed some answers before they showed their faces again. And, assuming that the Visa card had alerted the cops back at the motel, they could forget about credit cards taking them where they wanted to go. They needed to develop alternative resources fast. Which meant Harry Sinclair.

It took them nearly two hours to give Travis that much of the story. There were parts he didn't understand, and still more that he didn't want to. But as it dragged on, and his parents shared the details about who they really were, and who they really weren't, he found himself burrowing further and further under his Army blanket, finally wishing that they'd just stayed quiet and let him believe that things remained as they'd always been.

CHAPTER FOURTEEN

Eight-thirty had come and gone by the time Clayton Albricht finally returned to his office. Veronica was still there, of course—his personal assistant since his very first day in office—but she was the exception. The rest of the staff had flown the coop an hour ago. The senator walked heavily, his mind and his butt numbed by an endless series of meaningless meetings, with colleagues and constituents alike. Sometimes he swore that his life had become one long photo opportunity.

As he walked through the huge oak doors and entered his outer office, he felt a sense of peace pour over him. He'd worked for decades to get these digs in the prestigious Russell Senate Office Building, and now that he had them, every hour of the effort seemed worthwhile. In Washington, where power was measured by the square foot, Albricht's unobstructed view of the Capitol Building was the envy of all of his colleagues. With its two fireplaces, its intricately carved wood paneling, and its walls adorned with priceless works on loan from the National Gallery of Art, Chairman Albricht's office resonated with power.

"Hello, Veronica," Albricht mumbled as he dragged himself

through the doors. "I'm sorry to keep you waiting so long. Really, there's no reason for you to stay."

Nor was there much reason for her to leave. A widow with no kids, Veronica had precious little to go home to. She packed her stuff, nonetheless—an umbrella and rain hat were standard, regardless of weather—and headed for the door.

"A messenger dropped a package off for you," she said, plucking her overcoat out of the closet behind her desk. "The inner package said for you to open it personally."

Albricht noticed the package just as she mentioned it, sitting on the conference table in his office. According to the attached paperwork, it came from the *Washington Post.*

"It came from a newspaper," Veronica explained further. "The reporter said to give him a call when you get in. He said the story goes to press at nine."

"What story?" Albricht asked.

"Guy wouldn't say. Just told me to tell you to call him." Veronica walked as she talked, having learned a long time ago the hazards of sticking around after she'd been released for the day. "His card's on top of the package. See you tomorrow."

Albricht heard the outer door close before he had a chance to answer.

The package wasn't very big—standard eight-and-a-half-by-eleven, maybe a quarter inch thick. Reporter Tom Ford's business card was taped to the outside. If the hour were earlier, Albricht would have set one of his staff to the task of finding out who the hell Tom Ford was.

Helping himself to one of the wine-colored calfskin chairs at his conference table, Albricht shoved his thumb up under the seal and pulled open the Tyvek envelope, revealing a short stack of photocopied documents, along with a cover letter on *Washington Post* stationery.

Dear Senator Albricht,

Enclosed, please find copies of documents we recently received from an anonymous source, in support of allegations that you have regularly engaged

in pedophilic and homosexual activities. Because of the criminal nature of
these allegations, I thought you might want to comment before we went to
press with it.

Should you be so inclined, I have included my business card for your use.
As I'm sure this is very troubling news, you have my deepest sympathies, sir.
Under the circumstances, however, I have no choice but to go with the story.
Sincerely,
Tom Ford

Albricht's stomach seized as he tore the paper clip away and
turned the page. He gasped audibly at what he saw: credit card receipts for membership in some outfit called the Homosexual Freedom Congress and for subscriptions to a half dozen underground
publications specializing in pedophilic photographs.

"Oh, my God," he moaned. The blood drained from his head.
"Oh, my God."

These were his signatures and his credit card numbers, but he'd
never ordered any such materials! He'd authorized the legislation
that made it a federal crime even to possess such things, for crying
out loud. He'd even suggested the death penalty for the animals
who produced them. How could anyone think for even a moment . . .

Then, in an instant, he saw what had happened. What was it
that Frankel had said? *We'll both be on the news tonight* . . . Jesus.

His phone rang, and Albricht closed his eyes. It had to be the
reporter. Who else would call at this hour? He considered ignoring it but rose from his chair, anyway, his mind racing to put together a quotable quote but coming up empty. It was too soon, too
new. He needed his staff, dammit, and he needed them right now,
to put a respectable spin on it all, before he talked to the press. Before he said something he'd regret.

The phone rang a fourth time. As a practical matter, though, he
had to issue a denial. The sooner the better. Otherwise, the morning paper would tell the world that he "could not be reached for
comment"; code words interpreted by the public as a tacit admis-

sion of guilt. Still unsure of what he was going to say, the senator inhaled deeply, then lifted the receiver.

"Yes?"

"Hello, Clay," a voice said. "I see your light is on. Have you opened your mail yet?"

Albricht scowled. Even at the *Post*, reporters had the decency to call him Senator. "Who is this?"

"Why don't you call me Wiggins," the voice urged. "Impressive materials, don't you think?"

"I don't know what you're talking about." The senator stalled for time as he turned on the recorder.

Wiggins chuckled. "Of course you don't. Such shameful, horrible acts. I mean, really, Clay. Must you really turn to little boys for sexual relief?"

Albricht's hands trembled as he listened to this outrage, and he clenched his teeth tightly enough to cause pain. "I don't know who you are, Wiggins," he hissed, "but I've got a message for you to deliver back to Mr. Frankel. If he thinks that I can be blackmailed . . ."

Wiggins continued to speak, without breaking cadence. ". . . I can't imagine what the public reaction will be once the photographs are released."

The words jolted Albricht into silence; and though he recovered quickly, the damage was already done. He'd shown a moment of fear, and now his opponent knew who was stronger. "There can be no pictures of something that never happened," he scoffed.

Wiggins laughed again. "Oh, yeah? Well, I gotta tell you, Clay, they sure as hell look like you, with your pants down around your ankles. And that boy on his knees in front of you sure as hell isn't old enough to shave . . ."

Albricht sat down to avoid falling. As he saw the whole game played out before him, he knew right away that he had lost. The documents in the envelope proved Frankel's talents as a forger. Even if the pictures Wiggins described didn't yet exist, in these days of computer morphing—where any face could be put on any body—how difficult could it be? And once released, the pictures would scuttle his career.

The *Post* would run a censored version of the photos, while the smut rags would doubtless run the uncensored ones, and the truth would become irrelevant. Even if he were miraculously to prove that the photos were the hoax that he knew them to be, he'd forever be the brunt of jokes in every comedy café in the world.

His hands shook as Wiggins droned on, the condescending tone in his voice churning Albricht's bowels.

". . . of course, I suppose those receipts in the envelope could be explained away pretty easily. You could always claim forgery. God knows there are a million ways to get a man's credit card numbers." Wiggins paused, as if to make sure he had Albricht's full attention. "Are you with me, Clay?"

"What do you want?" Albricht growled.

"Just what's best for you and your family. I'd just hate like hell for these pictures to end up on the networks. I'll bet you'd have a hell of a time explaining *them* as forgeries. I mean, the media isn't exactly your friend to begin with, and given the corroboration of those receipts, well, that'd be just one hell of a mess, don't you think?"

Albricht closed his eyes, wanting to reach through the telephone to kill this man but able only to listen.

"Well, Clay, I've got to run. And listen, I'm sure you've recorded this call—maybe even traced it. You just say the word, buddy, and I'll be happy to come forward. Maybe I can even have these things blown up to poster size for the news conference. That'd be a hoot, don't you think?" Wiggins laughed one more time before the line went dead.

Albricht stared at the telephone for a long time after hanging it up. It was over. Everything. Just like that. A noble career brought to a disgraceful end. He could already hear his colleagues' conversations in the hallways: *He may deny it, but I've seen the pictures . . .*

Washington was a town of images, and no force on earth was powerful enough to counteract the images just described. Even if he could prove them all to be forgeries, the damage to his career and to his reputation would last forever. The traditions of the Washington press corps were clear: speculation of guilt sold newspapers; innocence was something for the courts to prove. Once proved, the media might even report on the verdict—on an inside page, of course, unless the story ran as a sidebar to someone's front-page insistence that the jury was wrong.

"God damn you, Frankel," he said aloud. The son of a bitch had warned him, hadn't he? Even as the anger swelled, a part of him admired the simple brilliance of Frankel's plan. It left him utterly defenseless. If Albricht declared the truth—that Frankel had created these documents to deflect attention from his own questionable past—the nation would collectively roll its eyes and dismiss him as paranoid. Meanwhile, insiders who knew Albricht well, and who knew exactly what was going on, would merely become an extension of the problem. They'd scramble like frightened rabbits to distance themselves from their wounded colleague, even as they extended a handshake toward the perpetrator of the lie. No one could know when they'd find themselves next on his list.

It all crystallized for Albricht in an instant. Folding his arms on the table, he lowered his forehead onto his wrists and moaned.

"I'm fucked."

CHAPTER FIFTEEN

Irene stood with her hands on her hips, mouth agape, as the manager of the U-Lockit Storage Company raised the door to unit 627. "I'll say they were prepared," she said.

Paul Boersky was more concise: "Holy shit."

"Look what they did to my wall!" the manager yelled. It proved to be the opening salvo of a diatribe about the trash who lived in the community and about the lack of respect his customers showed toward a poor businessman who could barely make ends meet. After thirty breathless seconds, Paul had one of the uniformed officers escort the man back to his office.

Finding this place had been a stroke of pure luck. Among the many tidbits collected from the Donovans' trailer in Farm Meadows was a bill that had arrived that day from U-Lockit. Initially no more or less interesting than any of the other slips of paper they'd logged for follow-up, the bill gained special significance when Officer Jason Slavka mentioned in passing that the storage yard was just a few blocks from the hospital where no one had ever heard of Jake's mother.

Even as she congratulated herself for such a valuable find, Irene realized that they were back to square one. The Celica was here, and judging from the size and the emptiness of the shelves, the Donovans had been more than able to compensate for the supplies they'd left behind in the trailer.

"You're authorized to say you told me so," Irene growled to Paul as they walked inside.

Unable to read his boss's mood so early in the morning, Paul said nothing as he strolled around the storage bay, surveying the scene.

Zeroing in on the discarded license plates and identification, Irene stooped down to examine them. "Look here," she said. "The Brightons are officially dead. And what do you bet they're clever enough to kill off the Durflingers, too? These guys are smart, Paul. They've got a ton of cash, by all accounts, and they're adept at changing identities. It's almost like someone trained them."

Paul sighed and arched his eyebrows. "At least we've still got the van," he said hopefully.

She laughed. "Undoubtedly with new license plates. Care to guess how many white vans there are in the world?"

As the crime scene technicians arrived with their cameras and their evidence bags and their fingerprint kits, Paul and Irene did their best to stay out of the way. By rights, Irene should have left Paul here to manage the scene himself, but truth be known, she didn't have all that much to do. In the absence of leads, an investigator's job was pretty damned boring.

"So who do you think trained them?" Paul asked out of nowhere.

"Come again?" She hadn't been paying attention. Her mind had been reliving Peter Frankel's third sputtering tirade in the last twenty-four hours.

"To disappear," Paul clarified. "Who do you think trained them?"

She scowled. "You're smirking. If you've got a theory, let's hear it."

Suddenly self-conscious of his expression, he made the smirk go away. "I was reading the Donovans' file last night at the hotel," he explained. "I didn't realize that Harry Sinclair was their uncle."

Irene saw where he was headed and dismissed him with a shake of her head. "If you read it all, then you know that he was investigated back in '83 and came up clean."

"No one with that much money is ever clean," Paul snorted. "Seems like an awfully convenient resource to have when you're on the run."

She considered that for a moment. "Sinclair would be crazy to get himself involved in something like this. Too much to lose."

Paul shrugged. "Hey, family's family. I think we ought to check it out. It's not like we've got a lot to lose. From where I stand, we've got a ton of evidence but not a single clue."

Irene weighed the idea. "Want to go for a phone tap?"

"Why not? God knows we've got probable cause."

A slight nod served as his order to go ahead.

"Great. I'll call the U.S. Attorney's Office." He moved quickly toward the overhead door, dodging the sea of evidence technicians. "Oh, by the way, Irene," he said, just short of the exit.

She looked over, eyebrows high.

"I told you so."

Carolyn screamed.

Jake rocketed upright in his seat, ready to do battle. His mind registered that it was light again, but he couldn't figure out what had happened to the dark. She was sitting up now, too, still in her seat, but barely. Her eyes were wild, unfocused. Her hands were poised in front of her, fingers spread, as if frozen in the midst of pushing something away. He knew then that she'd had The Dream.

"Carolyn!" he said sharply. "Carolyn, you're here. I'm here. Everything's okay." He wriggled as best he could across the center console and tried to pull her close. That's when the crying started. That's when the crying always started.

"Oh, God," she gasped, finally tuning into reality. "Oh, my God." She let herself be rocked back and forth in her seat, but she remained stiff in his arms, hugging herself instead of her husband.

"You gonna tell me about it this time?" he asked after a while.

She shook her head against his jacket. "No. I can't."

No, you *won't*, he thought bitterly. He wished he were a better man, but this game she played of keeping her past hidden away had bugged him forever. They were husband and wife, dammit. Two lives, one person. Three lives, really. They faced a whole future together, after facing down a whole past, yet she guarded her childhood horrors as if they were nuclear launch codes. Unless she was willing to be a wife, how could he ever be a husband?

He said none of this, of course, and right away he felt ashamed that he'd even think such things. These were the times when she needed him most, weren't they? And his job was simply to be there; to help her through the nightmare. He'd swallow his anger one more time, and a thousand times after that, probably. He kissed her hair and stroked it. She smelled horrible, a musky combination of dirt and sweat, but in some ways she was more beautiful right then than when she primped for a night out. This was Carolyn unveiled; the person she fought so hard to hide from everyone she knew.

A few minutes passed before she pulled away from him. She looked away as she mopped her eyes and her nose with a shirttail. "I'm sorry," she said.

"So am I." He stroked her face with the back of his hand.

Part of her still hadn't returned to the present. Jake had seen the mood last for hours. Last time, they'd had a fight over it, prompting him to leave the house and catch a zillion-calorie breakfast at I-HOP. Nothing like a pound of pancakes in your belly to douse your fires.

After a cold night in the van, he felt miserable. Shortly after they'd crossed into West Virginia last night, the skies had opened up, making the mountain passes slick and nearly unpassable. Rather than risk an accident, and the attention it would bring, he'd pulled into the parking lot of the Rebel Yell Motel outside White Sulphur Springs at about ten o'clock and declared it their home for the night.

As a precaution, just in case the cops who stopped them at the school had finally made the connection, Jake had changed their plates, driver's licenses, and registration one more time, transforming them into the Delaney family—James and Clarissa. Because

Travis was a kid, and kids never carried ID, Jake decided to limit the boy's trauma and keep his first name the same. For the time being, he'd just avoid using any last name at all.

Using an Army-surplus entrenching tool off one of the shelves, Jake had buried the old plates and IDs out in the woods.

He and Carolyn had discussed the possibility of checking into the motel but jointly vetoed the idea as something the police would be expecting them to do. They'd also thought about parking in a less-public place but decided in the end that a white van in a parking lot would draw far less suspicion on a rainy night than a white van pulled off into the woods.

True to form, Travis had slept soundly through the whole night, while Jake and Carolyn took turns pretending to sleep and watching for trouble. The direness of their situation still hadn't hit either one of them fully, although, as the hours stretched on, Jake found himself becoming progressively more bitter about the whole thing. What kind of warped individual could put another human being through this kind of torment? He berated himself for not having done something about it fourteen years ago, when all the evidence trails were still fresh, and when people might actually have believed as outlandish a story as the one they had to tell.

Such thoughts were counterproductive, he knew, but at zero-dark-early, in the hills of West Virginia, when you're sitting with a gun in your lap wondering if you'd actually have the guts to shoot someone to protect your family from harm, it was hard to keep your brain on track.

Finally, as the sun rose above the horizon, he'd had enough of waiting and decided it was time to move on. Carolyn had fallen back to sleep, though, and as he turned the key, she jumped.

"Sorry," he said, trying not to laugh at the outrageous look on her face.

It took her a second or two to figure out what was happening, and then she relaxed, bringing her hand to her chest. "Jesus, that scared me." She stretched and yawned noisily.

"Is Travis still asleep?" he asked, not wanting to turn all the way around to look.

She pivoted in her seat. "I think so," she said. "His eyes are closed, anyway."

They drove in silence for a long time after that, something clearly on Carolyn's mind. Jake didn't press, though. He knew she'd come out with it sooner or later. "You shouldn't have told him everything," she said at last. "Why get him so involved?"

"He's got to be aware of the danger."

"The poor boy must be scared to death."

Ah, the guilt card, Jake thought. *No one plays that one better than Carolyn.* "He needs to know enough to be careful. And that the stakes are huge."

"But you told him too much."

Here we go. "So you want me to *untell* him somehow?" God, he was sick of feeling defensive.

Jake possessed an arsenal of facial expressions, any one of which could launch Carolyn's temper into the stratosphere. It was this one, though—the smug, know-it-all smirk—that propelled her into orbit. "No," she snapped. "I want you to remember that he's only thirteen years old. He's just a boy."

"Got it," Jake said. "Thirteen years old. I've been wondering about that all morning. Thanks for the reminder."

She opened her mouth for another round, but then shut it again. She'd said her piece, and he'd said his. Getting along was important now. She let it go. Or tried to, anyway.

As the terrain became steadily more vertical, the roads shrank from four lanes to two; winding ribbons of black, snaking through endless miles of switchbacks and meandering curves. Jake hadn't been down this road in well over a year, and it was bad then. Now the worn, potholed roadbed bounced them like they were on a trampoline. Between the weight of the vehicle, its rear-wheel drive, and the hazardous road conditions, he found himself wondering if perhaps this ride wasn't the most hazardous aspect of their entire plan. Thank God for seat belts. Otherwise, they'd have been bounced through the ceiling by now.

Miraculously, Travis slept through it all.

Soon enough, the ride went from treacherous to positively boring. They'd skimped on engine size when they purchased the van, forgoing the optional V-8 in favor of the standard V-6, and now they were paying the price. The additional weight of the family, combined with the load of supplies, completely maxed out the vehicle's capabilities going uphill. Currently, Jake found himself trapped behind a tractor-trailer loaded with telephone poles, doing twenty miles an hour, with no hope of pulling past.

"Did you ever really think it would come to this?" Carolyn asked. Her voice carried an emotion that Jake didn't quite recognize. Sadness maybe, but not quite.

He answered her softly, not entirely sure what she hoped to hear. "I used to," he said. "You know, back at the beginning. In the last couple of years, though, I'd talked myself out of it. I let myself believe we'd made it. I let my guard down. I'm sorry."

She let his answer just hang in the air for a while, not saying anything. Then she ran her fingers into her hair and made a growling sound. "I'm not doing as well as I thought I would," she confessed.

He smiled. "I'll let you in on a little secret, if you promise not to make a scene."

He saw her head turn in his peripheral vision.

"Neither am I. In fact, I'm scared as hell." As more silence filled the van, he couldn't let pessimism prevail. "We'll make it, though. I *promise* you, we'll get out of this somehow."

For another full minute, they each pondered worries too awful to articulate. Carolyn broke first. "So what's next?"

He turned. "Next?"

"Yeah, next. Let's say we make it as far as the Den . . ."

"Oh, we'll make it, all right."

She waved off his defensiveness. "Yeah, okay. *When* we get all the way to the Den. What happens next?"

"We sleep?"

She rolled her eyes. She hated him when he was intentionally obtuse. "Come on, Jake! What do we do tomorrow? And the next day, and the one after that?"

He shrugged. "We live." He stated it as though it was the most obvious thing in the world. "We live, we wait, we make a life for ourselves as best we can. You know that. Then, when the time is right, we try coming out again and making the best of it. That's the plan; that's always been the plan. You know this."

"And that's what's been gnawing at me," she blurted. "You're right. It's always been the plan, but there's no future in it. We might as well all go to jail together."

Instantly, she realized she'd pressed the wrong button. Jake twisted his neck the way he did when he was angry, and he opened and closed his fists around the steering wheel. "I guess there's a reason why you're bringing this up now, after it's too late to do anything?"

"I'm just stating my concerns . . ."

He cut her off. "Then keep them to yourself. I've invested way too much time and effort into this to have you start tearing it apart now."

"Don't tell me what I can't say!" she declared. "If I have a concern, I'll damn well let you know about it."

"Why?" His tone was combative, but the question was real. "What do we possibly have to gain by your second-guessing now? The situation is what it is, and we are where we are. It's truly that simple. How many times did I ask you to come here with me?"

"And do what with Travis?"

"Bring him along! He'd have loved it."

She set her jaw angrily and turned to face out the window. "Well, Mr. Secrecy, you always were so paranoid about anybody finding out about this."

"Paranoid?" He couldn't believe what he was hearing. "We've got warrants out for our arrest—for *murder*. We're at the top of the Most Wanted list—at least, we were. And I'm *paranoid* for wanting to keep a few secrets?"

She held up her hands, as if surrendering. "Look," she pronounced. "I'm only saying that maybe we should have more of a plan than just heading out into the middle of nowhere to wait for God knows what."

He thumped the steering wheel with his palm. "And what would you have us do, Carolyn? Get on an airplane? A bus? A boat maybe?

Perhaps we could go back to the Rebel Yell and check in for the year. Hell, with the cash we've got in the bag there, we could stay at the fucking Plaza for a month! But you know what? There's people there, Carolyn. There's not a single plane, train, bus, or boat that we could get on without being spotted in a heartbeat."

She took a breath to argue, but he cut her off again. "No, wait. Listen to me. We've been planning this day for fourteen years, okay? You've got to believe that we've worked most of the bugs out. The place is ready for us, and we have to be ready for it. If you start losing confidence now, Travis is going to come unglued."

"What *about* Travis?" Carolyn shot. "We talked about schooling him ourselves, but I don't know what eighth graders are supposed to learn. Suppose we screw it up?"

Jake sighed. His planning had always centered around escape and a decent hiding place. The rest was just too unpredictable; and because it was so unpredictable, it was irrelevant. Now, in the heat of it all, she wanted a specific plan for every conceivable contingency. Why couldn't she see that this was a time for flexibility? Ever since this whole thing started yesterday, she'd focused on nothing but the negatives, and he was sick of it.

What the hell difference did it make if something went wrong at this point? They'd either recover or they wouldn't. It was that simple. Worrying about it only made everything seem more complicated.

"Christ, Carolyn," Jake said, making his voice suddenly much softer. "If we screw it up, we screw it up. Then we move on. Our hand is dealt, honey. It's too late to worry about a stacked deck."

She bowed her head toward her chest, and her voice got very small. "This is just all so unfair to Travis," she said.

Jesus. "Carolyn, look. Family first, remember? Everything else second. If we do our jobs right, Travis will grow up remembering this as one huge adventure."

She breathed through her mouth to rein in her emotions. It didn't take long. "God help us," she whispered.

Travis awoke fifteen minutes later, as Jake slowed the van at the top of Falls Ridge to make the left-hand turn onto a dirt road that would ultimately take them to Donovan's Den. "Where are we?" he asked groggily.

"Almost there."

"Where's 'there'?"

The answer became apparent soon enough. "There" was about two miles east of nowhere. The dirt road, such as it was, ended abruptly about a hundred feet in from the highway. From there it was grass and gravel; paradoxically smoother than most of the paved roads they'd traveled that morning. The aqua and white trailer—the Den—sat in the middle of an overgrown field, looking like a giant striped mushroom against the spatter-colored backdrop of the forest. Field grasses obscured the wheels entirely, reaching nearly all the way to the bottom of the high windows.

It had been too long. Carolyn remembered the place as being primitive, but no way was she prepared for this. Travis spoke her thoughts for her: "You've *got* to be kidding."

"Be it ever so humble," Jake announced, trying his best to conceal his own horror at the condition of the place, "there's no place like home."

"No way," Travis said emphatically. "No friggin' way!"

As the van came to a stop, the boy helped himself to the back doors and climbed out. His mouth agape, he led the family through the weeds toward the front door. If he used his imagination, he could swear that he saw a path leading right to it.

"What is it?" Travis asked.

"It's our home," Jake replied, his voice leaden with a threatening undertone. He'd already been through this discussion with Carolyn. He didn't relish a second round with his son. "Here, let me get the key."

"No need," Travis said, pushing the door open with a fingertip. "It's already open."

Jake drew his Glock from under his jacket and took over the lead, entering the door carefully, with the pistol stretched out in front of him and Travis close behind. "Anybody in here?" he called. The only response was the taunting buzz of a cicada.

Inside, the Den smelled like an old sponge, wet and dirty. Up front, in the kitchenette—which looked for all the world like a camp stove with a counter—the jalousie windows were opened just enough to let the rain enter and soak the Early American cannons-and-drums foam rubber seat cushions. The linoleum on the floor had peeled up around the base of the cabinets, exposing two parallel lines of yellow glue, which ran the length of the short hallway leading to the single bedroom at the other end from the kitchen. The total length of the place was maybe twenty-five feet.

"Looks like we've had some visitors," Jake said, holstering his weapon. A look from side to side constituted a complete search.

Travis slipped past his father, wedging belly-to-belly in the narrow galley. He said nothing; but the look of disgust on his face spoke volumes.

"I'd forgotten there's no electricity," Carolyn grumbled, eyeing the gas jets on the stove and the cotton mantles on the wall sconces.

"Oh, gross!" Travis exclaimed, ducking back out of the bedroom. "There's used rubbers all over the place!"

Carolyn gasped, momentarily curious about how Travis would recognize such a thing, and walked with Jake the eight paces to take a look. Sure enough, used condoms littered the mattress and the floor—seven of them, at first glance—looking like so many miniature crashed zeppelins.

"That's disgusting!" Travis declared again, making his way back toward the front.

"That it is," Jake mumbled. His words drew a look from his wife. "At least we know why our visitors were here."

Travis seemed headed for the door when he stopped short. "Wait!" he said, suddenly very agitated. "Where's the bathroom?"

His parents shared another glance. "Out back," Jake said simply. "I dug it myself."

Travis glared, his face a mask of disbelief. "No way," he said. "In the woods?"

Jake shrugged, suddenly ill at ease. "More in the field than in the woods, actually. It's got a shed around it."

"No way," Travis said again. He looked close to tears. "No fucking way!"

"Travis!" Carolyn gasped.

"No *fucking* way am I gonna *shit* in the *fucking* woods like some *fucking* animal!" He threw the door out of his way, catching it with his elbow as it rebounded off the cabinets, and stormed out of the trailer toward the woods.

"Oh, God—Jake, where's he going?"

Jake took a deep breath and let it out. "I'll go get him," he said.

"I'll go with you." She hurried to get ahead.

He grabbed her by the arm. "No," he said gently. "This one's for me, okay? He'll be all right."

Travis recognized the sound of his father's gait. He didn't even look up.

The reason he left the trailer in the first place was so no one would see him cry. Now they were coming to watch, anyway. As he swiped at his face, a stab of pain reminded him of Terry Lampier's gift from just two days before. As much as he thought his life sucked then, nothing compared to this level of hell.

When his dad sat down next to him on the deadfall that served as his bench, Travis ignored him. He hated this man—this liar. He hated them both. When his dad tried to touch his arm, Travis shook himself free and rose to his feet again.

"You knew this was going to happen one day, didn't you?" The boy made no attempt to disguise the accusation.

When Jake answered, his voice was just a whisper. "I guess I did."

Travis turned and finally made eye contact. The anger and the hatred were right there, burning red streaks into the blue eyes. "All these years, everything you told me—a lie. Was that story about the massacre a lie, too? *Did* you kill those people?"

"No."

Travis took a step closer, daring his father to fight. "I don't believe you," he spat. "You're a liar and a murderer, and I hope you get killed and go to hell!" He saw his father recoil under the impact of his words. *Good,* Travis thought, *I hope it hurts bad!*

Who was this man anyway? The father he'd known these thir-

teen years never would have tolerated this kind of verbal assault—
he'd have smacked his kid into next month. That his dad tolerated
it now pissed Travis off even more. He wanted a fight, dammit—
a knock-down, drag-out brawl where he'd get to take his best shot.

The enormity of it all was beyond his comprehension.

"You know, they taught it to us in school," Travis said at last, his
voice becoming unsteady. "They call it the Newark Incident. The
worst chemical disaster in history." He winced suddenly as his voice
cracked, and he pressed his hands against the sides of his head as
if to keep it from exploding. "Jesus, Dad! I mean, this is like the
Holocaust or the St. Valentine's Day Massacre! I mean . . . God, it's
got a *name!*"

Jake stood, too, and grasped his son's shoulders. Travis shook
himself free and backed further away. "I told you the story yesterday," Jake said as reasonably as he knew how, "and every word I said
was true. All your mom and I did was run."

"But you *lied!*"

"Look at me, Trav," Jake said softly.

Travis didn't *want* eye contact. That's how his dad always won
their fights. Still, the pull of his old man's gaze drew Travis's eyes
right where Jake wanted them.

"You're right, son. I *did* lie. I lied to anyone and everyone I've met
in the past fourteen years. Including you. There's no excuse for
doing what I've done, but even if I had it all to do over again, I still
can't think of how I would have done things differently. I'm sorry."
He cupped his son's chin in the palm of his hand and smiled. No
matter how hard an exterior the boy showed to his friends and his
classmates, Jake had always been able to look straight through to
his soul. "But you must believe that I'm *not* lying now."

Travis shook himself away. "Then why don't you just go to the
police? Right now. Just tell them what you told me, and we'll get it
all fixed." He was crying openly now, and as soon as he realized it,
he turned quickly away, to face the woods.

Jake tried to hug him one more time but with no success. "It's
just not that simple, Trav. It's been too long now. Whoever organized all of this had a plan. And it was a very good one. By sur-

viving, your mother and I set ourselves up to take the fall. The person who did this, he wanted us to look guilty, and by running away, we ended up doing our very best to help him out."

"Why *us*? What did *we* do?"

Jake sighed and stepped closer. God, it hurt him to say this. "It's not about *all* of us. It's about your mom and me. You're part of it only because you're a part of us."

Travis sat heavily at the base of a healthy oak, his back turned. He hugged his shins and buried his face against his knees as he fought to regain control. It was like someone had put a time bomb in the middle of his life, and now the alarm was ringing. Somehow he'd always believed that as he got older, he'd stop being just a trailer park kid; that life would somehow become fair. Now, as he fought back tears, he realized that fairness wasn't part of life's package.

Jake's heart withered under the strain of his son's sadness. His feelings of utter helplessness. He'd visited that place in his own soul many, many times.

Back in the early days, while they were learning to become invisible, Jake had dedicated hundreds of hours to mentally re-creating the events of that August afternoon in Newark. He knew, firsthand, that the "why me" puzzle could drive a person over the edge if dwelled on too long.

Whoever the architect of the "Newark Incident" was, and whatever his reasons, he could have killed the Enviro-Kleen workers *anywhere*, just as he could have blown up the magazine and its contents *anytime*. For some reason, the killings and the explosion had to happen together, of that Jake was sure. And it had to happen in such a way that somebody would get punished.

Inevitably, his thoughts always came around to the body that Adam Pomeroy had found just before the shooting started. That had to be it. The way Jake figured it, the asshole who put all of this together did it as part of an elaborate plan to hide a corpse. After all, what better place to put it than among a bunch of other corpses? Maybe the guy even knew that the fires and contamination would force the government to seal everything off and entomb the evidence forever.

Fourteen years ago Jake had tormented himself trying to solve the riddle of why Mr. X didn't just move the damn body and bury it elsewhere, but Carolyn eventually came up with a plausible theory: The EPA shutdown had caught Mr. X by surprise. Once the site was discovered and shut down, it was too late to go back in without being detected.

Over time, Jake and Carolyn had spun countless twists on every possible detail, but they always came back to that body. They'd even fantasized once about sneaking back inside and collecting the evidence that would prove their innocence, but the risks of getting caught or being poisoned by residual chemicals always seemed to outweigh the slim chance of finding the exculpatory evidence they sought. At best, it would have been a shot in the dark. And a dangerous one at that.

Now, as he watched his son fight off panic, the details of that long-forgotten pipe dream began to leak back into his consciousness.

You're crazy, he told himself. *A thousand things have changed since then.*

But a million others hadn't. If he'd read the newspaper articles correctly, and if the media reported the facts accurately, nothing in that magazine had changed since the day they'd escaped with their lives. Everything should have remained untouched.

It can work . . .

He shook his head, trying to knock the craziness out of his brain, but the flame of hope burned brighter the more he thought about it. Sure, there were risks. And they'd have to step into the open for a while, but by God, it could work!

And what did they have to lose? This was no life! What had he been thinking? The tragic flaw of their escape plan, he saw now, had always been that it stopped with the escape. The rest had been too unpredictable. What kind of future was there for them, huddled in some shithole of a trailer, living in fear of the moment when the lovebirds might return with more condoms? Once recognized, what would the Donovan family do then? How would they keep the lovebirds quiet? Kill them? Not hardly.

At least this new plan offered a glimmer of salvation. And if he and Carolyn died in the process, then at least their son would grow old knowing his parents had done their best to redeem themselves.

Sometimes honor lay more in the fight itself than in the outcome.

Even as he recognized the absurdity of the notion, Jake felt strangely energized, as if, in the space of a few seconds, years had dropped from his age. This could work!

"So is this it?" Travis asked, his back still turned. His voice sounded cloudy. "We just run forever?"

Jake took a seat on the ground next to his son. "Funny you should ask . . ."

Chapter Sixteen

For the first time in four decades, Clayton Albricht seriously considered just staying in bed. The press had been assembling on his front lawn all night, as he worked feverishly with his staff to figure out a way to control the damage.

He cringed as he heard the clip on the morning news of his press secretary telling the assembled reporters, "The senator vehemently and categorically denies that he has ever engaged in homosexual or pedophilic activities . . ."

Christ, even the denial was damning.

No one could prove, of course, that Frankel had anything to do with this, so it was out of the question even to suggest such a thing. That left Albricht with lame, paranoic claims of unidentified conspiracies to defame him. Every excuse he offered sounded comically defensive.

His wife, Alba, believed him, though. She'd seen too many careers plummet at the hands of others to think that any act of deception or cruelty was out of the question. At least the children were grown, she reasoned, and there was some comfort in that.

Still, Clayton and Alba had spent hours together on the phone with the kids, explaining what the media was about to release and assuring them that their father was not a pervert. By the end of the conversation, both kids agreed that it was a good time to take a quick vacation. Come eight o'clock tonight, Clay Jr. would be in Denali Park with his wife and two kids, and Amy would be basking in the sun in St. Thomas. Of the two, everyone agreed that Clay Jr. was less likely to be followed by the press. Alaska could get pretty chilly in October.

"This is the Big One, isn't it, Clay?" Alba asked as he hung up from his thousandth conference call with his senior staffers.

The instant the handset touched the cradle, it rang again. It had been like that all morning, with calls pouring in from all over the world. Apparently, it was an otherwise slow news day. The senator lifted the receiver and put it right down. Three seconds later it rang again. They both laughed.

Clayton made room for her next to him on the well-worn bedroom lounge chair. Countless stories and good-night kisses had been issued to the children from this very spot. He called it his thinking chair. "Not yet," he said, putting more levity in his voice than he felt in his soul. "Not as long as the supposed pictures stay out of the media. If they get released, then yes. This'll be the one that brings us down."

Alba rumpled his sleep-twisted hair, relieved that he'd finally been able to log forty-five minutes or so before dawn. "How are you holding up?"

He gave a wan smile. "I guess I'll be okay until I get an offer to be grand marshal of the Gay Pride Parade. Then I might have to jump off something tall."

"Not that there's anything wrong with being gay," she teased.

"Oh, heavens, no." He chuckled. Sometimes it made him dizzy to think of the number of times he'd had to abandon his moral stance on once-obvious issues. He secretly longed for the days when gay just meant "happy."

"Are you sure it's Frankel?" Alba asked.

The senator nodded as he rubbed his eyes with the heels of his hands. "It sure smells like him. It has to be."

"Can you beat him?"

He shrugged. The thought of sleep was particularly pleasing to him right now. "Well, I won't be charged with any crimes, if that's what you mean. You can't prove a case from receipts—or even from pictures—and even Frankel can't invent witnesses."

Alba stood and stepped behind the chair to rub her husband's shoulders. "He won't stop, you know. Even if you let him waltz through the confirmation hearings, he'll still have you under his thumb. It'll never end."

The senator leaned all the way back in his chair and grabbed both her hands, pulling them down to his chest, until she was hugging him from behind. "You know me better than that," he said. "I'll fight him underground for as long as I can. If I can expose him for what he is, we'll win. If not, then maybe it'll be time to move back to Chicago. Time to go home."

Deep down inside, Alba wondered if her husband hadn't grown tired of Washington, anyway. Life as a target for every bleeding-heart special interest was tough. Certainly, they could swing the financial aspects of retirement. Maybe this was all an omen that the time had come to quit.

"So what happens first, do you suppose?" she asked.

Clayton sighed again and pinched the bridge of his nose. "Well, the way I figure it, nothing happens until I want it to happen. The press will let this run its course for a couple of weeks, running my daily denials and the president's daily suggestions that I retire from office. After that, it'll get pretty hot, as the papers start collecting quotes from my own party, condemning me for godlessness and sanctifying you for your willingness to stand by such a horrible creature as me."

"Maybe I can go on *Oprah*," Alba teased.

Clayton laughed. "Pedophile Legislators and the Women Who Love Them," he added in his best announcer's voice. "If it goes the way these things usually do, we won't be invited to a single Christmas party, but come Easter, we'll be back on the A list. Then I announce my retirement at the end of the term, and in a few years we're back in Chicago, and I get to live off speaking fees and book advances."

"Sounds like you have it all planned, Senator," Alba cooed, rubbing his stubbly face gently with the back of her hand.

"Oh, I do," Clayton confirmed. "And best of all, I've got five full years left to figure out a way to break all of this off in Frankel's ass."

Alba drew back at that comment and smirked. "No pun intended, I assume."

"Jake, you're crazy." Carolyn seemed outraged that he would even mention such a thing. She turned her back on him and stormed into the trailer.

Jake followed, with Travis close behind, despite his father's warning to stay out of it. "Why am I crazy? This is a way to get our lives back."

"Bullshit! This is a way to get our lives ended!" She seemed close to tears.

"Like *this* isn't death?" He swirled his arms to take in the whole scene. "Christ, Carolyn, we've got to take a chance."

"Why now?" she insisted. "Last time we discussed it, you said yourself it was a stupid idea. What suddenly makes it any less stupid now?"

"You've been caught," Travis said evenly, stating the obvious.

"You stay out of this!" His parents said it in perfect unison.

Carolyn thrust her fingers into her thick hair, a gesture of ultimate frustration. "It's too late," she insisted. "The evidence is gone, and we're too old."

Jake tossed his hands in the air. "Okay, we're pushing forty," he conceded. "But you know what? Next year we'll be another year older. And so will the evidence. Now is a bad time only because we should have done it sooner!"

"And what about Travis?" She was grasping at straws now.

"What about me?"

"Stay out of this!" Another perfect chorus.

"What about him?"

"He's just a boy, Jake. We can't get him wrapped up in something like this. It's illegal."

"I'll just tell them that you forced me to do it at gunpoint," Travis offered helpfully, bringing the argument to a dead halt.

"Thanks a lot, buddy," Jake said, planting his fists on his hips. "With family like you, who needs prosecutors?" With just this glimmer of hope, Travis had become Jake's ally; albeit a conditional ally.

Carolyn worked her jaw muscles hard as she considered her husband's plea. "There's a million things that could go wrong," she said. Her voice had softened, and even Travis recognized it as the time to tread carefully. The right words now would make it a go. Say the wrong thing, though, and the option would be shut down forever.

"We only need a couple to go right," Jake countered. He moved closer. "Think of it. It's this for the rest of our lives, or we can take a shot."

She absorbed the words, looking first to Travis and then to Jake. "Suppose no one wants to help?"

Jake shrugged. "We'll never know unless we ask." He was careful to smile.

Closing her eyes, she sighed deeply and thrust her hand into her hair one more time. "This is insane," she moaned.

Travis cheered, "Yes!"

They jammed themselves into the mildewed kitchenette and discussed the details for a good hour, re-creating long-forgotten logic paths and mapping out the logistics of what had to be done and in what order.

With the initial plans complete, they headed back for the van. Jake started to lock the trailer's door, then paused, recognizing the futility of it. "My contribution to young love," he mumbled, and he put his key away.

CHAPTER SEVENTEEN

The Donovans needed a pay phone, but they may as well have been searching for the Holy Grail. In this part of southeastern West Virginia, it was hard enough to find buildings with foundations. The Gulf station up the road sported an international symbol for a telephone on the side of one of the service bays, but closer examination revealed that it had been out of service for quite a while—since, say, the Civil War.

They drove for fifteen miles, seeing nothing but shacks and endless forests, all situated on near-vertical slopes. "Why would anyone ever want to live here?" Jake wondered aloud.

Finally, they came to Homer and Jane's Roadside Diner, whose status as the only restaurant in this part of the state was plainly illustrated by the number of old cars and pickup trucks in the parking lot. The building was classic backwoods construction. The red brick center section may have had some charm in its youth, but as time had worn on, wooden additions had been slapped onto both ends of the place, with an eye toward nothing but efficiency and economy. Overall, the place had a droopy, unappealing feel. Not that it mattered; every window in the place displayed the profile of a live diner. More important, according to the sign affixed to the brick, Homer and Jane's had not only a telephone but rest rooms as well.

The van's suspension moaned painfully as Jake piloted the vehicle into the crumbled and pockmarked driveway. "What do you think?"

"I think—" Carolyn stopped before she could complete the thought. "Oh, God . . . take a look at the newsstand."

The gravity of her tone brought Travis forward. "What newsstand?"

Jake didn't see it either at first, but when he followed her finger, his stomach flopped. In the windows of their coin-operated dispensers, three competing newspapers—two from West Virginia and one from Washington, D.C.—displayed pictures of the world's most notorious environmental terrorists. Instead of the old Wanted-poster shots, however, the press was using current photos lifted from their driver's licenses.

"Shit," Jake said. "Looks just like us." Something about seeing the story in the paper made the threat to them more palpable.

"Well, we certainly can't go in *there*," Carolyn said. "Those people are eating breakfast. Half of them are probably reading about us as we speak."

It was a very good point. Wanted posters, as such, never posed much of a threat. People rarely made eye contact to begin with, and they certainly didn't remember pictures of people they'd never met. In a tiny community such as this, though, where everyone undoubtedly knew everyone else, strangers couldn't help but draw attention. When the focus of that attention was the very people whose pictures appeared before them in the paper, God only knew what might happen.

"I can go in," Travis volunteered. "I don't see any pictures of me."

Instinctively, Jake and Carolyn started to say no, but then stopped.

Jake arched an eyebrow. "What do you think?"

"C'mon, Mom, I can do it." Travis was anxious to prove himself.

"Hell, it's only a phone call." Simultaneous glares silenced him, and he rolled his eyes. "I meant, *heck*, it's only a phone call."

"This isn't a game, Travis," Carolyn scolded.

"I know that, but Jesus—um, I mean *Jeeze*—why risk you guys getting recognized when the only thing I have to do is make a phone call?"

Another very good point, drawing another shrug from Jake. "I don't see why not."

"But Harry doesn't know him from Adam," Carolyn countered.

"He'll know who I am after I tell him," Travis offered. "C'mon, you guys, just tell me what to say, and I'll say it. Then he'll tell me, and I'll tell you."

Maybe it really was that simple. "Have you ever made a collect call?" Jake asked.

"Uh-huh. Remember that time in Amarillo when the Tawingos' car broke down? I called you collect to tell you I was gonna be late."

Jake and Carolyn looked to each other for some sound reason to say no but couldn't find one.

"Okay," Carolyn said with an uneasy sigh. "Here's what we need you to say."

As he watched his son climb out of the back of the van and stride purposefully toward Homer and Jane's, Jake enjoyed a moment of intense pride. Here the kid's world had been turned completely inside out, and yet he truly wanted to help. Much was left to be done, of course, and this adventure was far from over, but as ridiculous as it sounded, Jake felt that they were more of a family at this moment than they'd been in years.

"I wonder how Harry will react," Jake mused aloud.

"I'm sure he'll be relieved," Carolyn said.

"Yeah, right."

Carolyn's maternal uncle, Harry Sinclair, owned more of Chicago's Miracle Mile than any other single investor. Widely known for his intense loyalty to his friends, and his ruthless business practices, Harry was both feared and revered, all depending on which side of the negotiation table he was seated. Harry was a man accustomed to winning, regardless of the cost. Rumors abounded of competitors threatened into submission, but none of the accusations were true—at least not in the sense that people imagined.

Harry Sinclair knew only one subject—business—and he played the game with a passion matched by only a few. Jake had met the man only twice, yet he had the old bastard's mantra down cold: "You can always tell a sucker," he'd told Jake back when he and Carolyn were just dating. "He's the guy who believes that the game is over when the other side gives up. Growing up on the South Side, I learned the *real* secret to winning. As long as the other guy can stand, the game's still on."

The lecture was the only form of speech that Harry Sinclair knew; and from that very first day, Jake couldn't stand the man. He was the embodiment of everything that was wrong about business—the very attitude that allowed the Pennsylvania coal-mining barons to send Jake's father into hell every day, knowing full well that the fetid atmosphere in those tunnels would corrode his lungs. For people like Harry, business was just a euphemism for crushing people who didn't have the means to fight back. They were bullies, pure and simple, differentiated from the schoolyard variety only by their expensive suits and silk ties.

During that first meeting, convened out at Harry's estate, and carefully orchestrated to intimidate the unsophisticated coal miner's kid who was sniffing around his niece, Harry laid it all out on the table. Sitting in his $2,000 chair and sucking on a thirty-dollar cigar, he told the story of a Korean grocer named Kim Po, who refused to sell his store to make room for Sinclair Plaza, a sprawling, fifty-story granite and glass office/retail complex on Michigan Avenue.

A man who prided himself on always playing by the rules, Harry got zoning approval to build his vanity tower, anyway, bringing his building within six inches on three sides and the top of Po's grocery. The Korean filed suit, of course, at which point Harry began his siege, filing a countersuit alleging emotional distress, and beginning an escalating war of legal fees which Po knew he could never win.

After six months of warfare, fought in the trenches of the courthouse, Po caved in and offered to sell his store. Harry refused. "I'd already spent that money on legal fees and architectural changes," he relayed to Jake. "I offered him forty cents on the dollar, though, and he turned me down."

With the value of his property dangling below the payoff price for the five college educations he'd leveraged against it, Po did the honorable thing. He dug in to make the best of things.

But, as Harry pointed out, he could still stand. When Sinclair Plaza finally opened, the old man made sure that the space just inches away from Po's store was leased to a competing grocery, which coincidentally specialized in everything that the Korean sold, only more of it at a lesser price.

Harry ended up declaring victory on the day he finally bought the ruined grocer's real estate as the only bidder at the trustee's sale.

Predators like Harry Sinclair drove federal regulators nuts. For the last two decades, they'd worked tirelessly to keep the old man honest. They'd nabbed him only once, back in the late seventies when the IRS found enough indiscretions to justify a five-year prison sentence.

To Jake, Harry would forever be a jailbird, even as Carolyn worshiped every step the old man took. As the only girl among a sea of boy cousins, Carolyn had always been Harry's "Sunshine," and the real estate mogul played his role to the hilt, bringing her silver dollars and chocolate bars every time he saw her. There was an unbreakable bond there, part of the great mystery that was Carolyn's childhood.

Distasteful business practices aside, Jake recognized loyalty when he saw it, and while he detested much of what Harry Sinclair stood for, there was no denying that the old man had come to Jake and Carolyn's aid at a critical time. As the entire world bore down on the Donovans in 1983, Harry provided them with everything they needed to disappear, from identities to cash—all just months after Harry himself had been released from prison and stood to lose a great deal in the transaction.

Sitting there in the van outside the diner, Jake shook his head in disbelief. *This* was the man from whom Travis was soliciting assistance? The punch line of an old joke popped into his mind, making him squirm in his seat: *We've already established what you are, madam, now we're just haggling over price.*

As he waited for Travis to return, Jake let his thoughts drift back to his *second* meeting with Harry Sinclair—Jake's first in the role of fugitive. The old man had sent a car to pick up Jake and Carolyn at a prearranged spot downstream from Buford. He remembered the driver's name to this day. Thorne: a sinewy, large-torsoed military type who rarely said a word but whose dark eyes continually cast a threat. The pickup had been late at night, as Jake recalled, and they drove straight through till morning to a house somewhere in southern Illinois.

Jake had slept most of the way, finally awakened by the heat of the rising sun. Carolyn was already awake, sitting upright and talking in hushed tones to Thorne. Jake stretched noisily, and slowly worked his way up to a sitting position.

"Hey, sleepyhead," Carolyn said happily. "About time you woke up."

"What time is it?" He was too sleep-dumb to think of checking his watch.

"About nine. We're almost there."

"Correction," Thorne interrupted. "We *are* there."

The only building in sight was a largish farmhouse planted in the middle of a huge expanse of green farmland. Thorne slowed the Cadillac nearly to a halt to catch a rutted dirt path. The house was gorgeous, in a uniquely midwestern way. Probably dating back to the 1920s, it vaguely resembled a squatty Aztec pyramid, anchored at its base by a huge, wraparound porch, and rising two more stories in classic Victorian style to a slate roof and an intricate collage of gables.

Harry was waiting for them at the front door, and Carolyn started to cry the instant she saw him. The years in prison had been hard. Heavy creases had invaded his boyish face. Last time they'd seen each other—could it possibly be eight years?—his hair, which now resembled a disheveled cotton ball, had been a lush auburn mane, carefully coiffed and proudly displayed. Despite his ever-present paunch, he'd always been obsessive about his wardrobe, sporting the very latest in men's fashions. Now his clothes just looked rumpled and old; not unlike the man wearing them.

Carolyn was out of the car as soon as it pulled to a stop, and she became a young girl again as she glided up the manicured path and into Harry's outstretched arms. "Little Sunshine," he whispered gently, "I've missed you so much." As she buried her face in his shoulder, he stroked the back of her head.

"Shh, Sunshine," Harry cooed. "Shh. Settle down now. Everything's going to be just fine . . ."

Jake watched it all from the driveway, trying to ignore Thorne, who seemed to regard Sunshine's husband as a threat. As Jake felt the driver's eyes burning through him, he found himself oddly aware of his hands, feeling fidgety as he fumbled for an appropriate, nonthreatening place to put them.

A minute passed before Carolyn pulled away from her uncle, and even as she did, he continued to hold her at arm's length, examining the face he hadn't seen in so long. "You're beautiful," he said. "You look like a Sinclair. You have your mother's eyes. And her mouth, too."

"So, her mom cussed, did she?" Jake quipped, trying to be recognized as something more than a lawn ornament. He smiled, but no one else did.

Harry's scowl spoke his mind: *Haven't you left yet?*

Jake extended his hand and stepped forward, bringing Thorne in close behind. "Hello, sir. Nice to see you again. You look well." Again, he smiled alone.

Carolyn half turned, keeping one arm wrapped around Harry and beckoning her husband with the other, as if to include him in a group hug. "You remember Jake, don't you, Uncle Harry? We dated back in high school? You had him to dinner once . . ."

"Of course." Harry took Jake in with an extended glare as he shook his hand. His face twitched a bit around the eyes, as if he smelled something unpleasant or was perhaps enduring a sudden gas pain.

The look prompted Jake to take a look at himself. At once, it seemed, everyone realized just how filthy the new arrivals were.

"Thorne," Harry commanded, "send somebody to get my niece and nephew some new clothes, will you? Plain vanilla, understand? Nothing fancy. What size shoes do you kids wear?"

"I'm a ten-D," Jake answered. "I think Carolyn's a five."

"Five and a half," she corrected.

Thorne looked from one visitor to the other as they spoke, and then back to Harry, who dismissed him with a nod. "Please come in," Harry offered.

"Nice place," Jake said. Dominated by tasteful yet not extravagant antiques, and accessorized with cloth wall coverings and Oriental rugs, the farmhouse felt lived in; well loved.

"Thank you," Harry acknowledged. "It's not mine. Actually, it belongs to a friend of mine. He agreed to let me entertain you here." He led the way into a spacious living room, where he lowered himself into a wing-backed chair. Overhead, one of the three fans churned the heavy air to create the illusion of a breeze. "Carolyn, why don't you and Jack sit on the sofa there?"

"It's, um, Jake, sir." Harry looked at him oddly. "As opposed to Jack."

Harry smiled. "Right. And you can call me Harry. So . . . what have you kids heard about the media's take on all this?"

"We haven't seen or heard a thing," Carolyn said. Since the explosion at the plant, she and Jake had been so immersed in staying beyond the reach of the police, they'd suffered a virtual information blackout.

"Hmm." The old man inhaled deeply through his nose and leaned back into the cushions of his chair, interlacing his fingers across his chest. "Well, I hate to break it to you, but you *are* the news. Very hot news, indeed. The minute you ran from that motel room in Buford, I'm afraid you lost any benefit you might have gained by turning yourselves in."

"But we didn't do anything!" Carolyn protested. "My God, surely we can prove that much!"

Harry inhaled deeply again, searching for the words that would cause this all to make sense. "While it *should* matter whether one is guilty or innocent, I've had some conflicts with the authorities myself, as you know, and I can tell you that culpability is frequently irrelevant. What *is* relevant is that you two seem to be the victims of a rather sophisticated conspiracy. Having kept one eye on the television for the last twelve hours, I've heard the words 'airtight case' dropped at least a dozen times."

"But how can that be?" Carolyn said. "If we just——"

"*Obviously,*" Harry cut her off, "someone *wants* the world to believe that you did these horrible things. And it appears that they've accomplished that goal. Accomplished it in a way that is beyond refute. Since your guilt is assumed, you must behave accordingly. Remember: the police don't differentiate between guilty fugitives and innocent fugitives."

Harry let the words hang in the air, allowing time for the Donovans to absorb them. Jake noted the old man's smile as Carolyn unconsciously sought her husband's hand and squeezed it lovingly. Clearly, it was important to Harry that she be happily married.

"So what do we do?" Carolyn asked.

Harry broke eye contact. "You disappear," he said to his hands. "You evaporate; cease to exist."

"For how long?" asked Jake.

Harry looked up. "Assume *forever.* There'll be a huge investigation, of course. Motives examined. Evidence sifted. My hunch is, the finger will still be pointing at you when they're done. Something about this smells. It's too neat and tidy. The game is rigged."

The enormity of what Harry was suggesting pressed down on Jake like a block of granite. "But what about our friends?" he blurted. "All our things are back at the apartment, and the car . . ."

"*Forget* about them. Forget about everything but survival." Harry had made it sound so effortless, so ordinary. Like pumping gas or buying an apple at the grocery store.

Carolyn shook her head fiercely, on the edge of panic. "There *has* to be another way."

"There *is* no other way," Harry insisted. "You asked for my advice, Sunshine, and now I'm offering it to you. There is no other way."

"What about money?" Jake asked. "And jobs? How are we going to support ourselves?"

Harry seemed pleased by these questions, as if comforted by the thought process behind them. "Thorne will bring you a briefcase in a moment," Harry explained. "In it, you'll find eighty thousand dollars. I'm sorry it can't be more, Sunshine, but what with my recent vacation courtesy of the IRS, my business is not what it once was."

Eighty thousand dollars! Jake's mind screamed. *And he's apologizing for it?*

Harry saw their looks of wonder and worked quickly to bring them back on track. "Listen to me, you two," he said, extending a reproachful forefinger. "This will be your survival money, and you must dispense it wisely. If either one of you spends it on a fast car or a night in Vegas, I swear to God I'll beat you both." What might have sounded like an empty threat coming from someone else sounded like the most sincere of promises.

"Now, I can help you to establish new identities," Harry went on. "My assistant, Thorne—he has contacts who can take care of things. But from that point on, you'll be on your own, do you understand?"

Carolyn nodded, but her mind had already left the conversation, racing ahead to God only knew what complications lay in wait. People couldn't just cease to exist! They had fingerprints. They had faces, and as Harry pointed out earlier, those faces were plastered all over every media outlet.

"Sunshine, you're not listening," Harry barked. "We don't have a lot of time here."

"What about our faces?" There, she asked it.

"Creating a new face is not as difficult as you might think. Or so I'm told. A new nose here, some collagen there, a new hairstyle—you'd be surprised how easy it is. The paper trail is the hard part—giving you not only a present to live in but a past to explain it. But don't worry about that. Thorne's friends will take care of you there. What's important is how you behave. You must never buy or produce or even own anything that you can't walk away from in a heartbeat. Even with the identity work we'll be doing for you, you must never forget that a single mistake can bring it all down. No homes, no stocks, no pets, and no kids."

"No kids!" Carolyn objected. "But we were planning a family!"

Harry laughed; a release of frustration. "For God's sake, Carolyn. You were planning a lot of things. And none of them involved any of this. Open your eyes. Kids weigh you down; slow you down. When it's time for you to move, you'll need to move instantly. You won't have time to run by the grocery store for Pampers and formula."

"Come on, Harry," Jake interrupted. "We've got to have some semblance of a life. What you describe—we'd be as well off going to jail."

Harry's eyes turned to ice, and he set his jaw angrily. "What I'm giving you *is* a semblance of a life. I'm trying to show you how not to blow it. You say you want kids. That's terrific. How screwed up do you want them to be? Here's the one absolute truth in your life from now on, and never, ever forget it: whatever you had planned for the next sixty years or so doesn't mean anything anymore, because you're not gonna have the chance to do it. Period. You're gonna have to move every year, some years more than once. You'll never get a job that requires a background check, 'cause that would be stupid. You'll never get another job in your chosen field, because you're more likely to run into people you know. And when we're done, you'll never be called Donovan again. Whatever family you have, you'll never talk to them again. Got a best buddy? Maybe the best man at your wedding? Well, to him, you might as well be dead.

"Are you understanding me, kids? You can't afford friends anymore. I know it's a raw deal, but it's all you've got. And if you can't have friends, then how the hell can you have kids? Don't you see? It's stupid."

Again, he let the words hang in the air. This was their first great lesson, and with it the weight bearing down on Jake seemed to increase a hundredfold. As he listened to Harry's speech, Jake realized for the first time the abiding injustice of it all. In the ensuing years, he and Carolyn would search repeatedly for the Greater

Good in all of this, but the bottom line—and the point Harry had been trying to make—was that there was no Great Plan; no acceptable reason for it all. It just was the way it was. Period. It was a lesson for which they hadn't been prepared; a lesson that Jake's complacency would ultimately allow him to forget.

"And Jake," Harry concluded, aiming a finger between his eyes, "don't ever assume that prison is an alternative to anything, do you understand? I'm tougher than you'll ever be, and it damn near broke me after five years. You two are looking at spending the rest of your lives there. If it comes to that, you're better off dead, do you understand? Dead is *better* than prison."

Jake and Carolyn both looked away. They held hands tightly enough to turn their knuckles white. Harry softened his voice, and as he did, his eyes moistened. "Sunshine, you know I'd rather cut off my arm than see you go through this. You know that, right?"

She nodded glumly, her eyes still cast downward.

"Now, there'll be temptations. Come Christmas, or maybe your anniversary, you'll want to call home; or maybe even call me. But you can't. The FBI is going to turn the world inside out looking for you, and the search won't stop in the next year or two or five. They'll know more about each of you than you know about yourselves, and every one of your friends and relatives will be watched. They'll be warned. The picture that the U.S. Attorney is going to paint of you will be so awful that there won't be a friend or relative who isn't tempted to turn you in. You can trust no one. Ever. Remember that."

Thorne arrived at the archway to the living room, briefcase in hand, waiting to be recognized. "Give us another minute," Harry said, and the assistant retreated.

Harry scooted forward in his chair and held his hand out for Carolyn's. She took it, linking herself to the two men she loved more than anything else in the world. "If there were another way, I'd take it," Harry said, his voice thickening. "Any other way in the world. But there isn't. The feds hate me, you know. Enough to be a risk to both of you, so I have to leave. If you get jammed up one day—I mean, really boxed in, and there's no other alternative—you call this number." He handed them a blue slip of paper, produced from his shirt pocket. "Read it, memorize it, and destroy it. I'll do whatever I can for you, but remember that the IRS and the FBI are likely to be watching me all the time. It's not impossible that a call to me would cause more problems for you than it would solve."

Cupping Carolyn's jawline tenderly with his fingers, Harry's eyes filled with tears. "Sunshine, if things go well, we'll never see each other again, sweetie." His voice disappeared entirely as he leaned forward and gave her another long, tender hug. Then it was time for him to go. He pushed Carolyn away.

As he stood, he extended his hand to Jake. "You can't imagine what your bride and I have been through together, Jake. You take good care of her."

Jake rose as well. "I'll do my best, Harry," he said.

Harry fixed him with a menacing glare. "Do better than your best. You protect her at all costs. From here on out, she's all you've got."

He exited quickly, leaving the Donovans alone in the living room. "Oh, my God, Jake," Carolyn said through bitter sobs. "What are we doing?"

Jake thought about that for a moment, chewing on his lower lip and trying to come to grips with it all. "I guess we're surviving."

"Excuse me, folks," Thorne interrupted, startling them both. "Mr. Sinclair said it was important to move quickly. We have some new clothes for you upstairs, if you'd like to change. And there's time for a shower, too, if you'd like."

Unable to think of a proper response, Jake just nodded, his expression blank. He looked like a man who'd just been handed a death sentence, his brain too overloaded with emotion to deal with the facts one at a time. With his bride tucked tightly next to him, he followed Thorne out of the living room and into the future.

CHAPTER EIGHTEEN

Travis's heart pounded furiously as he crossed the parking lot, stifling the urge to shoot a glance back toward his parents. This was his idea, after all, and he refused to look as frightened as he felt. In less than twenty-four hours, everything about his life had changed, and he was sick and tired of not having a role in it all. This was his contribution. At least now they'd all go to jail together.

As he climbed the four steps to the front door, he reviewed what he was supposed to say one more time in his head. Much of it made no sense to him, but his parents had assured him that it wouldn't matter; that Uncle Harry—whoever the hell he was— would know everything.

The aroma of bacon grew stronger as he approached the top step, and as soon as he pulled the door open, that aroma mingled with stale cigarette smoke and the sulfury odor of eggs. Homer and Jane's was packed and noisy, filled with people who looked like they might be on their way to work.

Travis paused in the doorway, holding up traffic for a few seconds as he surveyed the place and tried to locate the telephone.

"Make a hole, kid," said a man dressed all in denim and sporting a saucer-size belt buckle. Travis stepped out of the way, but the man nudged him aside, anyway. Not a push exactly, but it wasn't friendly, either.

A stern-faced woman approached from the other side of the diner, wearing a grease-stained waitress uniform and a scrungy hairnet. "Can I help you?" According to the guy who just asked for more coffee, her name was Peggy.

Travis smiled politely, trying to look the part of a wayward kid. "Yes, ma'am," he said. "I'm wondering if you have a pay phone?"

Whatever the waitress saw in the boy garnered more suspicion than empathy. "Are you here alone?"

What difference does that make? he didn't say. "Um, no, ma'am. My folks are out in the car waiting for me."

Peggy's eyes narrowed, as if to shoot him with X rays. Apparently, he looked like a vandal or something. Finally, she pointed to the right rear corner of the dining room, where he could just make out the image of a telephone through the thick haze of smoke.

He forced another smile. "Thanks."

Far from a culinary expert, Travis nevertheless surmised that this place was a dump. Every booth was either torn or tilted, and most bore more gray duct tape than aqua Naugahyde. He tried to look calm and impassive—friendly, even—as he strolled down the center aisle, surrounded by a dozen pictures of his parents, held up high for everyone to see while they read the morning news.

The telephone hung from the wall just outside the rest rooms, and, judging from the looming stench, someone had just pinched off a pipe-choker. Certain that everyone was watching, he lifted the receiver from its cradle and punched "0" plus the telephone number he'd memorized in the car. He used the same mnemonic, in fact, that his parents had used over the years to keep the number burned into their brains.

"I'd like to make a collect call to Harry Sinclair, please," he said to the operator after she'd picked up.

"Who's calling, please?" the operator asked.

Travis's heart stopped. What should he tell her? Mom and Dad didn't mention this question. He kept the operator waiting long enough for her to ask if he was still on the line. "Huh?" he said, startled by the voice's intrusion into his frantic thoughts. "Um, yeah. Yeah, I'm still here. Tell him it's Mr. Donnolly."

"*Mister* Donnolly?"

"No, Donovan!" he corrected himself quickly. *Shit!*

"Uh-huh. Which is it, sir?" Clearly, the operator trusted him about as much as Peggy did.

"It's Donovan," he said firmly. "Travis Donovan." *What the hell!* At this point, he'd sound suspicious no matter what he said. He tucked the phone in tight against his shoulder and looked around to see if anyone was watching. So far, so good.

A gruff voice answered on the fourth ring. "Yeah?"

"I have a collect call from Travis Donnolly for Harry Sinclair."

"Donovan!" Travis countered. *She did that on purpose!*

The line was quiet for a second. "Travis Donovan?" the gruff voice asked. "We don't know no Travis Donovan."

"I'm Sunshine's son," Travis added quickly.

More silence.

"Will you accept the charges?" the operator pressed.

The answer came slowly, suspiciously. "Yeah, we'll accept."

Travis let out a breath he didn't even know he'd been holding. "Thank you," he said gratefully. After the operator left them with a *click*, the boy said, "Uncle Harry?"

"No," the voice said sourly. "I'm a friend of his. Who are you really?" The threat in his voice was heavy; palpable even eight hundred miles away.

The sound of the voice launched a shiver down Travis's spine. "I'm really me," he insisted. "I'm Sunshine's kid."

"This isn't a joke, is it, kid?" the voice pressed. "This is the wrong number if this is a joke."

Travis swallowed hard. "N-no, this isn't a joke," he stammered. "M-my mom and dad need Uncle Harry's help."

Again, the phone line filled with silence. "Okay," the voice said finally. "Hang on a minute."

Travis nodded absently. "Okay," he said. Fact was, the guy on the other end had unnerved him enough that he'd stay right there all day and into the night, if he had to.

"Holy shit, we got 'em!" Paul Boersky whooped, drawing Irene's attention away from her mountain of paper. "The tap on Harry Sinclair's phone. Not three hours old, and we already got a hit!"

"Where?" Irene's voice buzzed with excitement. She had a call scheduled with Frankel in an hour and a half, and this was exactly the kind of scoop she prayed for.

Paul turned his attention back to the telephone and relayed Irene's question. "They don't have it pinned down completely, but it looks like it's from West Virginia. Some place called Winston Springs."

"Hot damn!" Irene rejoiced. "They're recording everything, I presume?"

"As we speak," Paul announced. The room came alive, with war whoops and high-fives all around.

While Paul stayed on the line for updates, Irene set herself to the task of siccing the West Virginia State Police onto her fugitives.

Harry Sinclair realized he probably should have mentioned his suspicions to Thorne. Truth be known, he'd been expecting the call since the news first broke yesterday, and while entirely unsure how he could be of much help, he remained committed to doing whatever he could.

He hadn't counted on the Justice Department, however. Periodically, they put taps on his phones, but never before at a time when they could do any real harm. Thankfully, Harry knew when the taps were to go into place, courtesy of a well-placed associate in the Chicago District of the U.S. Attorney's Office. Harry grew up with the guy's father back in the old days on the South Side and invested a few bucks in the deli he owned downtown. When the friend got hammered by the Health Department on some technical violations, Harry made a couple of calls to the Mayor's Office and got him off the hook. Even fronted the money to make the necessary repairs. Kids from the old neighborhood still knew what loyalty was all about.

The timing of Travis's call could not have been worse. As soon as Thorne told him who was on the line—and after he got over the shock of it being a kid—Harry knew they'd lit a short fuse. How short, exactly, he couldn't tell.

As Thorne brought the news, Harry instinctively checked his watch. "How long has he been on the line?" he asked.

Thorne shrugged. "Three minutes, maybe?"

Harry nodded. "Okay, scramble the call for a couple of minutes, then bring it up on the digital phone."

Over the course of the next three or four minutes, the kid's call would be transferred electronically all over the world, ultimately ending up on a private line in Harry's Dallas office—officially listed as the residence of a priest—and his staffer there would transfer the call at random to one of four digital phones at the house whose crystals were changed every four days, making them virtually impossible to track. Such precautions were a pain in the ass, but Harry had learned the hard way just how adept his competition was getting at electronic eavesdropping. Just two years ago, in fact, he'd lost a billion-dollar communications contract by a margin of less than a thousand dollars to a wiseass Texas redneck, and he knew then that the rules of engagement had changed. Now this business of call-scrambling was more the rule than the exception. That it also frustrated the occasional eavesdropper-with-a-badge was just so much icing on the cake.

The phone tap shouldn't have been a surprise, he supposed. God knew they'd slapped them on before, with far less cause. Nothing pissed off the Justice Department quite as much as the act of making a lot of money while employing thousands of workers. If you could do that, then you had to be doing something illegal. Unless you contributed to the president's reelection campaign, of course, and Harry would light a bonfire with his fortune before he gave a dime to that S.O.B. He'd already slept in the White House, thank you very much, and truth be told, the Four Seasons was a hell of a lot more comfortable.

The instant he got word of the tap, he'd set his lawyers to work getting it quashed. These things took time, though, and the FBI had undoubtedly snagged a recording of the kid's call being accepted by Thorne. That could be a problem. Didn't take much these days to establish enough probable cause to cut a warrant, and with that paper in hand, they'd tear his place apart looking for Sunshine. He sighed. The Justice Department lived for moments like this.

Harry's war with the feds dated back to the midseventies, when Chicago's congressional representative woke up one morning and realized to his horror that Harry was buying up much of the most valuable real estate in the city and that every penny of the tycoon's generous campaign contributions was going to the wrong party. Alleging unfair competitive practices, the congressman told an all-too-sympathetic president, who in turn whispered a few words to the attorney general.

And so it was, a few years later, that Harry Sinclair was sentenced to federal prison for income tax violations that would have netted anyone else in the country a wrist slap and a fine.

As outrageously unfair as it was, the experience proved a real eye-opener. Five years was a long time to live in a concrete room, denied privacy and sunlight, while choking down the double-fried slave shit they called food—although not nearly as long as the eight they'd slapped him with initially. Those were years that he'd never get back; places he'd never visit, deals he'd never close.

These days, Harry enjoyed the simple pleasures, rarely making an appearance in his palatial offices downtown. When the mood struck, he'd take a float in the pool or maybe indulge in a round of golf. He had managers now to handle the day-to-day crap. The time had come for him to reap the benefits of his empire.

Freedom meant everything to Harry; he wouldn't wish jail on anybody. Now his Sunshine's freedom was at risk again, and he couldn't bear the thought. He felt an emotion boiling in his gut that he hadn't felt in years—not since he'd stepped away from the negotiating end of the business. He felt himself bracing for war.

When he heard the chirp of a digital phone, Harry stood from behind his desk and strolled to the blue leather sofa along the opposite wall. Always a man of considerable girth, there was a jiggle now to his ample gut, where once it appeared to have been made of stone.

Thorne handed him the telephone. "Thank you," he said, then motioned for the other man to stick around. Pausing a moment to find the proper demeanor, he punched the connect button. "Yes?"

"Is *this* Uncle Harry?" a boy's voice said from the other end of the line, frustration growling in his throat.

"It is."

"Finally!" Travis blurted. "God, I thought I'd never get through to you. Jeeze!"

Harry said nothing while the boy ranted, waiting instead for him to settle down to listen. He caught on quickly. The flurry of words ended, replaced with an uncomfortable silence.

"Hello?" Travis asked. "Are you still there?"

"Are you finished?" Harry's tone carried a stern rebuke.

"Huh? Oh, yeah, sorry. I just . . ." Travis stopped himself in midsentence, and as he did, Harry watched in his mind as the boy calmed himself and got to the business at hand. "Okay, Uncle Harry, I'm Travis Brighton . . . No, I'm not, dammit . . . oh, sorry . . . I'm Travis *Donovan.* You don't know me, but . . ."

Harry interrupted. "I know who you are, son. Now, tell me what you want." Another deep breath from the other end and then a nervous chuckle. Finally, the kid found the handle for his tongue, and he recited the information that his folks had given him.

Two minutes into the monologue, Harry stood again and began to pace the carpet. This was the craziest thing he'd heard in a long, long time.

"Oh, *fuck!*" Paul Boersky slammed the phone down hard enough to knock a book off the desk. "They lost the call."

Irene, on the other line with the West Virginia State Police, told them to hold on for a minute. "Come again?" she said. *I dare you* went unspoken.

Never a great one at temper control, Paul launched a trash can across the conference room with his foot. "They're onto us. As soon as they took the call, they scrambled it. I don't know how, exactly, but they busted the tap. We got nothing."

Irene set her jaw, then shook it off. Murphy's Law governed all investigations to one degree or another, but never before had she handled one where Murphy was this much in command. She said nothing to Paul, whose tantrum seemed to have peaked, and turned her attention back to Sergeant Bower in West Virginia.

"I'm sorry, Sergeant," she said heavily. "We just got a bit of bad news on our end. Here's your opportunity to cheer up my day. Found the number yet?"

She heard some paper-shuffling on the other end before Bower spoke up. "Got it," he said. "Homer and Jane's Roadside Diner. I can have a unit there in twenty minutes."

Irene cringed. "Twenty minutes? Is that the best you can do?"

Bower chuckled. "This ain't the big city, Agent Rivers. Things take time out here. I can guarantee we'll do our best for you, how's that?"

Irene smiled. "I never doubted that for a moment. Tell your folks to be careful, though. The Donovans are slippery and they're desperate."

This time Bower laughed out loud. "My troopers work real hard to make our *customers* be careful around *us*, ma'am."

"Okey-doke, Sergeant. Then you just have your folks go do what they do best." She looked at her watch. *No chance*, she thought. Jake and Carolyn were specialists at staying ahead of the law. Christ, they'd already made it from Phoenix, South Carolina, to Winston Springs, West Virginia. If nothing else, they knew how to stay out of reach. No way would they still be there in twenty minutes.

Hanging up the phone, she turned to the task of calming Paul. Poor guy was working like a galley slave to keep his career afloat, and every time he fixed a leak, he took on another torpedo. Amazing how fragile a career could become. Like it or not, his was tied to hers, and hers was cloaked in a suit of eggshell.

✣   ✣   ✣

"There are grown-ups waiting to use the phone, young man." It was Peggy, now sporting a brand-new grease stain on the front of her apron, and an expression like she'd just drunk a quart of lemon juice.

Travis covered the receiver and tried his best to be polite. "Tell them to wait a minute," he said. Okay, so much for polite.

Peggy made a face, then flashed a two-fingered "V" in front of her nose. "Two minutes, smart mouth," she warned. "Two minutes, then you're off the phone." As she stormed away, Travis successfully fought the urge to flash a one-fingered sign of his own.

"Listen carefully, boy," Harry said. "Tell your parents that the FBI knows where you are. No need to panic, but they'll be on their way soon, I'm sure."

"I gotta go, then," Travis said hurriedly. Need or no need, the panic came, anyway.

"Wait!" Harry commanded. "I only need a half minute. I'll see what I can do about convincing this friend of your parents'—Nick Thomas, right?—to cooperate. For the time being, though, we've got to figure out a way to get you and your folks out of there. Are there any landmarks? A place where we can meet?"

Travis leaned away from the wall, trying to get a look out of the front windows, but all he saw was Peggy, who'd stationed herself in the middle of the aisle, fists planted on her hips. "I—I don't know."

Harry sighed heavily. "Okay, do you know which way the roads run? North-south? East-west?"

Travis shook his head, feeling embarrassed; like he showed up for a test without studying. "No, I don't."

Another sigh. Actually, this one sounded more like a growl. "All right. Listen. Here's what I want you to tell your parents. At midnight tonight, a white car will pull off to the side of the road, precisely two miles to the right of the diner where you're calling from. Got that?"

Travis wasn't sure. "To the right?"

"Yes, dammit, to the right. We don't know north and south, so we're doing left and right. You stand out on the road *facing* the diner and hold out your right hand. Exactly two miles in that direction."

"Okay."

"Don't say okay unless you've truly got it," Harry warned.

"No, really. Two miles. Got it." Sensing that Peggy was listening to every word, Travis pivoted back toward the stink of the rest rooms as he spoke.

"Okay, boy, now you all need to find a place to hide for the rest of the day. I don't care where it is, but when I say hide, I really mean hide. Until midnight, when you need to be at the rendezvous point. Are you still with me?"

"Uh-huh."

"Don't grunt at me, kid. I need yeses or noes."

"Yes, I'm with you."

"Wonderful. Now, pay very close attention to this part. At midnight tonight, a white car will pull up at the rendezvous point. That'll be your ride. The driver's name is Thorne, and he'll take care of you. When he gets out of the car and lights a cigarette, that'll be your signal to approach. Have you got all of that?"

Travis was terrified that he'd forget some detail, but he didn't dare ask him to repeat himself. "I think I can handle that," Travis said.

"Okay, then," Harry concluded. "Now, go back and tell your parents to get the hell out of there. Fast. If you've got a car, ditch it as soon as you can. And be in the right spot at midnight. Sharp."

Travis nodded. "We'll be there." He couldn't wait to get moving. "Anything else?"

Harry was quiet for a moment while he thought. "Yeah," he said at length, lowering his voice. "Tell your folks to be careful when they approach Thorne. Sometimes he misinterprets sudden moves."

From the tone of voice alone, Travis understood this to be perhaps the most important detail of all.

Harry pushed the disconnect button and relayed the details to Thorne—his personal assistant for nearly thirty years now. In order to survive in the business world, Harry firmly believed that you needed a watchdog—an attack dog, even. Somebody on the payroll who could discover the kind of information about competitors and politicians that could be used to keep them under control. You needed somebody to whom you could make a request, and never question that there'd be results. In Harry's company, that man was Thorne. Loyal as a lapdog yet fierce as a tiger, Thorne's unspoken job was to occasionally stack the deck a little. Only rarely did Harry have to rein him in anymore.

"Do they have a chance?" Harry asked when he was finished regurgitating his niece and nephew's latest plan.

Thorne shrugged. "I think it's risky as hell, but yeah, sure. Why not? There's always a chance. It'll take some time, though. A lot of logistics."

Harry shook his head. "We don't have time. *They* don't have time. We need to move quickly. Who do we know in Little Rock?" Washington contacts were a nickel a dozen, as were friends in Chicago, New York, and all the other major cities. Out in the boonies, though, pickings became awfully slim.

Thorne chewed on his lower lip and scowled. "I can't think of a soul. No, wait! Didn't that dermatologist friend of yours—Tim Vincent—move down there after they yanked his license in Wisconsin?"

"Oncologist," Harry corrected. "Cancer specialist." And yes, that did ring a bell. A friend from his college years, Tim Vincent had lost focus for a while about a decade ago and was nailed by some mutilated patients for all kinds of misdiagnoses, a few of which, it turned out, had resulted in the surgical removal of perfectly healthy body parts. The very thought of it turned Harry's stomach, but Vincent insisted in one tearful telephone call that it was all an accident, and he pleaded for help. Harry had waffled before finally caving in to his sense of loyalty. Leveraging some very generous gifts he'd made over the years to the Midwest's most prominent universities, Harry had been able to talk a few of Vincent's peers into taking it easy on him. He got to keep his license, as long as he agreed to take his practice someplace where they'd never have to clean up after him. Last Harry had heard, Tim had sobered up and was doing very well.

"Okay," Harry instructed, "give Tim a call. Tell him I send my regards and that I'll need him to put up some friends of mine in the next couple of days."

Thorne jotted notes on a scrap of paper.

"And if he can manage to make himself scarce while they're there, so much the better."

Thorne smiled. "Want me to roust your pilots and get the planes ready?"

Harry had to think for a moment on that one. "No, we've got the FBI watching us," he mused aloud. He snapped his fingers as the solution came to him. "Tell you what. Does Universal Waste still owe us a favor?"

Thorne laughed. "Didn't we guarantee Peter van der Horst's debt?" He didn't wait for a response. "I'll give him a call and see if he'll let us borrow a couple of planes and pilots."

"Just the planes," Harry corrected. "We'll use our own pilots."

Thorne nodded approvingly and jotted some more. "I trust you want me to go to Washington?"

Harry shook his head. "No. I'll go to D.C. I want you to make the pickup in West Virginia."

Thorne seemed appalled. "You're going to talk to the EPA guy yourself? Forgive me, sir, but I don't think—"

"There's no choice," Harry interrupted. "You can't be in two places at one time, and I want the fewest possible people involved in this."

Thorne shook his head vigorously. "With all due respect, Mr. Sinclair, I'm much more persuasive than you—"

"And much more *resourceful*. I need you to be with Sunshine." Harry ended the conversation by turning away, his ample gut heavy with the press of time. "I want to be in Washington this afternoon."

Thorne considered arguing but knew better. There was much to do.

"Oh, and Thorne?"

"Yes, sir?" He'd already stepped into the hallway but now returned.

Harry regarded him for a long moment. "You know how much Sunshine means to me . . ."

"I'll take care of everything . . ."

"No, listen to me. Don't go overboard, okay?"

Thorne bristled. He knew how to do his job. He said nothing as he left.

Alone again, Harry tried to sift through it all. It had been fourteen years, for God's sake! Without a snag. Now, at the first glitch, Sunshine and her dipshit husband wanted to throw everything away on this crazy plan. Unbelievable. Maybe it was just the panic talking. If he could just speak to Carolyn personally, then he'd be able to talk some sense into them.

But, of course, he could do no such thing. As much as he wanted to see his niece again—what did she look like now, as she closed in on middle age?—he understood that such a meeting was out of the question. Maybe if the kid hadn't called the house directly, but certainly not now. With the connection made at the FBI, the risk was too great.

Jake started the van as soon as he saw Travis walk back outside. He considered driving up to meet him but didn't, fearing that it might somehow attract attention.

"Where have you *been*?" Carolyn barked, the instant the door slammed shut. "We were almost ready to go in there after you."

"Sorry," Travis replied with a patently unsorry shrug. Over the next ten minutes, as they searched with progressively greater urgency for a place to ditch the van, Travis told them every detail of his chat with Uncle Harry.

Chapter Nineteen

Special Agent John Carnegie shifted position uneasily, daring to look away from his scope for just a few seconds.

He liked his work, on balance. It reminded him of his teenage years, when he and his father found true camaraderie hunting deer in the fall. Every Thanksgiving, they arose in the middle of the night and drove for hours before dawn, finding a spot to sit and wait, remaining still for hours at a time until their prey wandered in close enough to be taken.

So it was this morning, in every detail but the prey and the weaponry. From his spot on the edge of the woods, he sat perfectly still, watching the Sinclair compound for unusual movement or activity. Several cars had arrived over the course of the morning, but none of them contained anyone remotely fitting the description he'd been given of the Donovans. Those same cars had subsequently left, only to be subjected to a search a mile or so down the road. So far, the Donovans remained invisible.

By ten o'clock, he'd been on station for six hours, and his mind was beginning to play tricks on him. He'd heard noises that didn't exist; seen flashes of light in his peripheral vision. He knew that

such things were merely meaningless exercises commenced by otherwise unchallenged senses, yet they unnerved him, anyway. These
were the times he hated most—when he'd been on for longer than
his attention span, yet still was several hours from relief. Back in the
old days, when he did similar stints for the Marine Corps—only
then with a rifle—he enjoyed the benefits of a young man's brazen
cockiness. Now, as he approached his thirty-fifth birthday, he worried about what might get past him as his mind wandered.

His legs and his back screamed for relief, for a brief stretch; but
Carnegie was too well trained for that. Harry Sinclair—paranoid
tycoon that he was—enjoyed a reputation for countersurveillance,
and he was manic about personal security. If Carnegie moved, he
knew in his heart that Sinclair's men would see him.

To keep his mind active this morning, Carnegie had practiced
his times tables, through 25 times 25. When that grew boring, he
tried factoring four-digit numbers in his head. After a while,
though, that one gave him a headache.

About forty-five minutes ago, he'd been told on his radio that
the targets had contacted Sinclair by phone, bringing a brief rush
of hopefulness, but now the adrenaline had bled away, and he was
bored all over again.

Movement. Carnegie rolled his wrist to get a glance at his watch
and marked the time at 10:24. Returning his eyes to his spotter's
scope, he watched in fifty-power magnification as Harry Sinclair
himself walked out of the front door of his mansion and lowered
himself into the waiting limousine. Three staff members climbed
in with him, and the vehicle took off for the gate.

Carnegie thumbed his radio mike. "Target is moving toward
checkpoint one," he whispered. Despite the four hundred yards
separating him from the compound, he feared that the fall breeze
might carry his voice across the field.

"Checkpoint one's direct," a voice crackled from his earpiece.
"Attention all units, you're cleared to follow but not to intercept."

Way to go, Sinclair, Carnegie thought. *Be as stupid as you look.*

CHAPTER TWENTY

Nick Thomas's day had already been a bruiser, and it wasn't yet two. Mesmerized by this whole business of the Donovans' renewed flight from the law, he'd been unable to pull himself away from the early morning talk shows, thus destroying any chance he had of getting to work on time.

By the time he finally got on the road, forty-five minutes behind schedule, his mood had soured enormously. Then, to top it all off, a tractor-trailer had overturned on Route 66 at Gainesville, closing down all but the shoulder lane of traffic into the city.

It was already past eleven when he finally staggered into EPA headquarters on M Street, and his boss spent fifteen minutes pointing out that had he left on time, the traffic jam would never have been an issue.

Sometimes Nick wished he worked for the Postal Service, where people accepted homicide as a routine part of the job. As it was, he suffered his ass-chewing quietly and with as much dignity as the circumstances allowed.

As the story of the Donovans' capture and second escape un-folded on the news, Nick found himself entering corners of his mind where he hadn't ventured in years. What was startling was the clarity with which it all came back: the faintly sulfuric odor of the burning munitions, the fear that the odor had brought, even five miles from ground zero, and later, the persistent questions regarding why Nick had ever endorsed hiring such "unstable people."

The truth is, his close relationship with Jake and Carolyn Donovan had cost him a decent career. Had it not been for that miserable morning in 1983, Nick would undoubtedly have been in the Senior Executive Service by now; or better still, a lofty executive in the private sector. But things hadn't played out that way, and here he was, a GS-12 program specialist, manning a cubicle surrounded by up-and-comers, many of whom hadn't yet been born when he was graduating from college.

Some of those kids looked up to him as the experienced old hand, but the savvier ones avoided him like the plague. Ambitious careerists were wise to stay away from people like Nick. At this stage of the game, there were only a few reasons why someone with his background and education would be stuck in bureaucratic hell, and none of them were good.

He knew what the secretaries and the whiz-kid engineers had to say about him, and the names didn't vary all that much from the epithets he'd heard in his youth. By the time the term "nerd" had fallen out of fashion, the new and popular word "dweeb" had fallen right in to take its place. Over time, Nick had come to write the name-calling off as the price one must pay for being smarter than most of the population.

Such was life when you put your name on paper as the safety engineer at a hazardous waste site that killed sixteen people.

This morning in the shower, Nick tried to calculate the net cost of that single act of terrorism, and he realized no equation could handle it. In many respects, the corpses were the lucky ones. They merely died—relatively quickly, by most estimations. The courts then decided the value of their deaths, in the form of seven-figure settlements, and life went on. Even the loss of stockholder equity in Enviro-Kleen, and in their customer, Newark Industrial Park,

Inc., could be measured in finite terms, albeit in nine digits when all was said and done.

The emotional costs, on the other hand, were incalculable. The violence of that afternoon had cost Nick his marriage. At least that was how he saw it. For the sake of the kids, they still lived in the same house, but they hadn't shared a bed or a civil word in years. He'd told Melissa from the very beginning that his name was tarnished in his industry, but she chose to believe otherwise. When the truth of that assertion was ultimately borne out, and she realized she'd never have all the trinkets her friends thought were important, she'd written him off as a loser.

Then there were the hundreds of thousands of dollars in lost income from jobs for which he'd easily have been the best candidate, had it not been for the dirt associated with his name. At an intellectual level, he knew it was useless to feel sorry for himself, but sometimes he just didn't have the strength to rise above self-pity.

Nick never believed for a minute that the entire story of the Newark Incident had been reported. Everyone had been so damned anxious to bring the incident to a close and to seal off the site from further leakage that evidence had been gathered way too quickly and way too sloppily. He'd expected more from the FBI. They considered only one option: that the entire nightmare was a wild-eyed tyrannical act by two people whom Nick knew personally to be very ordinary. Rationally, he supposed their flight from the scene represented a de facto admission of guilt, but still, someone should have considered an alternative.

Nick was no cop, but as a safety engineer, he'd done more than his share of accident investigation work, and he knew from experience how persuasively and effectively hypotheses can drive investigations. Instead of allowing accumulating evidence to lead naturally to a conclusion, investigators locked onto a pet theory, then set out to prove it. In the process, they ignored contradictory evidence, mentally discounting it as irrelevant. It happened all the time in the media, but he expected more from the police.

In Nick's view, the Newark investigation had been driven by politics; and as with all things political, the investigation had an agenda. Publicly, that agenda was to render the area as safe as possible, as quickly as possible. Privately, Nick had always suspected something more. The president of the United States at the time had staked his entire reputation on the reconstruction of the country's defenses. The last thing he needed was for the public to be distracted by the horrendous consequences of an accidental "special weapons" release. If accidents like that were truly possible, then the dangers inherent in such weapons would overshadow everything else: On the other hand, if a release could be written off as the senseless ravings of a couple of lunatics, then the issue would not be the weapons themselves, but rather the people who abused them.

Nerve agents don't kill people. People kill people.

The bodies recovered from the exterior of the magazine most definitely had been shot to death, with a precision that simply was not possible via the random spray of small-arms munitions as they cooked off. And certainly, the one worker who was sick that morning—Tony Bernard—was murdered. Shot at point-blank range in his motel room. Terrible thing.

But why? Why would Jake and Carolyn Donovan go on such a rampage? And why on that *particular* day? Why not the day before or the day after? Or the month after, for that matter? Christ, they were scheduled to be there for half a year. Then again, such questions could be asked of any act of violence, he supposed. Why didn't Lizzie Borden wait another day? Or the Menendez boys?

And the note. By far the most damaging and inexplicable bit of evidence, it just never made sense to Nick. It seemed too pat. These two terrorists blow away over a dozen people, and then they go by to pick off Tony Bernard—they shot him in the face, for heaven's sake—and they top off the day by leaving a typewritten note in his room, confessing to the whole thing and ranting on about governments who choose to play God.

Puh-leeze.

Nick told the FBI agent in charge of the investigation—an arrogant control freak named Frankel—that Jake and Carolyn were not the sort to do such a thing, but the safety officer's protests were written off as the frantic pleas of a friend who simply refused to believe he'd been duped. The agent's condescending words rang clear in Nick's mind as he revisited those days: *Ted Bundy's friends were shocked as hell, too.*

The Donovans hadn't even *signed* the note they supposedly left! Their names at the end of the manifesto were typewritten. For Christ's sake, anybody could have pecked out the damned thing on their portable typewriter. But almost instantaneously, the sheet of paper became another piece in the "incontrovertible case" against the Donovans. To Nick, it all had the odor of a fish market on a hot day.

Still, the FBI was the FBI, and back then, he was merely Nick Thomas, suddenly unemployed and unemployable. If the Donovans were innocent, they were on their own. He sure as hell wasn't going to fall on his sword on their behalf.

So he'd pushed it all behind him. Or tried to, anyway; with growing success, until the Big Story broke yesterday. The stock footage shown on the news of the fire and the evacuation and the body recovery operation brought everything back with disturbing clarity.

And to think that there were still bodies sealed up in there . . .

His phone chirped twice, an inside call. Nick considered ignoring it but decided that his boss hated him enough as it was. He pushed the speaker phone button. "Yes?"

"Call for you on line seven," informed Maura, the group secretary. "Says it's really important."

He moaned. "Does it sound like a salesman?"

"Well, he spoke in complete sentences, if that helps."

Always the joker. "All right," he obliged with a sigh. "I'll take it." He thought he knew who it was. He'd made the mistake of expressing interest in a new computer system that his group couldn't afford and that he hadn't the authority to buy, anyway. He'd been dodging the guy for weeks. It was time to come clean.

"Nick Thomas," he said sharply, snapping the telephone off its cradle.

"Hello, Mr. Thomas," said an older voice he didn't recognize. "My name's Fox. I need to meet with you as soon as possible."

Yep, it was a salesman. Different one, but same technique. "I'm really bogged down at the moment," he said flatly. "Why don't you call me next week?" *Why can't you just say, "Thanks, but no thanks"?*

The voice remained calm but took on a very distinct edge. "Actually, Mr. Thomas, this is something of an emergency. We need to meet right away. Now. I don't mean to frighten you, and you're certainly not in any danger."

"Danger?"

"At least not right now," the mysterious Mr. Fox went on. "And neither are little Nicky and Joshua. In fact, they're still tucked away in their classrooms at Stephen Foster Elementary School. When they walk home at three-ten, I'm equally confident that they'll still be just fine."

A sense of horror drenched Nick like a bucket of ice water. This asshole was threatening his children! "Listen here," he said, raising his voice. "I don't know who—"

"If you raise your voice to me, Mr. Thomas, I will hang up the telephone, and then you'll never know what I wanted to talk about." The stranger paused for effect. "Am I making my point?"

As his fear peaked, Nick's will to fight drained right out of him; as if someone had pulled a plug. This guy knew his children's names. He knew their school . . .

"Mr. Thomas, are you still there?"

The voice startled him. "Yeah, I'm here."

"Good," said Mr. Fox, a smile suddenly materializing in his voice. "Really, I assure you that you're in no danger. But I need to meet with you. Right now. Look for a white Lincoln out in front of your building—on the M Street side. I'll wait exactly five minutes." The line went dead.

Shit! Nick stared at the handset for a long moment, wasting a good half minute of valuable time. He considered calling Security but instantly dismissed the notion. Whoever this guy was, he'd done his research. And whatever he was up to, he'd have planned a countermove if Nick did the obvious.

Besides, there was no time. That thought shot him out of his seat. *Time.* He said five minutes! God, if the elevator was cranky, it'd take him that long to get down to the lobby.

The handset bounced off the cradle as he tossed it down and headed for the door. His boss saw him tear out of his bull pen, and made a move to block his path, but then shrank away from whatever he saw. Even opened the door for him.

CHAPTER TWENTY-ONE

Irene placed the call from her car, on her way to catch the plane that would take her to West Virginia. She'd been dreading the deed all day, and once Frankel picked up on his end, she realized she hadn't been dreading it quite enough. As she took her drubbing, Paul Boersky sat quietly in the shotgun seat, pretending to be interested in the passing scenery.

"I've got to tell you, Irene, just how disappointed I am in your handling of this case."

Like you did it so much better in '83, she shot back silently. This was a call of atonement, not one of conflict—well, at least from her point of view. From the other side of the line, every call was an excuse for conflict.

"You have him and then you lose him, and then you have him again. Jesus, I need a scorecard just to keep up. What have our redneck friends been able to turn up?"

Irene checked over her shoulder and changed lanes, following the signs to Greenville-Spartansburg Airport. "Not much, I'm afraid. Nobody seems to remember seeing them, but a waitress remembers a kid spending a long time on the telephone. Didn't hear any of the conversation, though."

"Damn," Frankel spat. "So have the troopers given up?"

What a ridiculous question. "No, sir, not that I know of. In fact, the last time I talked to the guy in charge down there, he said he had every available trooper on the case. I called Les Janier in the Charlestown office, and he said he'd get some agents down there to help out. I'm on my way there myself, in fact."

"What about the surveillance we put on old man Sinclair out in Chicago?" Frankel asked, changing subjects. "Last report I got, they were following him out of the state."

Irene took a deep breath. *He's going to go ballistic.* "Well, there's a problem there, too, sir," she said. "Seems he was onto us somehow. He sent one of his associates on a ride, wearing a look-alike costume. Then, while we were distracted, he sneaked out another entrance to his compound and disappeared." There, she'd said it. At least the primary heat from this one would be focused on someone else. Ted Greenberg, probably—her Chicago counterpart.

Frankel remained quiet for a long time. She'd met the man only twice, but she knew he tended to turn crimson red when he was upset. In her mind, he was purple now. When he finally spoke, he seemed beyond anger, tipping the scale more toward fury. Hatred maybe. But he maintained perfect control of his voice.

"You realize, don't you, Irene, that we are the FBI? The most advanced investigative organization in the world. And these Donovans and their relatives are making you look like a complete idiot. A laughingstock for the entire world! Christ, I've seen Barney Fife turn out better police work than you!"

Why, thank you for the inspiration, Peter, Irene didn't say.

"You've got two days, Irene," Frankel concluded. "Two more days, and then I yank you off the case and bust you down to border guard. Are you understanding me here?"

"Yes, sir," Irene said. *Translation: I've got my confirmation hearings in six weeks, and you better not fuck them up.* "Perfectly, sir."

"Now, go out and act like a fucking FBI agent!"

✻   ✻   ✻

Nick saw the line at the elevators and said to hell with it. He flew down the stairs—six floors, twelve flights—passing two cliques of smokers huddled in the stairwell like high school students, sneaking their forbidden puffs where no supervisors were likely to catch them. Both groups looked startled at first, until they saw he was no one, then went on about their gossiping.

As he crashed out of the stairwell into the lobby, a security guard looked even more startled than the smokers, and he instinctively moved his hand toward his side arm. For the briefest moment, Nick considered blurting out the story—that some madman had been threatening his children—but instantly he pushed the thought out of the way. In response to the inquisitive look, he flashed the ID badge dangling from his neck.

"Late for an appointment," he said hurriedly. He didn't wait for a reply.

As promised, a white Lincoln was parked illegally, immediately outside the M Street entrance. He hurried toward the vehicle, then slowed his approach. How was he supposed to know if it was *the* white Lincoln?

As if to answer his question, the driver's door popped open, and a bull-headed man with white hair beckoned him over. "Mr. Thomas?" the man called.

Nick's breath caught in his throat. The voice was the same, minus the electronic distortion. He slowed even more. "Yes."

"Please climb in," the man offered with a smile. "Truly, you are in no danger."

No, just my children, Nick thought. He approached haltingly, like a dog obeying an order to come and be beaten for eating a sock. The man gestured to the passenger side, and the instant Nick's butt was in the seat, the vehicle started to move, even before the door was completely closed.

"Hello," the driver said, extending his hand across the seat hump. "I'm afraid we started off on the wrong foot. My name is not Fox. It's Sinclair. Harry Sinclair. Harry to my friends. May I call you Nick?"

Nick didn't bother to smile as he hesitantly shook the old man's hand. At first, the name didn't mean anything. Looking at his face, though, it came back to him. This was the man he'd seen on the cover of *BusinessWeek,* with a headline like "Mr. Connection." In the photo, the tycoon was awash in money, with cartoon politicians bulging out of his pockets.

"You can call me whatever you want," Nick said, still tight as a bowstring. "Where are my children?"

Harry scoffed and waved off Nick's concerns. "They are as I said to you on the phone. Perfectly safe at their school. I mean it, Nick, they're in no jeopardy. I'm afraid that in my zeal to meet with you, I may have led you to believe otherwise. I apologize."

The hell you do. Nick didn't know what to say, so he said nothing, concentrating his energies on an effort to keep his body from trembling as Harry piloted the Lincoln toward the Virginia suburbs. For the first time in a very long while, he felt real fear.

"You're on edge," Harry said. He flashed a smile that seemed to hold a genuine kindness. "I'll get right to the point, then. I have a niece who's in a bit of trouble right now, and she seems to think you can help her out. Her name is Carolyn Donovan. Ring any bells?"

For a moment, Nick could think of nothing to say. Then the words tumbled out: "I, um . . . I knew her a while ago, yes."

Harry smiled broadly at the recognition that was so plainly displayed on Nick's face. "I'm guessing you don't play a lot of poker, Nick," he said with a laugh. "Since you know her, I'll assume you know the nature of her problem as well."

Nick nodded, abandoning all efforts to be coy or elusive.

"Well, according to her son—they have a *son* now, by the way— whom I talked to this morning, Carolyn and her husband, Jack . . . do you know Jack?"

Nick scowled. "You mean Jake? Yes, certainly."

Harry stood corrected. "Jake, then. Whatever. Do you think they're guilty of the crimes they stand accused of?"

Nick's eyes narrowed. Obviously, there was only one right answer for this one. Happily, it doubled as his honest take on it all. "No," he said at length. "No, I never have. In fact, I told the FBI at the time . . ." He shut himself up abruptly. The time had come to answer the question, and nothing more.

"That's good," Harry said. "Because they vehemently deny any wrongdoing. In fact, confidentially, I must tell you that they wanted to turn themselves in from the very beginning; to prove their innocence. Alas, my faith in the judicial system was weaker than theirs, and I prevailed on them to disappear for a while. It's the sort of decision that can't be unmade. Now that events have taken this unfortunate turn, they feel that they can prove their innocence in this hazardous waste mess if they could just regain access to the site in Newark where it all happened."

Nick's jaw dropped. "No way," he said without hesitation. "You mean *inside* the magazine?"

Harry shrugged. "Presumably."

"No way. Absolutely not. The toxicity levels in there would knock down an elephant. They wouldn't even let me recover the bodies, for crying out loud."

"They?" Harry seemed suddenly intrigued.

Nick rolled his eyes. "The FBI jerks. And the EPA. They were so anxious to seal everything—"

"So, given the chance, you would have reentered?" Harry interrupted.

Nick paused, recognizing he'd just wandered into a trap. "Well, not without significant precautions. I mean, the protective equipment alone would . . ." He saw it. He saw what Harry wanted him to do. "I can't just requisition a bunch of remediation equipment!" he said. "That stuff costs thousands of dollars. They'd fire me in a heartbeat."

Deep wrinkles materialized in Harry's forehead. "Much as they would throw my niece in prison for a crime she didn't commit," he said. "She and her husband were hoping you'd be willing to help. That's why they called me. To see if I could talk you into assisting them in their efforts to exonerate themselves."

Nick's sense of dread bottomed out as he realized the choice he faced. One of the most powerful businessmen in the country— hell, in the *world*, for all he knew—had just confessed to committing a felony and had shared in detail the plans hatched by his own family to vandalize federal property. If he said yes, he'd become a part of the plot—a fellow felon.

"What if I say no?" Nick asked cautiously.

Harry gave a one-shoulder shrug. "Then I'd be very disappointed," he said. This time the smile seemed slightly less genuine.

Nick searched the old man's face for the hidden threat, for some sign of what might befall him and his family if he refused to cooperate. All he got for his effort, though, was the smile. If Harry read the fear in his passenger's eyes, he did nothing to dissuade it. He just smiled.

Men as powerful as Harry Sinclair didn't climb the ladder one step at a time; they knocked people out of the way, broke the ladder, then rebuilt it under themselves with no rungs on the bottom. A person like Nick meant nothing to a man like Sinclair—just another bug to crush if he got in the way.

This old man was too sharp ever to make an overt threat, and way too savvy to ever let Nick relax. So now Nick had a decision to make, and in the balance lay his entire future. He could fight or he could cave in; no middle ground. Truth be told, Nick was never much of a fighter, anyway.

When he finally renewed eye contact with Harry, he looked every bit as whipped as he felt. "What do you want me to do?"

CHAPTER TWENTY-TWO

Without any real alternative, the Donovans had parked their van in an abandoned barn about a mile from the diner. It looked abandoned, anyway. Sometimes it was hard to tell in West Virginia. The vehicle barely fit and was still visible through the gaping spaces between the wall planks, but with luck, no one would notice. At least, not for a while.

Leaving the van behind was tough for Jake. That vehicle—and the banged-up VW bus that preceded it—had always been the centerpiece of their escape plan. In casting it aside, he felt as if he were symbolically abandoning a second lifetime of planning and preparation.

Now it was official. They were walking the tightrope without a net.

The van was a storehouse for survival gear—clothes, ammunition, building supplies, food, and toiletries. Now these things were all useless to him. All but a few extra clothes. And the money, of course. Money was always useful. While Travis watched in wide-eyed astonishment, Jake and Carolyn transferred the banded bills into two zippered gym bags from off the shelves in the back.

That done, they chose a spot in the forest and settled in for the endless wait. Knowing they'd have to find their way out in the darkness, they decided to stay in closer to the diner than was probably prudent, still over a half mile from the designated pickup point. Jake had lobbied for a hiding spot further out, fearing the cops would turn the area inside out looking for them, but Carolyn took a different view. The way she saw it, only a crazy person would stay in this close. Therefore, the search would likely concentrate on the highway, some miles distant. A little high-stakes reverse psychology. In the end, of course, her logic prevailed.

Perched high on a hill and nestled in among jagged granite outcroppings, Travis watched in wonder as what seemed like hundreds of cop cars wore trenches into the highway below. "God, look at 'em all!"

Carolyn yanked the back of his denim jacket. "Travis, sit *down!*" she hissed. "They're gonna see you!"

Pulling himself free with a single jerk, he scoffed, "Yeah, right. They're gonna see me through all these leaves."

"It's fall," she countered. "The leaves are getting thinner every minute."

Travis laughed. "Do you really think—"

"This isn't a negotiation," Jake snapped. "Now, get down below the rocks and do what you're told."

Travis paused long enough to peek one more time, just to make the point before settling into his spot among the rocks. "This is so boring!"

Jake chuckled. "Under the circumstances, boring is good." In their hurry to get away from the van, Jake had snatched the wrong ammo bag, leaving the assembled magazines for the Glock on the shelves and taking the empties with him instead. Now, if only to pass the time, he busied himself with the task of loading 9-mm hollow points into his six remaining clips.

"Can I do one?" Travis asked.

"Sure." Jake felt the heat of Carolyn's glare without looking but paid no attention. Thirteen-year-old boys were poorly engineered for long periods of stillness, and if playing with bullets would divert him for a while, where was the harm?

The clip and the box of bullets were both heavier than Travis had expected. Watching his dad, it looked like you just slid the rounds into place, but when that wouldn't work, he looked up for assistance.

"Press down," Jake instructed. "Then slide in." He watched his son try it again, with little success. "That's the right idea," he encouraged, "but you need to press harder against the spring."

Hard was right! His thumbnails turned white from the effort, but finally, the first bullet slid home. "Cool."

"You know I don't approve of this, right?" Carolyn said.

Jake smiled uneasily. "That's why I didn't ask." He hoped to tap a vein of humor. The last thing he needed right now was a fight with his wife.

She didn't laugh, but she let it go. They'd seen enough confrontation for one day. Instead, she leaned back against her rock and stared up at the random splotches of brilliant blue sky through the patchwork canopy of leaves. The day was proving to be much warmer than the one before, and as the sun rose high to evaporate last night's rain, the humidity got trapped under the canopy, providing a last moment of summer before winter took over for good. If it weren't for the occasional siren and the incessant clicking of metal upon metal as her guys prepared for the worst, she might have talked herself into believing things were nearly normal; nearly peaceful. On a different day, she might even have fallen asleep.

"You know," Travis said, directing his words to his father, "you never answered my question."

Jake looked up. "Oh yeah? What question is that?"

"Whether you would have shot those cops. You know, back there at the school?" The boy kept his concentration focused on his hands as he spoke, studiously avoiding eye contact.

Jake tried to stay unfazed by the question. "What do you think?"

A casual shoulder twitch doubled for a shrug. "I dunno. I guess so."

Jake stopped what he was doing and placed his half-loaded clip on a rock, sensing that this went beyond a simple hypothetical. More and more, it seemed, as Travis closed in on adolescence, conversations were becoming complicated.

"There's only one reason to kill," Jake explained, peeling the words off carefully, as a gambler might deal a high-stakes hand. "And that's to protect your family."

Travis considered the answer, then went back to work on the clip, still making no effort at eye contact. "Even if it's a cop? And he's just doing his job?"

Jake looked over to Carolyn, who suddenly lost interest in playing possum. He softened his tone. "Where are you going with this, Trav?"

When Travis finally looked up, the innocence in his eyes had disappeared, bitterness residing in the spot once occupied by trust. "I'm just trying to figure it all out," he said. "I mean, all these guns and these bullets and stuff. You bring them everywhere, and you threaten everybody. I'm just wondering who you're going to kill."

If words were swords, Jake would have been in a million pieces. He didn't know what to say.

"That's not fair—" Carolyn tried.

Travis cut her off. "Why not? Am I supposed to think these guns are just for *show?*"

"Travis, please," she begged, rising up to her knees.

Jake waved her off. "No, let him talk."

"Yeah, let me talk," Travis mocked. "Let me ask my stupid-kid questions, right?"

It was Jake's turn. "Look, Trav, I tried to explain—"

"Why you lied," he blurted. "I don't think we ever got to the killing part."

"We're not going to shoot anyone," Carolyn said.

Travis dodged her grasp and stood, oblivious to his exposure above the rocks. "That's not what *he* just said!" He gave his father a withering look. "He said he was gonna kill to protect his family. Well, that's just great! And then they'll kill you! And I'll be . . ." His voice caught in his throat. "They'll just . . ."

Travis's eyes grew red as he contemplated a prospect he didn't dare to give a name. He searched for more words, but they just weren't there.

Carolyn stood unmoving, fearing the rejection she'd feel if she reached out to him. "Oh, honey, I'm so sorry."

Travis turned his back on her to stare down at the road some more.

Jake watched it all, without a word, respecting the boy's right to be angry. As husband and father, he wanted to go to them both, to somehow soothe their pain, but he sensed the uselessness of it. Pain was likely to become a big part of their lives, and to get through it, each would have to find their own way to cope. This wasn't a time for emotions. Maybe later, but not now. This was a time for rational thinking; for action. It was about survival now, not about feelings. Carolyn knew this as well as he, but she refused to stay strong.

This all had to happen one day, and here it was. This particular brand of resentment was all new to Travis, though. He was only just now tapping into its deeper levels, and as he did, he said hurtful, hateful things. But it would pass, Jake was sure. And if it didn't, so be it. May his son live long enough to resent him for a hundred years. Fact was, even a century of hate from his son couldn't begin to match the hatred Jake felt for himself.

As his vision blurred to a mass of autumn colors, Jake turned his attention back to the business at hand and began to slide bullet after bullet into his last spare magazine.

By six o'clock, the sun was gone, and a chill returned to the air, driving the Donovans once again into their jackets. The dampness which had felt so soothing in the warmth now brought shivers and misery. Carolyn had thought to stuff a goody bag with crackers and cans of tuna fish before they ditched the van, but forgot to grab a can opener. Thank God for Swiss Army knives.

Police activity up and down the road had died to practically nothing over the past five hours, luring everyone into a sense of security which Jake warned repeatedly was only an illusion. Each time conversation became animated, or the volume rose, he shushed them. Nothing serious was discussed during those hours, beyond catching Travis up on the real details of his heritage. It was as if they'd declared a silent truce, in which the only rule of engagement was not to engage the present or the future. That left them with only the past—well-worn, benign stories of Travis's childhood.

Come nine o'clock, it was time to move out, each of them carrying a bag of something. Travis offered to carry the cash but was relegated instead to hefting the extra food and clothes.

"Mom's in charge of the money, just like always," Travis observed, earning himself a playful shot to the head.

Darkness proved a formidable adversary as they picked their way cautiously toward the road, down the side of the hill. Loose rocks and coiled vines made footing treacherous, reaching out in the dark to force a fall. Excepting some dusty backsides, they all made it down without incident.

One of the challenges Jake had feared most was crossing the highway in the open to get to the far side, where the terrain was considerably flatter. A trio of people traveling by foot in the dark was bound to raise suspicion. As it turned out, the road was clear, and they crossed easily, dashing to the cover of the tree line on the other side. From there, they once again battled with darkness to walk the remaining three-quarters of a mile to the end of their journey.

By eleven-thirty, they were in position, more or less directly across the street from the pickup point. They huddled fifteen or twenty feet inside the tree line, invisible in the mottled moon shadows, and watched as the occasional car passed in front of the sheer rock face that defined the opposite shoulder of the road. Now, if they could just get warm . . .

After a day of being patient, the last half hour felt longer than the previous half day. No one spoke now, each choosing instead to listen to the stillness of the night—trying in vain to hear the hum of an approaching engine through the vibrating chorus of night creatures. As a single raccoon foraged for his dinner in a nearby drainage ditch, no one moved. A screech owl pierced the night with its haunting imitation of a crying child.

"Jesus Christ," Jake hissed, checking his watch. The luminescent green hands and numbers seemed exceptionally bright. "Where is this guy? He's late."

Carolyn gave him a disapproving glare. "What time is it?"

"Eleven fifty-seven."

"Then he's not late," Travis whispered, stealing his mother's thunder. "He said midnight sharp. It's not midnight yet."

"Close enough," Jake grumped.

"Relax, Jake," Carolyn said, a surprisingly calm tone masking her racing heart and fragile nerves. "Harry won't let us down."

Three minutes later, straight-up at midnight, a late-model white Cadillac pulled to a stop across the street, about a hundred yards short of them. "That's it!" Jake whispered. "Let's go." He tried to step forward, but Carolyn and Travis pulled him back by his jacket.

"Not yet," Travis scolded. "He hasn't lit his cigarette. Uncle Harry said to wait for the cigarette."

Jake pulled his jacket out of their hands. "Oh, for crying out loud. It's him! How many white cars do you think are scheduled to show up at this spot precisely at midnight? Jesus!"

"But Harry's instructions were exact!" Carolyn protested. "He said to wait until . . ."

Jake was done listening. He was tired, and he was wet. For the last thirty-six hours, he'd done nothing but follow Carolyn's orders. Do this. Do that. Stop here. Don't stop here. He was sick of it! Soon, he'd have Mr. Congeniality, Harry Sinclair, to deal with, too.

He hefted the two money bags and started for the car.

Fighting the urge to duck and dash around shadows, he opted to stroll out of the woods as normally as possible for the benefit of anyone who might be watching. Halfway there, he turned and beckoned for his family to join him, amazed at how thoroughly the shadows obliterated their images. He motioned, yet they didn't move.

"Come on!" he whisper-shouted. "Let's get this over with!" He waved at them one more time and they finally emerged from their camouflage, looking anxiously over both shoulders as they scurried to join him.

"Relax, Carolyn. You look like you just robbed a bank."

"I *feel* like I just robbed a bank." She sounded close to tears. "I don't like this. Harry said . . ."

Carolyn fell silent, and they stopped dead in their tracks as the Cadillac pulled smoothly away from the narrow shoulder.

"What the hell is he doing?" Jake gasped. He fought the urge to call after him.

Then they saw it. First, as a wash of headlights, then as a blue and white Ford with a light bar. West Virginia State Police.

"Oh, shit!" Jake hissed. "It's a setup."

"No!" Carolyn insisted. "Not from Harry."

"What are we gonna do?" Travis whined.

They were completely out in the open, too far from the tree line to make it back without being seen. Whatever they were going to do, they had to get it done in the next five seconds, or this would all be over. "The ditch!" Jake declared, pointing.

Moving as one, they dashed the three steps to the drainage ditch that ran parallel to the road, and dove in, sliding face-first in the gooey runoff and road trash.

Jake thought his chest might explode as he lay there, his eyes closed tight against the fear, listening as the cruiser drove on past. If the cop spotted them, they were done. Even his gun was useless. He couldn't get to it in time for it to do any good.

No one moved, even after the sound of the engine disappeared. A good minute passed before Travis broke the silence. "Is he gone?"

Jake sneaked his head above the ditch and slipped his hand to the grip of his pistol. Nothing but empty road, twisting out of sight in both directions. "Clear," he announced at a whisper. "Back to the trees!"

Jake grabbed Carolyn's hand, and she grabbed Travis's as they scurried back to the shadows and collapsed into the bushes.

"Oh, my God," Carolyn breathed. "I *told* you to wait!" She hit Jake in the chest, hard enough to hurt.

He said nothing. *When you're right, you're right.*

"Do you think he saw us?" Travis whined.

"No," Carolyn said unequivocally.

Jake wasn't so sure. "I don't know. Even if he saw us, he might not have stopped. We're armed and dangerous, remember?"

No one was sure what to do next. Their ride was gone, the police were cruising the area, and they were stuck in the middle of nowhere at midnight, without transportation. Five minutes passed.

"Do you think he's coming back?" Jake asked.

"Who, the cop or our ride?"

Jake shrugged. "Pick one."

Again, Travis answered for his mom. "I'm guessing: ride, yes; cop, not for a while."

Jake rumpled his hair, drawing an annoyed look. "I like the way you think." Two more minutes passed. Then three. Then five. "This isn't good," Jake whispered.

When Carolyn and Travis both missed their cue to argue, Jake's spirits slipped even further. Suddenly, capture seemed imminent. And what exactly would capture mean? Certain jail time, he figured, for decades, at least, if not life—or maybe even death. For the first time in years, Jake's mind recalled a tour he'd taken of a police station back when he was a Cub Scout—maybe ten years old. The best part of the tour had been the weapons locker, with all the rifles, pistols, and shotguns lined up like soldiers at attention; but the tour also included a peek at the detention cells, with their peeling paint and their metal beds and their toilets without any privacy. Even after all these years, Jake could clearly remember the tour guide reciting the dimensions of those steel-and-concrete boxes: six-by-eight. He didn't even know what the numbers meant back then, but he knew that it meant small. And he hated small.

You could suffocate in a cage that small.

In fact, of the entire Cub Scout den, he alone refused to cross the threshold to "try the cell on for size," as the cop had said. He knew how much other kids liked to fool around, and he remembered feeling terrified that one of them might think it would be funny to close the door on him. Even if they'd been able to find a key, there'd have been those minutes—however few—when he would have been locked alone in a tiny room, with everyone watching him and laughing at him as he sobbed and begged for them to let him out.

But it never happened that way. He'd said, "No thank you," to the police officer, and the police officer had respected his wishes. Still, the fear he'd experienced back then felt very, very real, even today, nearly thirty years later.

Neither surrender nor capture was a viable option.

"How long do you think we should wait?" Travis asked.

"Till next Thursday, if we have to," Jake said.

The Cadillac returned. "There he is," Carolyn said excitedly.

The mammoth white car returned to its spot in the road and parked. "This time we stay put until he gives the signal," Travis ordered. God, he was getting bossy.

Nothing happened for thirty seconds, and then the interior light came on. Right away, Jake recognized the driver as good old Thorne—the man without a sense of humor. Even after fourteen years, he hadn't changed a bit.

While the Donovans watched, the broad-shouldered man pulled himself out of the driver's seat and closed the door behind him. There was movement, but they couldn't tell in the dark what he was doing until a lighter flared in front of his leathery face.

"Now?" Jake prompted.

"C'mon."

They approached the car slowly but not stealthily, walking like regular people down a regular road in the middle of a regular night. "Remember," Travis whispered. "Don't startle him."

Jake smiled. "God, Trav, if he can't see us by now, I sure as hell don't want to be riding with him in a car."

"Just remember, is all."

"I'll try."

No one said anything until they'd approached within five feet of the driver, who, on closer inspection, had only one eyebrow, which stretched from ear to ear. He made no moves as they approached, but there was something about the way he smoked the cigarette that didn't look right. Then Jake realized that the guy was keeping his hands free.

How reassuring. And the hands wore gloves.

"Hello, Thorne," Carolyn said softly. "Nice to see you again." She gave him a perfunctory hug, and the tightly coiled man returned it, sort of.

Thorne did his best to squeeze out a smile. "Mr. Sinclair says hello. Your friend Nick will be able to join you tomorrow."

"That's *great!*" Carolyn exclaimed. "What about Uncle Harry? Will I see him, too?"

Jake checked his watch nervously. "Shouldn't we get going?"

Thorne ignored him. "No, Mr. Sinclair can't make it. The FBI's been watching him pretty closely since you guys popped up again." He seemed a little startled at the sight of Travis, who in turn did his best to keep his father between himself and the cold brown eyes. "What's this?" Thorne asked.

"It's a boy," Jake answered, his voice weighted with sarcasm.

Thorne's mouth smiled, but his eyes did not. His eyes never smiled, in fact. "I'd forgotten what a funny man you are, Jack."

"It's Jake," Travis corrected defensively.

Thorne regarded them both as if they were table scraps. "We've gotta get going," he said. He opened the back door and revealed a mess of luggage and newspapers strewn all over the seat and floor. "This spot's for you, kid," Thorne instructed. "Climb under all that stuff and cover yourself up good." He pushed a button on his key chain, and the trunk popped open. "You and your husband have to ride back here for a while, Sunshine," he explained. "They got roadblocks every place looking for you two. Can't stop us without probable cause, and with you back here, they got probable nothin'."

Jake pulled up short. "I'm not getting in the trunk," he said.

"Oh, yeah?" Thorne challenged, clearly amused. "Why not?"

"I'm claustrophobic."

The big man rolled his eyes. "Get over it, then. 'Cause that's how I'm driving you. It's that or walk. You choose."

Jake watched as Travis burrowed under the trash in the backseat, and Thorne helped Carolyn into the trunk. At least it was a big one.

Shit.

In the end, Jake took a deep breath, swung his feet over the edge, and lay down. Some decisions were inherently easier than others, he supposed.

CHAPTER TWENTY-THREE

Nick Thomas had every right to be at his desk, even if it was after one in the morning, just as he had every right to be grazing through the computer files on his screen. He'd written the damn things, in fact.

Why, then, did he feel like such a criminal?

This was crazy, he told himself as he pulled up the documents he needed, and printed them out. Topo maps, prevailing wind patterns, daily work logs—everything that had anything to do with the EPA's cleanup of the Newark site. The more he thought about this Sinclair character's explanation of Jake and Carolyn's theory, the more ridiculous it sounded. Talk about overkill. All of that destruction just to hide a corpse, which could have been hidden, anyway? It was absurd.

There was a certain logic, he supposed, that a blade of grass is best hidden in a bale of hay, but could the same hold true of bodies? If you stacked bodies high enough and violently enough, could you possibly hope to slip one through a crack somewhere?

Every twenty minutes or so, he fought a new urge to call the police and bring this all to a stop. To his knowledge, Nick had never before broken a law—unless you counted the occasional speeding violation. Even there, he allowed himself ten percent over the speed limit, no more. Now he couldn't *begin* to imagine the number of laws he was preparing to break.

If he ultimately found himself explaining his actions to authorities, he'd cast Harry Sinclair in the role of villain, threatening his own family with a horrible fate. Given the telephone ruse, he thought it would get him past a lie detector. Without such an excuse, people might figure out the real reason he was going along with this foolishness. And when they did, they'd know something that he'd only just figured out for himself.

The reality of it all smacked him in the head around ten o'clock— long after Sinclair had dropped him back at the headquarters building. The ninety-minute drive was over, and his assignment was clear. As Nick pieced together the plan in his head, he realized that for the first time in years, he felt truly alive. He'd stepped outside of his up-at-five, home-by-seven routine, and the presence of a little danger felt inexplicably invigorating. He felt guilty as hell for thinking such juvenile thoughts, and then he realized that even the guilt felt good. He couldn't remember the last time he'd felt true emotion like this, unburdened by second thoughts about what he *should* be feeling or what he *ought* to be doing.

For at least these few brief moments, he was working for himself. The only deadline he faced was the one he imposed upon himself by accepting this assignment, and deep in his heart of hearts, he knew that he was doing a job for which he was uniquely qualified. No one else in this massive sea of bureaucrats could dig up the details of Newark so efficiently—not his boss; not the fresh meat from college. He alone knew what to look for in these files, because he alone knew what he put there.

Knowing the layout of the storage magazine was crucial—too crucial to be left to memory. He and the Donovans had to know how to get in, and how to get out if something went wrong. Then there were the security concerns. He dove into the project with a zeal he hadn't enjoyed in years.

Reflecting further on it, Nick figured that at the end of the day, this was about friendship *and* about settling scores. About facing the image in the mirror every morning. He'd allowed himself to be railroaded into silence back in 1983, surrendering to the political forces who wanted the Newark Incident to just disappear. In his haste to cover his own ass, he'd sat quietly and allowed the EPA and the FBI to construct an ironclad case against his friends, never once speaking up to declare that the authorities were full of shit. It was too easy to remain silent. Even now he couldn't point to a single action he could have taken or a single speech he could have made that would have changed anything. But fact was, he didn't even try—and not only Jake and Carolyn but he himself had paid the price.

Then there were the bodies: the worst sacrilege of all. To this day, the entry team remained where they had fallen, denied the simple dignity of burial, all because the people in charge had placed their careers above human decency.

Well, Nick could fix that now. He could fix a lot of things, in fact.

It was one-thirty by the time he'd printed everything he needed, and then it was time to go. He placed the two-inch stack of papers into his briefcase and clicked it closed. He'd told his family he was headed to Arkansas for business, but left a note for his boss that he needed a few days off to attend to a sick relative in Oregon. With an overnight bag in one hand and his briefcase in the other, Nick walked briskly toward the door. He'd still have a short wait for his ride, once he reached the lobby, but that was okay. He knew the guard on duty that night, and for weeks the guy had wanted Nick to see pictures of his new baby.

As he headed for the elevator, Nick marveled at the value of this gift he'd been given. How often, he wondered, did a person get to travel back into his own past to set the future straight?

CHAPTER TWENTY-FOUR

How do they do this?" Irene moaned, resting her head in her hands. "They just evaporate. Like they were never here." Not counting the fitful forty-five minutes on the plane where she forced herself to sit with her eyes closed, she'd been without sleep for nearly thirty hours. The last time she remembered feeling this bad was when she'd graduated high school and spent seven days in a beach house playing drinking games. "What are we missing, Paul?"

Paul Boersky, looking remarkably natty in comparison, stared out the window of the state police barracks and considered his response. Built in the early fifties, the barracks was even dumpier than the squad room in Phoenix. By the look of the place, little had been updated since the first day of occupancy. The yellow cinder-block walls had been rendered even yellower by decades of nicotine, and while the floors appeared to have been recently waxed, the janitor would have been well advised to spend his time in a more fruitful endeavor, given the number of missing tiles.

"What are we missing?" Paul restated. "Not a thing except the Donovans." He turned away from the window and helped himself to a folding chair.

Irene lowered her forehead onto the Formica tabletop. "Very funny," she growled.

"I'm not trying to be funny," he defended himself. "I'm serious as a heart attack. I think we know everything that's out there to know. Problem is, we can't read their minds."

"We're the FBI," she reminded him. "Mind reading is in the job description."

He drained his Styrofoam cup, then leaned forward, forearms on the table. "Look, we know these two are getting help from Harry Sinclair."

Her head came up. "We do? We *know* that?"

He shrugged. "Okay, we don't have evidence to indict, but what the hell? I mean, they have their kid call him, and then he scrambles the call and disappears. That's quite a coincidence."

She weighed the logic. "So they're that much more likely to disappear for another fourteen years. Wonderful. Is this old man their only family?"

Paul replied through a giant yawn. "The only family they could turn to. Jake's parents are both dead—the mother just a couple of years ago and the father when he was just a kid. In fact, when Mama kicked the bucket, the Philadelphia office flooded the church and cemetery with undercover agents, just in case Jake showed up to pay his respects. On the other side, Carolyn's dad disappeared when she was little—you knew that. But her mom's in a home now, blowing spit bubbles and picking imaginary bugs off her blankets."

Irene winced at the imagery. "Sensitive as always. Okay, so we're not missing anything. Let me rephrase the question: How are we going to find them and get them back?"

Paul took a deep breath through his nose and let it go. "Well, as things stand now, we have to wait for them to make a mistake— something they seem unwilling to do. If we get a good solid connect between Sinclair and the Donovans, though—something better than a bloodline and a telephone call—we can get a warrant to dig deeper into Sinclair's contacts, to see who he's using to help them disappear."

She shook her head. Every argument became a circle all of a sudden. "Never happen," she sighed. "The Bureau's launched too many fishing trips against him over the years. The U.S. Attorney for the Chicago District is too intimidated by Sinclair's juice to go back to the well with anything short of a smoking gun."

She straightened in her seat and arched her spine over the chair back to stretch the weary muscles. "They're just so damned calculating," she said. "I keep thinking back to the moment I first arrested him." *Before I brought all this shit down on myself.* "He was so cool—arrogant, even. So pissed off that I would suspect him of using drugs." She chuckled. "As opposed to mass murder, for God's sake. What must he have been thinking? He had to be shitting bricks, but he never showed a thing. What does that say about a man?"

Paul answered without hesitation. "It says he's had a lot of time to practice. He's been preparing for this moment for over a decade."

No, there was more to it than that. What would breed that kind of complacency, that kind of self-awareness? Her mind replayed the details of the raid on Marcus Ford, and she saw Donovan standing there, revolver in hand. She remembered that hesitation that no one else wanted to talk about. Was he prepared to shoot? Was he planning to shoot? Why else would he be armed, but to effect his escape? He said it was for defense, but was that believable? Didn't everyone who took up arms do so with a notion to attack? Of course they did.

So why didn't he attack, then? Because he never stood a chance? Maybe . . .

An opening door interrupted her thoughts as a trooper who looked to be fourteen poked his head into the tiny classroom office. "Excuse me, Agent Rivers," the trooper said. "The sergeant thought you'd like to know that your boss is on CNN."

Eyebrows raised all around, and Irene and Paul shared a look before following the trooper out to the tiny lunchroom, where an ancient television sat wedged into a corner of the counter. From the looks of things, Peter Frankel was holding court with his fans in the press, standing behind a lectern bearing the seal of the FBI. A tangle of microphones obscured most of his chest. Irene had to hand it to him. Here was a man born to be on television. His white smile, blue eyes, and quick wit were everything J. Edgar could have hoped for.

"I don't think that's relevant at this point, Gail," the deputy director said in response to an unheard question. "What's relevant is justice. Senator Albricht is first and foremost a citizen of the United States, and as such, he is innocent until proven guilty . . ."

"What's he talking about?" Irene asked the young trooper.

The trooper laughed. "Apparently, the senator from the great state of Illinois has a thing for diddling kids."

Irene turned to Paul. "Was this on television this morning? Something about magazine subscriptions and club memberships?"

Paul shrugged. "Got me. I spent the morning sleeping."

"Yes, ma'am," the trooper interjected. "That's how he got discovered. Somebody leaked it to the press."

Irene turned her attention back to the television. Sooner or later, she figured, the Donovans would come up.

"Given his staunch opposition to your nomination as FBI director," a reporter asked from off-camera, "some have suggested that perhaps you leaked this information, sir."

Frankel's face turned sour as he regarded the reporter with a look of utter contempt. "I find that question offensive, Brett," he said, struggling for control. "You just tell those people that they're wrong." He pointed to another unseen reporter, and then, before the question could be asked, he turned back to Brett. "I'm the deputy director of the FBI, for God's sake. How dare you even imply such a thing." He paused for a long moment, silently daring the reporter to ask a follow-up. When Brett failed to do so, Frankel shifted his eyes again. "I'm sorry, Helen, it was your turn."

"Mr. Frankel, some fifteen years ago, the perpetrators of the Newark, Arkansas, hazardous waste incident got away on your watch. You yourself have called it the most embarrassing moment in your career. Now here we are again: Jake and Carolyn Donovan were in custody, and your agency lost them yet another time. Any comments, sir?"

As the question was presented, Frankel looked first pained, then a little saddened, and, finally, the tiny edge of a smirk appeared on his lips. "Have I told you how lovely you look today, Helen?" he quipped. Laughter burst among the reporters. When the noise subsided, he was all business again, talking around a boyish grimace of embarrassment. "What can I say? Yes and yes. We have our finest people working on the Donovan case, but as things stand, they're still at large, and we can use any help that the public is willing to offer to get them back in custody."

Irene laughed in spite of her hatred for the man. "God, he's good."

CHAPTER TWENTY-FIVE

Jake and Carolyn fell silent in the backseat of the Cadillac as Thorne left Little Rock behind and drove closer to Newark. They were only thirty miles out now, and Jake marveled at how little anything had changed in fourteen years. The road stretched on forever, ahead and behind, raised above the surrounding swamps on an endless ridge of tightly compacted fill dirt. It didn't seem possible, but he swore that even the billboards were the same. Faded by years of blistering sun and pounding rain, many had aged beyond legibility, but he could still make out the outline of a car here or a washing machine there. A roadside bar advertised "B er On Pr mis s" for the benefit of any passersby who wanted to get tanked before they continued on into hell.

"I swear to God those same letters were burned out last time," he said, pointing.

All Carolyn could do was shake her head. They had no business being here, she told herself. As they drew ever closer to the origins of their nightmare, the plan began to feel progressively more foolish. Certainly, Harry could have helped them to disappear one more time.

"What *is* this place?" Travis asked, his voice heavy with disdain. His folks had dragged him to some god-awful spots over the years, but this was worse than any three of them put together.

Soon they found themselves passing through a downtown area, such as it was, and approaching a squatty brick post office ahead on the left.

"This place look familiar?" Thorne asked from up front. It was the first time he'd spoken since releasing his passengers from the trunk six hours before.

Carolyn gasped as it came to her. "This is where you picked us up the last time." As she spoke, she squeezed Travis's hand.

"Never thought I'd be back in this fuckin' place," Thorne grumbled.

"Makes two of us," Jake agreed. "At least this time I'm dry and nearly clean." About three hours ago, they'd stopped for a brief roadside bathroom break and clothes change.

Planted as he was between his parents in the backseat, Travis had to crane his neck to see the post office as it passed by the window. "So where were you hiding till then?" he asked.

Jake pointed with a sweeping motion of his hand. "Up there in the woods somewhere," he said. "Not a lot different than last night, really."

"Except colder and scarier," Carolyn corrected. "God, we were scared."

Travis pondered that for a moment. "Okay," he said, as if settling an argument. "Tell me one more time. *Why* were you guys at Newark in the first place?" He looked to Jake for an answer, who in turn nodded for Carolyn to take the ball.

Nearly a century of prosperity in Newark came to a crashing halt in 1964, when President Lyndon Johnson shut down the 75,000-acre Ulysses S. Grant Army Ammunition Plant as part of one of the most expensive temper tantrums in history. In retribution for the incumbent governor's refusal to integrate his state's public schools, the Grant Plant was only one of countless federal facilities shut down, and the only one never to reopen.

Just like that, virtually overnight, the town of Newark died.

Until Harold Davis discovered a faint pulse. A twenty-something trust-funder back in the midseventies, Davis recognized the opportunity buried amid the local tragedy. Where everyone else saw endless acres of ugly, abandoned real estate, this ambitious entrepreneur saw a ready-made industrial plant, just waiting for the right customer. Moving quickly, and with great secrecy, he talked the bank out of enough cash to purchase all 75,000 acres for $5 million.

Harold Davis did nothing with the land itself for the better part of a decade, watching nervously as the market for Arkansas real estate plummeted, even as it went through the roof in the rest of the world. He never panicked, though. He knew in his heart that one day his patience would spell profit.

Finally, his dreams came true. The biggest peacetime military buildup in history began in 1981, when Ronald Reagan set out to resurrect the American armed forces from the smoldering ashes left by the Carter administration. Defense contractors sprouted like so many weeds in a garden, each of them fighting for a piece of the mass-destruction business.

Harold Davis knew instinctively what lay ahead for the CEOs who tried to find acceptance for their line of work in A List communities. Ultimately, weapons programs were about things that explode, and nice neighborhoods would want nothing to do with them. Finally, when the time was just right, Harold Davis stepped forward.

"Why not come to Newark, Arkansas?" he asked. "We'd love to have you."

The Chamber of Commerce nearly bankrupted itself creating brochures that put the best face on this rural community, and oh, were they pretty. "Newark, Arkansas—An Outdoorsman's Paradise." Of course, the buzz-builders didn't mention that people in Newark hunted and fished not for sport, but for food. The other town motto—"Like a Place from the Past"—translated to oppressive poverty and pervasive filth; where shoes remained unaffordable for a good ten percent of the school population and where dental care required a forty-five-minute car ride to Jefferson County.

None of this mattered in the longer view, of course, and Harold Davis knew it. If companies truly cared about living conditions for their employees, then places like Elizabeth, New Jersey, would have died years ago. Companies cared about money—specifically, about ways not to spend it. As custodians of a thriving weapons machine, the commanders at the Grant Plant had spent billions of dollars to construct thousands of buildings, designed for the specific purpose of developing and processing explosives. Say what you want about the Army, but they built their stuff to last forever.

When Harold made his pitch to boardrooms across the country, he sidestepped the community issues and focused instead on dollars. He offered a turnkey alternative to massive capital expenditure, and civic cooperation instead of endless zoning appeals. Some decisions are just easy.

In the twelve-month period beginning in April 1981, Harold Davis signed lease agreements with every one of the biggest names in the defense industry, worth over $100 million. With months yet to go before his thirty-eighth birthday, he'd made it onto the Forbes 500, and he didn't have to share his profits with a soul.

Then, in the fall of 1982, his good fortune turned.

First established in 1885, the Grant Plant had nobly served two great wars, and several lesser ones, and over time had become the repository for all manner and types of military toys. From rockets and bombs to bullets, nerve gas, and nuclear triggers, its storage magazines had seen a little bit of everything. Sometime after the Second World War, as activities began to diminish at Ground Zero—local residents' pet name for the place back in the fifties—operations within the sprawling facility became more centralized. Commanders transferred older, outmoded equipment and weaponry to storage magazines so far out in the miles-long stretches of identical bunkers that over time they were literally forgotten.

Before abandoning their stake in Arkansas, the commandant and staff of the Grant Plant had worked hard to ensure that every primer, shell casing, and propellant grain was transferred to suitable new homes elsewhere within the Army, but in retrospect, it seemed unreasonable to expect them not to lose something.

As corporate tenants arrived to claim and renovate their new spaces, they occasionally found odds and ends that didn't belong and needed to be properly disposed of. The Army was reasonably cooperative in helping to remove or destroy ordnance once it had been identified, but they were quick to point out that their help was offered only as a *favor* to Mr. Davis and his tenants. By purchasing the property, Harold Davis had bought all the problems that went with it. There was, in fact, specific language to that effect in the purchase contract he'd been so anxious to sign.

Davis's deal with the Army was simple: He would pay to have suspicious materials identified by private contractors and shoulder the burden of destruction for the garden variety of industrial hazardous waste. Uncle Sam, in turn, would take care of any weaponry they might find, but only after Davis had paid to have it identified independently. Bottom line, the Army didn't want its personnel chasing wild geese through the private sector. It was a gentleman's agreement, designed to make the area safe, while remaining profitable.

The first of the legal nightmares appeared late one winter, when the Environmental Protection Agency got wind of what was going on. Under hazardous waste regulations, it turned out, Harold Davis—as the owner of the property and therefore the "generator" of the hazardous waste—had a duty to report these waste sites as they were discovered, and his failure to do so had quickly run up over $1 million in fines, even as half the cases were appealed by his lawyers.

The specific horrors of Magazine B-2740 had been discovered by accident. A prospective tenant was touring one of the original, long-abandoned storage magazines in the outer regions of the plant in the company of Harold Davis himself when they discovered where, exactly, the United States Army had been stashing everything it wanted to forget about.

With no real choice, Davis hired Enviro-Kleen, which in turn hired unemployed chemistry majors to don impossibly hot suits to perform the ridiculously hazardous task of identifying the contents of the magazine.

". . . and so your dad and I became glorified garbagemen," Carolyn concluded, smiling at Jake. "To think of the rent Davis must have gotten off of the place while it was still up and working. It's hard to believe that the government just *abandoned* it all."

Jake frowned. "You're kidding, right? I wish they'd *nuked* it."

"That's kinda what happened, isn't it?" Travis interjected. "Nuked it, I mean. Poisoned it. Seems to me it's the same thing."

Chapter Twenty-six

In her haste to make an 8:00 A.M. meeting, Bonnie Jerome had time only to change out of her Nike walking shoes and into her pumps before scurrying down the hall to get checked off some- body's list for attending her umpteenth mandatory security brief- ing. Spies were everywhere, the speaker had told her, and the spies knew who she was. In fact, they knew who everyone was. If you worked for the FBI—from a file clerk to the director himself— they had your picture and a dossier. People like Bonnie and the technicians who worked for her were just as likely to be approached by a foreign agent as was anyone else—perhaps even more so, given that technical types had no arrest powers.

Mentally, she'd checked out of the briefing once the guy got to the part about foreign spies seducing unsuspecting sources at the popular Washington, D.C., nightspots. The thought of it made her smile. If last night's conquest—a hunky Georgetown student named Jonathan—was a spy, then he'd earned every secret he'd taken home with him.

The meeting finally ended, precisely three hours after it had begun, and now she could get back down to the business of being a computer geek. What she and her people did for the FBI could just as well have been done for any other agency in the government; or even the private sector. They made sure that the complex knot of computer systems—both hardware and soft—ran as smoothly as possible, thus keeping the world safe from the Red hordes, or whatever was the perceived threat *du jour*. In a town that was perpetually fissured by politics, Bonnie truly didn't care about any of it, so long as her cats remained well fed, her rent was paid on time, and these woefully out-of-date pieces of crap they called computers continued to process the information they were designed to digest. Her compartmentalized Top Secret clearance granted her access to just about everything the system had to offer, but none of it held her interest. Whatever she saw during the course of a day was forgotten by happy hour.

At least, that was usually the case. Today would be different. Just a few minutes after returning to her desk, she discovered in her inbox an urgent message directly related to the *content* of information within the system, rather than on the function of the system itself. She could think of only one other time it had happened—a security breach in one of the older systems in the network, the warning for which surfaced as an error message to one of her programmers. In that case, Bonnie had merely bumped it to the security people and was done.

This morning's message was different, however, and it came attached to a cover note written in hot-pink ink on a lime-green sticky.

> Bonnie—This popped up as an error message at 0321 hrs. this a.m. Thought you'd want to handle it. I'd do it, but I've got kids to put through school.
> —TR

He signed it with a dippy, ridiculous smiley face.

TR would be Ted Rosencranze, her assistant in charge of midnight shifts. Pulling the sticky off the printout, she read further. Apparently, someone over at EPA had tapped into a computer file

that had been tagged by one of the old Justice systems for surveillance, back in . . . she checked the date again . . . 1983! Somehow
the tag was forgotten, or maybe it expired. Anyway, for whatever
reason, it was never transferred to the new system. The instructions
were quite specific and, as such, rather unremarkable: in the event
that these files were accessed by anyone for any reason, the case
agent was to be personally notified right away.

At first, Bonnie didn't see what the big deal was. This message
contained nothing that Ted couldn't have handled on his own.
Then she looked more closely and saw the name of the case agent.

"Well, I'll be damned." She paused for a moment to figure out
what she should do. Finally, she shrugged and reached for her Bureau phone directory and thumbed through the pages until she
found the entry she needed. After one more short pause to collect
herself, she lifted the handset and punched in the extension.

A cheerful yet officious-sounding woman picked up after the
first ring. "Deputy Director Frankel's office," she said.

CHAPTER TWENTY-SEVEN

Nick knew he should be exhausted, yet the three-hour ride in the sleek Gulfstream jet had left him oddly energized. He could get used to this. The Gulfstream was a flying hotel suite, with lush seating, a fully stocked bar, and a miniature office, complete with a desk, computer terminal, telephones, and even a fax machine. Certainly, it was a far cry from the discount carriers he normally used, where service meant having some Cossack bounce a pack of greasy peanuts off your head while the passenger in front crushed your kneecaps with his seat back.

Nick was the plane's only passenger. Like a child on an amusement ride, he sat in every seat and played with every button and knob in the passenger compartment, just to see what they would do.

They'd touched down in Little Rock at about five in the morning, where a stone-faced driver met the aircraft on the tarmac and shuttled Nick the rest of the way to Newark. He and his luggage were deposited at an ancient, condemned motel complex a few miles from the industrial park. A long, low roof covered a row of decrepit doors and windows, each identical to the one next to it. Window, door, window, door; and so it went at exact intervals, along the covered sidewalk, for the length of the abandoned structure. An empty metal frame and dangling electrical connections doubled for a sign atop a rusted pole in the crumbling parking lot.

Nick recognized this place as the decomposed carcass of the Ouachita Grove Motor Hotel—the same fleabag where he'd stayed last time, when he was part of a high-spirited team of hazardous waste site workers.

The mute, faceless driver piloted the vehicle past the thoroughly vandalized motel office and back toward the strip of rooms. For the first time, Nick's stomach boiled with a sense of very real danger. Anything in the world could happen to a man out here, and no one would even hear the screams. Certainly, no one would find his body; the rodents would see to that. A place like this probably had rats the size of cattle. They'd have his bones stripped clean within hours.

What the hell have you gotten yourself into?

Once parked, the driver led Nick over the curb and up to room 24. The hardware had been ripped off long ago, but the silhouette of the numbers still remained in the chalky paint of the delaminated door.

Inside, a card table with four folding chairs had been set in the center of the room, under the skeletal remains of a ceiling fan. Overwhelmed by the stink of mildew and moldy foam rubber, Nick sneezed three times in the first half minute of entering the place. The driver produced a penlight from an inside pocket somewhere and, using its yellow beam to guide the way, found two battery-powered lanterns and turned them on. Next, he parted the tattered curtains on the window frame.

What did it say about the curtains, Nick wondered, when even the vandals left them alone?

"Here you go," the driver said. "I delivered a few boxes for you last night. That's them over there." He pointed to a spot in the back of the room where a dozen cardboard containers lay stacked in an awkward pyramid. "Your friends should be here shortly. I know the place looks creepy, but don't let it get to you. It's safe. No one will be by who's not supposed to."

As the driver let himself out of the room, Nick called after him, "Where are you going?" but the guy ignored him. It probably was none of his business, anyway.

Three hours had passed in silence, and Nick busied himself with the task of reading through the thick printout he'd brought with him.

It all came back quickly: the layout of the plant, the perimeter of the exclusion zone. He remembered it all so clearly, as if the intervening decade and a half had just dissolved from his mind. Preparing for the Newark cleanup had been his first solo shot as site safety officer, and he'd been determined not to blow it. If he'd done his job well, he'd have had it made.

Months before the entry-team cowboys showed up with their attitudes and their silver suits, he had been there with his assessment team, pulling samples out of the soil, air, and water to determine what might have leaked out over the years to threaten the fishes and the squirrels. It was nasty, filthy work—real wet-feet, dirt-under-the-fingernails stuff—the result of which was a stack of reports and maps and diagrams that empirically demonstrated just how little anyone knew about Uncle Sam's Arkansas root cellar.

Sometimes, though, the absence of information told as important a story as a computerful of data. As he reviewed the ancient charts and graphs there in the moldy motel room, he remembered the sleepless nights these papers had generated so long ago. It had been his responsibility to select the equipment the Silverados would use to make that first entry, and his sleep had been haunted by the penalties they'd pay if he miscalculated the risks.

In the end, of course, the reality had played out to be far more horrifying than any nightmare. He simply had not foreseen the possibility of a terrorist attack.

Not that the Silverados could have known that. Not that they cared. All they heard were the explosions, if they'd heard even that much. Sometimes, in the darkest days of his depression, Nick wondered how many of his dead friends had spent their last instant on earth cursing him for fucking up the one job he had to do.

Hardly a day went by—even before Jake and Carolyn resurfaced in the news—that he didn't think of those bodies; the way they dropped where they stood, strewn all over the roadway leading to Magazine B-2740. By the time anyone even tried to reach the exterior team, the corpses of those decon people and admin staffers were caked in soot. The ones closest to the open blast doors had melted into their moon suits, testament to the ferocity of the fire which had simply been allowed to burn. Further away, the bodies were just dead; so many lumps of flesh, contained within their protective garments, where their blood pooled out of sight.

Nick's mind replayed the recovery operations, where each of the contaminated bodies was placed inside an enormous rubber pouch that had been designed for just such a use, albeit with an eye toward a radiation accident rather than a chemical one. The bagged bodies had been taken to a staging area, where they were bagged yet again and shipped off to a military base for decontamination and autopsy.

Not the entry teams, though. Their bodies were deemed to be contaminated beyond recovery. Unlike biological agents, which would have been killed by the extreme temperatures, the chemical agents in Magazine B-2740 merely changed form as they were burned, recombining with the products of combustion to form wholly new, and potentially even more hazardous, compounds. The products of such reactions were reasonably predictable when the process started with known entities, but as more chemicals were added to the recipe, the list of potential combinations grew geometrically, quickly reaching the point where meaningful predictions became impossible. In the Newark Incident, where no one even knew what the original chemical combinations were, the possibilities were infinite.

During the fire itself, the magazine had been a boiling cauldron of fire, smoke, and chemicals as burning rocket propellant and high explosives ignited crate after crate of chemical warheads, raising the temperature within those walls to 4,000° Fahrenheit. According to the accident report—itself an educated best guess—the inferno created its own windstorm, sucking in huge quantities of air through the same opening through which the fireball was trying to vent itself, thus causing a continuous recirculation of the same poisonous atmosphere.

Faced with so much uncertainty, the professional whiners and camera hogs at the EPA did what they did best: they played it safe, declaring the building's threshold to be the absolute limit to entry. No one could take a step beyond the doorway without violating federal law. That the bodies inside were once people's sons, or that they were once friends of Nick's, was deemed an irrelevant detail.

He brooded on what he was about to do. *What if the EPA know-it-alls were right? What if we are walking into a toxic nightmare?* Even if he and Jake and Carolyn could figure a way to engineer the hazards down to the remotest possibility, how could he ever justify taking this kind of risk, just to put the past back on the right track?

As the sound of an approaching automobile pulled his attention back through the front window, he realized his answer had just arrived.

"I'm *not* staying here," Travis said firmly as he climbed out of the Cadillac and saw what was left of the Ouachita Grove Motor Hotel.

"Hush, Travis," Carolyn hissed.

"But I . . ." Jake's gentle hand on his shoulder told him that it was prudent to shut up.

Carolyn moved only her eyes as she took it all in, her jaw slightly agape. "Oh, my God," she whispered.

"One each, Arkansas-issue ghost town," Jake mused aloud.

"You guys actually *slept* here?" Travis asked.

Jake smiled. "Well, it wasn't quite this bad back then."

They all jumped as the door to room 24 opened, and Jake and Thorne simultaneously swung their hands to their holsters. Jake stopped the instant he saw who it was, but Thorne kept going, bringing a huge, chrome-plated .45 to bear on the new arrival.

"Freeze!" Thorne shouted.

Nick Thomas's eyes popped to the size of saucers, and he threw his hands in the air. "Jesus!" he shouted. "Holy shit!"

Jake threw a hand toward Thorne. "No! That's Nick! Don't shoot him!"

Thorne held his aim for another second or two, just to make sure, then brought the gun down. "Goddamn fucking amateurs," he grumbled, stuffing his weapon back under his sports coat. "You keep surprising people like that and you're gonna die young."

Nick haltingly lowered his hands, and his legs wobbled a bit as color drained from his face. Carolyn darted forward to help him sit down before he fell. "Holy shit," Nick said again. It seemed to be the entire breadth of his vocabulary. "Holy shit."

Travis started to chuckle but stopped when Jake thumped him on the head.

"I'm sorry, Nick," Jake said, hurrying over to help. "Are you okay?"

"He nearly shot me!" Nick declared. "You send some thug to drag me all the way out here, and then you point guns at me?"

"He's not a thug," Carolyn corrected, but no one seemed to hear.

Jake shrugged, looking a little pained. "We didn't know it was you, Nick. You just startled us."

Nick looked at him like he'd grown a third eye. "Startled you?" he said incredulously. "Jesus, Jake, you were gonna shoot me for startling you? Suppose it hadn't been me?"

Jake and Carolyn shared an uncomfortable glance, then changed the subject.

"So. What's new?" Carolyn asked, sparking a welcome laugh all around. She ventured a hug, as best she could there on the sidewalk, and Nick returned the effort.

"Jesus, you guys look awful," he said.

Jake helped Nick back to his feet. "How nice of you to notice. Diplomacy is still your specialty, I see."

Nick wanted to laugh—to lighten the moment—but he couldn't. "Seriously, Jake, are you all right?"

Jake's look said it all: *Are you nuts?* "It's been a tough fourteen years."

"And who's this?" Nick nodded toward the boy.

"This is our son, Travis," Jake said proudly. "And our fourteen years don't hold a candle to his last two days. He didn't know about any of this."

Travis offered a boyish, uncomfortable smile and extended his hand, just as he'd always been instructed.

"Nice to meet you, Travis."

The boy nodded, then took his hand back and chased a rock with his sneaker.

The sound of tires crunching gravel startled them all, but when Jake saw no aggressive movement from Thorne, he relaxed.

"That's the same car and driver who brought me here," Nick explained.

As the green Chevy pulled closer, Thorne waved to the driver, who slowed to a stop. The two of them chatted for a while through the window. When Thorne came up for air, he strolled over to Carolyn.

"Okay, Sunshine," he said. "I've got to go now. Mr. Sinclair wants me to keep a low profile. I'll leave the Caddy here for you to use."

"You can't go!" Travis said. "You're . . ." He shrank away from Thorne's piercing glare.

"Everything you asked for should already be in the room. Mr. Sinclair said he'd take care of all the other details, whatever they are. Just be sure to be back at the airport on time tonight." He delivered his entire speech to Carolyn, as if no one else was even there.

"Thanks, Thorne," Carolyn said with a smile. She offered him her hand, but he looked confused. "And thank Uncle Harry for me, too."

Suddenly, Thorne looked like he'd run out of words. He grasped her hand quickly, scowled, and disappeared.

"Well, you certainly have a way with criminal types," Nick said after Thorne had climbed into the car.

"Stop calling him that!" Carolyn barked. "I owe that man a lot."

Conversation stopped as everyone watched the Chevy leave. When it was gone, Carolyn abruptly shifted gears again. "So are we going to be able to pull this thing off or not?"

Chapter Twenty-Eight

Bonnie Jerome checked her watch. She'd skipped lunch to be ready for Frankel's return call, and now here it was nearly two, and her stomach was ready to consume itself.

To hell with him, she told herself. If Mr. Important didn't have the common decency to return a simple phone call, then she certainly wasn't going to wait around all day. What was it about the executive mind-set, she wondered, that made them think people had nothing better to do than wait for them to bestow their precious attention?

The really irritating part was, she didn't even care about the damn call. It was probably some computer glitch, anyway. With her luck, when Frankel finally rang back, she'd get an earful of just how important he was and how he didn't have time for petty issues like this. That was certainly the impression she'd gotten from his secretary when Bonnie refused to pass along the substance of the message.

"I'm cleared for everything," the secretary had pointed out.

"Not according to the message," Bonnie countered, after which the conversation had ended abruptly.

Maybe she should just call and get it over with; just leave a message with the secretary and get on with her day. Much as she hated to admit it, the prospect of talking to the heir apparent for the directorship had Bonnie a bit frazzled. All things considered, she'd be just as comfortable . . .

The phone rang, nearly launching her through the ceiling. It had been like this all day. Every time the phone chirped, she'd assumed it was The Man, only to find it was business as usual.

Don't seem overly anxious, she told herself.

The phone rang again. Bonnie hovered her hand over the receiver until it just started into its third ring. "Information Systems," she said, picking up. "This is Bonnie Jerome."

"Hold for Deputy Director Frankel, please." She recognized the secretary's voice from that morning, and she found herself on hold before she could say a word.

Here we go.

An abrupt click, and he was there. "Hello, Ms. Jerome, this is Deputy Director Frankel. I understand you have a message to relay to me?"

It was him! She recognized his voice from all of the training videos she'd watched and from his appearances on television.

"Um, h-hello, Mr. Frankel," she stammered. "Th-thanks for getting back to me."

"What is it you needed?" Suddenly his tone was flat; all business.

"Well, I work down in Information Systems. Actually, I'm a supervisor down here . . ."

"I know who you are, Ms. Jerome," Frankel interrupted. "This really is a very busy day. If you could get to the point?"

How does he know who I am? Bonnie's mind screamed. "Yes, sir. Well, overnight, we got notice that someone over at EPA had accessed a file that was apparently under surveillance at one time . . ."

"A file?" Where once there had been only annoyance in Frankel's tone, she heard a trace of interest.

"Yes, sir. A computer file. On a place called Newark, Arkansas?"

"Yes." The word came fast and hard, as if shot from a nail gun.

"You've heard of it, then?" she asked.

"Heard of it! Good God, Jerome, do you live in a cave?"

Whoops! Clearly, she'd revealed her ignorance. At FBI headquarters, everyone assumed that everyone else watched the news and read the newspapers. She struggled on: "In any case, the warning attached to the file said you were to be notified immediately if anyone accessed it. Of course, I nearly didn't bother you, since the access came from inside EPA . . ."

"Do you have a name?" Frankel interrupted.

The question caught her off balance. "Well, y-yes, sir. I'm Bonnie Jerome, in Infor—"

"Not you, for Christ's sake!" Frankel boomed. "The person accessing the file! Do you have a name on who accessed it?"

Bonnie jumped at the sound of his voice and inexplicably felt like crying. Why did he have to yell like that? She fumbled through the printout, looking for the name. It was always in the header, buried among the lines of seemingly meaningless text, yet she always had trouble finding it. "Here it is," she announced. "Shows up as a Nicholas Thomas."

She could hear Frankel whisper the name to himself, as if tasting the words. "*Nick* Thomas?"

Bonnie shrugged. Like he could see the gesture through the phone. "I suppose so," she said, but her words were wasted on an empty line.

Melissa Thomas was up to her elbows—literally—in clay when the phone rang. This was the first of her Christmas orders—for a rich museum patron in Los Angeles—and if she didn't get started on them soon, she'd be giving back a lot of money to a lot of very disappointed people. When she'd first thought of mailing out a catalog of her works, never in a million years did she think she'd get this kind of response.

"Lauren, can you get that, honey?" she called out to her five-year-old. "Tell them Mommy can't come to the phone." The thunder of footsteps sufficed as a delighted "yes."

Now, of course, Nick was off on some dead-end job interview, so not only did she have to fulfill all the orders but she also had to mold, fire, paint, and glaze five pots a day just to make the mailing deadline. It was doable, but a royal pain without a little help.

Melissa heard Lauren pick up the receiver and listened as she ran through the standard street-smart dialogue. "I'm sorry, she can't come to the phone," the little voice said, bringing a smile to her mother's face.

Kneading the clay was therapeutic, created a ruminative state. *If Nick could just move away from the past, this marriage could actually survive. But if he thinks, even for one minute, that I'm moving to Arkansas . . .*

"But he's not home," Lauren said to the telephone.

Whoa! That was a major break from the script. How many times had they discussed this? Lauren was never to tell anyone that people weren't home. Melissa stood, and turned the water on full with her elbow. The correct answer was always . . .

"He went to Noah's Ark," Lauren said.

What the . . . "Lauren! Who is that on the phone?"

"No!" Lauren said emphatically. "That's where he went! To Noah's Ark!"

Melissa turned off the water and grabbed a towel. "Lauren, answer me, young lady! Who is on the telephone?"

"Yeah, that's it!" Lauren announced proudly. "Newah . . . Whatever you said. That's it."

Melissa closed the distance quickly, but not quickly enough.

"Okay, you're welcome. Bye-bye." Lauren hung up the receiver.

"Who was that?" Melissa demanded.

Lauren shrugged. "I dunno," she said uneasily, clearly aware that she'd violated a rule. "Somebody who wanted to know where Daddy went."

Melissa sighed disapprovingly, then planted her fists on her hips. "Young lady," she said, "you and I are going to have a long talk about telephone behavior."

"I love what you've done with the place," Jake said, cringing in the dull light of the hotel room.

Travis was more succinct. "God, it stinks in here!"

"Is this the same room we had last time?" Carolyn asked.

Jake brought his eyebrows together, and he turned to get his bearings out the front window. "Maybe," he said, pulling on his lip. "Though I'd have guessed a little bit further down the row. It was close to here, though."

Nick led them to the card table, where he'd already prioritized everything they needed to talk about. As everyone settled into a chair, Nick touched Travis on the shoulder. "Hey, buddy, want to do me a favor?"

Travis looked to his mom and got a nod. "I guess," he said.

Nick brought a penknife out of his pants pocket. "Great. Take this knife here and open up those boxes, okay? Be careful, though. Use the blade to break the tape only. I don't want you to tear anything."

Travis's eyes grew inadvertently wider, showing a youngster's instinctive fascination with all things shiny and sharp. "Cool," he said. "You want me just to open them, or do you want me to take stuff out, too?"

"Just open them for now. I need to do an inventory."

Carolyn's head tilted curiously as she took in the pile of junk. "Is that the gear?"

Nick smiled proudly. "Yep. We should have enough Level A entry stuff for three people. Suits, air packs, and tools."

Jake shook his head in wonderment. "Where'd you get it?"

Nick frowned playfully. "Well, I can't say for sure. But I did happen to mention to your uncle that there's an EPA training school in Edison, New Jersey, that has a ton of this kind of crap. If a few sets disappeared, they probably wouldn't even know they were missing."

Jake smiled. "And I'm sure that Harry has *lots* of friends in New Jersey, huh, Carolyn?"

Carolyn blushed and set her jaw. "He has business acquaintances all over," she said defensively.

"And I know for a fact he can be very persuasive," Nick added.

It was like old times, mining each other's comments for maximum sarcasm. A playful enmity naturally existed between entry types, who tended to be rowdy, and toe-the-line administrative personnel like Nick, but Carolyn had always been the exception. Little Miss Safety, as the guys used to call her. Whereas the Silverados would forever ignore Nick's daily safety briefings—belching, farting, and grab-assing through every session—Carolyn was always the one to stand and tell everyone to shut up. There'd be groaning and smart-ass remarks, but Nick always figured them to be grateful to her in the end. They still got to be macho pigs, even as they absorbed the information that would ultimately keep them alive. Not because they *wanted* to hear that crap, you understand—real men breathed smoke and ate nails, don't you know—but because the wimpy lady said they had to. Everyone saved face.

God, that had been a good group of people. They'd worked hard, partied hard, and accomplished some pretty impressive feats together. What a waste.

As Travis set to work across the room on the boxes, the adults sat down in their impossibly uncomfortable chairs. Nick said, "Let's begin."

"Thanks for doing this, Nick," Carolyn said, straight from the heart. "I can't begin to guess why you'd put yourself on the line like this, but many, many thanks."

Nick's eyes softened, clearly moved. "I should have made this happen a long time ago," he said. "I can't compete with the hell you two must have been living, but that day ruined my life, too."

"We didn't do it, you know," Jake said abruptly. Then he looked embarrassed. "You never asked, but I thought I should tell you, anyway."

Nick smiled appreciatively. "Thanks. Actually, I never thought otherwise." The comment hung in the air for a moment. Clearly, there was more, but it would remain unsaid.

Nick smiled. "Well, whoever's setting you up for this has done one hell of a job." He turned to Jake. "Tell me about this body in the magazine."

Jake explained.

"*You* heard him mention the body, too?" Nick asked Carolyn.

She nodded. "Absolutely. You mean you didn't?"

Nick shook his head. "We weren't allowed on the ops channel, remember? Sean Foley was project manager, and he didn't want me *interfering*. Said if he wanted my input, he'd ask for it." The story stirred some old emotions, but Nick still found his way back to the task at hand.

"So do you think someone was monitoring the radio?" he went on. "That he heard you find the skeleton, and he just started shooting?"

Jake shrugged. "I don't know. I don't think so. I think he planned from the very beginning to kill everyone there."

Carolyn cut the chat session short. "Okay, guys, speculate on your own time. We've got a job here. Nick, you're the techno wizard. How likely are we to live till tomorrow if we go through with this?"

Jake shot her a disapproving look, then nodded toward Travis, who seemed oblivious to it all, lost in a sea of cardboard. The kid had enough to worry about without her posing questions in those terms.

"Actually, I think this'll be a fairly safe entry," Nick said cheerily. "But then again, I thought it could be done safely back in '83, too. We've got Level A gear just for the hell of it, but the real hazard this time is particulate, I think. No gas hangs around intact for fourteen years, and whatever liquids might have survived have long since evaporated; maybe even biodegraded. But that still leaves a shitload of really nasty dust, dirt, and soot. We sure as hell don't want to breathe any of that."

"Why?" Travis asked, looking up from his boxes. "What'll happen?"

So much for being oblivious, Jake thought.

Nick caught the look and smiled. "Well, Travis, we don't know for sure. Depends on what was in there to begin with and how it mixed during the fire. I'd expect some pretty severe respiratory distress. Maybe some systemic problems, too. Liver and kidneys, probably. Virtually everything affects them."

"That means you'd have trouble breathing and get really sick," Carolyn translated, earning herself a look that said, *I'm not stupid.*

"What about security?" Jake asked. "How big a problem will that be?"

Nick ruffled through his papers until he came up with the one he needed: an aerial photograph of the magazine and the surrounding area. "Actually, it shouldn't be too big a deal," he explained. "There's a general philosophy within the agency that people are not inherently suicidal. By putting up two concentric fences, here and here"—he pointed with the tip of his pencil—"and by posting signs every ten feet that say something like, 'Extremely Hazardous Area, You'll Die if You Go in Here,' we thought we'd pretty much discourage people from entering."

Everybody smiled.

"So, that in mind, no one saw a compelling need to have a resident security guard. Not only would it be a waste of time, but over eight hours a day, five days a week, who knows? Maybe he'd pick up an unmonitored exposure to something."

Carolyn was incredulous. "You mean, no one even watches the fence line?"

Nick shook his head. "Not exactly. If you look here on the map, you'll see that the old access road system—built in God knows when—still exists."

Clearly, Nick saw far more on the photograph than Jake did. Even as he followed the pencil, he still couldn't see what he was talking about.

"This road here is the closest one to the exclusion zone, about a hundred yards away, while this one here"—he moved the pencil—"is furthest away at about a half mile. We decided early on that it made sense to use the roadways as natural barriers and to build the outermost fences alongside them. Thus, three times a day, a rent-a-cop buzzes the place to look for any problems."

Carolyn interrupted. "Problems like . . . ?"

Nick shrugged. "Hell, I don't know. Anything, I guess. Holes in the fences? Birds falling out of the sky?"

The bird imagery made Travis giggle in the background.

Jake turned in his chair to face his son. "You're welcome to come on up here and join us, pal," he said with a grin. "Hate to have you straining your ears."

Travis flashed a sheepish smile, then returned to his cutting. "No, that's okay. I'm fine."

"I don't suppose you have a schedule for when those guards come?" Carolyn wanted to know.

Nick shot her his coyest smirk and held up another piece of paper from the stack. "Suppose again, Mrs. Donovan," he said. "So what time is it now?" He looked at his watch. "Two o'clockish. Next patrol is at three, and the one after that isn't till nine. I say we make our entry at three-thirty, do what we have to do, then be on our way back to Little Rock before dark."

Jake looked over to Carolyn, who met his eyes with an uneasy glare. So this was it. All the years, all the running, all the new identities, and all the lies ultimately came down to a simple decision just to go for it. Could it possibly be this easy?

"Sounds like a plan to me," Jake said.

CHAPTER TWENTY-NINE

As Irene watched the West Virginia countryside speed by, five thousand feet below, she tried to figure out why the Donovans would return to Arkansas—to the "scene of the crime" as it were. Christ, it sounded so clichéd, she hated even to think the words. These fugitives had worked so hard for so long to stay invisible, how could they possibly profit by stepping into the open like that? It didn't make sense.

But Frankel was convinced, and when you sat in the big office, your hunches carried the weight of law. What he didn't say was how he knew. Something about a hit on a computer field by some staffer at EPA, but between the sputtering cell phone connection and Frankel's clipped, pompous way of speaking, she couldn't get half the details she wanted. That was okay, though. She had staff back in Charleston to piece all that together for her.

Ironically, her team had just discovered the Donovans' white van, stashed in a dilapidated old barn, when word came from Frankel. It had taken a cool head and strong nerves for the Donovans to stay put like that in the middle of a full-scale search. Fact was, they'd

done exactly the right thing. Had they tried to bolt, they'd have
been caught for sure.

They always do the right thing, Irene mused. *It's really beginning to piss me
off.*

Judging by the equipment and supplies they left behind in the
van, they hadn't anticipated being caught in West Virginia. She figured that to be good news. The further she could knock them off
their plan, the more likely she'd force a mistake.

Best she could tell, they'd been planning an extended camping
trip. The van was loaded down with sleeping bags, lanterns, lamp
oil, and canned goods—everything they'd need to hide out from
civilization for weeks at a time, even with the approach of winter.
Even more interesting, they'd abandoned an arsenal of weapons:
three hunting rifles, a shotgun, and enough ammunition to invade
Mexico. Frankly, the weapons confused her. Should she be relieved
they hadn't taken them along, or concerned that there were even
more lethal weapons in the Donovans' possession?

Always better to err on the safe side. That's why the flyers on the
Donovans read "armed and extremely dangerous."

For a few minutes there—before Frankel's call—Irene felt certain she'd figured it all out. Clearly, the Donovans were experienced
woodsmen—a suspicion backed up by the magazines and literature
found in their trailer back in Phoenix—so she'd have bet a pretty
penny they'd be making a Von Trapp–style march over the moun-
taintops. In fact, she'd been in the process of mobilizing a search,
in cooperation with the U.S. Marshalls Service and the Park Service, when she got yanked away by her boss's hunch.

So how the hell did they get to Arkansas? Answer: they had help.
Paul could barely contain himself. He'd been first to suspect a connection with Harry Sinclair—the mystery man who'd yet to resur-
face—and sure as hell, it looked like he was right.

She closed her eyes against the din of the chopper and rested her
head against the bulkhead, trying to figure out if she'd done everything she needed to do. Why was it that she could never get ahead
of this case? Normally, investigations took on a rhythm, and once
you caught it, you could put together a plan to catch the bad guy.

Here she found herself arriving perpetually too late, only to find out that the Donovans continued to be slippery. This whole thing was taking on the bumbling quality of a Keystone Kops adventure. Assuming that Frankel was right—that the Donovans were in fact returning to the Newark site—then she could only assume they'd get in and out quickly.

But what do they have to gain by going back there?

She ran through the details of the case, ticking them off one at a time, and couldn't think of a single one she'd missed. The Little Rock field office had agents en route to Newark, and she'd notified the local police chief—a guy named Lundsford—to keep an eye on the site. If the numbers she ran in her head were correct, it would be another hour and a half, two hours, before any feds got on the scene out there, which made her exceptionally dependent on the abilities of the local cops. Remembering the bumbling antics of Sherwood and his crew back in Phoenix, the thought brought her little comfort.

Officially, the Newark Hazardous Waste Site was only about a hundred acres in area. Unofficially, the site extended to virtually all 75,000 acres. Some addresses just didn't lend themselves to corporate business cards. Of the few companies remaining in the business park, all were fly-by-nighters, representing new technologies in an industry known to vaporize inventors right along with their mistakes.

For Jake, it was like reentering a nightmare. Everything was close to the way he remembered it, but nothing was exact. Areas that had been so carefully cleared during the park's boom years had largely been reclaimed by the aggressive Arkansas undergrowth. Entire buildings had been swallowed up by field grasses, roads erupted by surging tree roots.

The big Cadillac looked comically out of place, dodging potholes and throwing gravel on its way toward the middle southwest section of the park. On this trip, the protective gear took priority over passenger comfort, forcing everyone but the driver—Nick—

to sit at impossible angles and hang on for dear life to keep from getting launched through the roof or crushed by a falling box.

"You sure you know where you're going?" Carolyn asked hesitantly.

"As sure as I can be." Nick shouted to be heard over the clatter of shifting equipment. "I studied the site maps pretty closely while I was waiting for you guys to arrive. So far, everything looks as it should."

"How much longer?" Travis wanted to know. His voice sounded strained against the weight of the breathing apparatus boxes.

Nick shrugged. "Two minutes maybe? Ten? No way to be sure."

Actually, it was four. The access road dead-ended at a chain-link fence, which stretched left to right in front of them for as far as they could see. Every few feet, at shoulder height, red-and-white signs had been posted on the fence, reading:

DANGER

HAZARDOUS WASTE SITE

UNAUTHORIZED ENTRY LIKELY TO CAUSE DEATH

DANGER

"We're here," Nick said simply. He made a sweeping motion with his arm, the latex gloves making his hands look oddly artificial. If there was one stupid mistake he didn't need to make, it was to leave fingerprints.

No one replied for a long moment as they took in the message from the sign. Carolyn grasped her son's hand and squeezed.

"I'd feel a lot better if that guy Thorne was here," Travis grumbled. The stinging no-confidence vote drew a look from Jake, but Travis held his ground. "No offense."

Jake let it go.

"So what do we do now?" Carolyn asked. "We can't drag this equipment a mile into the woods."

"There's a gate right here on the fence," Travis observed.

Nick shook his head. "No, they've got an alarm on the gate. We need to snip our way through."

Jake twisted his face incredulously. "They alarm the gate, but nothing happens if you cut the chain-link?"

Nick laughed. "Who in their right mind would want to break in, Jake? It's not like there's anything to steal, you know. The alarm just makes sure that the gate gets locked back up in case somebody has to come in to do something."

Amid the pile of equipment sent ahead by Harry Sinclair's New Jersey connections were two long-handled bolt cutters, which made quick work of what people with right minds purportedly would never do. When they were finished, the hole was just barely big enough for the car.

Jake winced at the sound of metal dragging along the paint.

Once through the hole, Nick steered the car back onto the roadway, which continued on the other side of the gate. Half a mile later, as advertised, they arrived at another fence and another gate. Nick threw the transmission into park and turned in his seat to face the rest. "Here we are," he announced. "Just your garden-variety certified hazardous waste exclusion zone."

"We're in the middle of the woods," Travis objected. "I thought there were supposed to be a bunch of storage buildings."

"Look again," Carolyn told him, pointing. "They're here. They're just overgrown."

At its heyday, this part of Arkansas had been mowed flat, turned into a grassy flatland extending from horizon to horizon; perfectly level but for endless rows of storage magazines which arose from the ground like so many swells in a grassy green sea. From the air, back then, the place would have looked like a mogul field on a ski slope, only green; and constructed at intervals that were far too precise and with lines too straight to have been a random creation of nature.

Today, from the ground, this part of the facility was so overgrown that nature had camouflaged everything. Trees now grew where roadways used to be, and thick undergrowth—kudzu, mainly, cohabitating with countless other varieties of the region's most hearty bushes, vines, and creepers—had long ago choked out any ground cover as fragile as grass. To the casual observer, these woods might have been around since the beginning of time, untouched by any human. On closer examination, though, beyond the thick tapestry of leaves and the random angles of the foliage, the repeating pattern of the land became obvious, rising and falling at precisely the same height and precisely the same interval. Like staring at one of those computer-generated 3-D art creations, the longer Travis examined his surroundings, the more the place began to look like the explosives storage facility it once had been.

The image solidified in his mind the instant he saw the first of the concrete-filled steel blast doors, set back in an overgrown tunnel, precisely in the center of one of the earthen mounds. Having seen one, it became easy to see others; dozens of them just by pivoting his head.

"Whoa," he breathed, his tone alive with wonderment. "This place is unreal."

"Are we safe, Nick?" Carolyn asked.

Nick's head bounced noncommittally. "Well, I wouldn't want to build my dream house here, but it should be pretty safe, yeah. Certainly for the short time we'll be around." He opened the door and stepped out. The others followed as he walked up to the fence and cut a hole big enough for people to pass through. That done, they all climbed to the crest of the nearest mound. "See there?" Nick asked when he got to the top. They all followed his finger. Two rows away, they could just make out a brownish black stain against the bright, fall-colored foliage. "That's where we're going," he said.

"God Almighty," Jake said, clearly overwhelmed. "It's a moonscape."

"Pretty close," Nick agreed. "Won't get much to grow there for the next hundred years." He looked first to Carolyn and then to Jake. "Ready to rock and roll?"

"Um, guys?" Travis said, an odd look on his face. "I—I don't know how to work any of the equipment."

Jake smiled and rumpled the boy's hair as he descended the steep hill. "That's good," he said. "Because you're staying here."

"I am not!"

Jake stopped midway and made his smile disappear. "It's not because you're not good enough, Travis, or not smart enough or not strong enough. It's because we only have three sets of gear. You need to stay back and keep an eye out for the security people. If you hear anything, you've got to let us know."

Travis looked for a moment as if he might argue but ultimately said nothing, choosing instead to help unload the car.

Deputy Sheriff Sherman Quill mumbled audibly to himself as he pulled his nightstick out of his Sam Browne belt and slid it into its spot next to the driver's seat. *I hate going out to this place.*

Ever since he joined the force, Newark Industrial Park had been the bane of his existence. Every time he turned around, there was some fucking thing going on out there, and with only the two of them in the department, he handled fully fifty percent of the calls. For some unfathomable reason, the local teenagers—local, hell, he'd arrested them from as far away as Little Rock—found it to be a romantic spot.

To date, no one had been stupid enough actually to climb the fence to fuck, but they'd come damn close, giving themselves away by jiggling the lock on the gates. But for the coils of razor wire along the top of the fence, he had little doubt that people would be scaling the thing every damn day. Crazy kids.

Now he was on his way to "check the place out," whatever the hell that meant. Apparently, some hotshot FBI lady had called the chief and told him to expect some kind of trouble out there. If Sherman had heard correctly—and he must have, else why would the chief have said it twice?—the same people who started it all way back when were returning to do it again.

"Don't make no sense," he grumbled, putting his ten-year-old Ford in reverse. "Ain't nothin' left out there to burn, for God's sake."

Damned entertaining thought, though, getting his hands on the son of a bitches who squeezed all the life out of this town. Sherman's family had come from these parts for generations; even stuck around during the bad times in the sixties, when Sherman himself was coming up as a teenager. People used to stick around, because sticking around was the thing to do. Now the kids were flying out of Newark as soon as their wings were big enough to support them. The luckier ones got to go to college somewhere and then get decent jobs. For the others—folks like Sherman, who struggled through high school with just enough Cs and Ds to warrant a diploma—it was damned difficult to find something that paid enough money to keep food on the table. As it was, downtown Newark had all but closed up. Places like the health clinic stayed open just because the state said they had to. God knows they had enough business to go around, just none of their patients had any money to pay their bills with.

Goddamned sad state of affairs is what it was. If Sherman could get his hands around those punks who made the whole world afraid of his hometown, then that just might be the best present anyone had ever given him.

One of the funny things about all this hazardous waste stuff was, no matter how much you rationalized the problem away in your head, and no matter how hard you listened to all those suit-and-tie experts the EPA sent out to tell you just how safe every-thing was, it was tough not to listen to the rest of the world. When everybody thought of Newark, Arkansas, in the same light as Love Canal or Chernobyl, it was hard to stand up as a resident and say, "No, no. My home is safe!" The instinct was to listen to what the other people had to say. The instinct was to avoid the place like the plague.

Which was why Sherman hated going out there so much. He'd signed on as a cop eighteen years ago to deal with crime and crim-inals. God knew they could be dangerous; especially on Friday and Saturday nights when the knife and gun clubs got together after an evening of drinking and hollering. But the biggest and the baddest guys he'd ever run into on the street were visible, living creatures. Well, the winners were living, anyway, and the losers didn't pose a hazard to anybody. Out there at Ground Zero, the worst hazards were invisible.

The suits from the EPA were very clear about that. The chemi-cals that were spilled out there were mostly odorless and tasteless, and the ones that weren't were so toxic that by the time you smelled them, you were already poisoned. They'd say this stuff, and then in the next breath, they'd tell Sherman and his neighbors that they were perfectly safe where they remained. How stupid did the government think they were, anyway?

What Sherman wanted to know was, how the hell could they be so sure that there was nothing wrong if there was no way to know the hazard was there in the first place? That just didn't make any sense.

So what did the EPA do to protect the community? They built a damn fence. They start with a hazard that nobody can detect, and then they try to throw a fence around it! Like the germs or the atoms or whatever the hell you called those toxic little monsters were afraid to cross a line drawn in the dirt. Who was kidding who here?

Sherman was no scientist; far from it, and he'd be the first to admit it. But he knew goddamn well that things that were invisible weren't going to stop at any fence line. They were going to get picked up by air currents, and they were going to be spread all over hell's half-acre, poisoning everything and everyone they came in contact with. Unless the government had come up with some special kind of force field that they hadn't told anybody about, and if they'd done something like that, why wouldn't they have said?

No, sir, a fence was just a fence, nothing more. It wasn't designed to keep out anything but people and animals.

Which made him reflect that, after fifteen years of inbreeding, some mighty scrawny, mighty strange-looking deer lived inside those fences. Sherman and his buddies—avid hunters all of them—had talked about that a lot over the years. One of these days, Sherman liked to say, one of them deer was going to talk back to him, and when that happened, he was leaving town for good.

God *damn* he hated this part of the job.

CHAPTER THIRTY

Clayton Albricht's closest staffers had redubbed his office the War Room. The place was bedlam as a dozen people manned fifteen phone lines, all in a united effort to save their boss's ass.

Everyone agreed early on that staying at home and running damage control from there was exactly the wrong image for the senator to project. Illinois's ship of state needed to look strong and steady, even as the hull leaked water by the tankerful.

Better late than never, Clayton started his day around two that afternoon. He had smiled politely and waved to the sea of reporters and cameramen as he backed his Oldsmobile out of the garage, but he refused to entertain any questions. "I'm running late," he mouthed through the glass. Man of the people that he was, the senator drove himself, alone in his car, while his chief of staff, Chris MacDonald, and his press secretary, Julie Baker, sneaked out the back door to drive separately in the cars they'd stashed a block away.

The media motorcade was something to behold. On the drive in to Capitol Hill from his home in McLean, Virginia, Clayton felt genuine concern for the other drivers on the road. The news vans

were so intent on photographing his every move that they'd forgotten some of the most basic principles of right-of-way. Entering
the Beltway, in fact, an NBC truck very nearly lost a game of
chicken to an eighteen-wheeler hauling gasoline. In the interest of
public safety, the senator turned on his flashers and slowed to an
unnatural fifty-five-miles-per-hour pace, thus allowing the camera
crews to get their obligatory shots of him driving to work. He wore
his blandest committee-meeting face as he navigated the right-hand
lane, and tried not to think about just how much he needed to
sneeze. Under this kind of scrutiny, he didn't feel like providing
easy footage for *Saturday Night Live.*

The parking garage under the Russell Senate Office Building
proved to be the great equalizer. Security restrictions prohibited
the cameramen and reporters from following him to his parking
space, so, for a few minutes, he was alone again to collect his
thoughts, absorbing the peace of the silent vehicle. This story was
barely a day old, and already it was spinning out of control.

Clayton sighed. It was going to be a very trying couple of weeks.

The elevator ride wasn't nearly long enough to suit him. By the
time the polished wooden doors opened onto the marble hallway,
the knot of reporters had re-formed, and they followed him all the
way to his outer office, where Julie Baker had already arranged to
have coffee and snacks brought in as appetizers for the vultures.

Finally, as he reached for the handle to his private office, Clayton turned and faced his pursuers for the first time. "Ladies and
gentlemen," he began, the softness of his tone forcing everyone else
to fall silent, "the stories printed this morning in the *Washington Post*
are entirely false. I have my suspicions as to what might have
prompted such vicious attacks on me, but until I have more details,
I truly have no more to tell you. The moment I have those details,
you'll be the first to know. Thank you very much."

The room exploded with questions, but he just turned and disappeared through the door. The center of activity seemed to be the
conference room at the end of the inner hallway to his left, so he
headed that way. Activity in the War Room ceased as the door
opened, and Clayton beckoned with two fingers for Chris Mac-

Donald to follow him. Activity resumed the instant the senator turned his back to the room.

"Good morning, Senator," Veronica said as Clayton entered her office on his way to his own. Under the circumstances of the day, she seemed far too chipper, but Clayton didn't mind a bit. Part of her job was to remain optimistic, even when everyone else's mood was in the sewer.

"Thanks, Ronni." Clayton accepted the cup of coffee she'd prepared for him, and allowed her to help him off with his car coat. "How are you holding up?"

Veronica made a snarling noise and curled her lip, digging deep furrows into the already wrinkled skin around her mouth. "Those reporters make me so mad," she fumed. "Sometimes I wish somebody would just blow every newspaper to kingdom come!"

Clayton smiled. "You know, Ronni, I've shared that very thought more than once this morning."

"I'll buy the explosives," Chris MacDonald chimed in, filling the doorway on his boss's heels. At fifty, Chris was the baby of the room; and at six-three, he was the tallest by six inches.

"This is where we really hope that the office isn't bugged," Clayton grumped. He led Chris into the inner office and closed the door behind them.

Without invitation—he didn't need one after all these years—Chris took his assigned seat in the leather chair in front of Clayton's desk. By now, he swore that the seat bore his buttprint. In the midst of chaos, Chris remained forever unflappable. And as a twenty-five-year veteran of Senator Albricht's political wars, Chris MacDonald was exactly the right man to have on your side in a crisis. Clayton knew it, and so did Chris.

"Let me have it," Albricht opened. He knew from his chief of staff's body language alone that the day had yet to bring its first bit of good news.

Chris opened the leather binder on his lap, exposing a rat's nest of papers and chicken scratchings. "It's just getting uglier, sir," he said evenly. "The distinguished gentleman from Arizona has called for your resignation from the chamber floor."

"Oh, now *there's* a surprise," Clayton scoffed, lowering himself into his high-back leather chair.

Chris produced a pair of drugstore-issue half-glasses from his suitcoat pocket and flicked them open with a jerk. He settled the white plastic monstrosities just so on his nose, then read from the transcript. "'So loathsome are pedophiles to the American people that the mere accusation of such deviancy lessens a legislator's ability to govern . . .'"

"Oh, Christ!" Clayton boomed. "This from a man who's fucked every pretty young thing on the Hill!"

Chris continued without breaking stride. "'. . . I'd like to believe that for the sake of not only his own reputation but that of this esteemed chamber, the senator from Illinois would have the common decency to step down and save us all the embarrassment of his inevitable fall.'" He looked up. "God, how that man does ramble!"

Albricht shook his head. "I don't suppose he mentioned the billions he's stolen from the taxpayers just to keep those useless Army bases open in his home state, did he?"

Chris smiled and pretended to search through his stack. "No, I don't remember seeing anything to that effect."

A moment of silence passed between them. Typically, Chris ended up being the de facto leader of these thrice-daily briefing sessions, but under today's circumstances, he felt that the senator should set the agenda.

Finally, Clayton began with a deep sigh. "Anyone from our side of the aisle weighed in yet to help?"

He already knew the answer, and Chris replied only with a look. As the feeding frenzy grew geometrically by the hour, both in size and in ardor, Albricht understood that his colleagues would pull away from him. He already felt it happening. The media had convicted him as the worst type of criminal, and try as they might to retain an open mind, the general public believed what the media told them. Some crimes—or even rumors of some crimes—were simply unforgivable to the average American, and a smart politician

would never provide such low-hanging fruit for his political enemies as to be seen within fifty feet of a man who fucks boys.

The more Clayton proclaimed his innocence, the more defensive
he looked, and everybody knew that only guilty people were ever
defensive.

Good God, Frankel was good. However he'd managed to put this
all together, he'd done a masterful job. But there was time. Clayton's
constituents wouldn't really have to get involved in any of this for
another five years. Fortunately, rhetoric alone didn't seem to do permanent damage anymore—a fact proved every day by the lying sack
of shit who currently owned the White House. It was all about the
length of a story's legs. When the media got bored, the public forgot. And there, the president and his friends had the advantage of
leading the media's preferred party. Still, Clayton couldn't imagine
how the story could stay active for another five years. Certainly, his
future opponents would dredge it back up, but by then, the voters'
passions would have dimmed.

"I want Frankel's head," Clayton announced.

Chris arched his eyebrows high. "You mean, you're still gonna
fight him for the directorship?" Politically, there was only one right
answer here, and it involved the consumption of a pound of crow.

The senator scowled and blew a puff of air through his lips.
"Fuck the directorship. I don't give a shit about that. I'll hang the
son of a bitch with his directorship. The higher he climbs, the bigger the grease spot will be when he hits bottom."

Chris suppressed a smile. His boss's colorful imagery was the
single attribute that had made the most popular politician in Illinois the most hated man in Washington. "Do I hear a plan brew-
ing here, or are you just dreaming?"

Clayton leaned forward in his chair and planted his elbows on
the mirrored mahogany of his desk. "That son of a bitch broke the
law, goddammit, and he did it with specific intent of hurting me
and my family. For the second time, I might add. I want to find a
way to ruin him, Chris, and when I'm done, I want the public clamoring for body parts!"

Chris's eyes narrowed. "What are you suggesting, sir?"

Albricht seemed startled by Chris's tone. "Don't look at me like that. I'm not suggesting anything illegal. Well, certainly not as illegal as what he tried to pull on me."

MacDonald scowled and fell silent. As he shifted in his chair, he closed the leather binder. "Senator," he said carefully, "I know how upsetting all of this is, but you've got to remember who exactly we're dealing with here. This is no minor political rival, sir. This is the FB-fuckin'-I. And he's got the full support of the president of the United States. You're the one presumed guilty here. If they so much as sense that you're jiggling the web they've worked so hard to spin, they'll slap you with a felony. The country loves Frankel, and they've shown an unending willingness to believe that grass is pink if the president declares it to be so."

Albricht completed the logic for him. "And everyone outside the Midwest thinks I'm Adolf Hitler."

Chris shrugged. "Well, you *do* want to kill off all those children and old people."

"Don't start with me." Clayton's forefinger threatened, but his wry smile was genuine. "So what do you suggest, Chris? Just sit and do nothing?"

MacDonald shrugged. "Well . . . yes. Politically, I think that's the best course. If you let it go, Frankel gets his big chair, and all the rest of this just runs its course and dies. In five years, if you still want this thankless fucking job, you'll still have an even shot with the voters."

Albricht leaned back again and spun his chair around to face the Capitol. He considered his chief of staff's advice carefully, then spun slowly back around to face him. "To hell with the political prudence. I'm older than fossil shit as it is. Last time Frankel had me in his sights, I just let him go. I took the politically expedient route, and now the cockroach has come back to infest me again. This time it's personal, Chris."

Chris shook his head and closed his eyes. "I won't do that, Senator, and it's not appropriate for you to ask. I will not . . ."

"For crying out loud, Chris, will you *relax*? I'm not suggesting that anyone break any laws, okay? I don't even want to stretch them a little. Just get people working on Frankel's background. In a perfect world, I'd have accumulated a ton of shit on him and fucked him on the witness stand during the confirmation hearing, but now that's not going to happen. *C'est la vie.* Frankel's still got enemies stashed all over the country, though, and I want you and your people to get to know every one of them."

"Under what auspices?"

Albricht shrugged. "I don't care. Keep it all unofficial. Just find the people who hate him, and take lots and lots of notes. Sooner or later, we'll have enough to choke him."

Chris opened the binder again and scribbled a few notes. "And how do you want to fund it?" he said, looking up.

The glare he got in return said, *Give me a break.*

"Gotcha." Chris stood. "And as for the media?"

Albricht frowned. "Tell Julie to keep 'em well fed."

His orders clear, Chris MacDonald rose from his form-fitting chair and left Albricht's office, closing the door behind him.

Alone again in the quiet, the senator spun his chair one more time to take in his favorite view. Chris's worries were all legitimate ones, and bombast aside, Clayton worried about continued retaliation from Frankel. Those pictures that Wiggins alluded to on the telephone scared the hell out of him. God only knew what hideous poses they'd attach his face to.

Much was at stake here. Truth be told, Clayton didn't give much of a shit anymore about his future in the Senate—he'd had a nice run, after all—but he cared a great deal about how the history books would record his tenure here.

The hell of it was, by actually caring about such things, people like Clayton Albricht were easy prey for the political predators of Washington.

Clayton Albricht had staked his career on middle-class morality, and it had cost him dearly. While his colleagues lied without remorse, he prided himself on his ability to hold the high ground of wisdom over the sewer of political correctness. Now, as he stood on the precipice—yet another hero ready to tumble—his innocence and his sense of fair play had become his greatest weakness, while his opposition grew stronger through a campaign of perpetual deceit.

Maybe it really was time to retire. He didn't much like the way the earth had been spinning recently, anyway. But he couldn't let Frankel go without a fight. If he did, then where would all of this stop? Maybe *that* was Albricht's legacy. Perhaps, at the end of the day, the senator's lifetime of legislative battles would be obscured by this one fight by the Good Guy to prevail over the Bad Guy. The white hat against the black hat, just like in the old movies of his youth.

Maybe, when the battle was over, Pretty Boy would learn that he'd gambled too aggressively on the public's willingness to believe sparkling blue eyes over the wizened countenance of a wrinkled old man.

However it might ultimately turn out, this was certainly a time to be careful. MacDonald had been right about the screams of misconduct and abuse of power if Clayton assigned his own staffers to dig up the dirt on Frankel. He needed help from someone else . . .

The inspiration hit him with a near-physical impact. Why he hadn't thought of it hours ago, he'd never understand. The time had come for some good old-fashioned Chicago-style politics.

And he knew of no better player at that particular game than his old friend Harry Sinclair. Forgoing the usual formalities, Clayton dialed the number himself.

CHAPTER THIRTY-ONE

A body bag with a window.

Jake had forgotten about the special breed of panic that rushed over him every time he sealed himself inside one of these damn suits. The world seemed very small when the only sound you heard was that of your own breathing. He checked to make sure he could reach his escape knife and found himself smiling. Not only could he cut his way out if he had to, but with the Glock still on his hip, he could shoot his way out as well.

Typical of training equipment, he supposed, this stuff was old yet functional. Prior to donning the ensembles, Carolyn had insisted that they perform perfunctory tightness-testing by flapping out the folds, much the way you'd shake out a rug, then laying them out on the ground. Once the folds had relaxed, and air entered the body, arms, and legs of the suits, they zipped them shut and rolled the legs up tight, forming a balloon of air in the upper part. With no obvious leakage, Carolyn proclaimed them safe to wear.

His air pack on his back, and his face mask in place, Jake wrestled himself into the body of the suit and awaited Travis's help to zip it up around him. As the hood settled over his head, Jake re-

membered with a dull ache in his gut that the last time he'd looked
through a similar Plexiglas face shield, it had a ragged bullet hole
through the center of it.

No one said anything. It had been a lot of years, but Jake remembered from the old days that this was the time of smart-ass
machismo, practical jokes, and snide comments. Now the under-
current of fear was palpable.

I just hope we're not chasing wild geese, Jake thought. If this didn't
work, they were flat out of options.

When all the players were at the same stage of readiness, Travis
stepped up to each of them in turn and pulled the heavy zippers
shut; first Nick, then Jake, and finally Carolyn, where he paused for
a long moment and said something to her that Jake couldn't hear.
The comment drew an extended embrace between the two of
them, and for just the briefest of instants, he was jealous. Somehow, as adolescence approached, Mom was becoming more important to his son than Dad; and he knew in his heart that it was likely
to remain that way forever. The realization triggered a catch in his
throat and blurred his vision, but he shook the emotion away. This
was neither the time nor the place.

When Carolyn was at last sealed into her Army-green butyl rubber suit, she initiated a round of thumbs-ups. Radios were not a
part of this bare-bones entry operation, but they'd developed a system of simple hand signals to convey essential messages, the most
critical of which was the universal distress signal—both hands
straight up in the air. Even in the old days, no one fucked around
with that one. You raise your hands over your head, and you'd better by God be in serious trouble, because people were going to risk
their lives to get you to safety super-pronto.

Nick paused long enough to duct-tape the combustible gas indicator to the sleeve of his suit before picking up the sledgehammer and leading the way forward. As unlikely as it was to
encounter a combustible atmosphere, fire was the single hazard for
which these rubber suits provided exactly zero protection. If the
detector vibrated against his arm, they would abort the entry and
decide what to do about it later. Each of them slung portable hand

lights over their shoulders, and Jake hefted the steel pry bar, while Carolyn took custody of the body bags.

Thumbs-up all around, and it was time to head out. They'd already breathed up five minutes' worth of precious air, and already their suits had begun to puff out from the pressure of their exhaled breath. Pretty soon they'd all look like the Stay-Puffed Marshmallow Man from *Ghostbusters*—one of Travis's favorite movies.

Jake shivered as the first drops of sweat blazed a trail down his backbone, despite the chill of the afternoon air. Inside of five minutes, he'd be soaked, with puddles of sweat accumulating in the tips of his gloves and the soles of his shoes. As he trudged off after the others, last in line, he paused for a moment to look back at Travis, who suddenly looked impossibly small standing there amid the empty boxes. Jake ventured a wave, but his son turned away.

"Well, I'll be damned," Sherman Quill said aloud as he nosed his police cruiser up to the main gate of the Newark site. Of all the times he'd been out to this godforsaken place, this was the first time he'd ever seen anything out of the ordinary, beyond the occasional teenagers locked in carnal ecstasy. Well, there was a first time for everything, wasn't there?

Somebody had cut a hole in the damn fence! And he could still see the tire tracks in the grass where they'd driven through the opening and down toward the exclusion zone.

What to do now, he wondered. The hole in the chain-link was nowhere near big enough for his full-size Ford with its light bar and whip antenna, and Sherman didn't have the tools with him to make it any bigger.

He pulled the white microphone from its clip and brought it to his lips. "Unit One to Control," he said in his practiced monotone.

"Go ahead, Unit One," the dispatcher replied.

"Hi, Nan. Listen, I'm out at the Newark site and we've got a bit of a problem here. Somebody cut a big old hole right through the fence. I'm gonna check it out, but I want you to see about getting some backup for me from State P.D., okay?"

"Okay, Sherm," Nan replied. In a town this size, formal radio procedure just seemed silly. "You gonna wait there till I check on availability?"

Sherman thought about that one for a moment. Wasn't a bad idea, actually, but he'd hate like hell to lose the bad guys if he waited, just as he hated the thought of scrambling the state boys only to find nothing there. "No," he answered at length. "I'm gonna go take a look-see while you call. I'll give you a shout on the portable if I need anything."

"You got it, Sherm." He could hear Nan dialing the telephone in the background while she spoke. "Be careful, guy."

Sherman smiled. Nan was the county grandmother. As dispatcher for both the police and the fire departments, she doubled as secretary and gofer for both.

"You got it," he said warmly. After returning the microphone back to its home on the dashboard, he climbed out of the cruiser, set his Smokey the Bear hat just so on his head, slid his nightstick into his belt, and slammed the door.

Travis watched intently from the top of the nearest mound as everyone disappeared from sight. He felt suddenly lonely. Without anyone around, the woods were way too quiet; and in the absence of noise, his ears played tricks on him. Every time he thought he heard a rustle in the leaves, it turned out to be the wind or maybe a squirrel. In his head, such noises were the telltale signs of approaching police with guns and dogs. So wild was his imagination, in fact, that he could have sworn he heard the sound of a car door being shut.

He knew the basics of the plan just from paying attention when no one thought he could hear. The trickiest part, according to his parents' friend Nick, would be to get through the heavy locks on the exterior of the magazine. He brought a thing he called a Dremel tool to do the job. It looked a lot like an electric screwdriver, but with a carbide disc at the end. He said it would cut the Golden Gate Bridge in half if you had enough time. Travis assumed that the sledgehammer and the pry bar were just backups in case the lock proved to be stronger than a bridge.

Once inside, they were going to put the body his dad kept talking about into a bag and cart it off someplace. After that, he didn't know what was supposed to happen. One thing was certain: Travis hated being out here by himself. The quicker they got it all done, the happier he was going to be.

Soon he felt relieved to hear the high-pitched whine of the little saw coming from the direction where they all disappeared. At least they were getting down to work. A few minutes later he heard the *tink-tink* of metal on metal, followed immediately by a metallic clatter, then silence. When no one reappeared after another minute or two, he concluded that Nick had been right about the lock and that they were inside doing whatever they had to do.

It'll just take a couple of minutes.

Those had been his dad's words back in the skanky trailer in West Virginia. When his mom kept rejecting the plan, Dad had assured her that it would "only take a few minutes." A few meant three, right? "A couple" meant two, and "a few" meant three. Or four, he supposed; five on the outside. After that, people said "about ten" or "about fifteen." So five minutes, then.

Travis settled into the colorful undergrowth and leaned back against a tree. He could do anything for five minutes. This was almost over. He wasn't worried. Everything was going to be just fine.

What's that?

Some sounds can be mistaken for other sounds; he'd certainly learned that lesson this afternoon. But only a cop's radio sounded like a cop's radio, and Travis swore to God that's what he just heard. His blood turned to ice. He brought his legs up and leaned forward until he was on his hands and knees, and he peered intently through the bushes. Something was out there, all right. He could see him moving out in the distance, slithering carefully through the trees, trying his hardest to be silent.

There was the radio sound again, but this time much quieter, as if the man in the woods had turned the volume down.

"Oh, God," Travis whispered, his mind racing. "They got us."

☆   ☆   ☆

Despite the wedge of light which sliced across the interior of the concrete tomb, the darkness seemed impenetrable—a black hole so dense that even the white light of the afternoon sun couldn't cut through it. Jake felt like a grave robber, nagged by a superstitious fear of waking the dead. He looked behind himself one more time to get his bearings before entering, and as he did, his mind replayed the last time he took in this view. It was mostly concealed by smoke and flames back then, but right there was the spot—directly across on the first berm there—where the man with a rifle, dressed all in jungle camouflage, squeezed off round after round, killing his friends and damn near killing him. He looked away, realizing that the memories of the past were far more frightening than the reality of the present.

They played their lantern beams through the blackness, revealing thousands of square feet of nothingness. The twisted remains of melted steel shelving rose from the concrete floor, standing guard above countless black lumps of charred, spent munitions. Remarkably, the skeletons of old wooden crates could still be seen among the ruins, somehow preserved by a quirk of physics that spared them from total annihilation by the white-hot fires.

As the entry team moved cautiously beyond the doorway and in toward the center of the ruin, their movements stirred dust devils of poisonous soot, which rose lazily from every surface to float in the air, creating a kind of dirty black fog.

They moved to the left, following Jake's lead. He and Carolyn had gone right on that day in 1983, and he remembered seeing the members of Entry Bravo—*My God, could I have forgotten their names already?*—waving their lights over their heads. That had been way off to his left. But was it past the door? He tried to remember if Bravo was standing beyond the seam of light when they announced they'd found the body, but the image just wasn't there. Perhaps this was going to be more difficult than he'd thought.

The harder Jake tried to peer through the gathering cloud of soot, the more difficult it was to see anything. His light beam penetrated only a foot or two ahead before being consumed by the poisonous cloud. It was here, though. It had to be: the evidence that would give them back their lives. As the darkness enveloped him, he stifled surging panic, keeping his mind on track by counting his breaths.

In and out, Jake, old buddy. One breath every five seconds. Twelve per minute. Seven-twenty per hour . . .

He nearly shit his pants when someone tugged on his arm. It was Carolyn. He could tell by her height. And she was pointing with her light beam to something on the floor. He had to stoop low to see what it was, and when he saw it, he gasped. It was a boot; the same type worn by every Enviro-Kleen entry team member, and in remarkably pristine condition. Closer examination revealed that it was still connected to the leg of a moon suit. He followed the lines along the floor with his light, over a bend that had to be a knee joint, past a waistline, and finally up to the hood. He touched nothing, and closed his eyes as he shone his light through the blackened Plexiglas facepiece. When he opened them again, he felt relieved to see that the fire had rendered the facepiece opaque. Still, in his mind's eye, he could swear he saw the empty eye sockets of the corpse's skull staring back at him.

Jake looked away. But for somebody's poor aim, or perhaps his own incredible luck, that could have been him. Or Carolyn. He swallowed hard to sink the wave of nausea before it could rise to his throat.

"That's one," he said to himself aloud, even though no one could hear. Hearing a voice reassured him, even if it was his own. "Now, where's the original?" The temptation to recover his friends' remains was overwhelming, but he reminded himself that such was not their mission here.

The remains of two other Enviro-Kleen workers—the rest of Entry Bravo—lay within a couple of feet of the first. Jake took some measure of comfort from their positions in death. The fact that their suits remained melted here and there, but largely intact, told him that they hadn't burned to death (his most horrid of horrid nightmares), and the fact that they lay sprawled rather than curled up told him that they had not suffered too greatly. Even as he thought these things, he knew that his conclusions were flimsy, but he chose to believe them, anyway.

Nick was the one who found what they came looking for. Six feet, at the most, beyond the furthest moon-suit-shrouded corpse lay a scattered pile of smaller bones—the bones of a child, it appeared. The meat was long gone off this body, and without any protective covering, it was barely identifiable for what it was. But there was no mistaking the vertebral structures of the spine or the looping shape of the few remaining ribs.

Nick's wild gesticulations with his flashlight drew Jake over toward him, and as soon as he saw the bones, he knew that their journey had ended. Before he could motion for Carolyn, she was there, body bag in hand.

Not a religious man by nature, Jake offered up a quick prayer of apology, begging forgiveness for the desecration he was about to perform. Blessing himself with the sign of the cross—something he hadn't done in more years than he could remember—he set about the grisly business of loading a small child into a rubber bag.

CHAPTER THIRTY-TWO

The man stalking them was definitely a cop. Travis got a glimpse of the hat and the badge as he stepped out into a clearing. From the way the cop was moving, he hadn't seen them yet, but he sure seemed to know where he was going.

As panic grew in his belly, Travis looked over his shoulder to see if the grown-ups were on their way back yet. It had been a lot longer than five minutes.

Shit! What do I do?

His father's last words burned in his brain: "Your job is to wait out here and watch for anything unusual." He realized now that it was just a bullshit job, because he was up to his eyeballs in unusual, but he had no way to warn anybody.

Dammit!

The cop was getting closer with every step, and Travis's sitting there with his forehead scrunched in confusion wasn't helping anything. He had to get word to them. Maybe he could shout.

Good idea, idiot, Travis chastised himself. *Why don't you just stand up and wave a flag, too?*

Okay, shouting was a stupid idea. At least from here. Maybe if he got closer . . . close enough to see what was going on, anyway.

He rolled out of his current spot, staying low to keep from being seen on the ridgeline, and then he slid on his butt down the other side of the embankment. On the far side, he found himself on another road, just like the one where they were parked, and facing another magazine, identical to the one he'd just climbed. Running now, he dashed around the next mound, rather than over it, and he found himself suddenly in the midst of the moonscape. Nothing lived here. No grass grew; no plants. Even the dirt seemed dead. Across another road, maybe fifty yards away, stood the open maw of the burned-out magazine. If he used his imagination, he thought he could see movement inside, but no people.

He considered yelling again, but it was still too far away. *C'mon, Trav, think . . .*

He needed to move closer. He could think all day, and he'd still be too far away to yell without being heard by the cop. But what about the dust? Jesus, how many times did they have to say it? The dust here would kill him if he breathed it. At least that's what they *thought.* But he was breathing it now, wasn't he? And he was still okay. Maybe the stuff had all worn off or blown away, like Nick said might be the case. In any event, he could always hold his breath.

He glanced nervously over his shoulder again, thinking he heard the squawk of the radio. Okay, he'd hold his breath. If he got in and got out quickly, it wouldn't be a problem. What other choice did he have?

Pausing there at the margin where green and red and orange turned to flat black, he took in five or six deep breaths, hyperventilating himself the way he saw swimmers do it on television before a big race. He could do this.

On your mark . . . get set . . .

Who the hell would bring a car out here? As Sherman Quill drew closer, he saw not only the car—a Cadillac, no less—but a bunch of boxes and equipment strewn all about. It still made no sense to him, but one thing was clear: whatever was going on, and whoever had done this, they were still here, unless they'd left on foot.

Maybe that FBI lady had been right. Maybe the Donovan gang

had returned to finish what they'd started. In an era where crooks were stupid enough to rob banks using notes written on the backs of their own deposit slips, as had happened in Little Rock just a few weeks before, Sherman had come to put no limits on the extent of stupidity he could expect from a lawbreaker. No matter how clever their crime, sooner or later, it seemed, it was always something truly stupid that ultimately brought the perpetrator down. Like returning to the scene of the crime.

Resting his hand on the grip of his .38 Police Special, Sherman approached the Cadillac cautiously, peering in the windows and scanning the trees for any sign of movement. "Well, I *will* be damned," he muttered, lifting his portable radio out of his belt.

"Unit One to Control," he said. He listened carefully for a response but got nothing. Somebody broke squelch, but if there was a message, he couldn't hear it.

"Unit One to Control," he tried again. "Nan? Are you there?"

Again, nothing. Not surprising, really. These low-band radios were a pain in the ass once you got them into the woods. If he had his patrol car down here, with its five-watt mobile unit, there'd be no problem. He briefly considered the option of going back for it, just to call in a report, but decided that would be silly. He was here, and the bad guys were here. He might as well take a look at what they were doing.

The conscious realization of where he was hit him like a smack in the face. Sweet Jesus, he was in the middle of the most hazardous spot on earth!

"You are out of your cotton-pickin' mind," he mumbled. He looked back again, and he considered the mobile radio one more time.

Make this collar and they'll be calling you a hero, he told himself. He drew the .38 from its holster, then started his long walk toward the exclusion zone.

Travis's big breath took him as far as the doorway and then about ten feet farther. If his folks had been closer to the front, he'd have been able to dash in, grab one of them, and then dash out again. As it was, there was no way for him to make it. His lungs screamed for relief, and as he turned to head back toward the door, the breath just popped out of him in a giant rush. Then, before he could stop himself, his diaphragm rebounded and sucked in a huge lungful of air.

Travis winced, closing his eyes tightly in anticipation of death, but nothing happened. There was a lot of dust, and it tasted like shit, but he felt fine, other than the urge to sneeze. Even the sneeze tasted awful.

Carolyn didn't hear anything, actually; she sensed a noise she didn't recognize through the layers of protective clothing. She pivoted her body to get a reassuring glance at sunlight, and there was Travis, silhouetted against the brilliant white background.

She screamed, "Oh, my God, Travis, no!"

She dropped her flashlight and Jake's pry bar onto the concrete floor, the noise reverberating forever in the concrete canyon, and ran to her son.

"Get out of here!" she yelled. "Oh, my God, get out of here!" She ran to her baby, scooping him up on the fly and dragging him out toward fresh air. In the rush of adrenaline, he weighed nothing. "Hold your breath, honey!" she yelled. "Hold your breath!"

But Travis couldn't hear any of it. "Hey!" he yelled indignantly. "Put me down! There's a cop outside!" *Jesus, she's strong!*

Jake saw the commotion and put it together in an instant. He followed his family out into the open, running as best he could in the bulk of his protective suit to catch up. *What the hell was he doing inside?*

Carolyn had the boy over her shoulder in a kind of fireman's carry that was as awkward as it was effective. With him wriggling to break free the whole time, she carried him out of the hideous stain of the exclusion zone and into the world of living underbrush. From there, it was another twenty-five or thirty yards down a small decline to a stream they'd seen on the aerial photo. She heaved Travis like a sack of potatoes off her shoulder and into the swollen, quick-running stream.

Good idea, Jake thought. She was going to try and decon him. But it'd be tough going in her moon suit. Pulling his arm out of his sleeve, Jake fished around his pants pocket for his knife.

"Hey!" Travis yelled. "Listen to me! There's a—"

Suddenly, he found himself immersed in frigid water, with his own mother holding him under the surface. As he struggled to rise to the top, she stepped into the stream with him, straddling him with her legs and crushing his rib cage with her knees. He could breathe, but not without taking a mouthful of water.

"Mom! Jesus! What the—"

She pulled at his soaked clothing, and suddenly he found himself shirtless. He tried to fight her, but there was nothing he could do. She was a crazy woman. Every time he thought he had a grip on something, it would slip out of his hands. "Mom! Stop! Ow, you're hurt—"

Now he was upside down in the water, face submerged, and she was yanking on his pants. As he felt them slip down past his butt and on toward his knees, he tried to kick and squirm, but it was useless. His choice was to cooperate or drown.

A new pair of hands appeared out of nowhere and grabbed him under his arms. It was his dad, and he was in regular clothes again, but with the air pack still in place. "Hold still," he yelled, his voice muffled by the mask. "We've got to get your clothes off! You're contaminated."

With two against one, there was little choice but to cooperate. One last hard yank ripped the pant legs clear of his feet while nearly yanking his legs clear of his hips. Once his pants were off, the struggling stopped, and Travis realized to his horror that they'd stripped him of *all* his clothes. He was naked!

As Jake struggled out of his air pack, Travis scrambled to cover himself up.

"Stay away from those clothes!" Jake commanded.

"But Dad, there's a cop—"

The sound of a gunshot killed the words before they could form in the boy's throat.

CHAPTER THIRTY-THREE

Sherman was getting too old for this crap: walking through the woods, trying to sneak up on people. Who the hell did he think he was, anyway? If he were halfway as smart as he pretended to be, he'd have waited for the backup that had to be on the way by now. Nan wouldn't have wasted even a second getting the call in to the state boys. So why did he keep on going forward? Another damn good question. Personal glory, he supposed. Because this was *his* town, and if the Donovans were down there like he'd been led to believe, he stood in a position to get payback—to punish those bastards for sucking the life out of the place he'd always known as home.

His heart fluttered like a butterfly as each step brought him closer to death; if not at the hands of the Donovans, then at the whim of his own body as he inhaled the unknown dangers floating in the air. He heard noises ahead; man-made ones this time. The realization made his heart pound even harder.

Why the hell would anyone . . .

He heard a yell. The sound of a child in distress. Sherman quickened his pace—something else he hadn't done in a very long time—and he hurried across the last roadway separating him from the foul-smelling desolation of the exclusion zone. The best speed he could muster was a moderate jog, and the out-of-sync swinging of the equipment in his Sam Browne belt slowed him down even more.

He chose to scale the final mound rather than go around it, in hopes that the elevation would grant him an element of surprise. Sherman expended enormous effort scrambling up the steep slope, using his left hand to pull himself up while gripping his revolver in his right. It was tough going until he cleared the top of the giant doors, and then the slope eased a bit, allowing him to scramble the rest of the way more or less on his feet.

The view from the top took his breath away. The world here had changed; an entirely different place than what he knew Arkansas to look like. Everything was monochrome, like an ancient daguerreotype photo.

"Holy Mother of God," he muttered to himself. He heard more yelling, again sounding like a small child, but it was from somewhere off to his left. He moved to head in that direction, welcoming the opportunity to break his gaze from the desolation before him, but movement in the doorway to the magazine itself made him freeze. As he watched, a man dressed in one of the green suits with which he'd become so familiar, courtesy of media obsessiveness, slowly crossed the threshold, carrying a bag in his arms. He transported the bag with care, as if there was something fragile inside. The spaceman look-alike moved carefully but deliberately as he walked to the perimeter of the dead vegetation and placed the bag on the ground. Then out of the grass he lifted another body bag—this one having a fluorescent orange color, which contrasted sharply with the olive drab of the first—and proceeded to flap it open. That done, he placed the green bag inside the orange one, then zipped it up.

Sherman's mind reeled at the impossibility of what he was watching. When the spaceman stood and headed back inside, Sherman knew it was time for him to act. He stood among the bushes that lined the crest of the mound and assumed a shooter's stance.

"Police officer!" he yelled. "Don't move!" But the man didn't even slow his deliberate gait.

Shit. He can't hear me.

He tried it again. "Police officer! Don't move!" Still no response. The man just kept striding back inside to continue whatever his mission was.

That really left Sherman with no choice. He took aim and pulled the trigger.

Five minutes earlier Nick had suddenly realized that he was alone inside the magazine. One second the three of them were inspecting the bones they'd found, and the next, Jake and Carolyn had dropped their hand lights and disappeared, leaving him there by himself. He figured one of the two had developed a problem and that they'd headed out together. He was a bit miffed—it was *their* butts, after all, that he was helping pull out of the fire—but that part of himself that was task-oriented swung into gear and he focused on what needed to be done.

As he loaded the skeletal remains into the green body bag, he marveled at how small the bones were and at what kind of madman it would take to kill such a small child in the first place, only to wreak all of this destruction to cover it up. One fragment in particular grabbed his attention, and for a moment, he wasn't even sure it was a bone. He spent a moment examining it, then tossed it in with the others. Better safe than sorry.

He desperately hoped that Jake's hunch was right—that by identifying the remains, they might have a shot at bringing the real perpetrators to justice. If ever there was a person who needed to suffer the wrath of the law, it was the monster who did this.

After he'd picked up every bone he could find and placed them inside the bag, he found the zipper in the dark and pulled it closed. The feather lightness of the package made his eyes moist as he carried it toward the door, and as he stepped over the remains of one of his colleagues from so many years ago, he realized that in another two minutes or so, he'd be done with the announced reason for reentering the magazine.

Then it would be time to pursue his own agenda.

The second body bag in the grass outside was Nick's addition to the plan. He'd anticipated the acute dust hazard inside the magazine and the enormously high levels of contamination the bodies were likely to carry. By bagging the bag, as it were, the hazard posed by their package to whoever was going to do the pathology work would be greatly reduced. When the doctor finally opened the package, he'd need to practice the same precautions as he would if he were dealing with the victim of a viral infection.

The absence of plant life spooked Nick. He'd hoped that enough time had passed for Mother Nature to begin to mitigate damages in her own way. No that there weren't a few hopeful signs. He noticed, for example, the absence of dead animals. If the dirt and the vegetation were toxic, then any creature who walked in here should become incapacitated and die. Such was not the case. In fact, as he donned his protective clothing, he'd noticed several squirrels scampering about, busily preparing themselves for the fast-approaching winter.

As he neared the blast doors again, he thought he heard something. Shouting maybe? He glanced around the horizon quickly, then dismissed whatever it was as something he didn't need to worry about. Probably Jake and Carolyn.

When a chunk of concrete exploded out of the doorjamb, however, and he felt the concussion of a gunshot through the rubberized fabric of his suit, he jumped a foot and whirled around in a crouch. There at the perimeter of the exclusion zone, maybe twenty yards away, he saw a man in a cop's uniform aiming a gun straight at him. He saw the cop's mouth moving, but he couldn't hear any of the words. Not that words were important. The business end of a firearm came as close to universally understood communication as anything he could think of.

Nick froze where he stood, and slowly raised his hands.

Jake reacted instinctively to the sound of the gunshot, ripping the mask off his face with one hand while drawing the Glock with the other, bringing it to bear as he dropped to one knee. In the same motion, he threw a forearm into Travis's chest, knocking him to the ground and out of harm's way. Even as he hit him, he knew he'd done it too hard, driving a blast of air out of the boy's mouth. No time to worry about that now.

"Ow, Dad!" Travis gasped, bringing an angry glare from his father.

"Quiet!" Jake commanded. "Here." He fished through his pockets again for his knife, then tossed it to the boy. "Help your mother out of her suit."

"But my clothes—"

"Screw your clothes," Jake hissed. "Just do what I told you."

Jake's eyes had taken on that same look that Travis had seen in the school and in the car when they were stopped. It scared him. He remembered again that his father could be a very dangerous man when he was threatened. Dangerous to everyone.

While Travis struggled with the folding blade, Jake wriggled out of his air pack harness and started inching his way up the incline, back toward the source of the shot. Maybe sixty yards separated him from the action, and it looked bad. He watched as a clearly agitated cop shouted commands to Nick, who just stood there, his hands in the air, doubtless unable to hear a thing the cop said to him.

"Shit!" Jake hissed. *What do we do now?* If push came to shove, he was a good enough shot to drop the cop at this distance, but that didn't seem like much of an option. Killing a police officer would render the rest of this exercise moot. If he murdered a cop, no one would give a damn that he hadn't killed the others.

By all appearances, the encounter had played itself to a standoff, as each player tried to figure out how to communicate with the other. For a shamefully long moment, Jake considered just leaving Nick there.

Family first, everything else second.

If Jake just guided Carolyn and Travis around the near side of the mound closest to them, they'd be able to make it all the way back to the Cadillac without the cop seeing or hearing a thing. Once at the car, they'd have a decent shot at getting out alive.

And forever after, you'd have to live with the burden of having sold out a friend. Suddenly, this had all become too complicated. He pushed himself up from the ground and moved to circle around the mound when the characteristic sound of ripping fabric momentarily diverted his attention back toward the creek bed. Carolyn was cutting herself out of her suit, with Travis's able, if somewhat hesitant, assistance. The boy was having a hard time getting much done with one hand covering his genitalia. Jake considered yelling at him but dismissed it all as irrelevant. Typical of a kid, modesty took precedence over everything.

Jake had work to do. He darted out of sight as quietly as possible, hoping to double back and come in behind the cop. "Just don't shoot yet," he mumbled, an indirect prayer for Nick's safety.

Once around to the front of the magazine opposite the exclusion zone, Jake ran full speed down the road to get to the other side of the mound. Last time he saw the cop, he was halfway down the other side of the berm, carefully avoiding the line where life stopped and contamination began. Jake's best approach, then, would be directly over the top. Judging from the displaced leaves and broken branches, it was the same route the cop had followed just moments before.

Jake scaled the hill easily, holstering the Glock until his footing was secure. Once near the top, he drew the weapon again and peeked over the crest, trying his best to stay hidden in the undergrowth. As he rose up to look, he realized with a rush that this was the exact spot where the sniper had made his perch fourteen years before. For the millionth time since that awful day, Jake's mind once again replayed the image of the man in camouflage, blasting at them randomly as they struggled to get out of the way of the giant smoke plume.

His thoughts tried to transport him back to that day, but he forced himself to stay in the present. He had some critical tasks to take care of right here. Without standing all the way up and exposing himself fully, all he could see of the cop at this angle was the back of the deputy's head and his shoulders. An easy kill shot, but he still didn't want to go there.

Honest, Judge, I had to blast him while he wasn't looking. Not likely.

If he tried to rush the cop, he'd no doubt hear the approach, and even though they were separated by only twenty feet, that was plenty of time for the cop to turn and fire. Similarly, if Jake just yelled for him to drop his weapon, he'd probably turn and draw down anyway, sparking a lethal exchange of gunfire, which, under the circumstances, Jake would probably win, but the result would once again be a dead cop. Back to square one.

Shit. Shit. Shit.

Then he got an idea.

"Federal officers!" Jake yelled, invoking the words and tone he'd heard in the body shop just three days before. "Don't move!"

The cop jumped at the sound of the voice and started to turn.

Jake fired a shot in the air. "I said don't move, goddammit! Now, drop your weapon!"

"But I'm a cop!" Sherman protested, once again starting to turn.

"And I'm the fucking tooth fairy!" Jake screamed. "Now, drop that weapon or I'll blow your fucking head off!"

"But I'm—"

"Now!!"

Sherman's shoulders sagged, and he shook his head as he opened his hand and let the pistol fall to the ground.

"That's a good boy," Jake coaxed, hoping he wasn't laying it on too thick. "Okay, now put your hands behind your head and interlace your fingers."

Sherman complied but bitched like an old rooster. "I'm a cop, goddammit! The bad guy's down there—"

"Shut up and listen," Jake interrupted. "I want you to step away from the weapon, back up the hill toward me." Again, the cop did as he was told, at which point, Jake was lost. He had no idea what he was going to do next. He truly didn't want to hurt the guy, but he didn't know what else . . .

"I've got him, Jake. You go ahead and cuff him." Carolyn's voice came from behind him and to his left, and she had her .380 in her trembling hand.

Sherman cocked his head at the sound of the new voice. "Jake?" he gasped. His shoulders sagged even further. "Jesus Christ."

Jake smiled as he holstered the Glock and moved cautiously toward the neutralized threat. "I'm afraid so, Deputy," he said. "You've been had. Now, the good news is, you're alive. Do what I tell you, and you'll remain that way. Just don't screw with me, okay?" The cop had no way of knowing that Carolyn could no more shoot a man than she could flap her arms and fly.

Sherman was a beaten man. He followed directions, but with his head bowed in shame. "How could I be so stupid?" he chided himself.

Jake didn't say anything as he pulled the handcuffs out of their holster in Sherman's belt. Gripping the cop's interlaced fingers tightly in his own hand, Jake led his prisoner backward to a sturdy young sapling and instructed him to sit down. Fifteen seconds later Sherman's hands were cuffed behind his back, the sapling preventing him from going anywhere.

"You'll never know how much I wanted to nail you, Donovan," Sherman growled, his fear masked by anger and embarrassment.

Jake said nothing. Instead, he took the cop's portable radio out of his belt and smashed it against a larger tree, thus putting the finishing touch on the worst crime of his life. *Thank you, God.*

"Come on up here, Jake," Carolyn urged. Her voice sounded a little shaky. "It's dangerous down there."

"I'm okay," Jake replied. She was right, of course; at least in absolute terms. The inverse square rule applied here—halving the distance squared the hazard. In relative terms, though, Jake didn't think he was in too much trouble. He needed to tell Nick that everything was okay, but when he turned to wave the all-clear, the other man was gone.

"Where'd Nick go?" Jake asked, glancing back to Carolyn over his shoulder.

"No idea," she said. "But come on up here. I don't want you down that close."

"You sound like my mother," Jake snorted. "I'll be there in a second." He stooped down to speak man-to-man with the cop.

"There he is!" Carolyn announced.

Jake looked up to see Nick dragging the remains of one of their old coworkers outside. "What's he doing?" Jake wondered aloud, watching as Nick went back inside again.

"The right thing," Carolyn answered. Her tone was one of total approval. "They'll have to bury them now. With the bodies visible to the news choppers, they'll have no choice."

Jake watched for a moment, then turned back to his captive, kneeling until they were eye-to-eye. "Look, Deputy, uh . . ." He glanced at the name tag. "Quill. My name is Jake Donovan. You know the name, I gather?"

"Fuck you, Donovan," Sherman spat.

Jake smiled. "Look, I want you to deliver a message for me when whoever sent you comes to find you."

"I'm not delivering anything."

Jake sighed. This wasn't going to be easy. "Okay, fine, Deputy. Don't deliver anything. Remember something, then. I could have killed you this afternoon, and you never would have known a thing. But I didn't, did I?"

"Only because I—"

Jake cut him off. "Look, I don't want to argue with you here. Fact is, I didn't kill you. My motivations can be whatever you'd like, but I'm telling you that you're alive because I don't kill people. Never have, hopefully never will. People don't want to believe that, but there you go."

Sherman broke eye contact and looked at the sky. By all appearances, if he could have stuck his fingers in his ears to keep from listening, he'd have done just that.

"When you write your report—and I'm sure you'll be writing a lot of them in the next couple of days—I want you to remember this: we're here to prove that we never did any of the things they accuse us of doing."

"Yeah, right," Sherman snorted.

Jake felt himself flush with anger and fought the urge to strike out at the man. He wanted to explain everything in detail; to tell Deputy Quill about the bodies on the inside and about just how miserable their lives had been. But he didn't. This cop was just a cop. At the end of the day, his opinion wouldn't mean a thing, anyway.

Jake stood again, intentionally towering over his prisoner, who now, finally, was beginning to look frightened. "Okay, Deputy," he said at last. "Don't believe anything. Just be sure to report it accurately, because what I'm about to give you is evidence: We didn't kill those people back in 1983. We didn't blow anything up. In fact, we damn near got blown up ourselves. Now, when your bosses ask you what we had to say for ourselves, you tell them that we didn't do a goddamn thing wrong. And we mean to prove it."

CHAPTER THIRTY-FOUR

Travis felt the first stab of pain about an hour into their drive back toward Little Rock. It wasn't much, really; just a slight pinprick in his chest, deep down. He'd felt twinges of it earlier, back when he was wrapping himself up in that policeman's pants, but he didn't say anything. He wasn't speaking to either of his parents. He was too pissed off about being stripped naked and nearly drowned. He'd saved their lives, dammit, and that was the thanks he got! As it was, he felt thoroughly humiliated. The pants might as well have been a dress, they were so huge, and he didn't even *have* a shirt. With the cop tied to the tree, there was no way to get his off of him, and he'd refused his father's offer to give him his own shirt, just on principle. As for the work of the day, Travis had retired. He didn't even lift a finger to help as his parents and Nick loaded stuff into the trunk of the Cadillac. His resolve to stay sullen and disinterested nearly broke when they built the bonfire to burn their protective clothing and equipment—everything that might carry a fingerprint—but in the end, he stuck to his guns.

So he just sat there, pressed up against the back door, sulking and feeling stupid. And pretending not to feel the pain delivered by every breath. If his parents hadn't been asking him every five seconds how he felt, maybe he'd have spoken up and told them something, but right now he didn't want to hear the lecture again about how stupid he was to go in there and to save their sorry butts.

He'd be okay. He was sure of it.

Ow!

That breath really hurt, and on both sides, too, making him want to cough. But as he drew in his breath to do just that, the pinpricks grew to razor blades, and the air made a rumbling sound deep down inside of him. When he finally coughed, if felt like it was in slow motion, as if something were blocking the air from escaping.

He looked over to his mom, just as she looked over to him from the other end of the backseat, and the look that twisted her face scared him more than the pain in his chest ever could.

"Travis!" she yelled. "Oh, my God, Jake. Travis!"

Jake whirled around to look at him from the front passenger seat and showed a look that terrified Travis even more. He said, "Oh, no," then scrambled over the seat back to join them in the rear.

What is it? Travis tried to ask. *What's wrong?* But his voice wouldn't work. The pain in his chest was worse than ever, and his heart raced at three times its normal rate. This time when he coughed, he could imagine someone ripping a piece of super-sticky tape off the lining of his lungs.

"Oh, my God! My baby! Jake!"

There was blood in his mouth now. And on his hands, too. Where did that come from? He needed to take a breath, but when he tried, he coughed again, and then he bled some more. He'd never seen his mother look so frightened. Or his dad.

Travis felt like he should be afraid. In fact, he remembered being afraid just a moment before. That *was* today, wasn't it? He wanted to talk, but suddenly, he didn't know how. And even if he did, he couldn't remember what it was that he wanted to say. He needed air. He forced himself to draw in a huge breath, and the pain came again, worse than ever, but, curiously, he didn't care much about it anymore.

His dad was in the backseat with him now, and from the look on his face, he was shouting something, but for the life of him, Travis couldn't hear a word of it. He tried for a second or two to watch his father's lips, to figure out what he was saying, but he became distracted by the way everything on the periphery of his vision had begun to sparkle.

Once the colors drained from the world, it was time to go to sleep.

CHAPTER THIRTY-FIVE

Irene was surprised to see George Sparks waiting for her as she stepped off the jetway and into the lobby of the airport. As supervisory agent in charge of the Little Rock field office, he should have had more important things to do than greet arriving passengers. Historically rail-thin, he looked like he'd put on a few pounds over the years, and what had once been a headful of flaming-red hair had receded to little more than a graying ring encircling a freckled pate.

Irene shifted the load of her garment bag to her left shoulder and extended her hand as she approached. "Hello, George," she said cheerily. "It's been a long time."

Sparks shot her a knowing smirk. "Yeah, I know," he said, reading her look for what it was. "But *you* haven't changed a bit."

She laughed. "God help you, George," she scoffed. "Haven't you heard that liars go to hell?"

He leaned forward and planted a friendly peck on her cheek. "This is Arkansas, my dear. The buckle of the Bible Belt. I'm already there." Back in the days when they went through the academy together, George was a proselytizing atheist, believing in essentially nothing but the Bureau and a good martini.

Irene introduced Paul, then let Sparks take her bag. "I heard you were out of the country," she said.

Sparks nodded. "Yeah, I've been in Iraq, working on my melanoma." He rubbed the top of his head. "Picked up quite a collection of hats over the past three weeks."

"Okay," Paul said, "I'll bite. Why was the SAC for Little Rock over in Iraq?"

George leaned forward a bit to see past Irene as they walked. "The world got real small," he answered. "Seems that what's left of the Republican Guard has been squirreling away chemical warheads. The U.N. inspectors stumbled onto one of their stashes and found serial numbers traceable to the Grant Plant."

"You're kidding," Irene said.

"No joke. Stuff was old as shit—dates back to the sixties—but the weps experts tell me it'll still work. Well, not anymore. They've got an incinerator out in the desert working overtime."

Paul made a face. "That's kind of *Twilight Zone*ish, don't you think?" he said. "All of a sudden, Newark, Arkansas, is the center of the universe."

George laughed. "Clearly, you've never seen Newark. Armpit of the universe maybe, but never the center. Come to think of it, it is sort of the Twilight Zone," he said, enjoying his own joke.

Irene changed the subject. "So to what do I owe the honor of such personal service?"

"I thought you'd want to know as soon as you got off the plane," George said, his tone becoming conspiratorial. "Your friends have already struck."

Irene stopped dead in the middle of the hall and nearly got run over by a frantic woman pushing a stroller. "You're shitting me."

He smiled at the frustration in her face. "I shit you not. We got the call about a half hour ago from Arkansas State P.D. Seems the Donovan gang cut through the fence to raid the original bunker."

She cocked her head, as if she hadn't heard correctly. "Come again?"

Sparks nodded. "Yep, you heard me. They broke back into the magazine they blew up in the first place." He started laughing. "Apparently, one of the local cops startled them, but they got the best of him. State boys found him tied to a tree in his underwear." The story struck Sparks as funny, and when he laughed it was a whole-body affair, bending at the waist, rolling his shoulders, and turning beet red.

Yuck it up, Irene thought bitterly. *You've still got a career.*

"His underwear?" Paul said incredulously.

Sparks gathered himself quickly once he realized that he was laughing alone. "Yeah. Best I can tell from the trooper who called in the details, the Donovans were in there to prove that they'd done nothing wrong. Don't ask, because I don't get it, either. Anyway, they had their kid with them, and he must have gotten himself exposed somehow. They stripped him naked, and he refused to go anywhere without any clothes on. So they took the cop's."

"His weapon, too?" Paul wanted to know.

George shrugged. "Trooper didn't say. What difference would that make? Christ, they're loaded for bear as it is, aren't they?"

They started walking again, in silence now, as Irene tried to make pieces fit. "They broke *in*? To prove that they're innocent." She shook her head and looked to Paul for some help. "I don't get it."

Paul shook his head. "I don't, either. Can't be much left in there. Certainly not enough to risk a kid's life . . ."

"That's it!" Irene said it with all the delight of a gold prospector. "That's how we get them!"

Sparks and Paul exchanged confused glances.

"The hospitals!" she exclaimed. "If their kid is injured, they're gonna have to take him to a hospital, right? All we have to do . . ."

". . . is get an alert out to every hospital in the state to be on the lookout for a sick boy?" Somehow, when George said it, the idea sounded less enthralling.

Paul liked it. "Of course!" he agreed. "Except I'd include the surrounding states, too. Just in case they bolted."

They exchanged glances again, in silent agreement.

"Okay, then," Irene pronounced. "That's our plan." She took her garment bag back from Sparks. "You two go get that rolling, okay? I've got to make a phone call."

"Who to?"

"Frankel," she said, turning away. "I'm tired of telling him that we've gotten left behind. He needs to know that we have a plan now." As she hurried off to find a telephone, she congratulated herself on her first big break in the case. Faith will out, after all. She knew if she waited around long enough, the Donovans would do something stupid.

Now, let's just hope that the kid got hurt. The thought triggered a chill, and a distant pang of remorse that she could even think such a thing.

"Come on, Nick, step on it!" The tone of Jake's voice had soared past desperation, to touch the outer boundaries of panic.

"I'm going as fast as I can," Nick shouted back. "Wrapping the car around a tree won't help anyone." *And neither will getting stopped for speeding,* he didn't say. Nevertheless, each rattling breath from the suffering boy in the backseat brought just a little more pressure onto the gas pedal.

"How far?" Carolyn asked.

"Last sign said twenty miles to Little Rock. I have no idea where the hospital is from there."

"He won't last that long!"

Even though his eyes opened from time to time, Travis had long ago lost consciousness. His skin had paled to the point of translucence, and as his breathing became progressively more labored, pink foam gathered at the corners of his mouth and at his nostrils. Jake had climbed in between Travis and the seat back, from which position he kept the boy leaning forward just enough to let the blood and drool drain without choking him. With little else to do, Carolyn used an ancient McDonald's napkin from her purse to wipe Travis's upper lip and chin. Every now and then, she'd lean over and kiss his hair.

"Oh, my baby," she said over and over again. "You'll be just fine . . ."

As the speedometer nudged one hundred miles per hour, Nick tuned everything out but the business of driving. He struggled not to hear the pitiful rattling of the boy's lungs or the crying and cooing of his parents. His job was to keep the wide-bodied boat of a car on the road and between the lines. Traffic was sparse along this ribbon of highway, and as he bore down on the occasional car in his path, he'd flash his headlights repeatedly, hoping they'd get the hint and move out of his way. Few did, but none of them made any stupid driving moves, either. He could only imagine what they had to say as he blew past them at half again their own speed.

The plan had been to get Travis to the nearest hospital, which everyone assumed to be in Little Rock. Now, a half hour into their high-speed flight, Nick had begun to question the plan's wisdom. Judging from sound alone, the kid was heading south fast. Without a more concrete set of directions, he feared that they'd simply run out of time.

Under different circumstances, he might not even have noticed the yellow diamond-shaped metal sign as it loomed up out of the distance. He'd seen them on roadsides everywhere, bolted securely to four-by-fours and driven deeply into the dirt, but they'd never had any special significance for him. But then, he'd never had such an immediate use for the service advertised: Rescue Squad.

He hit the brakes hard, struggling to control the speeding Cadillac as he slid into the turn. The deceleration launched everyone in the backseat onto the floor and ignited a chorus of angry, startled protests.

"What's wrong!" Jake shouted.

Nick gritted his teeth and closed one eye as the car slid to a halt on the front ramp of the Rescue Squad building. "Your boy needs medical attention more than he needs a car ride," he said.

"Where the hell are we?" Jake demanded, but Nick didn't answer. Instead, he jumped out of the car and jogged up to the front door for help.

Travis had fallen in a heap on the floor, and Carolyn struggled to help him sit up, but he had landed facedown, and the way his legs were twisted, it was a hopeless effort. "Oh, my God, Travis," she cried. "I'm so sorry, sweetie. Oh, my baby, my baby."

Jake planted his feet on the cushions of the backseat and tried to lift the boy, but with little success. Somewhere along the line, his son had gained some weight, and without a shirt to grab hold of, there just wasn't enough room in the cramped quarters of the seat to get the leverage he needed. In some dark corner of his mind, Jake suspected Travis was dead; totally limp, totally unresponsive. Yet he refused to let the thought come fully to the surface. His son was breathing, dammit. And as long as he was breathing, there was hope.

Jake was dimly aware of the sound of running feet, and then the driver's-side rear door flew open. He jerked his head to see two people—a man and a woman—standing there in matching white-and-green uniforms. *He* was a mountain; six-four, with a blond Santa Claus beard and matching gut. *She* stood maybe five-two if she stretched, and bore the concerned face of a schoolteacher.

The man spoke first. "Hi," he said jovially, even as he leaned in to take a look. "We're paramedics. I'm Bob Faylon, and this is my wife, Barbara. What seems to be the problem here?"

"It's our son!" Carolyn blurted. "He's only thirteen and I think he's dying. He inhaled some chemical residue and—"

Jake touched her shoulder gently and she cut her words off, but the damage was already done. He saw the recognition in Bob's eyes and realized that the big man had all the advantage on him. Recognition quickly transformed to fear, and that was the emotion Jake worried about most.

Jake answered the question before it was asked. "Yes, we are," he said softly. "And you're in no danger. We just need you to help our son."

Bob eyed the gun on Jake's hip and nodded toward it. "Then why don't you get rid of that?"

Jake looked down at his weapon and then back again. "Because you've got a half foot on me and about a hundred pounds," he said, making an effort to be completely honest. "But if you don't do anything aggressive, neither will I."

Bob backed out of the car and turned to his wife. "Barbara, go inside and call Communications. Tell them we've got the Donovans here. We need P.D., ASAP."

"I'd appreciate it if you wouldn't do that!" Jake called past Bob to his tiny wife. She froze, clearly not knowing what to do next. She looked to Bob for guidance, but his eyes never left Jake. This was a man who had been in his share of fights and clearly had confidence in his ability to win them.

"Are you going to stop her . . . Jake, isn't it?"

Travis barked out a horrid cough, distracting everyone for just the briefest of moments.

"Do something!" Carolyn cried.

Jake looked from his son to Carolyn and back to Bob. "No," he said at length. "I won't try and stop anything. I just want you to help my son."

Bob's eyes softened at the sound of the cough, and he nodded abruptly, his decision made. "Give me a hand here, Barbara," he instructed. He edged Jake out of the way as he climbed further inside the car. "We need to get him out onto the ground."

With Bob at Travis's shoulders and Barbara at his feet, they made it look easy, lifting the boy right out of the vehicle.

"Be careful," Carolyn admonished, worried that the sag in Travis's back might injure him. The enormous pants slipped a little as they moved him, and Carolyn told them to stop while she pulled them back up to cover his backside. Travis would have wanted it that way.

Jake and Carolyn huddled together in the chilly night air as they watched the paramedics work on their son. They said nothing. They just hugged each other and stared.

Bob was definitely the one in charge, and his face showed grave concern as he ordered Barbara to go inside and bring the ambulance out onto the front ramp. She wasn't three steps into her journey before he called to her again. "Call Communications," he instructed. "Have them cut numbers on this incident and tell 'em we need the state police chopper out here. We're gonna lose this kid if we don't fly him out."

Barbara disappeared at a fast jog.

Bob turned back to Carolyn. "What kind of chemicals?" he asked.

Carolyn shrugged. "I don't know. Old burned-up military stuff. You must have heard the story."

Bob nodded gravely as he produced a stethoscope out of his back pocket, and he pressed the diaphragm onto Travis's bare chest. He listened in one spot for a moment, then moved the instrument to another. And another. After about fifteen seconds, he pulled the bows out of his ears, then draped the stethoscope over the back of his neck. "You've got one sick little boy here, ma'am," he said. "His lungs are full of liquid, and judging from the bleeding, he's got some tissue damage down there as well."

Carolyn shook all over. "Is he ... Will he ..." She couldn't bring herself to ask the question.

Bob looked away. "I hope so, ma'am," he said gravely. "We're gonna do everything we can to make him as good as new." He seemed relieved when the overhead door to the ambulance bay rumbled upward, and the engine turned over. "There's some stuff I can do for him here, but we're gonna medevac him out to St. Luke's in Little Rock, where they can do a more permanent patching job."

The ambulance pulled up even with the Cadillac, and suddenly, the darkness erupted in brilliant white light, fueled by the halogen floods on the side of the vehicle. The brightness only emphasized the pallor of Travis's skin, whiter still in contrast to the redness of his blood.

As Jake and Carolyn watched in silence, Nick moved up quietly behind them. "Excuse me, guys," he said as gently and as lightly as he could, "but we need to get moving. A whole world of cops is gonna be here soon, and I don't want anything to do with them."

"I'm not going anywhere," Carolyn said firmly. Her tone left no room for negotiation.

Jake's breath caught in his throat. This was it, he realized. This was the end of it all. After fourteen years on the run, it all came to a crashing halt out in front of a building they'd never seen, in a town they'd never heard of. No shooting or shouting; they'd just allow themselves to be taken. Curiously, the very notion that had seemed so horrifying just hours before seemed inconsequential next to the loss of his son.

"I'm staying, too," he said.

Nick's jaw dropped. "You can't be serious."

Jake turned on Nick like a snapping dog. "He's my son, Nick! What would you have me do, leave him?"

Nick took a step back, startled by the attack. He didn't have an answer for that question, but he sure as hell hadn't come all the way to Podunk, Arkansas, just to be taken away in a police chopper. He'd done this as a favor, not as a sacrifice. He had his own family to worry about.

"You go with him, Jake." It was Carolyn. She'd found her voice again, and it was strong, unequivocal.

"Carolyn, I can't . . ." Jake felt himself losing control.

"You have to. There's no other way." She grasped his face in both hands and dropped her voice nearly to a whisper. "If you stay, we'll never see each other again. You know that. Giving up accomplishes nothing."

He looked suddenly like a little boy himself. His features knotted and he shook his head. "But what about you? What about Trav?"

To see her husband start to cry melted Carolyn's heart. "I'll be with him," she whispered, "for as long as they'll let me."

"But you'll go to jail . . ."

". . . and you'll get me out." She smiled, even as her lower lip trembled. "You're the only one, Jake. You and Nick—" She stopped herself and shot a glance over to Nick.

Nick waved off the sentimentality and turned away.

Jake looked at Carolyn for a long, long moment. They'd shared everything. Good times and bad. It couldn't end like this. They'd always been *together*. That's how any of this was able to work. How could he watch Travis be sent off to a hospital somewhere while

Carolyn was shipped off to prison? He didn't think he could make a go of it alone. What would happen if he failed? He realized in a rush of emotion that he'd never see either of them again. Never hear his wife's throaty laugh; never rumple his son's hair. He pulled Carolyn close, overwhelmed by a sense of helplessness. There'd always been options; there'd always been plans. Now there was nothing. Now he was alone. He couldn't . . .

"Jake, we've got to go," Nick said.

Carolyn pushed Jake away and reached up to wipe the tears from his face, ignoring her own. "He's right," she said. "You've got to go. I've got to be with Travis."

Jake shook his head. "Together forever, remember?" he pleaded softly.

"Family first," she corrected, straightening her husband's hair with her fingers. "This is the only way."

He wanted to argue. He tried to argue, but the words just weren't there. He allowed Nick to pull gently on his arm, and as they stepped away, Carolyn's face collapsed. She pivoted quickly and headed toward the ambulance, where Bob and Barbara were lifting Travis through the back doors.

"I love you!" Jake shouted after her, his voice thick and raspy.

He couldn't tell if she'd heard him over the rumble of the ambulance's motor.

CHAPTER THIRTY-SIX

Irene walked briskly through the throngs of reporters that had gathered outside Little Rock's Adult Detention Center, ignoring their shouted questions, concentrating instead on the ones she planned on asking herself. Paul had gone on to the hospital to stay with the boy, in case his condition improved enough to answer some questions, while George Sparks stuck with her. Once inside the jail, they were joined by Tom Flaherty, superintendent of the ADC, who greeted them warmly and seemed to be good friends with Sparks.

"How long have you had her?" Irene asked, keeping the pace moving down the hallway.

"About an hour," Flaherty answered. "Long enough to get her in-processed. Any word on the other one?"

She shook her head. "Not yet. He'll turn up, though. He's lost too much just to disappear." Maybe if she said it confidently enough, it would come true. Frankel wasn't nearly as pleased as she'd thought he'd be that fifty percent of the team was in custody. "No one's talked to her yet, right?" she pressed.

"Nope. Not beyond the standard in-processing crap, anyway. You know, name, rank, and serial number."

"Has she lawyered up?" This from Sparks.

"Not that I know of," Flaherty said with a shrug. "In fact, I'm not sure she even answered the name, rank, and serial number questions. I'm told she's pretty dejected."

Irene chuckled at that. "Yeah, well, her day's about to get a lot worse."

The three-person parade stopped at the edge of the security area, while Irene and George deposited their weapons in the shoebox-size lockers built for the purpose. Then they signed in, and Flaherty led the way to an interrogation room. Fairly modern as jail facilities went, the ADC was still a jail, and such places always left Irene feeling depressed. To her, there was a sense of hopelessness about incarcerated criminals that couldn't be dispelled by lofty claims of "rehabilitation."

"I'd like to talk to her alone, if that's okay," Irene said, stopping the procession at the door. "You know, woman-to-woman. I think she might open up more."

Flaherty couldn't have cared less, and while Sparks seemed disappointed, he didn't object. They'd be able to watch everything on the television monitors, anyway. His acquiescence came in the form of a shrug.

"Thanks, George." She turned to Flaherty. "Okay, then, let's go."

The jailer slipped a key into the interrogation room door, then pulled it open.

Irene paused while the door closed behind her, then stepped forward to sit at a conference table, directly across from the woman she recognized from pictures as Carolyn Donovan.

Frankly, Irene was surprised. As fugitives went, this one looked especially small; especially whipped. Ultimate Criminals—people who committed Ultimate Crimes—often failed to look the part, and this was certainly another example. Usually, though, behind the beaten look spawned by captivity, there burned an air of defiance; the spark of something despicable.

With Carolyn Donovan, there was only sadness. She sat slumped
in the padded metal chair, her right arm limp by her side, held im-
mobile by the handcuff on her wrist. Pale and drawn, she seemed
lost in the oversize blue scrub suit worn by all inmates. This
woman looked more like a mother than a criminal; more housewife
than murderer.

No wonder she's been able to stay free for so long.

"Hello, Carolyn," Irene said cheerily as she approached the table.
"I'm Special Agent Irene Rivers with the FBI. I can't tell you how
pleased I am to finally make your acquaintance." She helped herself
to a seat and folded her hands on the table. "As you might guess,
we've got two or three thousand questions to ask you." She meant
the comment to be lighthearted but feared it sounded cruel.

Carolyn didn't respond at all.

"Now, Carolyn, there are a couple of ways we can go about this,"
Irene went on. "You can sit there sullenly and silently, and in general make it all worse for yourself, or you can—"

"How is my son?" Carolyn asked abruptly.

The question caught Irene off guard. She paused for a moment,
wishing incongruously that she'd checked on his condition before
she entered. "I don't know," she said honestly enough. "But I have
an agent down there who'll be in touch with any developments."

"They could have let me stay with my little boy," Carolyn
moaned. She seemed dazed by her grief; drugged maybe.

Irene shook her head. "Actually, no they couldn't," she corrected.
"We've been trying to catch you for long enough, thank you very
much. The last thing—"

"They didn't even let me say good-bye to him. They just
swooped in with their helicopter and sent him off. I never even got
to kiss him good-bye." Her eyes were focused on a spot on the table
somewhere between them.

"You should have thought of that before you got him involved,"
Irene said, drawing a look that actually hurt.

"You people have no idea what you've done to us," Carolyn
snarled. "You think you have answers. You think you have evidence,
but all you have is stupidity and hatred. We've done nothing wrong.

We've *never* done anything wrong, but you people want to hurt us, anyway."

Irene felt oddly defensive. "I don't want to hurt you," she said. "I just—"

"You want to hurt my son," Carolyn interrupted. "Because by hurting my son, you can hurt me and my husband. That's what this is all about. Justice stopped mattering fourteen years ago. All that matters to you people is revenge."

Irene regarded the other woman for a long moment, searching her eyes for the scam; for the hidden agenda. The best criminals were consummate con men, and if you gave them half a chance, they'd work their way under your skin and fester like a bedsore. In all the years she'd been in the business of interviewing bad guys, she'd found precious few who owned up to their crimes. They all were innocent. Which made her speculate endlessly on the human capacity for self-delusion.

Evidence spoke for itself. As an agent of the Federal Bureau of Investigation, Irene bore the obligation to collect and analyze that evidence and to arrest people deemed by the United States Attorney to be violators of federal law. Guilt and innocence were the far loftier domain of jurors and jurists. She couldn't afford the luxury of feeling sorry for the people she arrested. As pitiful and grief-stricken as Carolyn Donovan appeared, Irene told herself it was irrelevant.

"You sound like you're ready to make a statement," she said, breaking the silence.

Carolyn raised her eyes and locked onto the other woman. At length, she nodded. "Okay," she said. She leaned forward, resting the weight of her torso as best she could on her single mobile forearm. "Okay, Agent Rivers, I'll give you a statement. Why don't we start with Newark, Arkansas, back in 1983."

"That works for me," Irene agreed. She nodded to the camera to her right, in the corner near the ceiling, as if to remind George Sparks that a one-on-one interrogation had been her idea.

Carolyn told the story her own way, at her own pace, refusing to be drawn onto the occasional side routes presented from time to

time by Irene's questions. She spoke for nearly a half hour, with
barely a break, starting with that first day amid the smoke and the
fire and the bodies and ending with Travis's injury that afternoon.
She carefully avoided any specifics on their aliases over the years
and mentioned nothing of anyone's participation outside of their
little nuclear family.

Of all the points she made, however, she emphasized one over
all the others: that Travis had never known a thing; that he was
purely a passive participant.

Her story was the most outlandish thing Irene had ever heard.
"You do know that we found the note you left at the crime scene?"
she asked.

"We never wrote a note," Carolyn responded easily. "Just as we
never hurt anybody. If you have a note, then somebody planted it
there."

Irene laughed out loud at the absurdity of it. "That's it? That's
your story? You want people to believe that someone planned all of
this? That someone went to all that effort merely to frame Mr. and
Mrs. Ordinary Citizen for some wild murder cover-up? Come on,
Carolyn, you can do better than that."

The prisoner stared some more, her eyes burning holes through
her captor on the strength of hatred alone. "God damn you," she
seethed. "Why bother to ask questions if you're so convinced you
already know the answers?"

Irene had heard this same question posed by dozens of prisoners in the past. "Because I'd like to hear you say it, Carolyn. I'd like
you to give me some indication I should trust you. That you're
going to be cooperative."

Now it was Carolyn's turn to laugh. "Trust? Cooperation?
You've got to be kidding. You people have made our lives a living
hell for the past fourteen years!" Her voice raised in pitch and volume, and she tried to stand, but the chair that restrained her arm
was bolted securely to the floor. "How dare you talk to me about
trust! If you people had done your jobs at the very beginning, none
of this would have happened! My boy . . . he wouldn't be—" Her
voice stopped working.

The interview was approaching the moment Irene had been waiting for: the point at which the prisoner's emotions swamped the protective walls she'd built around the truth. As she'd been trained, Irene slipped easily into the mother confessor mode: "We did our job, Carolyn," she said softly, soothingly. "We went in the direction that the preponderance of evidence took us. Please understand that there are no hard feelings here. You did your job, too. You ran, just as anyone who feared punishment would run."

"We ran because we had no *choice*!" Carolyn wailed. "We knew—" All at once, she realized what Irene was up to. She understood the game, and she brought her emotions under control. She remembered now what Lanny Skiles had told them so long ago, when he was indoctrinating them in the rules of the street. The police saw people as pawns, as things to be manipulated. They'd lie, they'd seduce, they'd do whatever it took to get you to string incriminating words together in a sentence. Once transcribed, those words would serve as a confession, devoid of any emotion, and carefully edited for the greatest possible damage.

Suddenly, she felt horribly, horribly tired. She couldn't remember all she'd said thus far, but she knew it was too much. Anger, fear, and hatred were all-too-natural emotions, and she could afford none of them. This game was for keeps, and it was time to change strategies.

She froze there for a moment, straining against her tether as she took a deep breath, held it for a couple of seconds, then let it go. Control flooded back. Breaking eye contact just long enough to soften her expression, she lowered herself back into her chair. "What time is it?" she asked.

Irene eyed her curiously, having trouble disguising her disappointment in losing the moment. "You have someplace important to go, do you?"

Carolyn rolled her eyes and chuckled. "You people really are bullies, aren't you?" The chuckle turned to a laugh. "This is one big power trip for you!" The laugh got louder, and even more genuine. Tears came to her eyes, and she wiped them away with her free hand.

"Okay, Agent Rivers," she snickered through her lingering smile. "If it makes you feel big, you just hide the time from me, okay? You're in control, by God, and I must say you wear it well."

Irene's jaw set as Carolyn derided her, and she found herself suddenly self-conscious of the people on the other side of the camera. Withholding the time was probably a petty move, but she certainly couldn't cave in now.

"Anyway," Carolyn concluded, "it's getting late, and I'm getting tired. Just let me ask you one question."

"If you must." Like there was a choice.

"You're not going to let yourself even consider the possibility of a conspiracy. You've made that plainly obvious, and in so doing, you've answered your own question about why we ran. Now, I'd like to ask you this: Why would we *return* to Newark, Arkansas, if not to collect the evidence I spoke of? You know from firsthand experience that we're adept at staying underground. Why didn't we stay there? Why did we expose ourselves?"

Irene played her hand with a flawless poker face. It was a damned good question. One that just might be worth pursuing. But this was time for the good guys to be interviewing the bad, not the other way around. One of the most basic rules of any interrogation was for the interrogator to remain in control at all times, and that meant never answering a substantive question from a suspect. Instead, she countered with a fresh one of her own.

"Your uncle, Harry Sinclair, is mixed up with this, too, isn't he?"

That one came out of nowhere and hit Carolyn like a slap. She tried to show no reaction.

"Like I said," she concluded, after dropping a beat, "I'm getting very tired. I think I'll stop talking now."

But Irene was only just beginning. Or so she thought. After a half hour of needling, prodding, insulting, and shouting, and not getting so much as a moment of eye contact in response, Agent Rivers finally gave up, and told Flaherty to take Carolyn back to her cell.

CHAPTER THIRTY-SEVEN

Jake was shocked that Nick's plan had worked so well. In all the confusion back at the Rescue Squad, his friend had transferred the orange body bag and the two money bags from the trunk of the Cadillac to the back of Bob and Barbara's Toyota pickup truck, which was parked, keys inside, just off the back ramp. No one seemed to notice as they turned off the tiny access road and back onto the highway, passing within thirty feet of the ambulance as it sat there on the front ramp, swaying ever so slightly from the frantic efforts to save Travis's life.

They traveled in silence. Nick didn't know what to say, and Jake, in a move to preserve some semblance of composure, simply allowed himself to become mesmerized by the yellow hash marks in the road. They flashed by endlessly, brilliant yellow dashes in the wash of the headlights, stretching forever, in a trajectory so straight that he wondered how a driver could stay awake.

Nothing mattered anymore. With Travis dying and Carolyn off to prison, this business of revenge and of staying ahead of the police seemed tragically irrelevant. Their only chance for a life together now rested squarely on his shoulders, but he had grave doubts that he could handle the burden. Giving up, giving in, just seemed so much easier. A relief, even, from the pain that grew like a tumor in his heart.

Why did I have to be so harsh with him?

He felt exhausted, unable to remember the last time he'd been without fear. It undercut everything. Even the most joyous moments over the years had been dulled by a pervasive sense of dread that it would be their last moment to laugh together. Thankfully, it hadn't been as bad the last year or two as it had been in the beginning. He'd finally gotten to the point where after a few months in one town, he'd achieve a certain sense of relief that they'd "made it" yet again, but then it would be time to move on, and he'd remember that their survival was only as secure as the first person who might recognize them.

The worst time came back in 1990, when one of the reality-based television programs did a piece on the Donovans and their years-long flight from the law. Millions of people watched that show, just as they did every Saturday night, yet, apparently, no one made the connection. Still, the pressure was crippling: walking through the grocery store or helping customers when he knew in his heart that half of them were searching their minds for a clue as to where they'd seen him before.

For Carolyn, the pressure had proved to be too much. That TV program, combined with the emptiness of anonymity and the demons from her childhood, had driven her to booze. He'd hated her for her weakness back then. How selfish, he'd thought, for her to try to drown out the miserable existence she'd helped him build, only to make it worse for the people she'd left behind to cover for her. Travis fared worst during those times, yet Jake knew without doubt that it was the sight of the boy's suffering that had convinced her to dry out.

He now realized and admired the courage it must have taken for her to shut down her only escape route. And he hated himself for never telling her.

If only he could just turn the clock back a few days. If he'd argued with Travis for just a little longer that morning, then none of this would have happened. If he hadn't taken a shortcut to avoid some of the traffic, or if he'd just stopped for a bite to eat, then the feds would have arrived before him, and he'd have driven on past the gathered knot of police cars. The randomness of life mocked him. After so many years of calculated planning and strategic moves, he sat now amid a giant clusterfuck, facing the prospect of never again seeing the two people who gave his life meaning.

Curiously, he and Nick passed only two cop cars on their way to the airport. About fifteen minutes into the journey, the cops came barreling down the road in the opposite direction, doing about a million miles per hour, lights flashing, sirens whooping. Nick said something at the time, but Jake hadn't heard it.

The plan, as relayed to Nick earlier in the day by his stone-faced driver, called for them to drive past the entrance to Little Rock Airport, to a strip mall located a few miles down the road. They were to park in front of a sporting goods store and wait for someone to pick them up. From there, presumably, they'd be ferried off in Nick's favorite Gulfstream to some new destination.

Problem was, their designated chauffeur would be looking for a white Cadillac, not a royal-blue Toyota. After sitting for five minutes without being approached by anyone, Nick suggested that they move outside, to sit on the hood, where whoever was watching could catch a glimpse of who they really were.

Another five minutes passed. Then ten. Finally, a car approached from the far end of the parking lot. At first, the driver appeared to be lost, cruising slowly down the line of shops, just a pair of headlights against the night. Then, without warning, the high beams flashed, and the big car took a hard turn to head right for them. Nick slid off the hood and retreated a few steps, while Jake slid his hand under his jacket to rest on his pistol. If it turned out to be the cops, everything would come to a noisy end right now. If it was marauding kids, they'd be sent scurrying on home. He hoped it was neither.

The vehicle slowed as it neared the Toyota, and dimmed its lights again as it pulled to a halt. There was a *click* as the door unlatched, and in the wash of the interior light, Jake recognized

Thorne's familiar face. The big man uncoiled himself from the car's front seat as Jake slid off the hood of the pickup.

"Where's Sunshine?" Thorne asked. His thick midwestern accent sounded somehow incongruous with his narrow eyes and V-shaped frame.

"The cops have her," Jake said grimly. "Travis got hurt, and Carolyn stayed with him."

"Mr. Sinclair is gonna be pissed." Thorne's tone made the observation sound like a threat.

"That'd just break my heart," Jake growled. Of all the ramifications inherent in Carolyn's capture, her Uncle Harry's being "pissed" didn't rank among the top one hundred.

"And what's this piece of shit you're driving? Where's the rental?"

"We had to leave it behind. We boosted this from a couple of paramedics."

Thorne's features twisted into a look of utter disgust. "And what about your package? Where's that?"

Nick reappeared, leaned over the edge of the flatbed, and hoisted the body bag. "It's right here. Looks like a small child."

Thorne didn't give a shit what it looked like. His expression never changing, he opened the trunk for Nick, then closed it again after placing the body inside. "Have you had those gloves on the whole time?" he asked Nick.

In all the confusion, Nick couldn't say, but he chose to think optimistically. "Don't leave home without 'em."

Thorne rolled his eyes. "Get in."

They did. Jake sat in the back with Nick, the two soft-sided money bags stacked between them.

As it turned out, the airport was merely a convenient meeting place. Their true destination lay about forty-five minutes further out and was accessible not by plane, but by car; down a series of progressively smaller, more primitive roads. Finally, the forest opened up again to reveal an antebellum mansion, rising like a medieval castle out of an endless expanse of cleared fields. Bright lights illuminated the facade of the brick residence, making it look like something from an amusement park.

"What's this?" Nick asked, but Thorne said nothing.

They swung the turn into the half-mile-long driveway, crunching gravel as the mansion grew to fill the entire windshield. Jake thought back to the last time he'd dealt with Harry's people, and he remembered the much more modest digs similarly located in the middle of nowhere.

"So much for keeping a low profile," Jake grumped.

"It's not about profiles," Thorne grumped back. "It's about protection. Out here, anybody comes, you can watch 'em for miles."

The driveway ended in a lazy circle surrounding a gaudy fountain which, as best Jake could tell, featured a flock of barfing swans.

"Go on in," Thorne instructed as he threw the transmission into park. "No need to knock. I'll take care of the package in the trunk."

Nick and Jake exchanged uneasy glances before climbing out of the car and scaling the wide marble steps leading to the double front doors.

Jake handed the gym bags to Nick and reached for the doorknob. He paused, then drew the Glock from its holster and let it dangle by his leg. He'd learned a long time ago to trust his instincts, for all the good they did him, and his instincts were unanimous in their advice to run back to the car.

He opened the door slowly, hesitantly. He checked first to see if anyone was concealed on the hinge side before stepping in. A shimmering, polished brass chandelier dominated the ceiling over the ornate foyer, whose sparkling walnut floors had been inlaid with an ebony and pearl family crest.

"Serious money *here*," Nick mumbled under his breath.

They moved softly in the heavy silence of the giant house, working their way to the right—toward the doorway of a small yet fabulously decorated room. Two lush, forest-green leather chairs framed a gorgeous fireplace, across from which sat a silk-upholstered sofa. Jake assumed this was what one would call a parlor.

"Hey!" a voice boomed from behind.

Jake led with his gun as he whirled to find Thorne walking briskly through the front door, dragging the body bag with one hand and carrying a cellular phone in the other. "Jesus, Thorne," Jake spat, breaking his aim. "You scared the shit out of me."

Thorne paused at the sight of the weapon and regarded Jake with disgust. "Put that fucking thing away," he commanded. "I told you, the estate is clean. We're safe here." He dragged the orange bag across the foyer and thrust out the phone. "Here," he said. "Mr. Sinclair wants to talk to you."

Mr. Sinclair can kiss my ass, Jake didn't say. He reached for the phone.

Thorne turned to Nick. "The rest of your shit's in the kitchen. That's where I'll put this."

Nick nodded and followed the other man down the hallway, to disappear behind the dramatic, sweeping stairway.

Jake brought the phone to his ear. "Yeah, Harry, this is Jake."

"Where's Sunshine?" the old man demanded, his words like daggers.

Instantly, Jake's hatred for this bully tycoon bubbled to the surface, just as pure and as bitter as it had always been. "Carolyn's not here," he said. The tone that he'd hoped would sound defiant sounded soft instead, like that of a child confessing to a parent. This was, after all, the man to whom he'd sold his soul in return for an easy way out. "I had to leave her behind." He took a minute to tell the story.

"So you just ran away!" Harry charged. "You just left her to those pigs!"

"There was no choice, Harry."

"Bullshit! There's always a choice!"

Jake said nothing, merely sat down heavily on the elaborate sofa. Of course there were choices, but what else—

"It's that goddamn kid of yours!" Harry roared. "I told you no kids! And you deliberately ignored me! Why didn't you listen?"

Jake was stunned, struck dumb. Whereas just seconds before, he'd felt his self-worth swirling down the toilet, now he was ready for a fight. *Goddamn kid?* How dare he! For a long time, he stared at the phone, his mouth agape.

"I asked you a question, Jake," Harry's voice buzzed from the earpiece.

"We *did* listen to you," Jake seethed. He found himself concentrating on his words, controlling his voice. "We did every goddamn thing you told us to do, and look where we are today."

"You *didn't* listen!" Harry yelled.

Fuck self-control. "We *did* listen!" Jake shouted back. "You said to run. We ran. You said to change our names and appearances. We did that, too. For fourteen fucking years, Harry, we've done every goddamn thing you told us to do! And yes, we had a son . . ."

Suddenly, the words caught in Jake's throat, and he paused, as if choking. And the horror of it all became clear. "I *had* a son," he repeated, and now his voice was barely a whisper. He'd just used the past tense.

Oh, God . . .

"He's the only thing we ever did right, Harry, and I think I killed him." He looked at the phone curiously for a moment, bringing it down to waist level, where he folded it shut and let it drop to the floor. The last person he owed an explanation to was Harry Sinclair.

With his elbows wedged into his knees, he leaned forward and ran his fingers deeply into his hairline. The hopelessness of it all took his breath away.

What kind of animal am I? he wondered. *Killing my own son, and sacrificing my wife, just to save my own skin?*

"Oh, my God," he whispered. "Oh, sweet Jesus, I'm so sorry."

And he came apart. He pressed his fists against his eyes to keep the sadness from spilling out, but it wouldn't be stopped. It gushed out of him in breathless, choking sobs, and suddenly, in his mind, he wasn't in Arkansas anymore. He was with his little boy, holding him steady as he pedaled his bicycle for the first time. Then he saw the pained expression that invaded Travis's face every time they told him that it was time to move to another town. The tenements they'd lived in, the roach-infested trailer parks. The bruises when Travis yet again refused to back down from the local kids who wanted to see what the new guy was made of.

God, Jake had tried so hard to be a good father, but in his zeal to keep his son in line, he'd never truly gotten to know the boy as a friend. The thought of it brought genuine pain. Suddenly, it was hard for him to take a breath.

And in his most heroic moment—when he was hoping to save our lives—all I could do was yell. And strip him of his dignity.

Jake wanted his family back. He wanted a group hug from the old days—a sandwich hug, where he and Carolyn were the bread and Travis was the jelly. The thought of never touching them again was more than he could bear. His mind played out a horror show, in which his only child lay trapped forever inside an airtight box, covered over by a ton of dirt, while his mother prayed for the moment when she could join him, every day suffering the torture of prison rapes and beatings.

Such a pillar of virtue, that Jake Donovan. Always willing to let women and children suffer in his place. There were words for people like him in our society: coward—the most exclusive group of villains; people who throughout history have willingly stepped aside to let others die in their place. Deserters and draft-dodgers came to mind. Or ship's captains who take the last lifeboat while their passengers drown.

Like falling down a well, Jake found himself tumbling deeper and deeper into the blackest misery he'd ever known. And the well of misery had no bottom; just more blackness. Everything he'd ever loved was gone now, and it was all his fault. How could a man live with knowledge such as this? Knowing that he'd killed his own blood, how could he ever face a mirror again? How could he face another dawn?

"Jake!"

The harshness of the voice startled him. It was Nick, and he seemed agitated. "What?"

"Are you coming or not?"

Jake felt disoriented, mentally numbed; as if a chunk of time had passed without his notice. He checked his watch and was shocked to see that a full half hour of his life had somehow evaporated.

"Coming where?" As he spoke, his throat felt thick.

"To the kitchen," Nick said, like it was the most obvious thing in the world. His face turned grave. "Are you okay?"

Jake stood uneasily, unsure whether to trust his balance. "Yeah, I'm okay, I guess. Just zoned out." A few seconds passed, and then his head cleared. He followed Nick into the foyer, then stopped. "What's in the kitchen?"

Nick clearly felt uneasy. "I wanted to take a look at these remains before we ship them off to Chicago. The best place I can think of to do it is in the kitchen." He responded to Jake's curious glare with an offhanded shrug. "Don't worry about it. Just something I noticed in the magazine. Probably nothing, but I thought we should check it out."

"What is it?" Jake pressed as he followed down the hall.

Nick remained evasive. "I'll tell you after we take a look. Like I said, probably nothing at all."

Body language alone told Jake that it was useless to press further.

The kitchen was huge; like something that belonged in the back of an elegant downtown restaurant. Stainless-steel appliances shined like mirrors. Copper pots and pans hung from the ceiling, suspended in midair, it seemed, over a gleaming six-burner stove. The black and white tile floor was so clean that Jake found himself stepping carefully, lest he find that it was still wet.

The orange body bag lay in a heap in the right-hand rear corner, placed there with all the care and respect that one would show to a throw pillow.

"What *is* this place?" Jake asked to whoever would care to answer.

"This house belongs to a physician friend of Mr. Sinclair's," Thorne explained. "He offered to let us use it for a while."

"Where is he?"

Nick smiled knowingly at the question. Apparently, this ground had been covered once before.

"Away," Thorne said. He spoke with an annoying, sanctimonious grin, as if responding to a joke that he alone had heard. Every move the man made seemed designed to keep people on edge. This was a man to be feared.

"What about contamination?" Jake asked.

Nick shook off the concern easily. "Don't worry. We've got some Saranex suits and some respirators. Shouldn't be a problem."

"Not us," Jake corrected. "The room. This is somebody's kitchen, for crying out loud."

"Don't worry about that," Thorne advised. "You need the room, you use the room. Our host won't mind."

Jake shared a look with Nick, but neither of them said anything.

"The stuff you said you needed is in the boxes over there." Thorne pointed. "Do you need me for any of this crap, or can I go sit down?"

As Thorne departed, Nick knelt to open the boxes. "Looks like it's all here." He lifted two sets of white, hooded coveralls out of the largest box and handed one of them to Jake, leaving ten in the box. "God, there's enough stuff here for an army."

"Easier to borrow by the box, I suppose," Jake mused. He rubbed the fabric of the coveralls between his fingers and shot a curious look. "What is this stuff?"

"Saranex," Nick said. "See what happens when you drop out of the industry for a while? It's basically a Tyvek garment with a Saran Wrap coating. Terrific stuff for low-level dust hazards."

Jake examined it more closely. "Feels kinda like Pampers," he said, drawing a chuckle. He flapped the garment with a loud snap, then thrust one leg into his coveralls. He had to push hard against the stiff folds. Suddenly, he stopped, realizing he'd forgotten something. "Thorne!"

It took a while, but in his own sweet time, Thorne reappeared at the kitchen door.

"See what you can find out about Carolyn and Travis, okay?"

The big man cocked his head and planted his fists on his hips. "And how the fuck do you want me to do that? Maybe I should just call the FBI and ask." Shaking his head with disgust, he turned and disappeared again toward the front of the house.

"Prick," Jake spat under his breath.

"He's all personality, that one," Nick concurred. "Don't let it get to you. He just doesn't get it."

Dressing for this level of protection was a far less complex task—more like dressing for surgery, but with a full-face respirator instead of a surgical mask. The respirator resembled a pilot's oxygen mask, with the addition of a clear Lexan facepiece, which formed an airtight seal around the entire face, from eyebrows to chin. In place of an artificial air supply, the respirators used two disc-shaped high-efficiency filters to knock any particulates out of the air before they could reach the user's nose or mouth.

With the coveralls on, and their respirators in place, Jake and Nick lifted the hoods to cover their hair and donned two sets of gloves—latex under heavier rubber—and approached the butcher-block table. The bitter sacrilege of examining a child's body on a surface designed for cooking was lost on neither man.

The orange body bag lay in a heap under a bank of fluorescent lights, not nearly as bright as Nick might have liked, but certainly adequate to the task at hand. It took a half minute or so to straighten the bag out enough to access the zipper. Like peeling a banana, the orange layer opened to reveal the green bag, which Jake lifted just enough to allow Nick to pull the outer shroud away and lay it on the tile floor.

"So tell me," Jake said, his voice muffled by his respirator. "What's the big mystery?"

"We'll see in a minute," Nick said. Jake noted the lack of eye contact.

"What is it?"

Nick ignored him as he fumbled with yet another rumpled bag in search of the zipper. Finally, he got it open. In the glare of the overhead light, they saw for the first time just how fine a dust they'd been exposed to: the consistency of talcum powder. Jake examined the fine coating on his gloved fingers and fought away a wave of despair. The body's natural filters were useless against so fine a particle size. Whatever Travis had breathed was free to travel into the deepest recesses of the boy's lungs; free to do its maximum damage. He closed his eyes and took a deep, purified breath.

Calm down, he told himself, fighting to find a ray of hope. *You're not a doctor. Quit trying to practice medicine. Maybe it's not as bad as you think.*

The bones were all jumbled together in a heap in the bottom

corner of the body bag. Nick reached in, up to his elbow, and pulled them out where he could see them. One at a time, he'd lift a piece to the light, turn it over in his gloved hands, then reach in for another one.

"What do you see?" Jake asked. It had been far too long since he'd taken anatomy and physiology.

Nick's eyes never lifted from his work. "Everything's pretty badly degraded from the heat of the fire," he said. "This one appears to be part of a vertebral column. See the ridge here?" He traced it with his finger.

Jake saw it. "Okay, so what do we know?"

Again, Nick ignored his question as he reached in for another piece. "Okay," he said. "This is the one I was looking for." He turned it over in his fingers—sort of a long *V* with some unusual ridges along its edge. Nick's shoulders sagged visibly as he dropped his hands to the table. When he looked up at Jake, his eyes had darkened, and even through the Lexan, Jake could see the creases in his brow.

"What is it?" Jake demanded, his heart suddenly racing. "What?"

Nick lifted the bone back into the light. "It's a jawbone," he said, his voice barely audible through the respirator.

Jake took the bone from him and held it up to his own face. "A jawbone! It doesn't look like . . ." Then he saw it. He dropped the relic back into the bag and grabbed the side of the table for support.

"It's a dog, Jake," Nick said. "Or maybe a wolf or a fox. But it's not human."

Jake bit his lip and closed his eyes against the conclusion that tried to force its way through his brain. "A dog? Who'd do all of this just to cover the death of a dog?"

Nick looked away.

"Bullshit!" Jake shouted. "No! We missed it, then!"

"Jake . . ." Nick moved to join his friend on the other side of the table. "Listen . . ."

"Fuck you! We missed it. It's got to be there!"

"But it's not." He put his hand on Jake's shoulder.

Jake slapped it away. "Oh, God," he wailed. A sound arose from his throat that was unlike anything Nick had heard from a human being: grief, unleashed in its rawest, most bitter form, rising as an agonized scream and reverberating off the tile walls, despite the muffling effects of his facepiece.

Jake pushed himself away from the table and stumbled toward the door. Suddenly, the huge kitchen seemed impossibly small. He needed to get out. Now.

He kicked open the door, bouncing a polished brass hurricane lamp off the wall and down onto the floor with a crash. Shards of glass skittered in every direction across the inlaid wood of the hallway. This couldn't be happening. They'd missed something. They'd had to. This was it. This was the whole plan. That skeleton was the key piece of evidence that would lead to their acquittal; that would give them their lives back!

Now, he realized, he had nothing. He ripped the respirator off his head and heaved it across the room, where it pulverized a vase that had once been supported on an intricately carved ebony plant stand. *"Fuck!!"*

Nick moved in behind him. "Jake, take it easy . . ."

Jake whirled on him, his eyes wild. "Fuck you, Nick! Fuck 'take it easy'!" He ripped at his gloves and threw them one at a time against the wall. "Oh, God, no!" His grief lit a fire in his brain, and he pressed his hands against the top of his head as he sat heavily on the floor. "Oh, God, oh, God, no."

Thorne's big, chrome-plated .45 was drawn and ready to shoot as he charged into the hallway. "What the hell is going on!"

Nick took off his respirator and nodded toward Jake. "It's like I feared," he said softly. "The bones weren't human."

Jake's face was a mask of anguish as he looked up to face the other men. "I killed my son," he gasped, "and I sent my wife away to prison for the rest of her life." He took a deep, labored breath before he could finish the thought. "For a dog."

CHAPTER THIRTY-EIGHT

Travis had had some wild dreams before, but nothing like this. It was all about pain. He was floating somewhere, he thought, but every time he tried to move, he couldn't. The more he tried, the more it hurt.

People were here in the darkness with him. They talked a lot, but they didn't make any sense. Lots of voices, but no one had a face. They talked in jibberish; about things he'd never even heard of. That was okay, he supposed, but why did it have to hurt so much?

His dick hurt. Somewhere, in the wildest parts of this dream, he remembered one of the faceless people jamming something into him down there. Something *big*. Not right, he thought, but then lost the thread of why he should object.

Drifting . . . He felt himself spreading out, traveling somehow. Over there—what was that?

Someone had set his lungs on fire. The fire got bigger every time he took a breath. Just like blowing on hot coals. Take another breath, burn another hole in your lung. That didn't make any sense at all.

Not when he could just stop breathing.

No more breaths for Travis, then. When they stopped, the pain would stop, too.

But he breathed again, anyway. He told himself to stop, but his lungs wouldn't listen. They just sucked in another finger of fire; another dose of airborne razor blades.

The image of a snake filled his mind. He hated snakes. This one was big, too. It had slithered all the way up his body and down his throat, doing mouth-to-mouth resuscitation on him, forcing him to breathe when he didn't want to. Hissing and biting his lungs with every breath.

I'm sorry, he said silently to the snake. *I'm sorry for whatever I did. Just stop hurting me, and I'll be good.*

The snake bit him again, a big chunk this time, and the pain brought tears to his eyes. Maybe he should just give up. But he didn't know how.

Jake felt drugged, like he was living someone else's life. The others had escorted him back to the parlor and deposited him in a chair, but he was only distantly aware of his surroundings. There'd always been hope before. There'd always been that glimmer of a plan—the one they could pursue when everything else had collapsed around them. They'd always had each other.

Family first . . .

Now it all seemed a horrible mockery. They'd never been in control at all. Whoever had put all of this together had built an airtight box around them, ruined them. Killed his son. Now there was only emptiness. Now there was only guilt.

And no one else seemed to see the helplessness of it all. Nick kept asking him what they were going to do next, treating him like he was still the leader of this operation. Didn't he understand that without Carolyn and Travis behind him, leadership meant nothing? Nick couldn't seem to grasp the obvious fact that there was no *next*. This had been *it*, all along. This was as far as the plan was ever designed to take them. He realized now just how ridiculous the gamble had been. He'd bet everything—*everything*—on a single roll of the dice, and he'd lost.

He felt the panic building again within his gut, but this time he didn't think he'd be able to stop it.

"Jesus, Jake, snap out of it!" Nick yelled. His frustration raised his voice an octave. "You've got your whole lifetime to feel sorry for yourself. Right now we've got some planning to do!"

"He's useless," Thorne said from his perch in the doorway. "He can't handle all this."

"Oh, yeah?" Nick growled. "Well, he'd *better* handle it." He put his hand on the top of Jake's head and rotated his face up high enough to make eye contact. "You're pissing me off, Jake! No one disputes that you've had a horrible goddamn day, but you're not the only one waist-deep in a shit bog here. We got caught, pal. All of us. There were witnesses. I might have gotten into this for differ-ent reasons than you, but—"

Jake twitched suddenly, as if something had startled him, and his eyes cleared. He clutched Nick's hand.

"What is it?" Nick asked, pulling away a little.

Jake was still struggling to connect the dots. "You're right," he said haltingly. "We . . . we got caught. *How* did we get caught?"

Nick scowled and cocked his head. "*How?* The cops found us. I guess when we snipped the fence, we made a bell ring somewhere."

Jake waved him off. "No," he said. That explanation wouldn't work. "You said that the response would come from a rent-a-cop. But this was a real cop."

"It's not like you haven't been in the news, ace," Thorne scoffed. "So they increased their security. They were probably expecting you."

They didn't see it yet. "Exactly, Thorne. They were *expecting* us. But why? Why on God's green earth would they ever expect us to go back there? If they really think that we blew the place up back in '83, that'd be the last place they'd expect us to go. I mean, what would be our rationale? Christ, if I had a brain in my head, I'd be in Arizona by now!"

"I'm not getting your point," Nick said. His expression, however, showed curiosity.

"Somebody was *expecting* us to go back there," Jake repeated, frustrated by his inability to make them understand. "They were *waiting* for us to go back. Something we'd never do if we were guilty."

Nick frowned. "But even if someone knew you were innocent, why would they assume your play would be to go back there—especially after all this time? Remember, the hide-a-corpse theory was all in our minds."

"Maybe they *didn't* see the Newark move at first," Thorne said, thinking. "But if there was a trip wire—I mean, if they were concerned you *might* go back, maybe they took precautions."

Jake wrestled with the trip-wire idea. "You think maybe the guy who framed us is someone local? Someone who has plenty of eyes and ears around Newark and got wind of our entering town?"

Thorne was indignant. "No way. It was a clean insertion."

Nick was lost in thought. *A trip wire has to be tripped.* Was there something there? "Maybe," he said at last, "we left an electronic trail of some sort."

Jake considered it for a moment, then dismissed it. "How, though? It's not like we bought plane tickets to get here or used a credit card for lunch."

Nick played a word association game in his head, trying to connect "electronic" with the events of the past two days. Just recently, he'd had to search his memory for a password . . . Now, what was that for?

He remembered. "Oh, shit! The computer file!" Nick smacked his forehead with his palm. "I had to log on to the computer back in Washington to get the records on the Newark site. When I accessed it, I rang a bell. Someone heard it. Given the timing of it all, they must have figured we were coming back. Dammit!" He stomped the floor.

"That's it," Jake said.

Nick hung his head low and rubbed the back of his neck. "Oh, God, Jake, I'm sorry. I should have—"

Jake waved the apology off as ridiculous. "How could you have known? Who would ever suspect . . ." He stopped in midthought. His eyes grew wide as an even larger idea formed. *Is it even possible?* "Holy shit, that's it!" he exclaimed.

"What?" Nick and Thorne said the word together.

Jake thought his heart was going to explode, and he held his hands out in front, palms forward, to calm himself down. Completely gone was the self-pity of minutes before. In its place, rising excitement. "Okay," he said, setting himself to begin. He might as well have said, *On your mark* . . .

"Let's go back to the basic premise. Whether they were watching the roads, or they were watching a computer file, the key here is that they were watching, right? I mean they had to guard against the possibility, however remote, that we might go back to Newark—to do something that would never make a bit of sense unless we were innocent and they were trying to hide something, right?"

"Who's the guilty 'they'?" Thorne interrupted.

Jake shook him off. "I'm getting to that. So, whoever this person is, they have the power to tap into the EPA computer files, right? They knew that if anyone ever wanted to reenter the magazine, they'd have to tap into the file first."

Nick shrugged, growing weary of the explanation and wanting to turn right to the end. "Right. Okay. So you're saying it's EPA? Somebody in my agency wants to keep you away from Newark? What the hell for?"

Jake shook him off, too. "No, you've got to think back further than that. When did the EPA get involved in the Newark site? Nineteen eighty-three maybe? Eighty-two at the earliest?"

Nick bobbed his head. "Okay, somewhere in there. What's your point?"

"From that point on, B-2740 was locked up tight as a drum, right? Sure it was. I was there when we took the lock off a year later. No one could get in."

"I think that's right," Nick agreed. It was tough to be definitive after so many years.

Jake paused while he mentally took the next step. "So the bad guys must have gotten caught with their pants down when the EPA threw a lock on the place. Whatever they needed to hide was locked *inside* the magazine. They had to sit on their thumbs for two years while everything was debated and paid for. First chance they got to go inside was when we opened the door for them."

Nods all around. The logic made sense.

"So EPA is out."

"Okay, hotshot," Thorne prodded, his patience gone. "Then tell us who."

Jake looked at Nick like he should already have made the connection. "Who can put a trigger on another agency's computer files, Nick?"

"The FBI," Nick joked, but when Jake didn't laugh, Nick's smile went away. "Come on, Jake, the FBI? You're crazy!"

"Think about it," Jake insisted. "It could probably be any federal agency—CIA, Secret Service, even IRS—but who has consummate ability to perpetrate a frame like this? Who can make a person look as guilty as they want to make them look? I mean, Jesus Christ, Nick, a note at the murder scene? Who the fuck would leave a note? And who has the authority to decide that such a preposterous thing isn't preposterous at all?"

Nick found himself nodding absently, beginning to buy into the concept. "And who was pushing for us to shut the scene down so early?"

Jake sighed as all the pieces began to fit into place.

Nick sat down heavily. "Oh, shit, this is huge. We're fucked."

The words made Jake recoil. "How are we fucked? We just figured it out!"

"You haven't figured shit," Thorne scoffed. "You can imagine any theory you want, for Christ's sake. Hell, aliens did it! Until you can figure out why—and prove it—Nick's right. You're fucked."

"It's the FBI," Jake insisted again. "More specifically, it's Peter Frankel."

Jake's conclusion, materializing out of nowhere, seemed to suck all the sound out of the room. Then, together, Thorne and Nick erupted with laughter.

"Well, now, *there's* some fine detective work," Nick mocked. "Peter Frankel in the library with the candlestick, right?" He laughed again.

Jake ignored the barbs. "He was in charge of the investigation back in '83, remember?"

"Of course I remember. But Jesus, Jake, there were lots—"

"And he was the one pressing to shut down the original investigation, right, Nick? At least that's what you told me. Every time you mentioned continuing, he just shouted you down."

Nick didn't want to see it. "I could have pressed harder—"

"No!" Jake shouted. "Open your eyes! He's the only investigator with the seniority to pull it off. He stopped the investigation as soon as he had the answers he wanted, and he was sure to get those answers because he planted the evidence himself. Who's to know? Since then, he's had all the time in the world to build his case. He's smart enough to know the value of those computer files if we ever decided to go back, and he's certainly well connected enough to put a tag on them that would ring a bell, as you say, if anyone accessed them. Now he's on the news again, every day, preening for the cameras and telling the world just how guilty we are. It's got to be him. He's the common denominator!" The silence from the others told him he was close to making a sale here. "Frankel's the only one with the power and authority to make it all work."

Nick turned to Thorne for some help. "Come on, Thorne, tell him he's full of shit."

But that wasn't what the other man's expression said at all. "You know," he mused, "I've actually run into this Frankel before. The prick's run a couple of witch-hunts against a good friend of Mr. Sinclair's. A senator, in fact. Frankel plays rough. And he sure as hell doesn't mind breaking the law if it suits his purpose."

Thorne scowled thoughtfully and locked eyes with Jake. "After watching what he put the senator through, I wouldn't put anything past him. And how tough can it be to fool the investigators when you're the investigator who needs to be fooled?"

Nick opened his mouth to argue but shut it again. "Oh, man . . ."

"But that still leaves us with why," Jake lamented. "Why would he do such a thing?"

Thorne finally stepped all the way into the parlor and helped himself to a chair. He crossed his long legs in front of him and folded his fingers across his chest. "Shit, Jake," he said, smiling. "The 'why' is the easiest of all. Blowing that place up—it's one of your classic moves."

"Now," Thorne concluded, "the trick is to prove it."

"It's not possible," Nick said. "Too many variables. Too much conjecture. Besides, nobody's going to listen to us, anyway."

"I suppose you could get some eager-beaver newspaper type working on it," Thorne offered.

"No," Jake said. "That'll just spook Frankel and drive him further underground. Besides, without proof, even the press would be nuts to push this one."

Nick stood up again and began pacing the room. "The whole problem is that the FBI has spent a decade and a half proving their own theory. They'll never be open to anyone else's ideas. Particularly not if we're pointing the finger at their boss."

This was not a new thought to Jake. "Then we have to get them to see it for themselves," he said. It was time for dramatic, decisive action. "Do we know where the lead FBI agent is staying? What's her name? Rivers."

Thorne shrugged. "Shouldn't be hard to find out. Why?"

"I'm going to pay her a visit."

Thorne shook his head vehemently. "Bullshit. That's suicide."

"I can make her *believe*," Jake insisted. "I've reasoned with her before, back in the body shop when all of this began. If I can set her on the right track, I think she'll be able to prove it to herself."

"No." Thorne was unequivocal.

"You've got a better plan?" Jake's frustration caused his voice to crack. "We're dead in the water here!"

The big man seemed to struggle for an answer, then looked away, his jaw set angrily. "Well, I got no part in it," he said. "There's no way Mr. Sinclair will allow himself to walk into a buzz saw."

Jake hiked his shoulders into an extended shrug. "Do you see him here?"

Thorne didn't bother to answer.

Jake shifted his gaze. "Nick?"

Nick recoiled at the thought. "I don't think so!"

"All you have to do is drive, okay? I promise. I need your help to pull it off. You'll never have to leave the car."

Nick cocked his head warily. "Look, Jake. You know I'm committed to helping, but I've got to start thinking about damage control."

"What are you saying?"

Nick looked to Thorne and got a supportive, understanding nod. "God's honest truth, I don't think you've got a chance. It's too big. I came here with the idea of staying away from the law. Now you're seeking them out." He broke eye contact. "I just can't do that."

"It's stupid, Jake," Thorne repeated. "Listen to him. There's got to be a better way."

Jake just stared. "And searching for better ways takes more time than I've got." He felt himself flush with anger as he realized they were abandoning him. Well, to hell with them. He'd make it all right, with them or without them. He looked to Thorne again. "Let me have the keys, then."

Thorne paused for a long moment before hesitantly handing them over.

Jake bounced the keys in his palm. "Some tough guy you turned out to be," he said bitterly. When his eyes landed on Nick, he just broke his gaze and headed for the door.

As Nick listened to the quiet click of Jake's rubber-soled shoes disappearing down the hallway, he looked to Thorne and felt ashamed. It was foolish, he knew—and sentimental—but he just couldn't let Jake down like this. Not again.

"God help me," he groaned, rising from his chair. "In for a dime, in for a dollar, right, Thorne?" He had to hurry to catch up.

Alone, finally, in the sprawling house, Thorne poured himself a drink and reached for the telephone. It was time to catch his boss up on everything that had happened.

CHAPTER THIRTY-NINE

The guards wouldn't tell Carolyn a thing. She'd begged. She'd cried. Still, no one would tell her how Travis was doing. She knew he was alive, but beyond that, they said nothing. More precisely, they insisted they had no information. Of course, if she found a way to be more forthcoming with details about Jake, well, they might just be able to scavenge up a tidbit or two. *Assholes.*

She lay on the concrete shelf that served as a cot in her isolation cell, bathed in the yellow light cast by the wire-reinforced fixture overhead. She'd unrolled her mattress, such as it was, but the threadbare Army blanket and plastic pillow remained folded and stacked on her bed, serving as a convenient footrest. Officially, her celebrity status was responsible for her isolation, but she knew that it was just more mind games.

She worried how much longer she could hold out. Fear was hard to manage when you were all alone, and the fact that her tormentors took such pleasure from her fear made it that much worse. She tried to focus on Jake and on all she knew he must be doing to get her out. They'd been married nearly fifteen years now, and he'd never once let her down. God only knew how he'd do it, but she had to keep believing in him. Without that hope, there was nothing.

She'd heard over the years that one of the worst adjustments to life in prison was the constant noise. The air handlers thrummed endlessly, keeping the place cold enough to hang meat and preventing even the few quiet moments from being truly quiet. Already, she missed the rushing sound of an autumn breeze, the silence of a snowy night. Over time, though, she knew she could adjust to mechanical noise. It was the human noise that frightened her.

She was all alone in her little four-cell isolation wing, yet the sounds of other inmates still reverberated off the walls. People conversed at the top of their lungs, discussing issues as mundane as the weather and as newsy as the addition of the Newark terrorist to the jail's population. "You ain't seen terror yet, missy," one inmate yelled. "Wait till you get out here alone with us! You'll wish you had some nerve gas!"

Carolyn just closed her eyes tighter and tried not to think about the future. These were tough, violent people, who'd been led to believe that she was just as tough as they. Once they found out how truly terrified she was, they'd eat her alive. The thought of institutional violence, with no place to run, made her stomach seize.

You can't think that way, she silently told herself. *You've had dark days before*. But never a day as dark as this.

She tried to think of Travis. When dark days had turned bright in the past, it had almost always been his doing. He had that smile, and that knack for knowing how to make her laugh; just as he knew exactly which buttons could launch her into orbit. She closed her eyes tight and concentrated just on the smile—the way his front teeth crossed ever so slightly, and the way his whole face lit up at any punch line involving a body part south of the navel.

When she concentrated on these things, the pain in her heart eased up a bit, and she nearly allowed herself a smile.

Then she saw him back inside the car, drooling and frothing, struggling for every breath. What he must have been thinking of her as she wrestled with him in the water, stripping him of his clothes and his dignity! Why couldn't he understand? Why did he have to be so angry at the end?

I killed my own son.

No! He wasn't dead, dammit. For all Carolyn knew, he was as good as gold again, and the jailers were keeping it from her just to torture her some more.

She found herself thinking back to the time three years ago, in Baltimore, when he stepped on a bottle, barefoot, and opened up a gash under the arch of his foot. The poor kid howled, begging her to stop as she dug the grit and dirt out of the wound. What he needed was a hospital; a place to get stitched up. But they couldn't take him to an emergency room. Too many cops there. If it had been life-threatening, sure. And probably, if he had torn any ligaments or broken any bones. But something as mundane—as painful—as torn flesh just wasn't worth the risk. The wound took weeks to heal, hobbling him well into the winter of that year.

Carolyn tried now to make the memories go away. What kind of parent would let her child suffer like that? *Praise Jesus, God made him tough,* she thought miserably.

And now he was alone.

A noise at her cell door startled Carolyn back to reality, and she sat up quickly, swinging her feet to the floor. She rubbed her eyes with the heels of her hands, surprised she'd actually fallen asleep. The lock turned, and the steel door swung open, revealing a Wagnerian jail matron named Gladys, in the company of a rugged-looking older man in the requisite gray pinstripes of a government cop, carrying the standard-issue leather briefcase.

"Got a visitor for you, killer," Gladys said. "FBI."

"Agent Wiggins," the man said with exaggerated patience, as if this weren't the first time he'd had to remind her of his name.

Gladys eyed him like he smelled bad. "Right. She give you any trouble, give us a yell." She closed the door on the way out. And locked it.

Carolyn eyed Wiggins cautiously, fearfully. He had a predatory look about him that made her instinctively uncomfortable. "What time is it?" she asked.

He seemed a little surprised by the question, as if such details as the time of day were somehow irrelevant. After dropping a beat, he looked at his watch. "A little after one," he said.

She had an instinct for people, and something about this guy put her on edge. That Rivers lady she'd sparred with earlier in the day had been a certifiable jerk, but in an officious, professional sort of way. She had a job to do, and that job was to put Carolyn away forever. With her, the rules of engagement were clear. Wiggins was different. He frightened her. And in a distant sort of way, she'd have sworn she'd seen him before. "I've already said all I'm going to say," she growled, masking her fear with testiness.

He seemed amused as he checked his reflection in the stainless-steel plate that served as a mirror over the toilet. After adjusting the knot in his tie and smoothing an errant hair, he helped himself to a corner of her cot. "Well, Mrs. Donovan," he said softly, "what you have to say really doesn't interest me much."

She narrowed her gaze. It was coming back to her. Something in the intensity of his eyes, his face. She considered calling the matron but abandoned the notion right away. What would she say to her?

He caught her quick glance toward the door and turned to look. "Oh, don't do something stupid, Carolyn," he said. "Fact is, you're in one hell of a mess. If you ask me, you'd have been much better off had you stayed in hiding."

She felt the color drain from her face.

"Damned unfortunate set of circumstances, you know? Bringing you back into the limelight and all. If you'd have just continued lying low—hell, if you'd just stayed away from Arkansas—we probably never would have had to meet again."

Meet again? Her mind raced to put the pieces together. *Again?* Then she had it. The guy on the hill. The guy with the gun and the camouflage. "Oh, my God," she breathed, bringing her hand to her mouth. She looked frantically to the door again.

"Don't do it," he warned, reading her thoughts. "That would be a huge mistake. So I see you remember." He smiled and shook his head slowly. "Goddamned worst shooting I've ever done. I don't know how you and hubby got outa that place, but I gotta tell you, when I saw you come stumbling out of that fire, I just couldn't believe it." He laughed softly. "I was so fucking scared of that smoke cloud, all I wanted to do was run. I just kept pulling the trigger till I had an excuse to get the hell out."

She stared, her mouth open, her brain overflowing. "But why?" The question sounded more like a gasp.

He eyed her and shook his head. "Actually, that's none of your concern," he said. His manner was all business again. "Your concern, Carolyn, should be to keep that handsome young Travis from getting hurt."

The sound of her boy's name passing this predator's lips made her want to throw up. "Don't you dare . . ."

He interrupted her with a laugh. "And you can stop me, right?" He laughed again. "Look, for what it's worth, I checked in on the little tyke just before I came here. Jesus, he looks so small and helpless there in that big bed, tubes coming out from everywhere." He shook his head pitifully. "Doctors say he's sick, sick, sick. But with the right care, he'll probably be just fine." He paused and looked straight through to Carolyn's heart. "Unless, of course, something terrible happens to him."

An icicle materialized in her chest, and for the briefest of moments, she thought she might pass out. There had to be a way to stop him . . .

"I've scared you," he observed. "How rude of me. Well, relax. I only kill adults. Well, mostly." He smiled. "Here, I've got something for you." He opened his briefcase and removed a pad of paper, a calculator, and his FBI credentials and placed them all on the cot next to him. He shot her a conspiratorial glance, then removed a false bottom, to reveal a coiled length of nylon clothesline, which he handed over to her.

"Here's how this works," he explained as he placed everything back into the briefcase and latched it. "With this rope, you can save your son's life." He pointed to the ceiling. "I think that light fixture there is plenty strong enough to support a tiny little thing like you."

The horror of what he was suggesting hit Carolyn hard. Without even knowing it, she started to cry.

"Oh, relax," he coached. "People hang themselves in jail all the time. So here's the deal. If you're still alive for morning roll call, poor little Travis will be dead by breakfast. See how simple that is?" He smiled and stood.

She stared dumbly at the rope in her hands, then back up at him. "But *why?*" Her voice was merely a sob.

He shrugged. "Because I said so, Carolyn. How's that?"

She just stared. It was too much to comprehend.

He bent close and took the rope from her. "Let's just tuck this in under the covers here," he said, laying the coil underneath the stacked blanket and pillow. "That way, the matron won't get wind of our little plan." He patted her on the head. "I've given you a lot to think about, Carolyn, and I apologize for that, but there's really no other way. Now, I can only imagine that you'll wonder at some point if maybe I'm bluffing. I'd wonder that if I were you." He leaned in even further, until bare inches separated their faces. "But I swear to you, if you let me down, he won't go easily. Do you understand?" He was whispering now. "I'll make him suffer. He'll *suffer*, Carolyn."

He let the words sink in for a long moment, then straightened. "Well, this has been fun." He called for the matron. "By the way, where did Travis get that scar on the sole of his foot?"

Carolyn's heart cramped hard, and suddenly she couldn't breathe. This man *had* been looking at her little boy.

"He's growing up *fast*, too, isn't he?" he added with a smile.

She felt ill. She wanted to rip this man's eyes out, but even as the image flashed through her brain, she knew the futility of it. Her mind swirled out of control, propelled by the purest form of fear she'd ever known.

A key slid into the lock. "I've got to go," he said heavily.

"Wait!" she insisted, even as she heard the lock turn. "How do I know you won't kill him, anyway?"

The door opened, and they weren't alone anymore. He flashed his humorless grin one last time. "You don't," he said. "Sweet dreams, Carolyn."

CHAPTER FORTY

All you have to do is *drive*," Nick mocked under his breath as he crossed the once-grand lobby of the Radford Hotel. He carried the pizza box on his shoulder, bearing the logo of Papa Lorenzo's Perfect Pizza Parlor. The box was empty, of course. Nick and his coconspirator had consumed the whole thing while sitting down the block in Thorne's rental car, working out the fine points of the plan. Tasted pretty good, actually, considering the fact that Papa Lorenzo and his staff all wore turbans.

Even though Little Rock was a small city by most standards, the task of locating a single needle named Irene Rivers in a haystack of several dozen hotels seemed hopeless at first. Then Jake got an idea. In fact, he seemed flooded with ideas. Good ones, even. An amazing turnaround, Nick thought, given the quivering mess he'd been just scant hours before.

Their approach was simple: divide the Yellow Pages in half and burn up a ton of quarters in pay phones calling front desk after front desk and asking for Irene Rivers's room. They were just shy of four dollars into their strategy when Jake got a hit on the Radford. After the phone in her room rang ten times without anyone answering, he just hung up, confident she was still out saving the world from the likes of himself.

Finding the hotel was only the first step, though. They still needed a room number, and for that, Nick needed to do some legwork. Between the two of them, his was the face that hadn't dominated the news.

The Radford was a big old place, which once had been the destination of choice for visiting presidents and celebrities. On the heels of more than a few slow years, though, the Radford had been unable to keep up with the Grand Marquis and the Crown Plaza, and its once-dependable clientele had shifted its loyalties elsewhere. The place was still several giant steps away from homeless-shelter status, but there was precious little charm left in the threadbare Oriental carpets and scratched cherry walls.

To be put up in a place like this was clear evidence that Irene Rivers had seriously pissed off her travel agent.

As Nick approached the two teenagers manning the front desk, they looked up simultaneously and smiled. "Hi. Can I help you?" one of them said.

Nick noted the similarity of the girls' features—even down to the matching zits on their chins—and he wondered silently if maybe they were sisters. He smiled back, trying his best to look a little sheepish while praying that his hands wouldn't shake.

"Hi," he said back. "You sure can." With hopes of making himself look more like a local, he spoke around a toothpick he'd picked up at Papa Lorenzo's. "One of your guests called and ordered a pizza. Unfortunately, I lost the little note with her room number on it. Got a name, though. Rivers. Irene Rivers. Can you give me her room?"

The Bobbsey Twins exchanged glances, then shook their heads in unison. "No, I'm afraid not," said the one on the right. "We can't give out people's room numbers to anyone."

"I can call her, though, and have her come down and pick it up," offered the twin on the left.

Nick's stomach knotted. He felt a burst of panic, then forced a smile. "No," he said quickly. "Please don't do that. Listen, truth of it is, I'm already running fifteen minutes late with this thing, and this is the second time I've lost an address tonight. Boss told me this Rivers lady is a pain as it is. If she gets ticked and calls, I'm sunk, know what I mean?"

The girls shared a *significant* look this time and nodded again. Obviously, they'd known some difficult customers in their time and maybe even worked for an asshole or two along the way.

"We really shouldn't . . ." hedged Bobbsey Left.

"Please," Nick begged winningly. "It's humiliating enough for a man my age to be delivering pizzas. I could really do without a lecture to go with it, you know?"

Another look. And a joint sigh. "Okay," said Bobbsey Right as she tapped the keys on her computer. "Just don't get us in trouble, okay? Room 405." She looked up and pointed across the lobby. "You can take those elevators over there."

Nick smiled and thanked them. He wandered over and pushed the call button, but it seemed forever before anything happened. Even the elevators in this old barn were tired. Fortunately, he was the only passenger. After the big doors rumbled shut, Nick pushed the buttons for both the second floor and the fourth, so that the floor indicator in the lobby would go all the way to Agent Rivers's floor, even after he exited on the first stop.

The hallway was bright enough, if somewhat narrow, in the style of old downtown hotels, and he encountered his first dilemma in trying to figure out what to do with the damn pizza box. Finally, he gave up looking for a trash can and just slid it under a Coke machine.

That done, he took the stairs down to a preselected side entrance on the first floor. Checking one more time to make sure that the stairwell was empty, he opened the door and nearly screamed. Jake was standing right there, not two feet away on the other side. "Jesus! You scared the shit out of me!"

Jake looked at him like he was crazy. "I told you I'd be waiting here."

"Yeah, but . . ." *Oh, the hell with it.* "She's in room 405. How're you gonna get in?"

Jake shrugged and craned his neck to peer up the stairwell. "I don't know yet. But I'll make it."

They climbed the first two floors together before Nick broke off to retrieve his elevator. "I'll wait for you in the car," he said. But his face said something else entirely.

Jake smiled. "I'll be there." He sounded none too convinced himself.

It was nearly two by the time Irene returned to her hotel room, exhausted. Her body was whipped, but her mind whirled way too fast to permit sleep. She'd hoped that the martini before dinner and the two glasses of wine with the entrée would take the edge off, but it was no use. Slice by slice, her career had been whittled away to virtually nothing these past few days, and all the alcohol had accomplished was to give her a world-class case of heartburn.

A hot bath was her last hope. She preferred them just this side of scalding, where the skin of her fingers and toes would prune up in minutes and the heat would suck away her ability to concentrate on anything but sleep. None of the worry mattered, anyway. Even with his wife and son in jeopardy, Jake Donovan still remained well out of reach. That part surprised her. She'd thought for sure he was more of a family man than that.

Still fully clothed, Irene plugged the tub and cranked the faucet all the way to hot. After a few seconds, she eased it back a bit, then closed the door behind her as she strolled back to the bedroom to change out of her suit.

They knew for certain now that Donovan was getting help from someone. The local cop in Newark reported a third party, as did the paramedics at the Rescue Squad building. Crime scene technicians had confirmed glove smudges in the Faylons' Toyota, but no extra prints yet. The Caddy was a rental—under a fictitious name—and as such had hundreds of fingerprints all over it. They'd run them all through the computer, of course, but it was a giant step between having rented a vehicle and being a suspect in a crime.

Agents from the Chicago field office had been following through on Irene's pet theory involving Harry Sinclair, but after a day of turning his house inside out, no one had found a single piece of evidence to implicate the old man. Old Harry had even shown up at the house again, after a day of what he called "alone time." Apparently, occasional stretches of unaccountability helped him cope during his periods of heavy thinking.

Ted Greenberg in Chicago had sent a tape of Sinclair's interview via courier to George Sparks's office in Little Rock. Irene had listened to a copy in the car on the way to dinner. It was funny, really, hearing Ted work to trip up the old man.

"So, how do you explain the phone call from Travis Donovan?"

"I suppose he wanted to talk to me."

"Did he?"

"Why don't you tell me."

"Look, Mr. Sinclair, it's in your best interest to cooperate here."

"Consider me the poster child of cooperation."

"Fine. Did you speak to Travis Donovan?"

"I'm afraid our connection was broken."

"So you didn't speak to him?"

"If the connection was broken, how could I?"

"Please answer the question, sir. Yes or no." The frustration in Greenberg's voice jumped right out of the cassette. "Did you or did you not speak over the telephone with Travis Donovan?"

"That would be very difficult without a connection, don't you think?" Equally obvious was the amusement in Sinclair's voice.

And so it went, for forty-five minutes, with Harry Sinclair neither incriminating nor perjuring himself. It occurred to Irene that the old man would make a great politician. In all likelihood, the interview would have continued ad infinitum had Sinclair's attorney not shown up and put a stop to it. He'd already talked an appellate judge into nullifying their warrant and slapping a stay on their wiretap, due to a lack of evidence.

What the hell? she told herself. It was a dead end, anyway.

She undressed quickly and clumsily, kicking off her shoes and wriggling out of her suit. She paused a minute to check a spaghetti spatter on the front of the blouse and made a mental note to send it out to the cleaners first thing tomorrow, before it had a chance to set.

Next came her weapon, a black S&W .40-caliber semiautomatic, which she unclipped from the waistband of her skirt and dropped with a thunk onto the dresser. In less than a minute, she was naked, ready to soak. On her way back toward the bathroom, she paused for a moment to view herself in the mirrored closet doors, first full-face, then profile.

"Not bad for forty-two," she told herself. Then, to remember what she looked like at twenty-two, she sucked in her stomach until she couldn't breathe. "It sucks to grow old," she grumbled. Hearing the vernacular, she reminded herself just how much she was beginning to sound like her kids.

I've got to call them, she thought. *First thing tomorrow. It's been two days.* And two days alone with their father was more than anyone should be asked to endure.

By the time she finished brushing her teeth, the water level had reached the danger line, and she had to take care as she lowered herself into the steaming bath not to slosh anything over the sides. It was wonderful; better, even, than she'd hoped. In the oversize tub, the water came past her breasts, just high enough to tickle the underside of her chin. The tension and the worry drained away as she leaned her head back against the tile and closed her eyes. This was heaven. If only she'd thought to turn out the lights, she could've fallen asleep right there.

In fact, she'd nearly nodded off when she heard the bathroom door open.

"Don't scream," Jake warned as he took aim at Irene's left eye. "In fact, don't say anything. If you try to call for help, I'll kill you."

Irene didn't move, other than to begin trembling in the scalding water.

"Do you believe I'll kill you?" Jake asked.

The fugitive's face was blank, yet his eyes remained warm. The contrast petrified her. She nodded. Yes, she believed him.

He nodded along with her. "Good." He pulled a towel off the metal rack next to the sink and handed it to her. "Here," he said. "Cover yourself up."

She reached for the towel too quickly and caused a wave of water to arch over the porcelain edge and slap down onto the black and white tile floor. As she tucked the towel around her body, she realized with a shudder that she was staring down the barrel of her own gun. A humiliating end to a humiliating day.

"What do you want?" she demanded. The strength she heard in her voice surprised her.

"How's my son?"

She glared at him, her fear dissolving quickly into anger. "Who do you think you are, charging into my hotel room—"

"You know who I am," Jake interrupted. "And if you truly believe all the bullshit they say I've done, then you should be scared shitless right now. If you don't believe it, then you should know just how angry and unstable I have a right to be." He helped himself to a spot on the vanity and drew one knee up to help support the weight of the pistol. "Either way, it seems that you should think twice before pissing me off."

She continued to glare. There was fear in his eyes now, and combined with the complex assortment of other emotions he projected, she didn't know what to make of his stability. Perhaps it was, indeed, time to be careful.

He took a deep, shaky breath and tried again. "I'm not asking you for state secrets, Rivers. I'm a father whose son is sick. Now, please answer my question. How is he?"

The way she broke eye contact said more than her words ever could. His shoulders sagged.

"They say he'll live," she said softly. "But it's too early to tell the full extent of the damage to his lungs."

Jake felt the sadness return and closed his eyes. *At least he's alive,* he told himself. This was a time to focus on the positive.

He heard movement in the water and his eyes snapped open, freezing Irene in midlunge. If her foot hadn't slipped, she might have made it.

"Don't!" he yelled, more loudly than was prudent this late at night. His finger was half a pull away from killing her, and she seemed to know it, her full attention focused on the barrel of the pistol. "Sit down!" he commanded sharply. "Goddammit, Rivers, don't do that to me!"

She did, indeed, sit back down, and she watched as Jake struggled with his emotions. Sure as hell he'd have killed her, and from all appearances, that fact scared him nearly as much as it scared her.

A full minute passed before anyone said anything. Then he asked, "Have you seen him? Travis, I mean?"

She nodded. "Yes, I've seen him. He seems to be resting comfortably. They've got him in pediatric ICU, and he's on a respirator, but he doesn't seem to be in any distress."

He considered that for a moment, then nodded to himself. "That's good," he said absently. "It's good he's comfortable. We can handle anything as long as he's alive." Another long pause followed. "Do you have children, Rivers?"

The question made her uneasy, but there seemed to be no threat in it. "Uh-huh," she said. "Two daughters."

He nodded again, though she wasn't at all sure he'd heard her answer. "Kids are a hoot, aren't they? Nothing makes you laugh as hard or cry as hard as a kid." Again, he seemed to disappear into a distant room in his mind.

"Why are you here, Donovan?" she said, interrupting his thoughts. "No offense, but for an intelligent guy like yourself, this is a stupid place to be."

He looked up again and chuckled. "So I've heard. Well, I'll admit it seemed a much better idea when I was planning it than it did once I got here. But sooner or later, I figured I had to trust someone. You're it. What does that tell you about my available options?"

"How did you get in?" *Get him talking about himself,* she thought, remembering her hostage negotiation training. As long as he felt like he had a friend, he'd be less likely to harm the hostage. She must have skipped the lesson on what to do when the negotiator and the hostage were the same person.

"You'd be surprised how many master keys they've got lying around the Housekeeping Department at this hour," he said.

"That's smart," she said. "I'm not sure I would have thought of that."

The comment brought a smirk to Jake's face, and then the smirk turned to a smile and the smile to a laugh.

"What?" Clearly, she didn't like being laughed at.

"Why, Agent Rivers, I believe you're trying to suck up to me. Is that one of the lessons in Hostage 101?" He laughed again.

She scowled. "I don't know—"

"Please," he interrupted with a wave. "Spare me. If it sets your mind at ease, I don't want anything from you except conversation, okay? If you just stay put and do what I tell you, I'll be on my way in just a little while. As you might imagine, I feel a little exposed here." He eyed her towel and chuckled again. "Well, okay, maybe not as exposed as you, but still . . ."

She smiled in spite of herself and pulled the towel a little closer.

"So, tell me, Rivers, do you really believe that we killed all of those people back in 1983?"

Her eyes narrowed as she searched for the right answer.

He sighed. "Relax, okay? This isn't a quiz. It's a fact-finding mission."

She shrugged. "Well . . . yes."

He considered the answer. Certainly, it was no surprise. "That all makes perfect sense to you, does it? That my wife and I—neither of us with the slightest hint of a violent past—would shoot our friends, blow up half the state, and then leave a *note?*"

She shrugged. "With all due respect, Donovan, crooks have been known to do some pretty stupid things. Zealots, in particular, have a long history of stupidity."

"Zealots." He said the word softly, as if testing its flavor. "So that's what we were, huh? Zealots? I suppose the record is full of documented examples of our zealous causes? Or was this environmental thing our first?"

"Look Jake . . ."

"No, you look, *Irene,*" he pressed. "Have you found any evidence at all to substantiate this zealot crap? Registration cards for the American Nazi Party, maybe? How about—oh, damn, who was it that burned all the campuses in the sixties?—SDS, that's it. Students for a Democratic Society. Have you found that? How about the

NRA? Have you been able to dig up a single example of Carolyn or me being zealous about *anything?*"

Irene rolled her eyes. "Come off it, Donovan. Even Fidel Castro had a first time. The evidence speaks for itself. Frankly, this little campaign of yours to dream up a conspiracy about some skeleton is kind of sad. Maybe if you'd come forward at the time, but really . . ."

He recoiled a bit at the mention of the skeleton, but then he realized that she must have interviewed Carolyn. "That proved to be a dead end," he said. At this point, honesty could only help.

"I beg your pardon?"

"The skeleton we came after turned out to be a dog. Must have wandered in and died before any of this happened."

Now she was really confused. "So, what—"

"But getting back to the note," he said, gesturing with the gun as if it were an extension of his forefinger. "You're telling me you don't find that even a little absurd? A little *convenient?* Jesus."

She didn't know where this was going, so she remained silent. She figured he'd get to his point sooner or later.

"Have you investigated many arsons, Rivers?"

She shrugged with one shoulder, the abrupt change of subject putting her on edge. "My share, I suppose."

He nodded approvingly. "I thought so. I remember seeing on television once that sometimes arson is used to cover up an entirely different crime. Has that ever been your experience?"

She regarded her visitor for a long moment before answering. "Let's say I've heard similar rumors."

"Okay, fine. Let's say that. It wouldn't be out of the question, then—I mean, it wouldn't be inconceivable—if you found out that such was the case in Newark back in '83, right?"

Irene didn't like being cross-examined by a murderer. "The water's getting cold, Jake. Please get to the point."

"Fair enough." It was time to play the Big Bluff. "Living underground as I have these past years, I've developed some interesting friendships with people who have access to information you wouldn't believe."

"And Harry Sinclair is one of them," she interrupted.

Jake was ready for that. "Who?"

She rolled her eyes. "Right," she groaned. "Go on."

He shrugged it off. "Well, this information, I'll admit, is not always put to good use, but it's proved to be very reliable." He paused for a reaction, got none, then moved on. "These friends have recently given me proof that your boss, Peter Frankel, was up to his elbows in illegal activities back in the early eighties . . ."

"Oh, please!" she scoffed. "I don't even need to listen to this."

"Hear me out," he insisted.

She looked poised to argue but then seemed to give up. "I guess I don't have a lot of choice, do I?"

Okay, here we go. It was time to sell guesswork as fact.

"Frankel was a senior guy in Little Rock, wasn't he, back in '83?"

"Are you telling me or asking me?"

"I'm trying to get you to open your mind, goddammit!" Jake barked.

She smiled smugly. "Then you're wasting your time here."

Okay, fine. False start. He tried again. "Well, if you do some research, you'll find that he was in charge of the whole investigation back then. Fact is, he was senior enough to be involved in just about everything coming out of your Little Rock office."

"As the supervisory agent in charge is wont to do," she interrupted.

Bingo. Guess number one confirmed. "Well, my people tell me that your boss knew all about the chemical warfare shit that was stored back in that magazine but had reason to keep it a secret from everybody—including *his* bosses."

"And what reason might that be?" She pretended to be amused, even as a tiny light came on in her brain.

"Lots of money to be made in illegal weapons sales, you know."

Irene's heart skipped a beat as she recalled George Sparks's recent mission to Iraq. To Jake, the recognition registered only as a slight tic in her right eye and a slight parting of her lips. Like a silent sigh. She said nothing, and she recovered quickly.

"So he's having this regular yard sale out of Uncle Sam's general store, when bingo! up pops the EPA and slaps a lock on the door.

He's cut off from his supplies, and all the evidence in the world is just sitting there waiting to convict him."

"You're guessing," she hedged. "You don't have any evidence."

Jake was encouraged, even as she hit the nail on the head. It made too much sense for it not to be true, but he was powerless to verify anything. If he did his job right, she'd do the research for him.

"Oh, there's evidence," he bluffed. "You already see it in your head. I know you do. You don't want to, but it's there, isn't it? If you want the same proof I have, all you have to do is look for it."

"Where?" she pressed. "Where do I look for this earth-shattering revelation? Who do I talk to?"

"C'mon, Rivers. People can die for answering questions like that." It was the response he'd rehearsed in the car with Nick. *Mystery masks any lack of substance.*

She shook her head vehemently. She refused to buy into it. "Why not just blow the place up, then? Why go to all the effort to kill so many people if he was just trying to hide some evidence of missing inventory?"

Her question stopped conversation dead. Jake narrowed his eyes and allowed himself a bitter smile. "Why kill so many people . . ." He savored the words as he repeated them. "You ask that question when it's one of your own, yet you assume simple insanity when it's Carolyn and me. Strange, huh?"

She acknowledged the point by looking away.

"Think about it, Rivers," Jake urged, his tone growing more insistent. "Assume for just a second that I'm telling the truth here—that Carolyn and I are innocent. Now look at the facts. If you want to truly hide a secret, it's not enough merely to destroy it. You've got to provide an alternative explanation for the destruction. The last thing Frankel wanted was an open-ended investigation. Without evidence to point to someone else, the trail might very well have led back to him. As it was, he got his bad guys on the first day and got the entire episode cleared up within a couple of weeks. Because of who he was, no one questioned anything."

Irene considered it, and the more she thought, the more frightened she looked. "How could he have known that you and Carolyn would survive? If he was planning to pin this elaborate conspiracy on you, how could he know you'd get away?"

Jake watched her for a few seconds, waiting for her to see it for herself. "The name Tony Bernard mean anything to you?" he asked.

It took her a moment to place him. "Yes. He's one of the people killed that day. Back at the motel room."

"And why was he back at the motel? Do you remember?" If this was going to work, she had to put some pieces together for herself.

Irene closed her eyes. She'd just reread the file that morning, but it felt like years ago. "He was sick, wasn't he? Some stomach thing."

Jake waited, but she still didn't get it. "Awfully odd, don't you think? Young man like that suddenly too sick to work, and then these murderous barbarians go all the way back to the motel just to pop him—and to leave a note?"

Irene's eyes grew intense enough to spark a fire as the pieces fell into place. "You think that Tony Bernard was the original patsy?"

Jake smiled. "In fact, I know he was," he lied.

"But what about his illness? There were witnesses—"

"And how tough is it to give somebody a bellyache? I saw him that morning, too. He was heaving his guts out. He thought it was something he ate. I bought it at the time, just like everybody else did. But hell, we all ate the same stuff at the same place. Why was he the only one to get sick?" He let the words settle for a few seconds. "When Carolyn and I survived, Frankel had to shift gears a little, but he stayed with essentially the same plan. I figure that Tony was killed as an insurance policy. No telling what he might have known."

She considered it all for a moment longer. "And if you and your wife had gotten arrested, it wouldn't have mattered a bit, would it?" she thought aloud.

"Not with the case that Frankel put together," Jake agreed. "And the further false evidence I'm sure he would've found if he was pushed to the wall. Plus, when emotions run as high as they did after Newark, the standards for evidence decrease. Why scour the bushes when the answer is delivered to your door? People want a quick conviction in these things. In the end, nothing we said could have gotten us off."

Her head spun with new possibilities. It had never occurred to her to believe Carolyn's story. Was it possible the Donovans were telling the truth?

"So how's Carolyn?" Jake asked, another radical change of subject. Irene looked at him, confused. "I trust you've spoken with her?"

Irene nodded. "She's fine. Frightened, angry, and sad, but otherwise fine."

He smiled. "Good. Next time you see her, will you tell her I love her? And that I'm doing my best to fix everything?"

She saw a chance. "Why don't *you* tell her, Jake? Let me take you in, and we'll get this all straightened out. I promise you, I'll pursue every lead you give me."

That one made him laugh. "You're kidding, right?" She wasn't, and he knew it. "Well, I appreciate the offer, but forgive me if I decline. I'm not entirely convinced that trusting you this much hasn't been a huge mistake. Somehow my faith in the criminal justice system just isn't as strong as it used to be." As he spoke, he dropped the clip out of Irene's weapon and started thumbing the bullets into the toilet. He saw her look of disgust and smiled. "I know, it's kind of gross, but I can't very well leave you with a loaded gun, can I? I don't think either of us wants the hassle of a shoot-out at two-thirty in the morning."

"So what's next?" she asked cautiously.

He shrugged. "I guess that's up to you. You need to decide if your job is about justice or simply about following orders." With the bullets removed, he dropped the clip into the bowl, then drew his own weapon before snapping the last of Irene's bullets out of the chamber and closing the toilet lid. "I do have one last thing for you to think about, though."

"I'm all ears."

"I know you've been wondering why we came back here today, and I've done my best to explain that. We came for that dog skeleton, and it was a horrible miscalculation. Stupid reason, isn't it? Made no sense. So how come you were expecting us?"

Without waiting for an answer, he slid down off the vanity and turned the doorknob to let himself out. "By the way," he said with a grin. "I was hiding in the closet when you came in, and I have to agree. You're not bad at all for forty-two."

Sleep now was out of the question. Irene considered trying, anyway, if only in deference to the time of night, but even as her body screamed for a place to lie down, her mind spun like a top.

Donovan's visit had left her stunned. All day long, she'd tried to think of a sound, logical reason for the couple to return to Arkansas. Clichés notwithstanding, smart criminals never returned to the scene of the crime. And after fourteen years on the Ten Most Wanted list, the Donovans had proved themselves to be very smart indeed.

After fishing the ammunition out of the toilet bowl—thankfully, she'd flushed after using it last—she'd strolled back into the bedroom, where she found her weapon in the middle of the king-size bed. She didn't bother calling to alert anyone about Jake. He'd be long gone as it was, and the last thing she needed was another documented getaway.

Pulling on the lightweight flannel nightgown she always kept stuffed in her garment bag, she sat heavily in the hard-back desk chair in front of the faux-wood desk. The Donovan file lay in her briefcase, just out of reach, but she didn't want it right now. She wanted to reconstruct the case against them from memory.

What did the Bureau have, really? The note. Sixteen dead bodies. The fact of their survival and escape. What else?

Nothing. The thought made her gasp. What had seemed so ironclad—so obvious—only an hour ago now seemed pitifully superficial. Fragile almost. There was enough there, she supposed, to win a conviction in the hands of a skillful prosecutor; but suddenly, there seemed to be huge holes in the case. Holes big enough for a skilled defense attorney to drive a Mercedes through.

Maybe that's what this was all about, she mused, resurrecting her natural cynicism. Maybe their return and the attendant shenanigans were merely stunts, designed to build a case for reasonable doubt in the minds of a future jury. Lord knew that the standard for acquittal was getting lower these days. Maybe this was just a high-stakes roll of the dice. They'd made their stand, and if they won, they'd be able to reenter society as full-fledged citizens. Was such a plan truly out of the question for people as intelligent as the Donovans? Especially if they had Harry Sinclair's money behind them?

Certainly, it wasn't as absurd as Jake's assertion that Peter Frankel was involved in arms trafficking and murder.

So why *did* the Donovans return? Why didn't they just disappear one more time? They'd made it, for heaven's sake; they'd dropped completely off the radar screen after they snagged their kid from the school. Certainly, Sinclair would have helped them one more time. Why risk so much just for a jury stunt?

And why the hell would they just give up like that, after all this time on the run?

But they didn't give up, did they? Their kid got hurt, and they sought medical attention. If that hadn't happened, would they have disappeared, anyway? Dammit, why weren't these questions in her head when Jake was in her bathroom?

Maybe hurting the kid was part of the plan. Certainly, that would garner more sympathy from the jury. Wouldn't it be harder to send grieving parents up the river than it would a pair of hardened killers?

Perhaps. But she'd seen the pain on Carolyn's face. And on Jake's. As a sometimes-negligent parent herself, Irene easily recognized parental guilt in others, and the emotions she saw in the Donovans today were as genuine as any she'd ever seen. There was no faking that kind of pain.

What was Jake's challenge to her? *Is your job about justice or merely about following orders?* She wondered bitterly if salvaging a career might be a noble third option.

So if the day finally came to testify against the Donovans in open court, could she sell a jury on the idea that all of this conspiracy crap was merely an absurd stunt to deflect attention away from their heinous crimes? Absolutely. And in so doing, did she believe in her heart of hearts that justice would be served? The answer to that one scared her.

But Frankel? Jesus.

Jake's claims of hard evidence were a bluff, and she knew it. Clearly, lies were not his strong suit, even after so many years of living one. Still, even though she wished with all her heart that she could dismiss his theories as crazy, she had to admit that he made a lot of sense.

What was it he asked on his way out? The question she was supposed to ask herself? Ah, yes. Frankel was the one who told her that the Donovans were coming to Arkansas. Something about a computer geek at EPA. So what was the big deal there? They put triggers on computer files all the time. If someone tried to access it, then a warning . . .

Then she saw it. "God *damn* it," she breathed. "He *knew* they'd go back, sooner or later."

Her face flushed hot as the pieces fell into place. *Oh, God, this is suicide.*

Now it was just a matter of proving her case without detonating her career. Fact was, she found herself liking this criminal named Jake Donovan. Much as it sickened her to think it, he seemed far nicer—and far less likely to take another life—than Peter Frankel ever had.

Moving quickly to make the most of the few hours remaining before dawn, she opened her briefcase and slid her laptop out from under the Donovan file. Damn thing took forever to boot up, but once running, the rest was a breeze. The Internet was never busy at this hour.

Chapter Forty-One

Despite the sprawling opulence of the mansion-in-the-meadow—Jake had it pegged at about ten thousand square feet—they remained clustered in the tiny parlor. Never much of a brandy connoisseur, Jake had developed a taste for Armagnac in the hour since he returned from the Radford, made even more discerning by Thorne's observation that the stuff sold for four hundred dollars a bottle.

Nick had crashed shortly after they'd returned, claiming the love seat as his own and leaving the two chairs for Jake and Thorne. Harry Sinclair's right-hand man looked exhausted, yet he remained awake and attentive while Jake recounted all that went on in Irene's hotel room. He seemed particularly intrigued by the part about finding the "FBI lady" naked. Under different circumstances, Jake might even have considered this little chat a bonding session, but he never doubted that Thorne's single purpose was to report everything Jake said back to his boss.

"I think Rivers is pretty sharp," Jake concluded. "I'm sure she'll do the legwork we need to get done." *Did I just say that?* He wondered if he wasn't trying to convince himself. The fact was, the odds were even that she'd take his information straight to Frankel, at which point Jake was screwed. No, correction—they were *all* screwed. Possibly even the mighty Harry Sinclair, given Irene's question about his involvement in all this—the one detail he'd omitted from his report to Thorne.

As the big man started to doze, Jake was seized by melancholy, and the image of Travis fixed itself in his thoughts. Was there at least a safety net for his son—a level below which he wouldn't fall? Jake wanted to believe that even if the fight to prove his and Carolyn's innocence dragged on, the boy would be cut loose and—

What?

It worried Jake that even if he saw his most fervent wish fulfilled and Travis staged a full recovery, the likelihood was that his son would become a ward of the state.

A thought materialized out of nowhere. It was a wild one—one that was formed more from exhaustion than logic—yet in the space of seconds it grew from merely a seedling notion to a fine compromise to a question in need of speedy resolution. He turned urgently to Thorne and tapped the man's knee, startling him from a fragile sleep.

"I've got a question for you."

Thorne raised an eyebrow.

"What do you think Harry would say if I asked him to take charge of Travis while all of this business plays itself out?"

"He'd say no," Thorne replied grumpily. He'd been enjoying his shut-eye.

"Why?" Suddenly, Jake was wide awake. He sat up straight. "I mean, he's family, right? The courts would surely be inclined to grant temporary custody to family. Christ, Carolyn thinks the sun rises and sets with the old bastard."

Thorne shook his head. "It's a question Mr. Sinclair anticipated. The answer is no."

"It'd be better than shuttling the poor kid from stranger to stranger," Jake countered. "At least Harry could give some stability."

"Your boy isn't Mr. Sinclair's problem," Thorne said simply. "I mean, as kids go, yours ain't so bad, but a kid's a kid. You know of any kids Mr. Sinclair ever had? I don't. He doesn't like them."

Jake wasn't about to let it go. "But what about Carolyn? His Sunshine? I mean, she's—"

"She's *different*," Thorne interrupted. He thought about saying something else but then stopped himself. "She's different."

In that instant, Jake saw a look in Thorne's face that came as close to tenderness as a man like him could ever generate. "Tell me about her childhood," he said softly.

Thorne's eyes narrowed. "What do you want to know? She was a kid. Mr. Sinclair liked her."

"But she has nightmares. Horrible ones. She wakes up screaming, yet she won't talk about them. I know nothing of her parents. When I try to probe, she just pulls away."

Thorne looked away, uncomfortable with the topic. "Then she doesn't want you to know," he said. "You should just let it go."

"So why does she adore Harry the way she does?" Jake pressed. "What is it about that ornery old man that makes her melt at the mention of his name?"

Thorne just shook his head. These questions were not even worth answering.

"Did Harry abuse Carolyn?" Jake asked out of nowhere.

"What?"

"Did Harry abuse my wife when she was a little girl?" Jake said it again firmly, without hesitation. "There's signs, sometimes, that she was molested as a kid. She pulls away occasionally, she frequently doesn't sleep. And the nightmares. I just thought that maybe . . ." His voice trailed off. He'd never verbalized his concerns to anyone before, and he was shocked by the emotions that welled up within him.

Thorne's eyes hardened. "So you think Mr. Sinclair raped his niece? And that afterward she decided to *adore* him?" He leaned heavily on Jake's word.

Jake shrugged. "I don't know. There's so much weird psychological bullshit you read about. I thought maybe . . ."

"You really got it bad for Sunshine, don't you?" Thorne seemed surprised.

Jake looked away, embarrassed. "More than you could know," he said.

Thorne inhaled deeply through his nose and let it go through puffed cheeks. "Mr. Sinclair's little sister, Rebecca—she wasn't very tough . . . very confident about herself," he said softly. "She was sick a lot as a kid, and as she got older, she started into that whiny teenage shit, where she thought she was ugly and no guys would ever like her. I never knew her back then, you know, but Mr. Sinclair was very bothered by her attitude. Said she was a pretty thing, but how do you make a kid sister listen?"

He shifted again. "So when she's eighteen, along comes a twenty-five-year-old dickhead named Mike Skepanski. Him I knew, and you could tell just from looking at him what a useless pile of shit he was. Mr. Sinclair hated him. Hell, *everybody* hated him. Everybody but Rebecca, of course, who fell in love with the guy and married him. Just weeks out of high school, knows nothing about anything, and she's attached to this jerk for the rest of her life."

As he spoke, Thorne's story took on a momentum of its own, seeming to propel him more than he was propelling it. "Well, he does a stint as a construction worker for a while, but then the poor baby cuts his hand and doesn't want to do that anymore. So he sits around the house for a few months until some stupid fuck offers him a job as a security guard. He takes it, because he's allowed to carry a gun and the gun makes him feel like a big man.

"That doesn't work out either, of course, because he's a worthless fucking loser. Seems to me, he got caught sleeping on the job, or some such thing, and he got fired. It's like this his whole life. He can't hold a job, Rebecca's miserable, and in the middle of it all, Carolyn is born." Thorne allowed himself a smile as he looked back to Jake. "Now, I gotta tell you, I'm not much into kids, but Carolyn was a cutie. Big eyes, always smiling. And for the first time, Rebecca begins to think good thoughts about herself, you know?" The smile went away. "Until the Polack starts knocking her around just for the hell of it. Rebecca never said a word to anybody. Instead, she got heavy into drugs and booze and shit."

He fell quiet for a moment, clearly girding himself for the rest of the story. "So I get a phone call one day that scares me. Rebecca's not right, you know? And she wants to talk to her brother. I think that's the first time I got clued in to the drinking. Well, Mr. Sinclair talks on the phone and comes out breathing fire. He grabs me, and we go driving all the way up to Milwaukee. He wouldn't say why we were going up there, but I couldn't drive fast enough to suit him.

"We pull up to their crappy little house about six at night, and as we get outa the car, we hear these screams. Not like angry screams, you know? Like terrified screams. Little-girl screams. We go inside and run upstairs, and there they are, all three of them in little Carolyn's bedroom. She's maybe nine, ten years old now."

His voice trailed off. Another deep breath, and he recrossed his legs. "The Polack is drunk off his ass, beating the living shit out of both of them. Little Carolyn was screaming for him to stop, crying and crying while he just beat her with his fists."

"Oh, my God," Jake moaned. He felt ill.

"Rebecca was out of it," Thorne went on, his voice growing thicker. "She'd already been pounded numb. Maybe it was the drugs, but she was never the same." He paused. "Mr. Sinclair took the girls to the hospital, and I took care of the Polack."

The tone and the body language told Jake that Thorne was done, but he couldn't let it end there. "What did you do?"

"I didn't do anything," Thorne said, shrugging. "But Mr. Sinclair made sure that Rebecca and Sunshine had everything they needed." He locked his gaze on Jake and scowled.

"What did you do with her father?"

Thorne's eyes narrowed, and his jaw set. His position sort of uncoiled as he leaned back and placed his palms on the arms of the chair. "You ask a lot of questions, Jake. Are you sure you want to know the answers?"

Jake paused just long enough to convey his uneasiness. "Yes," he said at length, "I want to know. I think I *ought* to know."

"Okay," Thorne said, leaning his elbows on his knees. "This is just between you and me, right? Mikey and I went for a little drive in the country. We talked for a little while, and then I blew his fucking head off." He smiled, still pleased with himself after all these years. "He's fertilizer now, and as far as I know, no one even reported the bastard missing."

The words hung in the air like a bad odor, churning Jake's stomach. At the same time, they left him feeling oddly fulfilled. "You *murdered* him?"

Thorne responded silently, with one of his humorless smiles.

"Does Harry know? I mean, did he *tell* you to kill him?"

"Of course not," Thorne scoffed quickly, unequivocally; like it was the most ridiculous question in the world. "Mr. Sinclair doesn't operate that way. He thinks I put the Polack on a plane to anyplace two thousand miles away, with instructions never to be seen again. He assumed I did what he told me, and I never bothered to correct him."

Jake didn't buy it. "Come on, Thorne! Do you expect me to believe—"

Thorne cut him off with a raised hand. "You still don't get it, do you? My job is to make problems go away. Ninety percent of the time, Mr. Sinclair has no idea what I do. In fact, he pays me a lot of money *not* to keep him informed."

"But if he knew—"

"He'd be upset—oh, yeah," Thorne said. "But like I said, Carolyn—she was a cutie. And myself, I've always been partial to permanent solutions."

Travis had been in this tunnel once before, and like last time, he wasn't alone. Those same faceless voices floated all around him in the dark, saying things he couldn't quite make out.

The snake was still down his throat, but it seemed to have settled down. It wasn't biting him anymore. Jesus, though, his mouth was dry. He tried to swallow, but the snake wouldn't let him. It wasn't hissing at him anymore, either—at least, not unless he wanted it to. The snake had given him back control of his breathing. That was nice of him.

Something was dragging him toward a light, and as he got closer, he gradually realized that he wasn't in a tunnel at all. He was asleep. Try as he might, though, he couldn't get himself all the way awake. The voices kept getting louder and louder. If he wasn't mistaken, someone was saying his name.

What nightmares he'd had! Chases and chemicals and screaming and fighting. Whatever he'd had to eat before bed last night, he hoped he'd never make that mistake again.

What was last night, anyway? The light grew brighter still.

But he wasn't floating anymore. In fact, he felt anchored down, as if glued to the floor. He tried to move, but his chest hurt like hell. Like he'd been beaten with something. Was that what this was all about? Maybe he was still in the dirt recovering from his fight with Terry Lampier, and the rest had all been a wild dream.

The light rushed toward him now, with frightening speed. The voices grew louder and clearer, and sure enough, someone was saying his name.

Travis opened his eyes, yet he still didn't know where he was. He tried to talk, but something in his mouth wouldn't let him. His old friend the snake.

A face appeared above him, a lady he didn't know, with a smile that trimmed the edges off his fear. "Hi there, Travis," she said. "Welcome back. You had us worried for a while."

Hours had passed, she was sure, but there was no way for her to know what time it was. Clocks weren't the only human niceties denied to residents of the isolation wing. So was any view of the outdoors. The only reality residents were allowed was the one provided by their jailers. How easy it was, she'd thought at one point during the night, to manipulate people's thoughts and fears. Her light had stayed on all night, but she supposed it would have been just as easy to keep it off. Days and days without a restful sleep, followed by days and days of darkness, were pretty much guaranteed to alter a body's sense of reality. And to what end? Any end they chose, she assumed.

She hadn't moved in a very long time. She just sat there on her concrete cot, fingering the rope that Wiggins had left behind and trying to make peace with God. *Was* there a God? Despite everything that had happened to her over the years, she couldn't help but feel that there was another place, better than this one, and a presence—a *force*—that wanted her and Jake and her little boy to be together. If not here, then there.

What was she to do? What options did she have? She could kill herself or kill her son. That part was clear, but what then? What guarantees were there that Wiggins wouldn't kill her little boy, anyway? Maybe this was all bluff to begin with . . .

No, she told herself quickly. *He was dead serious. He'll kill my baby.*

For a long while, she debated the option of reporting all of this to the matron, but ultimately, she rejected it as unworkable. They'd never believe her, and in the questioning that followed, she'd miss her deadline to die.

Roll call. She didn't even know when that was. It had to be in the morning, she figured, but what time? Judging by the rhythms of the place, the critical hour was approaching. Late, late that night, the noise had died down to just a few rude conversations as inmates dropped off to sleep. Now the noise was picking up again; nothing like it was before, but it wouldn't be long.

The slipknot was the first thing she tied. Nothing fancy—nothing like the looped nooses that Travis liked to tie in every piece of rope he ever got his hands on. Just a simple slipknot, tied the same way she'd learned years ago, in Brownies.

Memories of her childhood—the most horrible ones—tried to sneak their way into her consciousness, but she ran them off. *For the last time*, she realized with some measure of relief. Perhaps that was the silver lining within this darkest of clouds. She'd never have to face the nightmares again.

It was time to think about Jake. And about Travis. About the good times.

Snagging the light fixture with the running end of the rope

turned out to be quite the challenge. She fashioned a lasso of sorts in the middle of the clothesline and tried to rope the fixture, much like a cowboy would rope a horse. With the fixture well out of reach overhead, there could be no screwups, no second chances; no way to loosen a fouled knot.

It helped if she stood on the cot. After four or five flubs, she finally got it and in so doing, felt inexplicably elated. The next challenge would be to lean out far enough to actually extend her neck into the dangling loop of rope.

A bell rang somewhere, startling the hell out of her. "Roll call!" someone yelled. "All right, ladies, rise and shine!"

Carolyn's heart raced now as she heard footsteps approaching down the hall.

"Front and center, Mrs. Donovan!"

Standing on tiptoes and straining like a kid trying to see over the fence at a ballpark, she just barely hooked the noose with the point of her chin and opened her jaw wide to drag her head in further. She filled her brain with images of Jake and Travis. The images she wanted to take with her. She whispered that she loved them.

"It's a new day . . ."

That's when she lost her balance. The noose came tight—impossibly tight—as she swung away from the cot in a wide arc, her toes straining instinctively to touch the floor, which remained just an inch out of reach. For an instant, she wondered if the thin clothesline might actually pop her head right off her body, and she clawed at the spot where the rope dug into her flesh.

Then her vision flashed red, and there was nothing more.

CHAPTER FORTY-TWO

The Orion News Database was available to everyone who could afford the subscription fee, which was easily high enough to keep the riffraff from jamming the server. Such concerns were not a problem, of course, for the FBI, and once inside the database, Irene could locate every article written on any subject within the last fifty years, as compiled from over a thousand daily, weekly, and monthly periodicals.

Somewhere, buried among all those words, she figured there had to be an item or two about the Grant Plant's past. Never much of a computer whiz, she was walking blind here, having always depended on staffers to take care of this kind of research. She learned right off the bat that success and failure lay in the selection of well-defined search parameters. Underestimating the scope and power of the database, she tried *Newark+Arkansas* in her first attempt and was greeted with an invitation to scroll through 627,838 items.

Yikes!

Her second attempt cut the number of hits in half by setting date parameters between 1980 and the present.

"Getting closer," she told herself. She leaned back in the impossibly hard desk chair. There had to be a way to get a handle on this. Problem was, the 1983 explosion and its aftermath had dominated every news outlet for so long that those were the only references she could find. She needed to filter out that information somehow.

She concentrated her next search on a year-by-year examination of articles up to, but excluding, the date of the explosion, and even then, she was pulling up more than a hundred articles at a time, mostly from hunting and recreation magazines.

Finally, she surrendered to the inevitable. "Okay, Irene," she'd grumbled, about forty-five minutes into the exercise. "Why don't you ask it what you're really looking for?"

She entered, "Newark+Arkansas+Frankel/1-1-80 thru 8-21-83."

In her heart, she'd hoped the screen would flash an error message. Instead, she got seventeen hits, sixteen of which dealt with the same story: the apparent murder/suicide of an Army general named Dallas Albemarle and his wife, up in suburban Virginia. She decided to go back to those later and concentrated instead on the seventeenth hit, from a periodical called *The Freedom Report: A Journal Dedicated to Preserving Democracy.* The article quoted highly placed, unnamed sources in reporting that Special Agent Peter Frankel was actively investigating a plot to sell chemical weapons out of a "secret location" in Newark, Arkansas. The article went on to say that the investigation had been fruitful but that no arrests had been made, and from there, launched into a blathering tirade about the looming threat posed by Third World powers.

"Well, there's his hard evidence," Irene told herself. Frankly, she'd been hoping for something more concrete.

After a giant yawn, and yet another battle with the chair over control of her spine, she turned her attention to the list of suicide stories. As she read through them, they even rang a distant bell. Seems that the kindly General Albemarle was the man responsible for overseeing the shutdown of the Ulysses S. Grant Army Ammunition Plant, back in 1964.

That's why the name rings a bell. He's the guy the EPA wanted to crucify, back when the hazardous waste site was first discovered.

Inexplicably, the general had shot his wife to death in the bedroom of their home in Clifton, Virginia, and had then driven all the way out to Manassas Battlefield Park, to blow his own brains out at the base of a statue paying tribute to Stonewall Jackson. Each of the articles quoted the same source—Special Agent Peter Frankel of the FBI—in reporting that General Albemarle had been distraught over the recent death of his daughter and by his likely implication in the then-developing chemical weapons scandal in Newark. According to Frankel, the general had made his intentions clear in a suicide note found in the couple's bedroom.

"First in line with a quote even then, eh, Peter?" Irene mumbled, clicking on through the stories. The coincidence of the note was not lost on her.

Odd, she thought. *Some guy nobody knows blows his brains out, and the story is picked up all over the country. Yet an investigation into illegal weapons sales pops up only once.* Now, *there* was a telling tribute to the credibility given *The Freedom Report* by its journalistic brethren. *Probably devoted the rest of the issue to flying saucers and Elvis sightings.*

On a whim, she compared the dates on the weapons article to the one on the dead general. The story from *The Freedom Report* ran just three weeks before the general did the big nasty.

How about that?

Truth be told, Irene believed in mere coincidence. They happened all the time—sometimes so wild they defied logic. As a matter of fact, in a very real sense, most violent crime against innocent people boiled down to just that: a tragic coincidence for the victims involved.

She understood better than most, then, that the presence of two people in the same place at the same time didn't necessarily reflect intent on anyone's part. There comes a point, though, when coincidences stack up so high that it takes more effort to justify their randomness than to accept them as something more complicated. This business with Frankel was rapidly approaching that point.

It was time to stop being an investigator for a little while and become a casual observer. If she were to accept only Donovan's side, she could place Frankel with at least one other dead party, and she could place him at the Little Rock field office with the opportunity to pull a fast one with his investigatory prerogative; all within the time frame when weapons could have been sold out of his backyard. Wouldn't be the first time such a thing had happened, after all. Sadly, it wasn't uncommon at all for a cop to get involved with the very crime he's investigating.

Hmm . . .

She clicked back to the beginning and initiated another search, this one running permutations of dates, places, and names, but all with the common denominator of "chemical+weapons." After half a dozen tries, the list became manageable, and within an hour, she'd found what she was looking for.

"Well, I'll be damned," she said. The coincidences just went over the top.

When the phone rang a minute later, she didn't even jump. It was nearly six o'clock, and she'd been waiting for the switchboard to get around to their promised five forty-five wake-up call.

"I'm up, thank you," she said as she lifted the receiver from the desk.

"Irene?" Hearing her name stopped her from hanging up.

"Yeah?"

"Hi. This is George Sparks," the voice said. "I just got a call from the county lockup. Carolyn Donovan hung herself in her cell."

The matron peeked in through the observation window and went right to work. As she worked her master key with one hand, she pushed the transmit button on her portable radio with the other. "Unit Four to Central, we got a swinger in Isolation Two." Her voice sounded hurried but not panicked.

"Fresh or stale?" a voice came back.

"Still swingin'! Get Medical down here quick!"

The prisoner's face was purple from the increased pressure in her head, and her hands and feet were still twitching. The matron knew from her rookie training five years ago that as long as the victim's neck wasn't broken, and she hadn't burst something in her brain, this one was salvageable. Kind of a waste, though. Hardly seemed worth the effort to save somebody, just so the government could later issue her a termination slip.

Working alone—although she could hear the pounding of running feet in the hallway—the matron locked her arms around Carolyn's waist and lifted, hoping to take some of the strain off her neck. No matter how high she lifted the body, though, its torso flopped over to take up the slack. Burying her face in the victim's clothes like this made the matron's skin crawl. If the approaching footsteps hadn't been so close, she might have let her sway for a while longer.

The duty paramedic arrived first, a college student named Dan. Rather than burst in, he strolled. "Hi, Gladys. Whoa!" he exclaimed with a wince, recoiling just a bit. "Ain't she pretty?"

Gladys was too busy to laugh. "Shut your mouth, Mr. Stand-Up," she snapped. "Give me a hand here."

"Always the boss," Dan sang out cheerily. Precious few people were permitted to carry knives in the cellblock, and he was one of them, in anticipation of this very event. Then again, he never went down there unless someone was either dead or dying, and even then he'd often wait until all the inmates were locked down. He preferred to work in a controlled situation.

He removed his Leatherman from its holster on his belt, fished for the knife blade, then reached high to saw through the nylon. When he was done, both prisoner and matron fell in a heap on the floor. "You okay, Gladys?" he asked, suppressing a grin.

"No, I'm not okay. Get this bitch off of me!"

Two more staff members arrived at the door, one of them wheeling a crash cart, loaded with all the equipment necessary to perform CPR.

Dan knelt next to his patient and paused a moment to don latex gloves. With the tension of the rope removed, her color looked nearly normal, other than some bruising around the area of the rope burn. He pressed two fingers deeply into the flesh of her neck, just slightly off midline, and arched his eyebrows high.

"Hey, we got a live one," he announced. "Pulse is a little thready, but it's there. Time to go to work, people. Anybody called Fire and Rescue yet?"

"On their way," someone said.

Over the course of the next thirty seconds, Dan found nothing but good news. His stethoscope found good lung sounds on both sides, as well as a patent airway. One of the most critical complications of what the incident report would euphemistically call a near-hanging was the fracture of the larynx, the voice box. Vascular as hell, a fractured larynx would bleed like a son of a bitch and swell up to the size of a grapefruit, cutting off the flow of air through the patient's windpipe. That would have required him to do an emergency tracheostomy, a procedure he hadn't tried in over a year. As it was, the rope seemed to have avoided the critical structures of the throat entirely.

Dan plucked a penlight from his breast pocket and flashed the beam first into one eye and then into the other. The pupils performed as they were supposed to, contracting uniformly to the beam of light.

"I've got normal breath and lung sounds and perfect pupils," he announced to the still-gathering crowd. None of them knew the exact significance of his words, but the banter helped him concentrate. "Quite an audience," he observed lightly.

There wasn't much to do, actually. The patient was stable; breathing on her own and clearly perfusing oxygen. In the world of the road doctor, that was called a save. To kill some time, he started an IV of dextrose and water, flowing at just a high enough rate to keep the patient's veins open, in case something catastrophic happened and she decided to crash. With the line in place, they could administer virtually any drug they wanted to.

"Hey, Doc!" someone called.

Dan looked up. He loved it when they called him Doc. "Yeah?"

"I got somebody from the FBI on the phone. Wants to know if this one's gonna get a bed or a coffin."

Dan laughed. "Tell 'em that Dan Schearer's on duty. I only do beds."

Barely 6:00 A.M., and the streets of Little Rock were still deserted. That didn't stop Irene from using the bubble light and siren, though. Paul sat planted in the front seat next to her, looking like he still hadn't come to grips with morning. Irene had given him only five minutes to pull himself together and meet her in the lobby.

They'd got to within three blocks of the jail when George Sparks called on Irene's cellular to inform her that Carolyn was still alive and en route to St. Luke's Hospital. The turn Irene executed in the middle of the street would leave marks on the pavement for years to come.

For his part, Paul pulled his seat belt tight. Between being ejected out of a good night's sleep, Irene's driving, and the absurd tale she relayed from the night before, he'd have sold his soul for a stiff drink right about now.

"Say that again slowly," Paul said, his tone dripping disbelief.

Irene smiled and nodded her head. "Yeah, you heard it right. I think this whole mess was started by Frankel and that he's still running it."

Paul gave a low whistle. "Jesus, Irene, if I ever piss you off, will you at least give me fair warning?"

She laughed. "This isn't a grudge," she insisted. "I'm telling you, it's a solid case."

"Referred to you by none other than Jake Donovan," Paul finished. "At least there's no conflict of interest."

She changed lanes. "Don't get me wrong. I don't think we have an indictment here, but I'm telling you the pieces fit." She ran through the coincidences of the notes and the locations. "And let's not forget the munitions George Sparks was tracking down in the desert. But here's the real kicker. You ready?"

"Holding my breath. You do see that parked car up there, don't you?"

Actually, she hadn't. She swerved violently to the left, then back into her own lane, siren and horn screaming the whole time.

"Sorry about that," she said sheepishly. "Woke you up, though, didn't it?"

He answered with a look.

"Okay," she went on. "Here's the kicker. Let's assume that the arms were stolen and sold in the early eighties."

". . . by our boss."

She waved him off. His defeatist attitude really grated on her sometimes. "Doesn't matter. Not for now, anyway. Just assume they're being stolen and sold."

"Got it. Stolen. Sold."

"Bite me, Boersky," she growled. "Well, what do you know? Up until then, nary an article was published on chemical warfare incidents anywhere in the world. Then, starting in early '84, we got incidents popping up all over the world. Iran, Iraq, Libya, even Tokyo, for crying out loud!"

Paul looked at her disapprovingly. "And because people are getting gassed, you think Frankel did it? I'm afraid I don't see the nexus."

She tried again. She pointed out that no one incident was enough to draw a conclusion, yet taken together, as a tapestry of events, it all started to make sense. Frankel was the common denominator. He was in the article about General Albemarle, he was involved in the right-wing rag's prophetic allegations about Newark, and he friggin' *ran* the investigation after the explosion. Then, there was the business of the notes and the inherent flimsiness of the case itself.

"Tell me this," Irene challenged. "Why didn't Frankel keep digging? Why doesn't the file have interviews with friends and coworkers and teachers?"

"It does," Paul scoffed. "The file is full of them. I've read them."

She shook her head emphatically. "Uh-uh. No, you haven't. Look again. What are those interviews really about? The investigators back then were trying to *catch* the Donovans; they weren't trying to build a case against them."

"What's the difference?"

"There's a huge difference! You look through those files again, and you'll see it. Frankel and company only asked questions about where the Donovans might have run to. Nothing about whether they might have done it. No one ever noticed the sloppy work, because everyone thought they already knew the answer. Frankel was going to rest his whole case on the note and their escape."

Paul let the words settle into his brain while she negotiated a treacherous series of turns through the center city. "And that other guy? Tony Bernard? He was just a bonus kill?"

"No. At least not at first. I think he was the original patsy. But when the Donovans survived, the bad guys had to regroup in a hurry. That meant killing Bernard."

"And leaving a note."

She nodded. "Yes. And leaving a note. Chances are, there was a whole other note already drafted, to frame Bernard. How big a deal could it be to rewrite it?"

"You're crazy, Irene."

CHAPTER FORTY-THREE

Travis was tired of the pain. He was tired of being checked and poked and peeked into. Most of all, he was tired of this tube they'd shoved down his throat to help him breathe. It helped some that it didn't hiss anymore unless he told it to; unlike before, when it made him breathe whether he wanted to or not.

The hissing snake. When he was first climbing out of the deep cave of his unconsciousness, in those horrible moments when the line between reality and fear was blurred, all he could think about was the snake in his mouth. He'd panicked, clawing at the tube with both hands to pull it free. They said he was strong, too. It took two doctors and a nurse to keep his arms pinned to the bed. The struggle didn't last long, of course. Somebody injected something into his IV line, and right away, everything changed. He wasn't afraid of the snake anymore. In fact, he wasn't afraid of much of anything.

Gushing apologies, and assuring him over and over again that he'd done nothing wrong, the doctors and nurses went on to put fleece-and-leather handcuffs on his wrists—they called them re-straints—and tied his arms to the metal bed rails. "We can't afford to have you pulling that tube out," one of them explained.

He understood, but he wished there was a way to make them trust him again. Better still, that there was a way for him to rub his nose. He'd have apologized by now, but he couldn't make a sound. Apparently, this mile-long piece of plastic went right between his vocal cords and kept them from working. They told him not to worry, though. At the rate he was going, the tube would be out in a day or two. "Remarkable progress" is what they called it.

Of course, the mere fact that he couldn't talk didn't stop anyone from asking him questions. Tons of them. Can you feel this? Can you hear that? Can you squeeze my hands? On and on, with his only possible reply being a nod of his head. Happily enough, as far as he could tell, he'd given nothing but right answers.

He just wished that they'd get their act together. Every new face that came to see him asked the same questions as the face that preceded it. And the winner in the category of most frequently asked question by a doctor in ugly clothes was: *Does it hurt when you breathe?*

Thank God the answer to that was finally a no. If he never had to endure another night like last night, he'd die happy. Now, if they could just do something about the damned monitors. Between the hissing of the respirator and the incessant *bleep-bleep* of the EKG, he felt like he was going nuts. Those sounds made him think too much about things you were never supposed to be aware of—things that the body was just supposed to do. He kept waiting for that time when the noise didn't happen. He knew from television that that would be the moment when he died.

Try to block it out.

He wanted his mom. He knew it was wimpy to think such a thing, but it was the truth. She loved him more than anything, and if she were here, he could relax a little more; let her do his worrying for him. If it weren't for the cops, he knew she'd never have left his side. She'd have just sat there, holding his hand and talking nonstop about nothing.

He worried about her. He could still see that look on her face in the car, right before his vision had begun to sparkle. He didn't like seeing his mom wrapped that tight. It brought back memories of the awful days when she was drinking, and he berated himself for being the cause of a potential relapse.

He missed his dad, too, but in a different way. Dad could take care of himself. But Mom needed him.

A lady named Jan—she called herself a physician's assistant, whatever that was—told him his mom and dad were both okay but that they wouldn't be able to come by to visit. He didn't know what that meant, exactly, but in his heart, he knew they'd come for him sooner or later. They'd have to. He'd seen the look in his dad's eyes as he took him away from Mr. Menefee's school. Sometimes his dad was too intense, but once he set his mind to something, there was no stopping him. Just ask the FBI. The thought made him smile.

Of all the doctors and nurses he'd met in the past few hours, Jan was far and away his favorite. Besides her quick smile and her perfect teeth, she always took the time to explain stuff to him. It was like she could read his mind, zooming right in on the questions he wanted most to ask but couldn't. If he was alone and he had a question, all he had to do was turn his head to the right, and she'd catch his eye through the window separating his room from the nurses' station. Seconds later she'd be right there by his side.

She was the one who told him about the heart monitor; how the shape of the little squiggles on the screen showed that his heart was working perfectly. "That's your good-news monitor," she said.

He'd seen those green tracings a million times on television and never even thought about them. Up close, though, it was cool. That those sticky white pads on his chest could record every contraction of his heart made him wonder at the science of it all. Maybe one day he'd become a doctor himself, he decided. Or maybe a physician's assistant. From what he could tell, they had the best of all worlds: they got to do all the cool stuff without having to go to school forever.

"I want you to think of me as your mom away from home," Jan told him. "If you need anything at all, just press the call button here on your controller." She showed him a beige plastic box that was roughly the shape of a fat letter *T*. "I'm gonna loop it around your bed rail here so you can reach it easily. Just push the button at the bottom here."

As she demonstrated, he thought he could hear a distant *ding* out in the nurses' station. He tried it once, and it worked, but between the restraints and the IV crap dangling from his arm, it wasn't easy.

As always, Jan interpreted his look correctly. "Maybe later this afternoon we'll lose the restraints, okay? For right now, though, I think it's the safest way to go."

He nodded, but his face showed his disappointment.

She leaned in close and said in her most conspiratorial whisper, "Hospitals suck."

That brought a smile, despite the intrusion of the tube. The buttons along the top of the controller were marked "Television," and he tapped them with his finger.

Her expression darkened, and she broke eye contact. "Um, in your current condition, the doctor said you can't have any television."

Right away, he knew she was lying. Well, okay, fibbing. He liked her too much to think she'd lie.

"Tell you what, though," she added quickly, clearly announcing the birth of a new idea. "I'm going off duty soon, but I'll be back tonight at six. How about I bring in a VCR and a bunch of tapes so you don't get too bored?"

He nodded again, but without much enthusiasm. *Too late for that,* he thought. It wasn't possible for time to crawl by any more slowly. *I just hope it's not a lot of little-kid Disney stuff.*

She patted his hand and left. That was an hour ago, probably, and nothing much had happened since.

The sound of sudden activity startled him. Normally a quiet, laid-back place, the nurses' station exploded with activity. Through the window to his right, he saw everybody launching from their seats, tipping over chairs and coffee cups as they hurried off, out of his field of view. They looked scared, too, like maybe there was a fire or something. He tried to sit up to follow the action, but they were gone.

He lay back onto his sheets to begin the task of counting ceiling tiles when he saw a doctor peer in at him through the window. Yet another new face.

Gee, I wonder what he's going to ask me?

The doctor moved on, and a few seconds later Travis could hear him talking to somebody outside his door. Finally, he entered and closed the door behind him. "Hello, Travis," he said.

He wore the tie and the lab coat of several doctors he'd already seen, but this guy looked different somehow. He made Travis feel uneasy. Maybe it was the way he smiled. The lips pulled back the way they were supposed to, but there was something missing. Something important.

This guy also seemed like he had all the time in the world. Where everybody else in the hospital always seemed like they were trying to do a half hour's work in ten minutes, this doctor moved like he was on his lunch break. And why on earth was he putting on surgical gloves? Travis watched as he twisted the miniblinds shut.

"Just want us to have a little privacy," he said.

Now, *that* was *really* weird. So far as Travis could tell, nobody in the hospital gave a rat's ass about privacy. So many people had seen him naked by now, it almost didn't embarrass him anymore. So what was this guy up to? Whatever it was, it made him feel nervous as hell.

Who are *you?*

The doctor turned to him after darkening the room. "I talked to your mother last night . . ."

George Sparks went straight to St. Luke's Hospital and was waiting in the emergency room when Carolyn's ambulance arrived at the double doors. Little Rock was a violent town for its size, and nothing about this case caused anyone to get particularly excited. From all indications, in fact, as relayed via radio from the ambulance, this one was borderline inconsequential. An attempted suicide. Big deal.

Clearly, things had changed between the last radio transmission and the moment the gut bucket backed into its designated spot.

The crew seemed agitated, hurried, as the doors flew open, and they struggled clumsily with the cot. The E.R. doc, a Generation Xer named Oscar LeGrand, saw the flurry of activity through the windows and left his current patient in midsuture to see what was going on. Sparks followed.

As the doors opened, the pulse of air brought a rush of profanities and cries for help from the patient, who obviously had found her way back to full consciousness.

"He tried to kill me!" she shouted. "And he's going to kill my son, goddammit!"

The paramedics exchanged rolled eyes and knowing smirks. This was a live one, all right. "Okay, Carolyn," one of them said. "We hear you, honey, but just relax, okay? I don't see a single murderer out here."

Dr. LeGrand met them halfway. "I thought she was unconscious." He reached casually to Carolyn's handcuffed wrist to take a pulse.

"Well, she was until about a minute ago," the older of the two paramedics said. "Then she just came out of it. Bam." He snapped his fingers. "Just like that. Screaming all sorts of paranoid shit about hit men and murder plots."

LeGrand raised an eyebrow. "How about little green men? She say anything about those?"

Everyone laughed.

When a uniformed Little Rock cop showed up in his cruiser to assume custody of the prisoner, Sparks fell back a little. He hated this medical shit, anyway, and if someone else could do the fighting while they transferred her from the ambulance cot to the gurney, that would be just fine with him. This was Irene's case, anyway. Once she arrived, he was history. Now, he just hoped that Carolyn wouldn't say anything worthy of paperwork.

Watching the wrestling match, he noted the strength the woman showed, kicking and yelling. She even tried to bite the cop once, at which point Sparks gained a lot of respect for the man for not coldcocking her outright. *Could be on drugs?* he thought. He'd heard some caches of PCP had been discovered recently among the prisoners at the lockup.

All at once, Carolyn's eyes cleared, and she settled down, zeroing in on the cop's badge. "Oh, my God," she said, her voice giddy with relief. "You're a cop! Oh, thank God. You've got to listen to me! You've got to help me."

The uniformed officer seemed uncomfortable with the sudden attention, and he smiled sheepishly to the others around him.

"Looks like love to me, Officer," LeGrand joked.

Carolyn shot a hateful glare at the physician and focused in again on the cop. "Please listen to me!" she pleaded. "No one will fucking listen to me!"

"I'm right here, ma'am," the cop said, shrugging. "Say what you need to say."

"Let's try five milligrams of Valium," LeGrand said to a nurse. "Before she strokes out on us." The nurse went to work preparing the shot.

"God, no! Don't!" Carolyn yelled at the doctor. Then she turned quickly back to the cop. "A man came to my jail cell last night. I know this sounds crazy, but it's true, I swear to God. He said if I wasn't dead by morning, he'd kill my little boy. He was dressed as an FBI agent, and he said he'd kill Travis."

The cop scowled. "Isn't your son upstairs here? We got a guy assigned to his room."

LeGrand accepted the syringe from a nurse and inserted the needle into an injection port in the IV line. "Everything's going to be fine, Carolyn," he said.

She pleaded again, "No, don't do that! He'll . . . kill . . . Please . . ."

The medical personnel nodded approvingly as the patient lost consciousness. Meanwhile, the uniformed cop looked back to Sparks, who arched his eyebrows. "What do you think?"

"Well, the FBI part is bullshit," Sparks said quickly. "So's the rest of it, I'm sure. But *she* certainly seems convinced."

The uniform looked over at Carolyn and then back to Sparks.

"Shit, I can't leave her," he said. "I should get word to the man on the kid's door. I mean, what the hell?"

George agreed. What the hell, exactly. He checked his watch and sighed. "Okay, tell you what. You stay here and watch Sleeping Beauty, and I'll go upstairs and tell your buddy."

"If you wouldn't mind, I'd sure appreciate it."

"No problem."

Travis heard his heart skip a beat on the monitor as the doctor mentioned his mother's name. Something was terribly wrong. He could tell, just from the way the man spoke.

"She was really sad, kid. Worried as all get-out about you. She's in jail, you know."

No, he didn't know! The heart monitor was beeping like crazy now, and Travis knew instinctively that this guy was trouble, with a capital *T*. He wished Jan were here with him. Or even another doctor. Any adult would do, just to keep him from being alone with this guy. The way he talked, the dead look in his eyes. In an instant, Travis knew that this was one of those guys whose cars he was never supposed to get into when he was a little kid.

His fingers touched the call button. *If you need anything . . .*

Wiggins caught the movement and quickly pulled the controller out of the boy's reach. "Whoa, buddy! You're not gonna go tattling on me, are you?" He laughed.

Travis's eyes were wide, wild. They darted to the window for help, but all he saw was a wall of beige plastic.

"No, that's right, Travis," the doctor said, reading his thoughts. "It's just you and me. Everybody else is too busy to help you." He dropped his voice to a whisper. "Seems a little kid's heart stopped down the hall a ways. Terrible, terrible thing. Somebody pumped a whole shitload of potassium chloride into her IV line and stopped her heart dead like a slab of hamburger." To make his point, Wiggins pulled a capped syringe out of his lab coat pocket and dropped it in the trash can at the foot of the bed. "They tell me this shit stops a heart forever."

Travis tried to yell, tried to struggle against the restraints, but nothing would work. This guy was crazy! This guy was a murderer!

"You just keep floppin', boy. You look like a fish in a boat." He chuckled one more time, then struck out with a hand to squeeze the sides of Travis's face. The force of his grip sent darts of pain through the boy's jaw as his teeth battled with the hard plastic of the ET tube. "You just settle down now," Wiggins commanded. "Or I'll give you more of the same." A second syringe appeared.

Oh, shit! Oh, God! Travis froze, his eyes darting from the needle to his attacker's face and back again. He pleaded silently for mercy but got only an icy glare in return. The blood in his mouth tasted hot against the chalky dryness of his tongue.

Wiggins watched the terror build in the boy's face and smiled contentedly. "Yeah, that's right, kid. You show some respect." After holding his grip for a few seconds more, he turned his attention to Travis's respirator. Dropping the full syringe back into the pocket of his lab coat, Wiggins traced the connections with his finger, petting the tubes lightly as he followed them from the spot where they left the bellows, all the way up to the connection at the boy's mouth.

He paused, and his voice softened. "Before we go on, I just wanted you to know that none of this had to happen. I told your mother specifically what she had to do to keep me from hurting you, but she just wouldn't listen." He made a clicking sound with his tongue as he shook his head sadly. "Does it hurt when you breathe, boy?"

Travis felt the panic build like pressure in a volcano. The heart monitor chirped too fast to count, and no matter how hard he pulled, his lungs couldn't draw enough air through the respirator. His terror had left him deaf. He knew that the doctor had asked him a question, but he had no idea what it might have been.

"Pain's a terrible thing," the doctor went on. "Especially for kids. You don't like pain, do you, Travis?"

The reference to pain—and the way it was asked—brought Travis's ears back on-line. He shook his head vehemently. *Please don't hurt me! Please, oh please, oh please!*

Wiggins winced, as if he could feel the boy's panic in his own gut. He pointed to the heart monitor. "You're scared, aren't you? Yeah, look at that. A hundred and eighty-four beats per minute." He thought about his words. "That's good," he mused. "It's good I've scared you, 'cause that's what I promised your mother I was gonna do. Before I killed you."

Oh, God! Jesus! In a desperate effort to get away, Travis lunged forward in his bed, pulling hard against the unyielding restraints. Wiggins recoiled a half-step, then punched him hard in the chest, rocketing him back against the sheets. The impact drove the wind out of his lungs and reignited the fires from the day before.

Please don't!

"Don't try to fight me, kid," Wiggins growled. "That's a mistake every time." He wiggled a finger at the respirator. "Now, Travis, did you know that this machine here is what keeps you breathing on schedule?" He patted the top of the control panel as if it were an old chum. "Every bit of air you breathe has to come through this part right here." He tugged on the end of Travis's ET tube, where it attached to the hose from the machine.

Travis was beyond panic now, and he struggled in vain one more time to reach the controller. Wiggins seemed amused by the effort. For the first time, the smile seemed genuine.

"Want to feel something really scary?"

No! Please, God . . . No!

Wiggins snapped the respirator connection away from the end of the ET tube. Travis winced, expecting to suffocate, but in the midst of his terror actually felt relief when the air still flowed into his body.

Then Wiggins put his thumb over the hole.

The pediatric floor was a welcome departure from the emergency room. Hospitals were disagreeable places no matter what, but at least up here, the paintings of *Sesame Street* and comic book characters on the walls gave everything a lighter feel. Had to be tough, Sparks supposed, to work with kids who'd been deprived of their childhoods by illness. At least kids had the sense of natural optimism to make such a tough job feel worthwhile.

He stepped off the elevator and paused, trying to figure out where to go next. The pediatric floor spanned out before him, arranged as a giant rectangle that was dominated in the center by a sprawling nurses' station. He looked in all directions, but he didn't see a cop. Conscious of the racket his heels made against the spit-shined tile floor, he walked on tiptoes over to a lady in blue scrubs. Thoroughly absorbed in notes she was jotting on a clipboard, the lady didn't acknowledge him. He cleared his throat.

"Excuse me," he said lightly.

The nurse held up a finger while she finished writing a thought. "I'm sorry," she said when she was done. "Can I help you?" She wore an orange stethoscope draped casually over the back of her neck, with tiny stuffed koala bears hugging each of the earpieces. A huge yellow button over her breast pocket read, "It's a wonder-ful day!"

"Hi, I'm George Sparks, with the FBI." *Even the nurses are happier up here.* He returned her smile and flashed his credentials. "You've got a patient up here named Travis Donovan, I believe? I need to speak with him."

The nurse's smile morphed into a frown, deep furrows tracking across her forehead. "Travis Donovan? On the pediatric floor? Hmm . . ." She rolled her chair over to a stack of files and riffled through them. "I don't see a Travis Donovan here," she said. "You're sure he's a peds case?"

George shrugged. "Well, I know he's thirteen years old."

"That'd make him a peds case," the nurse confirmed. She rolled her chair toward a computer terminal and tapped a few keys. "We don't have anybody by that name on the floor here," she explained, pausing while the computer whirred. "I'm trying to check the ad-missions file. Maybe they put him someplace else. The name sure rings a bell . . . Wait a minute! He's the kid with the parents, right?" Now she got it.

Her characterization made George smile. "That's the one."

She smacked her forehead with a palm. "Duh," she said. "He's in the hospital, all right, two floors up in pediatric ICU."

Travis's lungs screamed for relief as he kicked and squirmed on his bed, trying to break free from Wiggins's grasp. As he thrust his head violently in an effort to get away, his attacker's hand never loosened, and he could feel the long plastic tube shifting from side to side, deep inside his chest. His eyes begged for mercy, but it was like pleading with a shark as he dragged you deeper and deeper into the water.

His sheet was gone now, kicked off onto the floor, and his body's struggle to breathe had pulled his sweaty, smooth skin taut against his thin frame. The bones of the boy's chest seemed to rise out of his skin as his diaphragm strained to pull in a breath, and his abdomen seemed to collapse, his navel heaved so far into his belly that it looked like it might actually touch his spine.

Please stop! Oh, God, please make him stop! I'll be good! Tears poured from his eyes as he realized he was going to die. He started to hear the same rushing sound in his ears that he'd heard in the car, and the colors started to drain again from his surroundings . . .

Wiggins let go.

The rush of air into his body made Travis feel suddenly dizzy, as if somebody had put his bed on a lazy Susan and spun it. There wasn't enough air in the world now to fulfill the boy's need. He sucked in huge lungfuls, and he ended up swallowing nearly as much as he breathed. He gagged once and tried to vomit, but nothing came up.

He was alive! The feeling of relief was overwhelming.

"Told you that would be scary, didn't I?" Wiggins said, smiling. "I timed that one. A minute and a half. That's it. Felt like a much longer time, didn't it?"

This asshole wasn't done! He said that already, didn't he? *He said he was gonna kill me!* Travis remembered the syringe, and his panic bloomed even larger than before.

Wiggins just kept talking, like he was trying to figure out where to have dinner. "I mean, it felt like a much longer time to me, and I was just standing here. For you, it must've seemed like an hour."

The fight had left Travis exhausted, soaked with sweat. Even through the fear, he could smell his own body odor, and it was horrible. His muscles told him to quit, but his brain shrieked at him to keep fighting. He tried to move his right hand again and could feel the fleece lining slide a little further down his wrist. If he used his imagination, he could almost feel the restraint sliding off his hand.

Wiggins seemed suddenly tired of this game. "Want to go on that ride one more time, or shall I just get on with my business?" Holding the syringe directly in front of the boy's face, he took his time sliding the blue plastic cap off the end of the needle. "I think you've probably suffered enough," he said as he shot a spider-silk stream of poison into the air.

Pediatric or otherwise, the ICU was anything but cheerful. It had the same rectangular design, but it was much smaller. This was a place for very, *very* sick children, and under the circumstances, the larger-than-life mural of Barney the Dinosaur looked horribly out of place; sacrilegious almost.

The place was bedlam. Over on the far side of the nurses' station, a cast of thousands swarmed like gnats around the bedside of a child who looked way too small to have a problem so big. Sparks recognized the look of helplessness in some of the faces, and he knew what it meant. He turned away. It had been a long, long time since he'd dealt with death real-time, and the fact that the victim was a kid made it worse.

"What happened?" George asked as he approached the uniformed guard at Travis's door.

The commotion down the hall had obviously unnerved the cop as well. "Can I help you?" he asked in a half-polite, half-surly tone.

The agent flopped open his black credentials wallet. "George Sparks, FBI."

Recognition flashed in the cop's face. "Oh, sure," he said. "I know you. Bill Rubie." He turned his gaze back down the hall. "I don't know. Best I can tell, the kid just died. They've got every doctor in the state trying to bring her back." He looked at his shoes as he sighed. "Makes you think." When he looked up, he was past it all. "What brings you here?"

"Travis's mother tried to hang herself in jail last night," Sparks explained, eliciting a pained groan from Rubie. "I was downstairs when they brought her in, and she was babbling about some plot to kill her kid. I told one of your buddies I'd relay the story to you, so he could stay put with the prisoner."

"And who's supposed to be hatching this plot?"

Sparks started a chuckle, then stifled it as he remembered that death was nearby. "The FBI," he said. Traces of a smile remained.

Rubie rolled his eyes. "Ah. I see. Well, the only folks who've been in with the kid are doctors and nurses, and they've been coming in by the truckload."

Sparks reached for the doorknob. "Have you checked in on him yourself?"

The cop shrugged. "I see him when the door opens, but other than that, what's to check?"

George considered that for a moment, then nodded. "Good point. Mind if I peek in on him?"

The cop made a face that spoke his words: "Suit yourself. There's a doc in there right now, though. Said he wanted to have some privacy with the kid."

Sparks paused, his hand a half inch from the knob. "I'll wait," he said. "I hate the body fluids business, anyway."

Rubie laughed at the turn of phrase. "I don't know how they do it," he agreed.

Travis closed his eyes at the sight of the needle. This was it, fifteen seconds from now, he'd either be alive or he'd be dead, all depending on what he did next. Concentrating exclusively on his right hand, he forced his thumb as far in toward his palm as it would go. His wrist hurt as his thumb formed an X with his pinky, making his hand as small as it would ever get. He yanked once, very hard, and spun his wrist in the fleece. There was resistance for maybe half a second, and then he was free!

He moved faster than Wiggins could react. The needle was poised under Travis's suspended IV bag, just an inch from the brown rubber injection site, when the boy made his move. With no idea what might happen, Travis grabbed a fistful of IV tubing and pulled. The swiftness of the move caused Wiggins to jump back as the tubes came free of the bag and flopped like so many clear snakes across the boy's legs.

Furious, the killer lashed out and smacked the boy across the face. Travis felt something rattle inside his mouth, but he ignored it. Instead, he shifted his attack to the EKG monitor on his left. He needed some attention, right this very second, and this seemed like the way to get it. As Wiggins recoiled for another blow, Travis rolled to his left and smacked the side of the heart monitor as hard as he could, sending thousands of dollars of machinery crashing to the floor.

"What the hell was *that*?"

At the sound of the crash, Sparks and Rubie spun together and dashed through the door, into Travis's room. Neither was prepared for what they saw. A doctor was beating his own patient!

"Hey!" Sparks yelled. "What the hell . . ." The instant the man turned, Sparks knew he was no doctor, and the rest of the situation crystallized. He reached for his weapon.

The attacker moved with remarkable speed, launching a vicious kick to Sparks's hand, just as the pistol cleared its holster. The weapon skittered across the floor. A second kick—really a continuation of the first—folded Rubie's knee backward onto itself, rendering him instantly useless.

Sparks tried to brace for a fight but, in reality, never had a chance. He saw something moving in the doctor's hand, and then George's whole world flashed red. His head erupted in agony as the syringe needle came around in a horizontal arc and buried itself into his right eye. He heard a snap as the point impacted bone and broke off. He screamed; an inhuman howl that rose up from a place deeper than his throat as he clutched his hands to his face and fell helplessly to the floor.

"Oh, God! My eye! My eye!"

Rubie was screaming, too, as he squeezed his ruined knee with both hands, as if he could clamp off the flow of pain. The scream ended abruptly; cut short by yet another kick that at once crushed his larynx and drove his lower jaw with jackhammer force into his upper jaw, severing his tongue in the process.

Rubie collapsed backward onto the floor. Struggling for breath, but choking on blood instead, he was dimly aware that someone had lifted him by his hair, but felt nothing as the doctor smashed his head like a melon against the hard tile floor.

Everything was moving too fast for Travis to process it all. He didn't see it all in detail, but he saw the blood and he heard the screaming, and he found himself wishing more than anything that he could scream, too. So much noise. So many people, all running in to see what was going on.

"Oh, shit!" someone yelled. "Jesus Christ! Get us some help up here!"

God, there was so much blood! Travis was mesmerized by it all. And so were the hospital staffers, until they realized that their real patient was a naked little boy, whose color suddenly matched that of his disheveled bedclothes. All at once, they descended on him, shouting orders to each other as they reconnected his respirator, yanked out old IVs, and went about the business of establishing new ones. No one talked; everyone yelled. But for his role as a pincushion, he might as well have not been there.

Where is he? Travis's mind screamed as he searched the assembled faces for the man who'd tried to kill him. He slapped at each of the hands that approached him, fearful that the murderer was still there. He didn't see him, but that didn't mean he wasn't lurking around somewhere, waiting for his chance. He'd done it once; he could do it again.

The hands fought him back; they were all over him, pushing and prodding and poking all the places they'd pushed and prodded and poked before. Everyone talked at him, told him to relax, but no one even seemed remotely concerned about what happened to the asshole who did all of this.

They had more pressing matters to worry about: like the guy on the floor whose screams sounded more animal than human; and the other one, whose brain matter formed a slick coating under people's feet.

Travis closed his eyes and wished for it all to go away. He wanted his mom and his dad. He wanted to go back to Farm Meadows to smell the mildew and the accumulated trash. He wanted to die—quickly and easily this time. He wanted to be anywhere but here.

Somewhere, from outside his darkness, a hand gently touched his cheek, and a voice said, "Travis, honey, are you okay?" It was his mother's tone but someone else's voice. He opened his eyes, and there was Jan. She gave him her warmest smile. "I only got as far as the cafeteria," she explained softly. "I was worried about you."

He reached up to hold her hand, but someone told him to hold still. He tried to shake his arm free, anyway, but whoever was working on him down there fought him back.

"Let them do their job, Travis, okay?" Jan soothed, stroking his shoulder. "You're okay now. I'll be right here. Nobody can hurt you if I'm right here, now, can they?"

He relaxed and closed his eyes again. He felt her hand in his hair, petting him gently and whispering about things that didn't matter. Her touch reminded him of how his mom would sit with him all night long whenever he'd get sick as a kid. He thought about his dad's laugh; how he'd always howl at the dirty jokes that his mom would pretend to be offended by.

He thought about all the horrible things he'd said and felt about them on their last day together, and in that moment, he knew he'd never see his parents again.

CHAPTER FORTY-FOUR

Irene made sure that her badge was showing from the waistband of her skirt as she wandered with Paul into the emergency room at St. Luke's. From the level of activity, she expected to see the carnage of a train wreck. People ran in all directions, shouting orders, and in general creating bedlam out of disorder. She tried twice to ask a hospital staffer what was going on but was soundly ignored.

Across the way, she noted the still form of Carolyn Donovan, unguarded and likewise ignored by medical personnel as she lay on her back on a gurney, both wrists cuffed to side rails. "They just leave her there unguarded?" she asked Paul incredulously.

He answered with a question. "What the hell is going on in here?"

One thing was certain: she was going to have a long talk with the Little Rock police chief about his chain-of-custody procedures. Leaving a fugitive like Carolyn Donovan alone was inexcusable.

"Look there." Paul pointed.

The commotion seemed centered around a bank of elevators, where Irene saw a cluster of doctors and nurses waiting for the doors to open. A cop nearby had his weapon drawn, and she suppressed the urge to draw her own. She was still twenty feet away when the doors opened, and the waiting crowd came alive. Amid the cluster of legs, she could see the wheels of a gurney being brought off the elevator, and above their heads, she could make out the characteristic slumped posture of someone in the midst of performing CPR while straddling his patient on the cot.

The knot of people moved as one down the tile floor back toward the trauma rooms, leaving a thick blood trail on the tile floor. As they passed, she thought she saw a police uniform shirt in a heap at the foot of the gurney.

The other cop—the one with his gun still drawn—looked like he needed to sit down but followed the procession, anyway. She snagged him as he passed, snapping the badge from her waistband and holding it up where he could see it. "What's going on?" she said quickly. "And why don't you put that weapon away?"

The cop looked scared to death. He glanced first at the badge and then to her face. Finally, his eyes fell to the gun in his hand, and he sheepishly slid the weapon back into its holster. "Somebody killed him upstairs," he said, clearly dazed by it all. "Guarding some kid. Got one of your guys, too." He shook himself free of her and hurried to rejoin the group.

Irene looked to Paul. "One of our guys?"

They got it at the same instant. "Sparks!"

Bleary-eyed and numb after his fitful three-hour nap, Jake had just lifted himself out of an overstuffed chair in the lavish TV room, on his way back to the kitchen for a second cup of coffee, when the Special Report graphic caught his attention. Flanked by pictures of Carolyn and Travis, the local Little Rock newscaster nodded slightly to acknowledge his cue and started right into the story.

"Police sources confirm that they foiled an attempt this morning to suffocate the teenaged son of the famed terrorists Jake and Carolyn Donovan as the boy lay in the intensive-care unit of St. Luke's Hospital, recovering from injuries sustained yesterday as he reentered the Newark Hazardous Waste Site . . ."

Jake froze, his mouth agape, as he zeroed in on the announcer's words. The station cut live to a young reporter on the scene at the hospital, who used the most graphic, sensational terms he knew to describe the details. As the reporter spoke, the screen showed close-ups of blood smears on the tile floor of the Emergency Department.

"Ironically," the reporter went on, "this attack on young Travis Donovan happened on the same morning that his mother reportedly attempted to hang herself at the Adult Detention Center . . ."

Jake's breath escaped in a rush as he sat himself heavily onto the arm of the chair. *This isn't happening . . .*

Back to the announcer in the studio. "Brian, we're receiving reports in the newsroom that Carolyn Donovan had alerted hospital officials of the attack on her son, but that nothing was done about it. Do you have any details on that?"

"Well, Perry, as you might imagine, rumors fly like snowflakes during times like these, and we're working as hard as we can to separate truth from fiction. We've heard those reports, too, but we've thus far been unable to confirm them. Frankly, just in the last half hour or so since this story broke, police and FBI officials have started to clamp down on hospital personnel, and it's getting harder and harder to get confirmation on anything . . ."

The reporters continued chatting like this, mostly repeating themselves to fill time, but Jake stopped listening, as if his brain was already full, unable to process another word.

Clearly, Frankel now knew that his secret was out. And he was trying to shut the Donovans up.

"I'll kill him," Jake seethed. Deep in the pit of his gut, disbelief transformed to anger, and anger to fury, as it suddenly dawned on him that a peaceful solution was no longer possible. "That asshole is dead."

When he turned, the figure of Thorne standing in the doorway startled him. "I heard the news," he said. "I'm sorry. At least they're still alive." He filled the entire door frame, his legs spread, fists on his hips, intentionally blocking Jake's exit. "Maybe you should sit down."

Jake glared, his jaw locked. "You can't stop me," he growled.

Thorne cocked his head curiously, looking for all the world like he was suppressing a laugh. "Actually, I can. I will, in fact."

"I'm gonna kill him," Jake repeated.

Thorne stepped closer. "Who, ace? Who you going to kill?"

Jake's eyes locked onto Thorne's and wouldn't let go. "Frankel."

The big man cocked his head to the other side. "Right. The deputy director of the FBI, and you're just gonna walk up and blow his ass away?"

Hearing his thoughts spoken by someone else made Jake feel stupid. He set his jaw and looked away. "It won't be easy, I'm sure, but I'll get it done."

"Uh-huh. You really think it was him, do you? The most famous guy in law enforcement, and he just walked into St. what's-his-name's and tried to kill your kid?"

"He tried to *suffocate* him, Thorne!" Jake yelled.

"No, *he* didn't!" Thorne yelled back. "Somebody else did! And my money says it was the same somebody who tried to hang Sunshine." An eyebrow twitched. "Unless you think she really tried to kill herself . . ."

Jake scoffed and waved off the very thought as ridiculous.

"What's going on?" Nick shuffled into the TV room barely conscious, his hair standing erect on the left side of his head.

Jake took ten seconds to catch him up, while Nick fell into a sofa. "Oh, my God . . . what the . . ." He was trying to absorb it all.

"You're angry, Jake," Thorne cautioned, clearly bothered by his version of the story. "You can *think* till the cows come home that Frankel is responsible, but thinking doesn't make it so! And you can't just walk up to a guy as powerful as him and blow his brains out. The world already thinks you're a nutcase. Why prove them right?"

Jake's shoulders slumped as he felt the wind leave his sails. Thorne's words made sense, and he hated him for it. "So what do you suggest? Just sit?"

Thorne mulled over his answer before offering it. "Yeah," he said finally, with a shrug. "Until you can prove some of this stuff you think you know, you're stuck in neutral. Try anything, and they'll throw away the key and the ring with it." He pulled on his lower lip as he considered a thought. "What we need is to get our hands on the guy who actually worked the hits. I bet he could tell us everything we want to know."

Jake shook his head in disgust. "And how likely is that?"

"Pretty damned, I'd say." Nick's sudden contribution brought heads around in unison to see a face transformed into a mask of dread. "Especially since we know where he's going next."

Thorne didn't see it yet, but Jake did. "Oh, my God."

"Frankel knows I'm involved," Nick explained, his voice barely audible as he rubbed his temples with his fingertips. "Once I went into the computer, he knew. What he doesn't know is how much I've said, and that seems to be his biggest fear." His eyes widened as he raised them up to lock onto Jake's. "My family's next."

Consciousness came instantly, without transition. "Where's Travis?" Carolyn shouted to the room.

Her answer came from very close by. "He's fine," Irene said. She was perched on an examination stool, next to the bed, and she looked as tired as anyone Carolyn had ever seen. Her normally fine features were ravaged by deep lines tracking across her forehead and down both sides of her mouth.

"Someone's going to attack him," Carolyn announced, oblivious to the hours that had passed.

Irene looked at the floor. "He already did," she said heavily. "But Travis is fine. Quite a resourceful young man you've got there."

But I don't *have him*, Carolyn thought bitterly. *You do.* She didn't know whether to rejoice or to scream. She'd told them, goddammit, and no one would believe her. No one would even listen, not for a minute!

"I'm sorry your warning wasn't taken seriously," Irene concluded.

"Was it the same guy?"

The question drew Irene's eyes back up to meet Carolyn's. "Same as the one who came to your cell last night?"

"So you know?"

Irene nodded. "Well, we know now. The coincidence of your suicide and the attack on your boy was too much, so we checked back at the jail. We've got a picture from the security camera, so there's a good chance we'll be able to identify him. Fact is, he got away."

You won't identify anything, Carolyn thought. "At least your capture rate is consistent," she snarled.

Irene grew visibly more tired as she sat there. "I know you're upset," she said measuredly. "God knows you've got a right. But you should know that this animal who attacked your son also killed a seven-year-old girl." Her voice became stronger. "Doctors say he gave her a massive injection of potassium chloride—the same stuff they use in executions. She never had a chance."

The words hit Carolyn hard. "Why?"

Irene shrugged. The conversation was mother-to-mother now. "Who knows for sure? We think it was because he wanted to direct attention elsewhere while he attacked your boy."

"But wasn't there a guard—"

"He was killed," Irene interrupted. Then added, just to make a point, "Trying to save Travis. And a very good friend of mine was horribly wounded. Their efforts are the reason why your son is still alive."

"And your vendetta is the reason he was there in the first place." It was the wrong time and the wrong place to pander for Carolyn's sympathy.

Irene absorbed the barrage and changed the subject. "Your husband came to see me last night," she said, drawing a distrustful look. "He told a very interesting story about your innocence and about arms being sold out of a magazine in Newark."

Carolyn listened with her eyes closed, hoping her face remained impassive—bored, even—as her mind raced to figure what she was talking about. "So where is he now?" she asked.

Irene gave a wry chuckle. "As you say, my capture rate is consistent."

The sale of weapons out of the magazine was an interesting twist, Carolyn thought—one she hadn't considered.

"He wanted me to tell you he loves you."

The words brought Carolyn's eyes around, searching for the scam. This Rivers lady was good. She almost looked sincere. But Carolyn had played the mind game with her once before, and she wasn't inclined to do it again. She listened silently as Irene told of Jake's theories and of her own efforts to verify them.

"Your situation is really very desperate," Irene concluded. "People are trying to kill you and your family, and the only way we can protect you is to have you in custody. You and Travis are safe now—we'll see to that—but as long as your husband is out on his own, he's in very grave danger."

Finally, Carolyn had to laugh. "You've got to be kidding. After fourteen peaceful years on the run, the *only* time my family has been attacked is when we've been in your custody. From where I sit, there's no more dangerous place in the world."

Carolyn's face darkened as her eyes burned a hole through her captor. "This sympathy simulation is a nice try, Rivers. And deep down, I'd like to believe you might actually give a shit. But you put it best yesterday. We all have jobs to do. I've failed at mine, so here I am. Now it's all on Jake. He's my last hope for getting our lives back. I just don't believe you have as much incentive."

Irene looked for a moment like she might argue again but then stopped. Interpreting the silence as a victory, Carolyn decided to press. "Now, I'd like to see my son. Please take me to him."

Irene glanced toward her prisoner again, then looked away. "I only wish I could. The doctor doesn't want you moved with your neck injury."

"Then bring Travis to me."

Irene pressed her lips together and shook her head. "I can't do that, either. He's still tied to the respirator and the monitors."

Carolyn felt the anger flare in her belly, burning off the hazy cobwebs left by the drugs. Threats and furious invectives flooded into her brain, but in the sudden clarity of the moment, she knew such words would be wasted; maybe even harmful. She took a deep, silent breath, and when she spoke, she made sure her tone was the very essence of reason. "He's my son, Rivers. My only child, and someone is trying to kill him. You have to let me see him."

Irene regarded her for a long moment, the exhaustion of the preceding days weighing on her like an anvil. "I'll see what I can do," she said finally. The words sounded hollow even to herself.

Carolyn was done talking; Irene recognized the signals now. The agent closed her eyes and tried to massage away her booming headache. An odd mix of fear and guilt boiled in her gut, making her wish for the first time that she'd chosen a different career. The Bureau was supposed to be the good guys, dammit. If her suspicions were correct, this poor woman who lay tied helplessly to her bed had endured more hardship than anyone should ever bear.

Over the course of her career with the Bureau, Irene had absorbed a lot of hate from a lot of fugitives, but never before had she felt crippled by it. She wanted to tell Carolyn that she believed her story now; wanted to tell her all about Frankel and to apologize on behalf of the federal government. But that was out of the question. Fact was, they couldn't *prove* anything. Yet.

As if on cue, a gentle rap on the door drew her head around. Paul Boersky beckoned her into the hallway and from there, hustled her into an empty room.

"I gather from all this stealth that we guessed right?" Irene opened.

Instinctively, Paul looked over his shoulder. "This is scary as shit, Irene," he whispered. "Looks like the Donovans nailed it. I talked to a guy in Records—you owe him a hundred bucks, by the way—who dug into Frankel's files for me. Your rag mag was right. From 1981 to early '82, our fearless leader ran an investigation out of the Little Rock office into arms sales shenanigans out of Newark. Apparently, there were a few leads that seemed to head back toward the last Army commander of the place—your suicidal buddy, General Albemarle. Seems that the case dried up, though, all of a sudden like.

"Then Albemarle—a freakin' war hero, from the Second World War through Korea and even a touch of Vietnam—blew his brains out in 1982, just after the EPA discovered this weapons stash. His note said it was the pressure of the investigation." Paul looked up from his pad and sighed. "It's just too close, Irene. I think we got him. He blew up the magazine to cover the missing inventory, and the people to deflect the attention."

Irene stared off to a spot on the floor, lost in the meaning of it all.

"You still with me?" Paul asked.

"Huh? Oh, yeah, sure. Just getting a headache."

He snorted. "Yeah, well, tape it up, because this gets better. Remember Tony Bernard? The guy at the motel?"

She nodded. "Yeah."

"Okay, well, listen to this. He was the only son of a couple of flower children. Real doper types, who dragged baby Tony through all kinds of hippie shit at Berkeley, and later got his picture in the *Chicago Tribune* as a—and I quote—'young rioter' during the Democratic convention back in '68."

She looked confused. "I don't get it."

"Sure you do. What better bio to hang a 'crazy environmentalist' tag on? He was the one who was supposed to go down for the whole thing, not the Donovans. They just got tagged because they had the poor taste to survive it all. With them alive, Frankel had no choice but to kill Bernard. Whatever holes the sudden change left in his plan, he just covered over with a little hysteria."

Irene's eyes got wider, and she took a deep breath. "Holy shit," she said.

"The holiest," Paul cheered, still at a whisper. "Here we were worried about career damage control, and instead, we strike gold!"

Irene shot him a glare.

"What?"

"You're nuts," she declared. "We don't have squat here."

"Bullshit."

She realized she'd made him defensive, and she waved it off. "No, that's not what I mean. It's a good case, and I think we've found the answer, but Frankel's not just going to cave. Christ, he's got a confession and a truckload of circumstantial evidence. Certainly as much circumstantial evidence as we have."

Paul shrugged. "Reasonable doubt, right?"

She laughed. "Oh, yeah, this is great news for the Donovans. They're home free, if we ever get them to trial. But you were talking about your career. If we can't put Frankel away, then all we'll do is set the Donovans free and shoot ourselves in the feet."

Paul opened his mouth to argue, then shut it again. "Shit."

CHAPTER FORTY-FIVE

Melissa Thomas loved her big old house. She just wished she had the money and time to take care of it the way her mother and father had. The house and its surrounding six and a half acres of woods were her parents' legacy for their only child. And their curse. Her parents had been dead nearly ten years now, yet Melissa still couldn't afford to replace the furniture she'd known as a child. Wisely invested, her inheritance would spin off enough cash to pay the property taxes every year, with enough left over for three college educations. But that defined the limit of the Thomas family's solvency.

Still, the place was home for her; the repository for all her good memories. And, more recently, for her bad ones as well. Although solidly built at a time when carpenters took pride in their work, the place was beginning to show serious signs of age. The roof needed replacing, the walls screamed for a coat of paint, and the soil had begun to erode away from the foundation out front. It was a real worry. They couldn't afford to have the work done by a contractor, and Nick was worthless with tools. He couldn't drive a nail if it had tires and a steering wheel. So the repairs went undone, waiting for that time when they'd find themselves with a few dollars they didn't already owe to someone else. Nick's solution was just to sell the place. Typical. Address a temporary problem with a permanent solution. Kill a fly with a shotgun.

Ticked off as she was about Nick's being gone at the precise time she most needed his help—she'd received twelve more Christmas orders just this morning—she had to admit that it was kind of peaceful, just her and the kids. At one level, that's all she ever really wanted out of a marriage, anyway. And if this job interview could somehow jump-start his dead career, then maybe it would be good for all of them. This whole business with the Donovans in the news made her a bit nervous, though. If Nick were anyone but his spineless self, she might even have been worried.

The pot on her wheel was giving her fits. The Aztec Urn, as it was called in the catalog, had a long fluted neck that ordinarily would have been the simplest thing in the world to fashion, yet for some reason she couldn't get the proportions right. And this was her third try.

"Dammit!" She stopped the wheel and hammered the misshapen pot back into a lump of red clay with the palm of her hand. What she needed was a break, but she knew better than to take one. Not just yet. Once this one was molded, she'd have a full load to stick in the kiln, and then she'd reward herself with a late lunch. She should have grabbed a bite when she fed Lauren at noon, but she hadn't been hungry.

That reminded her: Lauren hadn't made a peep in a long time. Probably still watching her *Lion King* video. Melissa sighed. She knew her daughter needed more stimulation, but Melissa just didn't have time to be a mommy anymore. Next year, though, her baby would start school, and everything would work out just fine.

Maybe I'm trying too hard, she thought as she started up the wheel again. That was often the root of her creativity problems. Sometimes she'd get so tense about doing it "right" that she'd lose the feel for the clay. She tried closing her eyes this time. The tiny foam earphones on her head filled her mind with the peace of Copeland's *Quiet City*, and as the haunting sounds of the solo trumpet ebbed and flowed with the melody, the base of the pot magically formed in her hands.

A shadow fell across Melissa's face, and her eyes snapped open. A man she'd never seen before was standing in the archway that separated her studio from the kitchen. He held a package of some sort in his arms. In the green-filtered light cast by the tinted jalousie windows, the package looked almost human. A doll maybe? And it was dressed in the same outfit Lauren had been wearing.

Melissa screamed.

Nick slid the telephone receiver back into its clamp and thrust a hand angrily through his hair. "Dammit!" He looked at his watch. "It's after two, for Christ's sake. I thought these planes were supposed to be fast!" Under the circumstances, the Gulfstream could have been rocketing through Mach 3 and it still wouldn't have been enough.

"Stay off the phone," Thorne growled for the thousandth time. "Every one of those calls is like a trail of bread crumbs for the feds."

Nick responded with an angry glare. At that moment, reinforcements from the FBI didn't sound like such a bad idea.

"She could just be out of the house, you know," Jake offered.

Nick shook his head. "No chance. She's buried in catalog orders. She wouldn't leave the house if it was on fire." He sat back down in the overstuffed captain's chair and rested his forearms on his knees. "She does this all the time when she's really busy. She just turns off the phones. We've got one of those answering services through the phone company, and she just checks the messages at the end of the day. Drives me nuts. Suppose one of the kids was sick at school or something, you know?"

"They have a place to go, though, right?" Jake asked. "I mean, once you get word to them, they can leave right away?"

Nick opened his mouth to answer but closed it. He hadn't thought that far ahead. "I guess they'll just stay in a hotel."

"Make sure they pay with cash," Thorne warned. "If we miss this guy, he's gonna be pissed. The last thing you want is another electronic trail."

Nick's features sagged. "I don't know that I have that kind of cash."

"Don't worry," Jake said, smiling. He patted the ever-present gym bags. "I've got you covered there."

A speaker popped overhead, and the pilot asked everyone to return to their seats and to fasten their seat belts. They'd be on the ground in about ten minutes. Their destination was the Manassas Regional Airport, a discreet commercial airstrip in the far-west Virginia suburbs of Washington; large enough to accept corporate jets yet small enough to allow passengers to remain anonymous.

Thorne crossed his legs comfortably and folded his fingers over his knee. "So, ace, what about you? Now that you're fishing for sharks, what happens when you pull one in?" His lips bent back into the condescending smile Jake had come to hate so much.

"I'll make him talk," he said, simply enough. He tried to sound decisive, but they all knew he was in over his head.

"Uh-huh," Thorne grunted. "And suppose he doesn't want to cooperate?"

"He will. He has to."

"But suppose he *doesn't*?"

Jake looked at Thorne carefully, knowing exactly what he was driving at, but refusing to address it. "He'll talk," Jake said. "Most people's tongues loosen when they have a gun pointed at their heads."

Thorne smiled, stared out the window. "The question is, is our man 'most people'?"

Melissa shot to her feet, sending both her potter's wheel and the Aztec Urn crashing to the floor. "Oh, my God!" she yelled. "Lauren!"

The whole room shook as she bounded across the floor of her studio, the cord from her headphones dragging the CD player to its death off the edge of its little table. "Lauren, baby! Oh, God, honey, are you all right?"

The little girl didn't move, her body so still and limp that the man seemed to have difficulty holding on to her. As he passed her on to her mother, they both tried to scoop up a dangling arm, but it seemed intent on staying free. Melissa was gone in an instant, hurrying past the stranger without so much as a thank-you.

The man followed without an invitation.

Melissa ran as best she could over to the high-ceilinged great room and laid her treasure gently on the sofa. "Lauren, honey, wake up. Wake up, sweetie . . ."

"She'll be okay," the stranger offered.

His voice startled Melissa; she'd forgotten about him. "How do you know? What happened to her?" The first thing she noticed as she looked up was the coldness of the man's eyes. The second thing was his gun.

"She's not good at following orders, is she?" he said.

It had been years since Jake was in an airport, and even this little one out in Virginia's boonies had five times more people milling around than he was comfortable with. This kind of travel should have been done only at night, but Nick was such a basket case that they'd had to come back early. Thorne insisted it was the most foolish thing they could do, that professional killers only worked at night, but Nick was equally adamant that they had to warn his family. With the telephone unplugged, the only alternative was to fly in. It wasn't like he could call the local sheriff's office and have them deliver the message.

Jake tried his best to stay invisible, wearing his sunglasses and baseball cap. He stood outside as Thorne took care of the rental car details. If Nick paced any more frantically, people were going to start looking for the maternity ward.

Finally, Thorne emerged from the sliding glass doors, car keys in hand, and they followed him across the parking lot to the cluster of five rental cars: four Escorts and a Grand Marquis. Thorne treasured his comfort. "Put your gloves on, people," he instructed as he thumbed the remote to unlock the Grand Marquis's door.

"I'll drive," Nick said, stepping in front of Thorne. "I know where we're going."

Thorne held his ground—and the keys. "Good. Then you sit up front and tell me where to go."

Nick shook his head, eyes desperate. "But . . ."

"I'm driving, Nick," Thorne said simply. "Now, we can argue about it, or you can fight me for it, but when we're done, I'll still be behind the wheel. You're wrapped way too tight to drive anywhere."

"We're wasting time, boys," Jake chided as he climbed into the backseat.

Defeated and deflated, Nick considered his options and quickly let it go. As he settled into the shotgun seat, and Thorne slid in behind the wheel, Nick gave his instructions in a burst. "Left out of the airport onto Nokesville Road. Follow the signs toward Warrenton." He checked his watch. "And for Christ's sake, step on it. This is taking way, way too long."

Melissa's mind was a complete blank. She felt dizzy, and her legs wobbled as she tried to figure out what she'd *really* heard. *Not good at following orders?*

"You look confused," the man said with an odd smile. "Let me clear it up for you. I'm here to let you save your children's lives."

"Who are you?" Melissa breathed.

The man chuckled. "Everyone always asks that. Like it matters." He smiled. "You can call me Wiggins, if you'd like."

She still couldn't move. "But why . . . What . . ." Her brain refused to function in complete sentences.

"I know it's confusing," he said apologetically. "But I really don't want to hurt your children any more than I already have."

Her eyes grew huge, and they shot back to her helpless little girl.

"Really," he said. "She'll be fine. I'm afraid I had to get a little rough with her as she tried to squirm away. Once she got a whiff from my magic handkerchief, though, she settled down. She should be under for at least an hour."

Melissa's face lost all color.

"You know, you really shouldn't let such a little girl answer the door," he chided. "No harm done, though. She'll be awake just in time to greet little Nicky and Joshua as they come home from school."

Melissa's world started to spin, and she sat down hard. She figured she'd fainted, because barely a second passed before he was right there, his face just a few inches from hers, his pistol pressed against her temple.

"Now don't go wimpy on me, Melissa. There's no time. We've got a lot of work to do before the boys get home."

"Please don't . . ." she sobbed.

"Just think of your children as Thanksgiving turkeys," he whispered. "And how awful it would be to be carved alive."

"Something's wrong," Nick whined. "I can feel it."

To Jake's eye, the scenery hadn't changed in the last twenty minutes. Hell, it hadn't changed in a year. Heavy woods just led to more heavy woods, the monotony of the landscape broken only by the occasional house or gas station. Rural Virginia was no different than rural South Carolina or rural Arkansas. Only the terrain and the foliage changed. The isolation was a constant.

From Route 28, they took Vint Hill Road to cross over to Route 29, and from there, on into Warrenton. After that, the turns and the route numbers came too quickly and too frequently for Jake to keep track. No one even bothered to name the roads out here. They just stuck a number on a post.

Soon the woods began to give way to fields and rolling hills. Stone walls took the place of barbed wire along the roadside, some of them in pristine shape, others crumbling under a century of neglect. Multimillion-dollar mansions alternated with more modest farmhouses and barely habitable shacks.

"How much further?" Jake asked. Anything to cut the tension.

"About three miles."

"Now *sign* it," Wiggins instructed. They were in the master bedroom upstairs, gathered around a tiny antique writing desk.

"No one's going to believe any of this," Melissa sobbed. Her tears dropped heavily onto the mauve stationery, smearing the ink of her suicide note.

He smiled. "You'd be surprised what people will believe. Now hurry up and sign it. You're running out of time. It's after three."

But the note was all wrong! She didn't hate herself, and she wasn't hopelessly lonely. She loved her children, and they loved her right back. Even the stuff about Nick was all wrong. He wasn't the best husband in the world, but she could have done a lot worse. This whole thing made no sense.

If she signed the note—every word dictated by this madman—what would her children think of her as they grew older? They'd spend their entire lives hating her for abandoning them; for filling their minds with memories of finding her dead body.

"I won't do it," she declared.

Wiggins's eyes flashed—a second of anger that disappeared instantly, replaced by his professional calm. He glared straight through Melissa's eyes, into her brain. "Fine," he said. "Don't sign it. I don't want you to sign it." He snatched the note from beneath her hand and crumpled it up tightly, stuffing it into his pocket. When his hand came into view again, it held a knife. He snapped it open, revealing a finely honed three-inch blade. "But don't say I didn't warn you."

She winced, anticipating pain, but panicked when she saw him heading out of the bedroom toward the stairs. "Where are you going?"

He never slowed, didn't say a word.

"Oh, my God!" she yelled. "Lauren!" She bolted out of her writing chair and ran after the killer. She caught up with him at the top of the stairs and tried to tackle him, but he didn't even seem to feel the impact. She fell to the floor and tried to hang on to his ankle, but he just kicked himself free.

"Please!" she yelled. "Please! I'll do it! Please don't hurt her."

"I told you, Melissa," Wiggins said calmly as he marched down the sweeping, carpeted staircase. "I told you this would happen, but you didn't believe me." His heels clicked as he stepped onto the hardwood of the foyer. "I'm going to have to get *really* creative with the boys."

"No!" she shrieked. "I'll do it!" She sailed down the steps, barely touching them as she charged at him. "Touch my little girl, you son of a bitch, and I'll kill you!"

She was five feet away when Wiggins stopped suddenly and

whirled, thrusting his hand into the air like a traffic cop in an inter-
section. She skidded to a halt and nearly fell.

He glared at her and brought the point of his knife within inches
of her face. "Are you asking for a second chance?"

She nodded frantically. "Yes."

"Then ask me." His voice was barely a whisper.

"I am," she whispered back. "I'm asking you for a second chance."

He smiled. "Ask me to let you kill yourself."

She tried. "Please," she said. She choked on her voice as she began
to sob. She slumped to her knees. "Please . . ."

"Say the words," he insisted, "or I'll field-dress your little girl right
there on the sofa."

She tried again. Really tried, but the words wouldn't come.
"Please . . ."

"Say the words!" he boomed, his voice shaking the glass on a curio
cabinet.

She was helpless now. Terrified. Fear and sadness flowed from her
soul like a raging river as she finally croaked out the words. "Please.
Let. Me. Kill myself."

Wiggins stood over her, admiring his handiwork. Finally, he
stooped down to her level and used one finger on the point of her
chin to raise her eyes to meet his. "I don't normally give second
chances," he whispered.

"That's it!" Nick yelled. "The white mailbox on the right. That's
my driveway!"

Thorne hit his signal and slowed to make the turn. All very legal.
All very slow.

"Goddammit, Thorne, move it!"

"Look!" the driver snarled. "If our target is already there, I'm sure
as hell not charging up the driveway into a trap! It won't make a difference, anyway . . ."

Jake saw the words cut divots out of Nick's heart.

". . . and if he isn't there yet, then we've got nothing to worry
about." He cleared the mailbox and began inching his way up the
long driveway, scanning the horizon for threats.

"Whose van is that?" Jake asked, pointing to the end of the driveway. The block lettering on the side read "Mike's Plumbing."

"Oh, shit," Nick breathed. "Step on it, Thorne."

Thorne hesitated, then stopped. "This isn't good."

It was three-twenty now, and the boys' bus would arrive out front at any minute.

This time the note was short and sweet. "Good-bye." She'd addressed it individually to all of her family, and she'd signed it without objection. With her children's lives in the balance, her own meant nothing.

Wiggins led Melissa to the little balcony overlooking the foyer and handed her the rope. It was clothesline, really; an eight-foot nylon tube with little tufts of white stuffing sticking out of either end. "Tie this onto the railing," he instructed.

She moved mechanically, like her hands were suddenly a couple of sizes too big. Much to her surprise, though, they didn't tremble. She was terrified, yet resigned to her fate. It was for her children.

Wiggins watched her work, observing every detail.

She tied the knot carefully, making sure it would hold, even as she feared that the railing itself might not stand the strain of the jolt. Probably wouldn't matter, anyway. Once her neck snapped, the rest would be academic.

"Very good," Wiggins praised. "Now, you see that little loop I tied on the other end?"

She looked at him quizzically, then nodded.

"Good. I need you to pull some rope back through the loop to form a noose."

She did what she was told, looking up for confirmation that she was doing it right.

"A little bigger," he said.

And bigger it grew. She knew that a single screwup would kill her children. She had doubted that once, but not anymore.

He backed away now, putting some distance between himself and his victim. "Okay, Melissa," he said softly. "The rest is up to you now." He walked down the stairs to watch the action from the foyer.

She looked at him strangely; like she suddenly didn't know who he was. She still didn't understand why, but the time had come to kill herself. She prayed it wouldn't hurt too much. She eyed the rope in her hands, then slowly and deliberately slipped the noose over her head, adjusting it just so on her neck, with the knot lined up to her spine.

She was crying now, though still amazingly calm as she slung one leg over the railing, and then the other, moving carefully to keep from falling. Like it would matter. The tiny ledge beyond the white wooden rail spindles protruded just enough to support Melissa's heels; and even then, she had to jam her Achilles tendon into the spaces between them. With her hands behind her, knuckles white against the dark wood of the banister, she looked like the bowsprit of a great schooner. The tears flowed freely now as she looked down at her murderer.

"You're doing great, Melissa," he coaxed. There was now an easy gentleness to his tone that she found more frightening than his anger. "You're almost there. Just take a step."

She looked down at him, wanting to beg; hoping to tap into a tiny vein of compassion. But there was no pity in those eyes. There'd be no reprieve. She tried to speak but found her throat packed with sand. She swallowed dusty air and tried it again. "Promise me you won't hurt the children," she croaked.

He put his fists on his hips and shook his head. "We've already been over this."

"Promise me."

His eyes narrowed as his features hardened. "Jump, Melissa. End it. Now. They'll be home soon."

"*Promise* me!" A fierceness returned to her voice. It wasn't a request anymore. It was a demand.

He found it amusing. He stared at her for a moment longer, then finally shrugged. "Okay," he said. "I promise. Now jump!"

She glared down on him, trying to kill the bastard with the strength of her hate alone. When he refused to break eye contact, though—when he chose instead to smile up at her—she knew the battle was lost. Out in the family room, she heard the mantel clock chime the half hour. Nicky and Joshua would be home at any minute. She had to get this done.

Forgive me, she thought, and she adjusted the rope one last time behind her. Then she let go. And jumped.

"He's in there," Thorne whispered, and he climbed out of the car. Jake followed, sliding out of the backseat. "How do you know?"

"Because that's what I'd drive if I thought I might have to dispose of a couple of bodies. Call it intuition."

Nick stayed in the car as Jake and Thorne played commando, sneaking quietly up the grassy slope toward the house.

"Fuck this," Nick spat. In one smooth motion, he slid over to the driver's seat and slammed the gas pedal to the floor. The rear wheels dug trenches in the grass as the big boat of a car launched forward, the acceleration slamming Jake's door shut.

He passed his partners in a blur, rocketing straight toward the front of the house. He covered the three hundred feet in no time at all, destroying a dozen azaleas and a thirty-year-old boxwood as he slid to a stop on the front walk.

Stealth be damned, he jumped out of the car and dashed full speed up the two steps to the front door. When he found it ajar, he panicked and flew into the foyer. "Mel—oh, God!"

Melissa saw the door fly open, even as she leapt into the air, and the reality of her rescue hit her like a bolt of lightning. Her body jerked and arced wildly as she abandoned her suicide and turned in midair, clamoring for a handhold on the railing. Her left hand nicked it but missed, and she brought her right around in a giant overhead arc, catching the polished banister in her palm.

She slammed heavily into the ledge and the spindles. A splintering *crack!* startled her, and for just a fraction of an instant, she feared that the wood had snapped. Then the bolt of agony reached her brain, launched from her ruined shoulder. Suddenly, the railing felt white-hot in her palm, and as her grip started to slip, she said another prayer for her children.

☆   ☆   ☆

Nick had never seen the man before in his life, but he knew from his eyes exactly who he was. The entire scene registered with the speed of a camera flash. The murderer in the foyer. His wife struggling overhead.

Little Lauren, looking sleepy and disheveled, took it all in from the kitchen doorway.

Wiggins moved toward Nick with viper-speed. But for an extra two feet of separation, Nick would have died right there. As it was, Wiggins had to close the gap by a step, and Nick used the half-second delay to dive out of the way. As he skidded across the floor, his attacker changed course.

Nick saw the kick coming, and he rolled to his right, just as he heard Lauren's panicked voice yell, "Daddy!" The kick missed, but Wiggins adjusted one more time, settling for a crushing blow to Nick's ankle. He stomped on it; like someone else might stomp on a bug.

Nick howled in agony. He tried to pull his leg away, but the foot just flopped to the side, like it didn't even belong to him. His vision seemed to liquefy. Again, he saw the kick coming, this one to his head and moving a million miles per hour.

Lauren screamed one more time.

Thorne moved with tremendous speed, sailing across the foyer in no time flat. For the final ten feet, he was airborne, arriving shoulder-first and launching Wiggins into the opposite wall. The murderer hit hard, knocking a curio cabinet off the wall and sending the shattered remains of Melissa Thomas's most prized pottery skittering across the floor.

Thorne recovered quickly, but Wiggins was faster, sweeping the newcomer's legs out from under him with a vicious roundhouse kick. Wiggins was on him the instant he hit the floor, and suddenly, the struggle looked like something you'd see in the halls of a high school: a wrestling match, with only a few punches thrown—and those to little effect—as each man struggled for dominance over the other.

Jake moved in, weapon drawn, and pulled Nick out of the way by his armpits. "Help my wife," Nick groaned, and he pointed over-head.

Melissa looked like she was trying to swim, her legs kicking use-lessly in the air as she dangled from her one good arm. *What the hell?* Jake wondered, and then he saw the rope. "Oh, my God!"

The two fighters broke apart as Thorne's head snapped back and a smear of blood flooded the lower half of his face. Thorne coun-tered with two savage lefts to the killer's mouth. A tooth hit the floor, and the men locked it up again.

Jake took the stairs two at a time. As he arrived at the top, he saw the angulation in Melissa's ruined shoulder and realized for the first time just how desperate her situation was. If she let go, she was dead.

Melissa greeted Jake with a look of faint recognition. "You—" she said, not completing the sentence. She eyed the Glock in his fist and gurgled out something like "Shoot him."

Jake didn't bother to respond. He needed the killer alive and prayed Thorne would be able to hold his own while he concentrated on saving this woman's life. He examined the complex knot on the railing for just a second before abandoning it as hopeless. Reaching over the top, he grabbed a fistful of shirt and heaved her high enough to where she could regain her foothold on the ledge.

"Shoot him!" she said, air returning to her lungs.

He helped her climb back over the banister. "I can't," he said.

A heavy thump and a crash whipped his attention back down the stairs as Thorne and Wiggins exploded apart, each tumbling back-ward onto the wooden floor. Thorne landed in the broken glass.

Wiggins landed on Lauren.

"Mommmmeeeee!!!"

In an instant, Wiggins had the little girl in his grasp, his forearm around her middle, squeezing her hard enough to turn her face red. The Beretta appeared in his other hand, and he brought it toward the little girl's head.

Melissa and Nick shrieked in unison, *"No!!"*

On the floor, Thorne rolled to his side, and there was a flash of silver as he slapped his own weapon out of its holster. A tongue of flame six inches long jumped from the muzzle of Thorne's big .45, and the house rocked with noise as Wiggins's gun hand left his arm. Fingers flew through the air like chips from a log, and the Beretta dropped harmlessly onto the polished hardwood surface of the foyer.

The impact of Thorne's bullet spun the attacker into the wall with tremendous force, but he never let go of the girl, who flopped in his arm like a doll.

Jake flew down the stairs as Thorne drew a bead for his kill shot. "God, Thorne, no!" He slapped at the chrome-plated .45 even as it rocked the house one more time. "We need him alive, goddammit!"

"Get the fuck out of my way!" Thorne yelled, and he brought the gun around one more time.

But he was too late. Wiggins had shifted arms again, the tattered stump of bone and tissue painting horrifying red stripes across Lauren's pink coveralls. She stood tall and still in his arms, though, her feet dangling by his knees as his knife blade pushed into the underside of her jaw, just far enough to draw a bead of blood.

"Put the piece down or I'll cut her fucking throat!" he commanded.

Thorne never broke his aim. "Like I give a fuck," he growled. "Go ahead and cut it. I'd love to see your brain on the floor."

"Oh, my God!" Melissa shrieked.

Nick was standing again, his weight on his only good foot. "Thorne!" he yelled. "For Christ's sake, put your gun down. That's my daughter!"

"Then make another one. I'm gonna kill this fuck."

Wiggins smiled, even as he backed out of the foyer, toward the kitchen. "You gonna shoot right through her, tough guy?"

Thorne shrugged. "If I have to."

Jake didn't know what to do. He knew without the tiniest doubt that Thorne couldn't have cared less about that little girl. Jake moved in behind him, his own weapon drawn, as together they backed the killer through the kitchen, toward Melissa's workroom.

"Don't kill him, Thorne," Jake said softly, nearly whispering in his ear. "If you kill him, it's all over. We don't have squat for real evidence. That's what we're here for, remember?"

"Stay out of my way, Jake."

Melissa and Nick joined the group, helping each other move as best they could. "Nick!" she wailed. "Stop him! My God, who are these people? What are they doing here?"

Thorne never broke eye contact with his target as he hissed, "Do me a favor, Nick, and get control of your wife."

"Fuck you!" Melissa shouted. She darted out in front of Thorne, blocking his aim, and facing Wiggins eye-to-eye.

Nick panicked. "Melissa, no!"

"Please let her go," she pleaded. "I tried . . ."

Wiggins was gone. Keeping the flailing, sobbing little girl between himself and his pursuers, he glided out of the kitchen and through the glass doors of Melissa's studio.

"Get out of my way!" Thorne shouted as Melissa tried to block his path.

"He'll kill her!" she screamed. She grabbed Thorne's jacket in her fists. "Let him go!"

Thorne settled the issue with a slap that sent Melissa reeling.

Jake stood watching, horrified. He saw Nick's wife hit the floor shoulder-first and heard her scream in pain. Nick shot him a look of pure hatred as he hobbled over to help her. Jake stared for a moment, absorbing his friend's anger, but there was nothing to say. He hurried to follow Thorne into the yard.

CHAPTER FORTY-SIX

Out back, the grass gave way quickly to woods; small scrubby stuff up front, backed up by a thick forest of brilliantly colored young hardwoods—a final insult to the property's nearly forgotten heritage as a farm.

Movement drew Jake's attention to his left as he saw a flash of Thorne's back disappearing among the colors. He followed at a dead run. With the sun resting low on the horizon, streams of light painted a confusing mosaic through the leaves, making it difficult to keep Thorne in sight. Jake couldn't see their quarry at all.

When Thorne stopped, Jake was with him in an instant. "Where are they?"

Thorne gestured for silence, using the muzzle of his pistol as an extension of his vision as he scanned the forest for movement. "I saw him," he whispered. "He's here."

The words triggered a chill. Where could he be, then? He didn't have that much of a lead. "There!" Jake pointed. "Isn't that blood?"

In the distance, they heard Melissa's plaintive voice. "Lauren! Lauren, honey, we're coming!"

Out in front, and off to the right, they heard a child's muffled cry. Together, they moved toward it, following the blood trail and listening for additional noise.

"Lauren!" This time it was Nick's voice, and they were getting closer.

Soon the woods opened up again, to reveal another cleared field, with a dilapidated barn growing up out of the center. Jake and Thorne stopped at the edge of the clearing.

"What do you think?" Jake whispered. "Are they inside?"

Thorne shook his head. "He's too smart to corner himself."

"Then why . . ."

A rustle of leaves just inches to their left brought both men around, their guns bearing down on the terrified face of little Lauren. She screamed, yet even at five, she understood the unasked question. "He dropped me!" she shouted.

Jake saw the flash of steel the instant he broke his aim. Wiggins came from nowhere, lunging out of the foliage, propelling his knife in a huge downward arc. Jake got an arm up but couldn't deflect it all. He grunted as the glancing blow left a wake of torn flesh down the side of his ribs, and he tumbled for cover in the leaves.

The speed of the attack caught Thorne off guard, but once he recovered, he struck like a snake, firing two quick punches, one to the stump of what used to be Wiggins's hand, and the other to his face. The gunman went down hard but rolled fluidly to his feet. As he took a martial-arts stance, or a pitiful imitation of one, he seemed to notice for the first time that his right arm was four inches shorter than his left. He shifted his eyes to the stump, and in that instant, Thorne dropped him with a chilling elbow shot to the jaw.

Thorne was out of control. He muscled his trophy off the ground and punched him again. "Who are you, you son of a bitch?"

The man said nothing. For an instant, Jake wondered if the guy was already dead.

This time Thorne's fury took the form of a savage kick to the gunman's testicles. The mystery man made a gagging sound and tried to clutch at himself, but Thorne launched him back with yet another kick, this one to his face.

"Stop it!" Melissa shrieked, appearing with Nick at the edge of the clearing.

"What's your *name*, asshole?" Thorne yelled, preparing for another kick.

"Wiggins!" Melissa answered for the gunman, even as she ran to be with her daughter. "He already told me his name is Wiggins!"

Thorne shook his head. "I want to hear it from him."

"Not here!" Nick yelled, clearly torn between joining his wife and confronting Thorne. His skin gray with pain and fear, he chose the latter. "Not in front of my daughter, Thorne!"

Thorne looked thoroughly disgusted. "Do you know what this rat turd tried to do?"

It was Jake's turn. "This isn't the plan," he said, shooting a glance toward the terrified little girl who sat hugging her knees at the base of a tree. The blood from her chin left a sweat trail down the front of her neck, which Melissa tried to wipe away with her one good hand. "Let's stick with the plan."

Thorne laughed loud and hard. "Plan! What plan? You don't have a fucking plan, Jake!"

Jake felt his face flush. "We agreed—"

"*We* didn't agree to shit!" Thorne declared. "*You* came up with the pea-brain idea that Mr. Terminator here would spill his guts. All we had to do was say 'pretty please.'" He laughed again and launched another kick to Wiggins's ribs. "Just like *Murder, She Wrote*, right, ace?"

"But my daughter—" Nick said.

"What about her? Get her the fuck outa here, if you want. I'm not stopping you!"

Nick swallowed hard, then glanced nervously over toward his wife and daughter before whispering, "You can't do this *here*. I don't want that kind of involvement. That's not what I signed on for."

Thorne set his jaw angrily. A long moment passed as he struggled with his temper, and when he finally spoke, his voice trembled. "You're in this up to your eyeballs, Nick. Remember that. Don't

you dare think even for a minute that you're not a part of it all."
He leveled a forefinger and lowered his voice. Anger burned in his
expression, genuine loathing. "You do yourself a favor and think
real long and real hard before you go soft, you hear?" He let the
words sink in for a moment. "Now, why don't you and the missus
go back to the house and clean up? Jake and I will take care of what
needs to be done. Tomorrow morning, you can tell your kid all
about how real nightmares can seem." He paused again, for effect.
"You've got a secret now, Nick, and I expect you to keep it. Now
get the fuck outa here. Go find that hotel you were talking about
and make sure it's a million miles from here."

"Suppose someone *sees* you?"

That one caught Thorne off guard. He scowled as he considered the question. "What's inside that barn?" he asked, pointing.

"It's just a storage shed," Nick said as Thorne began dragging his
prey in that direction.

Thorne called over his shoulder, "You're with *me*, ace!"

Jake ignored him and took a step closer to his old friend. In the
distance, he could hear children's voices calling for their mom and
dad. "Is that your boys?"

Nick nodded. "I guess they just got home."

Jake nodded back. It was an awkward moment. "Look,
Nick . . ."

"You're welcome, Jake, okay? Let's just leave it at that."

Jake stood still for a moment, wanting to say something but unable to construct the sentence. Finally, he nodded. "Okay, Nick.
Thanks. And I'm sorry."

Nick nodded, too, but looked away. "I'm glad I could do my
part. Now, just do us all a favor and end it."

"About your wife . . ."

"Just end it, Jake. I'll worry about my wife."

It was a sickening thing to watch. Wiggins sat bolt upright in the
middle of the dusty skeleton of a barn while Thorne secured the
man's neck directly to the twelve-by-twelve center support column
with five loops of duct tape. A tourniquet at the gunman's wrist,

fashioned out of an old rag and a screwdriver, kept him from bleeding to death, even as blood and snot continued to leak freely from his shattered nose. With the man's neck secured, Thorne went to work on his arms, binding them with loop after loop of tape, just above the elbows.

"You like to be called Wiggins?" Thorne growled as he worked. "That's fine with me. What I want to know is who you work for. And why. Every little detail." Thorne tore off the last piece of tape and tossed the roll aside. "Won't it be fun?"

Jake had never seen Thorne so animated, so entertained.

"Who do you work for?" Thorne paused for just a beat—barely long enough for the man to have formed an answer, even if he'd wanted to—then loosed a backhand smack that scattered a bloody mist into the air.

Jake felt his stomach turn and moved his head to look away when the most amazing thing happened. Wiggins smiled. His teeth—what was left of them—were shiny with blood, but the son of a bitch thought this was funny.

And that *really* pissed Thorne off. He fired a kick into the prisoner's tattered hand. Wiggins's face knotted up tight against the pain, but as soon as the wave of agony passed, the smile returned.

"Jesus Christ, Thorne," Jake moaned. "Is this it? You're just going to beat him to death?"

Thorne stayed poised for another shot but moved his head to see Jake. "Actually, that's up to him. He doesn't have to die. I'll stop as soon as he starts talking."

Wiggins actually chuckled. And earned himself a kick in the ribs.

It was an obscene cycle. Wiggins seemed to grow stronger through the beating, refusing on the strength of his spirit alone to use the one key Thorne had given him to unlock his dungeon of pain. And the more he held out, the more vicious Thorne's attacks became.

After maybe three minutes, Jake actually found himself feeling sorry for the son of a bitch. Then he thought of Travis's face, and he made himself imagine the suffering his son must have endured.

He thought of this animal hanging Carolyn in her jail cell, and he conjured the images of the grief endured by the family of that little girl in the hospital, whose only involvement in any of this was to have the misfortune of getting sick at the same time as a stranger down the hall.

The rage Jake summoned up was enough for him to root Thorne on for another minute, but ultimately, it was of no use. He found himself desperately searching for an alternative to prolonged beating. What was infuriating was the man's defiance. This asshole's life lay in their hands, yet his battered, swollen eyes continued to say, "Fuck you."

Standing there, Jake had a kind of epiphany. He realized that in this battle of wills between professional painmongers, winning and losing were not measured by who had a heartbeat at the end of the day. A man won when he denied his adversary the pleasure of witnessing a breakdown. Men like these had inflicted too much pain, too many times, merely to be beaten into submission. Pain didn't frighten them anymore. Neither, apparently, did the thought of death.

So what did?

Frantically, he scanned the interior of the barn, searching for the answer. The far wall was lined with tools: wordworking, painting, plumbing. *Nothing there.* Just to the right of those was a narrow shelf stacked high with all manner and types of chemical supplies. All of the labels were turned out just so, with the hazards warnings clearly visible. He looked away, then snapped his head back again. *That's it!*

"Stop!" Jake commanded, freezing Thorne in the middle of an open-handed backswing.

"Stay out of this, Jake," Thorne said. "If you can't take it—"

"Shut up. It's my turn."

"*Your* turn?" The thought seemed somehow unthinkable.

"Yeah. *My* turn. He tried to kill *my* family. I get to take my shot at him. Can't do worse than you, right, Thorne?"

The battered man actually grinned.

Thorne hesitated, then shrugged and backed off.

With Thorne out of the way, Jake walked past the prisoner toward the storage shelf, out of Wiggins's field of view. What he needed had to be here somewhere. "Here's how I see it, buddy," he said to Wiggins's back as he rummaged through the containers. "Death is the gold medal for people like you. Pain gives you a hard-on. It's sick, but what the hell? So's making a living killing women and children."

He rummaged through all kinds of chemicals, pausing for just a second at a bottle of insecticide before moving on. Ah! He found one that would work perfectly. Now he needed a rag.

"With that arm of yours, I figure you're pretty much out of business," he went on. "Once word gets out in your circles, I imagine things'll get pretty intense for you."

"What the hell are you doing?" Thorne barked, his hands on his hips.

Here's one. Jake found an old rag on a bench. "Just pay attention, *ace.*" He needed gloves, too, and they were right next to the rag. Leave it to Mr. Safety to have rubber gloves in his shop.

He strolled back to the prisoner and stooped down in front of him. "The way I see it, we're wasting our time here, right? You're betting you can hold out just long enough for Thorne here to kill you. That lets you off the hook and somehow earns you special bragging rights in hell. Am I close?"

The gunman just stared defiantly, his left eye all but swollen shut, his right one not much better.

Jake's expression changed as he pulled the black rubber gloves onto his hands and opened up the brown glass bottle. As the cap came off, the faint stench of rotten eggs filled the air.

He held up the bottle and displayed the label as a sommelier might display a good bottle of wine. "Sulfuric acid," he explained. "Great for cleaning concrete, but man, you've got to dilute it. Otherwise, it burns like shit."

He tipped the bottle and poured a drop of the clear, concentrated liquid onto Wiggins's pant leg, just above the knee. Instantly, the cotton began to degrade, and the rotten-egg odor became unbearable. Soon it was joined by the smell of burning flesh as the acid ate away a chunk of flesh about the size of a dime.

The man's eyes were wide now. This clearly was beyond what he'd mentally prepared himself for. Pain he understood. Now his imagination was taking him into uncharted territory.

Jake smiled. "As I said, death comes too easily to you. The consequences don't mean anything. For all I know, after you finished with my son, you went out and had a pizza." The very thought of it made Jake's hands tremble. Wiggins saw the tremors and smirked.

"The hands?" Jake asked. "You think that's funny? A sign of weakness?" He smiled. "Well, you got me. I've never been much of a killer. Even the thought of killing a worthless coward like you makes my stomach flop."

Thorne had had about all he could stand. "Oh, for Christ's sake . . ."

"Shut the fuck up, Thorne!" Jake yelled. The suddenness of the outburst made Wiggins jump. Jake turned back to his prisoner. "Seems to me we're a bad match, Wiggins. I don't want to kill you, yet you seem content to die." He moved in very close now, close enough to smell the other man's bloody breath. And he whispered, "If you don't talk, I'm gonna make you live."

Wiggins shot a look to Thorne that said, *This guy is nuts.*

"You're right," Jake said, answering his thoughts. "I'm over the edge. Out of my fucking mind. And here's my one-time-only offer. You've seen how this stuff works. You've felt it burn. Well, the next dose goes in your eyes."

He fell silent, allowing the impact of his threat to settle in. "Really, that's it. One splash and it's all over. Ten seconds later your eyeballs are charcoal, and we're done here. We'll just let you go."

Wiggins's eyes grew wild as he glanced again toward Thorne. Jake caught the glance and smiled. He had him. "Imagine what it would be like not to see. You couldn't find your victims, even if you had two hands to kill them with."

He pulled away now, as his words took their toll. He actually enjoyed the look of horror in Wiggins's eyes. "You'll be ugly as hell, too. Repulsive burn scars all over your face. Everyone will point and whisper. Get a load of *that* guy, they'll say. Not that you'll be able to *see* the finger-pointers, of course."

Wiggins's breathing picked up, and his red, swollen eyes darted back and forth between Jake's face and the bottle.

"Okay, then, let's start with something easy. Who are you working for?"

The man said nothing, looking once again for Thorne to resume the beating. Panic was written all over him.

"Don't look at *him*, look at *me*," Jake said, his face showing cold fury. "It seems so right, don't you think? I don't get to see my family again, and you don't get to see anything. I'll count down for you. At zero, the lights go out. Five . . ."

Wiggins watched with growing terror as Jake soaked the rag with acid. The excess trickled off onto Wiggins's pants, instantly burning a half dozen holes into his legs.

". . . four . . ."

The rag was soaked now, disintegrating under the onslaught of chemical as Jake brought it ever closer to the man's face. The odor of sulfur brought tears to his eyes.

". . . two . . . one—"

"Frankel!" Wiggins yelled it loud, screamed it, really, in case Jake might not have heard it. "Peter Frankel hired me!"

The rag was only an inch away, and Wiggins shut his eyes tight, as if that would actually stop anything. For just a second, Jake kept the rag suspended there, letting the stench pour off it, then he pulled it away.

He turned to Thorne, who himself looked unnerved by the display. "Okay, Thorne, I think he's ready now."

Two hours later it was done. A wall of silence, it turned out, was just like any other wall. Once cracked, it just kept crumbling. Wiggins gave them everything they needed, and they never had to lay another hand on him. He was a broken man, and Jake accepted that he'd been the one to break him, though he wasn't sure how he felt about it.

When the gut-spilling was done, he pulled Thorne off to a corner of the barn. "So what's next?"

"With him?" Thorne said, gesturing without turning his head.

Jake nodded. "Yeah, with Wiggins or Dalton or whoever he is."
During the interrogation, Wiggins had given up his birth name:
Clyde Dalton. "What do we do with him?"

Thorne gave Jake another one of his condescending looks. "What
do you *think*? Three of us go for a ride, two of us come back."

Jake's stomach knotted. He'd spent nearly half his life running
away from a murder charge. *It just doesn't seem right . . .*

Thorne read the look and rolled his eyes. "Relax, Jake. You
won't have to do shit, okay? This one will be on me."

They heard a noise and turned. Wiggins was gone! Disappeared!
The tape that had once bound his neck dangled limply off to the
side.

In that split second, Jake had only one thought: *How does this guy
keep going?* He was surprised Wiggins could even stand.

Thorne stomped the dusty floor. "Fuck!"

They both drew their weapons. "Where'd he go?" Jake asked.

Thorne glared. "Not far."

"Is there a back door?"

"How the *fuck* would I know? Go look for one." Then, to the
dusty air, he added, "You're a dead man, Wiggins!"

It was dark now, inside and out, and the single bank of fluorescent lights overhead did little to lighten the shadows in the barn. Jake
couldn't bring himself to move forward. Death was out there somewhere—his *own*, in all likelihood, and he didn't want to face it.

"Go on," Thorne ordered. "I'll go—"

A loud *thok*—like the sound of a well-hit baseball—cut his
words short as Wiggins's good hand brought an ax handle slicing
out of the darkness onto the top of Thorne's head. Thorne
dropped instantly, unconscious even before his knees buckled. In
the instant it took for Jake to react and swing his Glock around,
Wiggins rewound his swing and let it fly against the muzzle of
Jake's weapon. Another home run, launching the pistol deep into
the dark shadows.

Jake saw the third swing coming from a mile away and ducked,
stumbling over Thorne's thick form on the floor as he scrambled
for the chrome .45. Wiggins kicked it away and brought the

makeshift club down hard against the wooden floor. Twice evading the club by inches, Jake brought his arms in close and rolled quickly to his right—a maneuver he hadn't tried since he was a little kid rolling down his next-door neighbor's hill.

Wiggins kept coming; amazingly fast, frighteningly strong.

Up on all fours now, and fighting for balance, Jake found himself back at the post that minutes before had been Wiggins's personal torture rack. He felt the next blow coming through the air, dodging without looking. The barn shook as the ax handle splintered against the twelve-by-twelve post.

But Wiggins held on, his club transformed into a ragged spear. He lunged, but Jake was on his feet again and able to maneuver around it. Grabbing a claw hammer from a nearby shelf, he heaved it in Wiggins's direction, buying himself an extra second as a glancing blow off the man's shoulder spun him in an awkward pirouette. Jake opened the distance by two steps and spotted a pitchfork resting in the corner. In one fluid motion, he brought it round and faced his attacker.

For an instant, Jake thought Wiggins's momentum would impale his guts on the tines, but the man reacted quickly, skidding to a stop with barely an inch to spare.

He locked onto Jake's gaze and smiled. The blood on his face and in his mouth wasn't shiny anymore; it had turned a crusty brown.

"Guess you win, Donovan," he said, looking warily at the tines. At this point, even the slightest twitch on his part might bring them surging forward. "Looks like I'm your prisoner, after all."

Jake knew his attacker was playing for time. He stared at the killer's heart and wondered how hard he'd have to push to split it open. He locked his jaw, tensed his muscles. *Decision time.*

Wiggins thought he saw something in Jake's eyes . . . *Hesitation?* "Want to tie me up again?" he asked, stealthily leaning back to pivot.

"No thanks," came a voice from behind. In a long-drawn-out moment that Jake would later look back on as impossibly distended, Thorne, who'd materialized out of nowhere, fired a kick to the base of Wiggins's spine, plunging the killer belly-first into the pitchfork.

Jake held on against the impact and stared, mesmerized, as Wiggins's eyes widened, and his mouth opened and closed uselessly. The killer struggled to find a breath as the rusted steel tore through his gut, but the best he could do was cough up a torrent of blood. Fixing Jake with one last amazed look, he collapsed.

"Fucker almost split my head in half," Thorne declared as Jake struggled to support the dead man's weight on the tines. His arms and shoulders screamed at the effort, but they seemed somehow separate from his body. Seconds passed. Finally, he released his grip and slumped with the corpse onto the earthen floor.

Jake followed Thorne in the plumbing van as they drove hours into the night. Paved roads gave way to dirt roads, which finally became fire trails. When they stopped, Jake had no idea where they were exactly, but civilization was far away.

Once parked, Thorne strolled up to Jake's window. "How'd your passenger behave himself?"

Jake just glared. If there was humor in any of this, he didn't see it.

Thorne gestured with his hands. "Well, this place is as good as any. Help me dig the hole."

They'd wrapped the body in a threadbare wool blanket to carry it out of the woods surrounding Nick's house and laid it in the back of the plumbing van. Now, as they hauled it out into the crisp night air, the Army-green fabric had transformed to a dark copper color, and the smell of death was overpowering.

They worked silently to dig the hole, using tools taken from Nick's barn. They dug it just deep enough to shelter the remains from hikers and hungry animals. The body made a wet sound as they dropped it into the earthen scar, and for the millionth time that night, Jake successfully fought off the urge to vomit.

The next order of business was the van itself. Smeared with blood, and no doubt covered with fingerprints, it had to be destroyed. They drove it a mile or so back down the trail, primed it with whatever was left in the bottom of a two-gallon gas can, then ignited it with a road flare.

None of it was as gratifying as Jake had hoped. As recently as that morning, he'd fantasized about killing the man who'd attacked his wife and child, but now that he was watching the last of this nightmare being consumed by flames, he just felt . . . guilty.

He walked back to the rental and slid into the shotgun seat, slamming the door behind him. Thorne dropped the transmission into drive and started back down the mountain. Neither of them spoke as they watched the billowing black smoke cloud envelop the trail.

"He blew away your friends, Jake," Thorne said at last. "Tried to kill your family. Nearly killed me. Almost killed you. All *we* did was balance the account."

Jake stared straight ahead, still silent, only now comprehending that—at least to some extent—he'd become what everyone thought he'd been all along.

He checked his watch and sighed. Two-fifteen. Finally, it was a new day, and come hell or high water, it would all be over before the calendar turned another page. He leaned back against the head-rest and closed his eyes.

Sleep came instantly.

CHAPTER FORTY-SEVEN

The doctors were allowing Carolyn to sit up now, her spine forced into alignment by a corsetlike back brace and a hard plastic collar. The severe spasms hadn't started until late last night, but when they arrived, they came in waves, racking her body with sheets of agony. The doctors wanted to give her something to ease the pain, but she'd refused. With a killer on the prowl targeting Travis and her, she wanted to be as alert as she could be.

Her resolve weakened, however, beginning around three in the morning, when a series of shattering muscle spasms drove her to the edge of lunacy. She approved a dose of muscle relaxant, and since then, she'd been fairly comfortable, if not entirely lucid.

The neck pains were worst, predictably enough, and the doctors weren't ready to say for sure whether or not she'd done irreparable damage up there. At least they weren't talking paralysis anymore. She'd officially dodged that bullet. And if she were going to stroke out as a result of increased cranial pressure, she'd have done it by now.

All kinds of good news this morning. Best of all: Travis was going to be okay. The lung damage had not been as devastating as they'd feared. A lot of fluid remained in his chest, but time and respiratory therapy would take care of that. In another month, he'd be feeling normal. Three more after that, and he'd *be* normal.

Thank you, God, for sparing him. She didn't bother to pray for herself or even for Jake. But for them, none of this misery would have happened in the first place.

She found herself crying, her emotional defenses weakened by the Flexeril. Why wouldn't they let her visit her son? Couldn't they see that by punishing her they were punishing an innocent child? Travis needed his mother. All children need their mother, for God's sake! Why couldn't that Rivers lady see the damage she was inflicting? Why couldn't she see for herself that by keeping them apart, she was retarding Travis's recovery.

"Excuse me, Mrs. Donovan?" a voice said. "Are you awake?"

Carolyn wasn't sure herself until she opened her eyes. In the dim light of the darkened hallways, she saw a tall young nurse standing in her doorway, with a uniformed cop by her side. "Mm-hmm," she croaked, her throat thick from disuse. "I'm here."

The two forms approached together, and for just an instant, she wondered if she should be frightened.

"My name's Jan, Mrs. Donovan, from the pediatric ICU. I've come to take you to see Travis."

As the sun rose in McLean, Virginia, news crews began to stir from their uneventful all-night vigil outside Senator Albricht's home. The morning on-air talent was arriving now, in time for the prenetwork morning news shows. Red-eyed second-stringers could go home now, relieved from their fruitless wait for some dramatic overnight development.

It took a special breed to find status in the act of being awake at such an ungodly hour, but in the prestigious Washington, D.C., news market, face time meant everything. It didn't matter that the average viewer was too comatose ever to remember what the face looked like. It was all about paying your dues.

Clayton just didn't get it. He'd held a lot of jobs in his lifetime, from buck private in the Army to summertime tar slinger for a roofing contractor. He respected any job that earned an honest wage, but for the life of him, he couldn't figure out the allure of the news business. Reporters never built anything, never contributed to the greater good. Instead, they made their living by fanning the flames, doing whatever they could to tear down the hard work and reputations of others.

He left the window shaking his head. Under the weight of his exhaustion, his cynical streak had begun to show. Maybe Alba was right. Maybe it was time to leave legislation to the young bucks and mend the fabric of his soul.

First, though, he had a reputation to mend and a debt of his own to call. When he'd last spoken to Chris MacDonald, around eleven last night, his chief of staff reported that he was ready to launch on Frankel the minute Clayton gave the go-ahead. With only a little exaggeration, Chris said, they could fill the USAir Arena with people who would pay their own expenses to get a shot at nailing Frankel to a tree. They'd accumulated countless examples of Frankel's ruthlessness and could prove beyond a shadow of a doubt that the man was a flaming asshole.

Unfortunately, they'd yet to find anyone willing to testify that they'd seen him break a law.

"It's not that they haven't *seen* him do it," Chris was quick to clarify. "They just won't say it under oath."

"Suppose we subpoena them?" Clayton had asked.

Chris laughed. "Does the expression 'I can't recall' ring any bells?"

Indeed it did. He'd even used it a few times himself over the years.

So here it was, morning again. The horrid rumors were a day older, yet the good guys weren't a single step closer to ruining the man who started it all. It was a difficult time, Clayton told himself—one that called for patience. And another cup of coffee.

He walked carefully as he passed his sleeping bride. In hopes of inducing a full night's sleep, Alba had finally resorted to taking an antihistamine, which seemed to be doing the trick. Clayton was pleased. She'd been looking way too tired. This morning he wanted her to sleep until she was slept out. He'd actually turned off the ringers on all the telephones upstairs, just to keep the place quiet. He figured that whatever crises might have arisen during the night could wait till morning.

Padding down the hall to his converted bedroom office, he lifted the stack of faxes that had accumulated during the night. Much of the pile were letters of support from fellow senators, and as he read each of them, he jotted a handwritten note on his personal stationery for hand-delivery later in the day. Once read and responded to, he sacrificed the originals to the shredder, reducing the pages to so much confetti.

For the most part, the rest was unremarkable bullshit from constituents. A few nervous supporters demanded clarification of his real role in all of this controversy. These he saved. By the end of the day, Chris would take care of it all.

The rubber tires of the wheelchair rolled silently across the polished linoleum as Jan eased Carolyn to Travis's bedside. "He's just sleeping," the nurse whispered. "We've given him something to help him rest. He's going to be just fine." She lowered the bed rail and moved Carolyn in as close as the chair would allow. "Stay as long as you like."

He looked so—*young*. Barely a lump under the stark white sheet. "Look at you," Carolyn whispered, the words barely audible even to herself. "You're just a baby." And to her, at that moment, her son looked just as he once was—as he looked, in fact, the last time she just sat and watched him sleep. In her mind, the strong, lean features were chubby again, the disheveled mop of hair a mere sheen of corn silk. Those were the happiest days—the days full of promise. Now there was only the reality of atrocities committed against his youth.

The muscles of her neck rebelled as she reached out to brush a greasy tendril of hair off Travis's forehead. There really was no baby left in him at all, she realized. He still had those eyelashes, though—Bambi lashes, she called them, just to get a rise out of him. He'd get so mad . . .

The lashes fluttered, and then his eyes opened; unfocused, and heavy with sleep.

"Hello, sweetie," she whispered. "It's only me. Go back to sleep."

The eyes closed again, and right away, she knew he hadn't heard a thing. She wanted him to be awake, though; she wanted to tell him so many things. But he needed his sleep and the rest that came with it. Leaning back again, to ease the growing spasm in her neck, she lifted Travis's hand from where it lay on top of the sheet, and kissed it, careful not to disturb the IV lines. In the yellow darkness, she studied his long, slender fingers. The nails needed trimming, as they always did, and they were dirty. Amid all the sterility and all the technology clustered around his helpless form, those dirty fingernails seemed like a final remnant of boyhood.

"I love you, Travis," she whispered.

The fingers flexed in her grasp. A sleepy attempt to let her know he was there with her, after all. His eyes fluttered open again, and it looked for all the world as if he was trying to smile; but in the end, he just couldn't make it happen. His lips faltered, then started to tremble around the ugly white-tipped tube that continued to rob him of his voice. He looked at his mom for a long moment, and through his gaze, she could feel his fear and his anger.

"Travis, honey, I'm so sorry. I'm so—" Suddenly, her voice stopped working.

He fought hard for control, shutting his eyes tight and folding deep lines into his forehead. But it was a losing battle. Tears bubbled up from behind his eyelids and tracked lazily over the pale, taut flesh of his cheekbones. He squeezed his mother's hand tightly now, as his body began to tremble, and his mask of bravery folded in on itself. Filtered through the respirator, his sobs were merely whispers against the silence of his room, rendered even more pitiful by the rhythmic hum of machinery that a child should never have to see.

She kissed his hand again and rested her forehead on his bed rail, ignoring the darts of pain from her neck. Her baby needed her now. And she'd stay right by his side for as long as it took for him to smile again.

*   *   *

It was nearly eight o'clock when the senator reluctantly turned the phone back on, and within two minutes, it rang. *Here we go again.* He considered ignoring it but took a deep breath instead. "Hello?"

"Hi, Clayton," the familiar voice said from the other end. "This is Harry Sinclair. I think we've got a breakthrough on that matter we discussed the other day."

The senator's heart skipped a beat. He'd discussed only one issue with his longtime friend and contributor, and for him to announce a breakthrough, it had to be momentous. "Good morning, Harry. Sounds interesting."

"What are you doing for lunch this afternoon?"

Chapter Forty-Eight

Thorne hadn't driven much through D.C. and had trouble finding the address he needed on Connecticut Avenue. He had to circle the block a few times before he finally hit his signal and turned into a narrow alley between two commercial buildings. The one on the left advertised itself as an appliance store, while the one on the right—the one that proved to be their destination—had no writing on it at all.

"We're here," he announced.

Jake seemed unaware that they'd even stopped. Without a word, he refocused his eyes from the spot he'd been watching on the dashboard, to take in their immediate surroundings. Seemingly satisfied, he pulled on the door handle to let himself out.

"Hey," Thorne said.

Jake paused. "What?"

"Relax. You're about to win. You can smile now."

Jake looked at him for a long moment, wondering if he should even bother to respond. Wiggins's death, the disposal of the body—it still weighed heavily on him. Smiling was the *last* thing he felt like doing.

"He was an insect, Jake. A parasite. And we squashed him. Let it go."

Jake nodded, not out of agreement but out of resignation, and emerged slowly from the car. He stood up straight, as if to walk away, then turned back again to lean into the driver's-side window.

"Thanks, Thorne," he said. "And thank Harry for me when you see him."

The big man picked up the money bags from the floor of the front seat. "Here, don't forget these."

Jake waved his hand. "No, you keep it. One way or another, I won't be needing it anymore."

"You nuts?" Thorne scoffed. "Mr. Sinclair doesn't need this back."

"Tell him to give it to charity then," Jake said. "I don't want it."

Thorne eyed him for a long moment, then shrugged. "Suit yourself," he said. He threw the shift lever into drive. "Say, when you catch up with Sunshine, you tell her to give us a call, okay?" he said.

"Sure," Jake replied, and watched as the Grand Marquis pulled away from the curb.

He climbed the front stairs to the door, where he took a deep breath before ringing the bell. Instinctively, he avoided looking into the security camera, pretending instead to inspect his shoes. After a few seconds, the door buzzed, and he stepped inside.

As he crossed the threshold and waited uneasily for his eyes to adjust to the darkness of the room, he began to see just how wonderful a place he'd entered: a restaurant where the aroma of fine foods was every bit as opulent as the furnishings. Typical of Washington town houses of the Federal era, this one seemed to extend forever, from front to back, with a wide stairway interrupting the center hall about halfway down, on the right-hand side. Off to either side, in what would have been the living room, dining room, parlor, and library, he could just glimpse the white linen and exquisite crystal.

He stood in the entryway, his back to the wall, waiting for someone to greet him. "Anybody here?" he called softly.

A second later a tuxedoed maître d' appeared from behind the stairway and strode down the hallway. "Good afternoon, sir," he said cheerily. "Mr. Donovan, I presume."

Jake accepted the man's firm and vigorous handshake. "And you must be Eddie Bartholomew."

Eddie nodded. "I've heard a lot about you, Mr. Donovan."

"Call me Jake."

"And you can call me Eddie." He led his guest as far as the reception lectern, then stopped. "I've spoken to Mr. Sinclair," he said, "and he has vouched for you, but still, you must understand that we have rules here at the Smithville." He removed an ornate wooden drawer from somewhere off to the side of his stand and placed it on top of the lectern. "Place your weapons here, please."

Jake found himself suddenly on edge. Thorne had explained in the car that the Smithville was neutral ground—the local equivalent of Switzerland—but this guy Eddie Bartholomew was a bundle of conflicting images. Dangerous yet polite; gracious yet brutish. Nonetheless, Jake understood the rules, and he placed his Glock inside the box.

"Any ammunition, too, please," Eddie said. "Saves us an anxious moment when we use the metal detector."

"What, you don't trust me?" Jake quipped. He meant it as a joke, but Eddie took it seriously.

"No, I don't," he said. "Nothing personal, you understand. I don't trust anyone. Can't afford to." He smiled.

Jake didn't bother. There was no humor in it, anyway. He dutifully produced the two extra magazines from his jacket pockets and added them to the pile in the drawer.

"Is that all? No knives? No backup pieces strapped to an ankle somewhere?"

Jake shook his head. "That's it."

Eddie made a face that showed surprise, but he didn't argue. "Mr. Sinclair assured me there would be no violence this afternoon."

Jake had to quash a brief rush of amusement as he realized that under the top layers of gracious suspicion, there lay within Eddie a bedrock of fear. "Don't worry," Jake reassured. "My mission today is merely to talk." He glanced over his shoulders. "Where's the rest of your staff?"

The maître d' shrugged and tossed his head to the side. "They've taken a few hours off. Given the guest list for your meeting, it seemed prudent for all concerned. Mr. Sinclair also assured me that you'd be finished before the dinner rush begins."

"I don't think that will be a problem at all," Jake said.

The answer seemed to please Eddie, who closed the gun drawer and led the way around to the staircase. "Follow me, please," he said. "I understand that you need a place where you can remain out of sight."

Jake grumbled under his breath, "That's the story of my life."

This time Paul drove. In fact, by the time they'd taxied all the way to the midfield terminal at Dulles, and they'd ridden the bus to the place where they could catch a second bus to the car rental counter, Paul felt like he might as well have driven all the way from Arkansas.

With the zero notice they'd received to get here, they were lucky to have caught a flight as it was. Add that confusion to the disturbing lack of detail on the purpose of the trip, and what Paul had was a barrelful of question marks.

"I'm glad this makes sense to you, Irene," he said as he navigated the treacherous, narrow lanes of Route 66 through Arlington. "Because it sure beats the hell out of me."

She watched out the window, squirming with a desire to move faster through traffic. He drove like an old woman, sticking to posted speeds and prompting angry blasts from other motorists. "What's to make sense? When the chairman of the Judiciary Committee tells you to come to a meeting, you come to a meeting."

"Without telling anyone? That's not right. It's not the way things are done. Christ, we didn't even tell the field office here."

She shrugged, still avoiding eye contact. "He's a senator. If he wants secrecy, we'll give him secrecy."

"That's improper as hell, Irene! Who the hell is this senator to be giving us orders to begin with? I'll bet you a week's pay this has something to do with his alternative-lifestyle crap, and when it surfaces in the press, we're gonna get screwed."

Finally, her head came around. "No, Paul. *I'm* gonna get screwed. You're just sitting in the car, remember? Besides, he said it was about the Donovans. As case officer, I'm the one he *should* have called. Nothing improper in that at all."

"Then why doesn't he want me in the meeting?"

She rolled her features into a bored, condescending scowl. "That'll be the very first question I ask," she said, groaning. "Truthfully, my guess is that he's turned up something on Frankel, and he's as scared of his conclusions as we are."

As they crossed the Potomac, Route 66 became Constitution Avenue, and from there, it was only a matter of navigating the one-way streets up to Connecticut Avenue, where Senator Clayton Albricht would be waiting. Given Paul's cynicism, she didn't bother to mention that she'd agreed on the telephone to surrender her firearm at the door. Frankly, she didn't need any more of his shit right now.

By the time Clayton Albricht arrived at the Smithville at three-thirty, the luncheon crowd had come and gone, leaving the ornate cavern empty. Other than Eddie Bartholomew, he didn't even see any service people.

According to his telephone conversation with Harry Sinclair, if Clayton could convince Irene Rivers to travel to Washington in secret, and Peter Frankel to come to the Smithville for another afternoon rendezvous, then all this boy-fucking bullshit would go away. It wasn't Sinclair's way to be specific in such things, any more than Clayton would have welcomed specifics over the telephone.

He moved to sit near the archway, as close as possible to the entrance. From there, he could see for himself who came and who left the restaurant, but Eddie Bartholomew wouldn't hear of it. "Please," he said as he led the senator toward a spacious table for four in the rear corner of the room. "You'll be very comfortable over here."

Albricht considered arguing but didn't bother. Eddie seemed wrapped pretty tight this afternoon. A man who was none too stable on a good day, it was best not to push him.

Barely five minutes passed before he heard the heavy front door open and shut, and among the muddled conversation out in the hallway, he heard the unmistakable arrogance of Peter Frankel.

Jake listened to it all from the top of the stairs, where he sat crouched out of sight. If he wanted to, he could crane his neck far enough to catch a glance at people's legs as they arrived, but what was the point? He'd see them all, soon enough, from head to toe.

He felt like a kid with a secret—ready to bust if he didn't share it soon.

When Frankel entered the foyer, Jake's blood pressure topped the scale. Just breathing the same air as that son of a bitch was nearly more than he could tolerate.

And Eddie Bartholomew was just as cordial as could be. They exchanged pleasantries at the lectern, and as Frankel handed over his firearm, Jake could hear the famous television smile in his voice.

Just a few more minutes, Jake told himself, *and I'll shove that smile out your ass.*

"You sure this is it?" Paul asked incredulously as he backed into the narrow alleyway. "There's no sign or anything."

Irene checked her notes one more time. "It's the right address."

He shook his head. "I gotta tell you, boss. This one doesn't feel good to me."

She shrugged, even though she shared the sentiment. "Well, we're here. If it's the wrong place, then I won't be gone long at all." She opened the car door.

"I'll be here if you need me," he said.

She sensed danger as she climbed the front steps to the town house, and she found herself noticing every detail of her surroundings. The steel staples in the marble steps; the boot scraper on the stoop. Someone had spent serious bucks on this place. She waited patiently after pushing the doorbell, even though she never heard anything ring on the other side. To make it easy on whoever was watching the security monitor, she stared directly into the camera lens. She fought the urge to rest her hand on her pistol grip, figuring that this kind of security bespoke a certain paranoia on the other side. The last thing she wanted to do was make people more nervous than they might otherwise be.

Finally, the door buzzed, and she pushed it open. Eddie was waiting for her, smile already in place. "Ms. Rivers?"

She nodded. "*Agent* Rivers, yes. I'm here to meet someone."

Eddie beckoned her inside. "Senator Albricht, of course. We've been expecting you, ma'am. You've heard of our unique security precautions?"

Another nod. She hesitantly produced her S&W from the waistband of her skirt and placed it on the lectern.

Eddie swept her body quickly with the metal detector, then ushered her forward with a sweeping motion of his hand. "Please go on in. The others are waiting for you."

Others? she thought. *As in, more than one?*

The senator sat facing the door, and as soon as she entered the room, his face beamed. "Welcome, welcome," he said, rising from his chair.

They'd never met, but she recognized him from the news. It was the other man—the one with his back turned—who looked remarkably familiar. As Frankel turned in his seat to greet the new arrival, his face mirrored the shock Irene felt in her belly.

"What the hell are you doing here?" they both said in unison.

Jake sat on the stairs now, waiting for the right moment to come down. The sudden explosion of voices startled him at first, then brought a smile as he imagined what must be going through everyone's mind.

If they thought they were surprised now, they need only wait half a minute.

He took a huge breath and concentrated on his nerves. He had to remain calm through this. Finally, he had the audience he'd dreamed of, and at last, he knew what had to be said. Now all it would take was a little salesmanship. After fourteen years on the run—after all the days and nights of worry and of lies—it all came down to this.

A single roll of the dice.

His mind shot back to his last big gamble, where his hunch had turned on him and cost him so much. This one was it; his very last shot.

Jake stood tall, and paused long enough to straighten out his filthy clothes before descending the stairs. Eddie was waiting for him at the bottom. "Are you ready?"

"No," Jake snorted, but Eddie started walking, anyway, escorting his next guest into the dining room. Once moving, they never stopped. Jake strolled on into the lions' den, just as if he were any other diner.

CHAPTER FORTY-NINE

Conversation stopped dead as Jake entered the room. Irene recognized him first. "Oh, my God," she breathed.

Her reaction drew Frankel's head around, and he reacted explosively. "Donovan!" He leapt from his seat and instinctively reached for the weapon he'd been forced to surrender at the door, but Eddie moved in quickly to dispel any notions his guest might have had about picking a fight.

The senator just stared, his face forming a giant O.

"What's he doing here?" Frankel demanded. He turned to Albricht. "What the hell kind of game do you think you're playing?"

The senator shrugged, clearly befuddled yet mildly amused. "I have no idea. Agent Rivers?"

Irene eyed Jake cautiously, then suppressed a knowing smirk of her own. So Jake was going right to the top. "Not a clue," she lied.

Eddie placed a beefy hand on Frankel's shoulder. "Please take your seat, sir," he said.

Frankel tried to shake the arm off, but it was like shedding steel. He sat. With a nod from Jake, Eddie backed out of the room, leaving the group alone to discuss whatever was on their minds. Jake pulled a chair around to the end of the table so he could face everyone at once.

"Thank you all for coming," he said.

"Look, Donovan," Frankel seethed. "I don't know what you're up to, but I'm not—"

"Relax, Peter," Jake said easily. "I'm just here to turn myself in to Agent Rivers. I'm just not up to the chase anymore."

Frankel fell silent, his mouth open, frozen in midsentence.

Jake smiled serenely at Irene. "But first, I thought I'd make my official statement."

"I think not," Frankel blustered. "This is neither the time nor the place—"

"Shut up, Peter," Albricht commanded. "The man's come a long way."

"The hell I will!" Frankel boomed.

"It's tough to have a big secret, isn't it, Peter?" Jake taunted. "Especially when everyone's about to hear it spilled."

Frankel rose again from his chair. "Agent Rivers, keep an eye on this man while I—"

Jake rose, too, and shoved Frankel hard. He fell backward, his legs entangled in the chair, and ended up halfway under the table. "Sit the fuck down, Peter!"

Irene made a move to intervene but stopped herself. It just looked too good.

Frankel sputtered profanities as he pulled himself back into his chair. "Go ahead, Donovan. Just keep racking up the charges. We'll have to clone your ass just to live long enough for early release. Rivers, you're a witness."

Irene sucked on a cheek. "At this point, sir, I'm not sure what I've seen."

For the first time, Jake heard real equivocation in Irene's voice, and he moved quickly to capitalize on it. "Does the name Wiggins mean anything to you, Peter?"

Frankel ignored him, but Jake didn't miss the barely audible gasp from Albricht.

"C'mon, Peter," Jake taunted. "Surely you must know him. I hear he goes by the name Clyde Dalton, too, if that rings a bell. He certainly knows you. I had a long chat with him just this morning, in fact. He said you guys go all the way back to Nam together."

Frankel just stared at the table, his jaw locked.

"You guys worked SEAL team insertions back then, right? You drove the boat and he did the wet work." Jake glanced over at Irene. "You might want to take notes, ma'am," he urged. "This should all be verifiable stuff."

Irene seemed momentarily stunned by the request, then embarrassed that she hadn't thought of it herself. Frankel glared as she pulled her notebook out of the pocket of her suit jacket, then patted herself down in search of a pen. Albricht lent her one of his.

Jake went on. "Wiggins said that after the war, you guys sort of went your separate ways. You joined the good guys, while your buddy chose more interesting pursuits. Seems he became quite proficient at killing people."

"Where's this individual now?" Irene interrupted.

"He left the country," Jake lied, staring the whole time at Frankel, who in turn stared at Irene with enough intensity to cut her in half. "Just pay attention. It'll all come together for you in a minute."

He nudged Frankel's shoulder playfully. "How am I doing so far, Peter?" When Frankel didn't respond, Jake laughed. "Yeah, I know. Scary, isn't it? So anyway, let's fast-forward to the eighties. Here you are, this Young Turk, moving through the ranks, making your mark on the Bureau, when along comes this case in Arkansas where an aging general named Albemarle is lured by the Iraqis into selling chemical weapons as a way to finance his only daughter's medical bills." Jake looked again to Irene. "You found some evidence on that, I assume?"

She nodded. She knew exactly where this was going.

"So here comes Peter Frankel, supercop," Jake continued, "and you find yourself the perfect crime. Nobody but this Albemarle clown even knows about this stash of weapons in East Jesus, Arkansas. He's making himself a fortune. So you offer him a deal. If he cuts you into the action, you'll cut off your investigation." Jake leaned forward, forearms on the table. "What was the split, Peter? Sixty-forty? Seventy-thirty? Knowing you, you had to be fucking him pretty deep.

"Well, logistically, you can't sell all your weapons at once, right? People might notice the comings and goings. So you dribble them out, a piece at a time, for a shitload of money. If I did my math right, and if your pal Wiggins was telling the whole truth, I figure that this went on for a good six months. Maybe more. Then you get blind-sided." Jake feigned a gasp and clutched his chest. "Somebody finds your stash and reports it to the EPA! Well, what's a body to do now? Overnight—literally—you're out of business."

Jake leaned away from the table again and made a show of tapping his temple. "Now, here I've got to do a little guessing, but my money says the good general got a serious case of the guilts and wanted to punch out. Pretty close?"

Frankel didn't move.

"But you can't let that happen. So you call up your old buddy Wiggins to stage a suicide. I mean, why not? The guy's already dishonored, he's lost a kid. He's got plenty of cause to off himself. You leave a note, you pop him, and you move on. How simple can it get?"

As the story droned on, Jake watched with satisfaction as Frankel sank further into his chair. He could only hope that the son of a bitch was suffering.

"But you can't just kill one, can you, Peter? I bet it's hard as hell to know when to stop the killing. Just to be safe, you pop the old man's wife, too, in case she knows something."

From there on, Jake concluded, it was just a comedy of errors. "You had this grand plan to cover your tracks: Slip something into Tony Bernard's food to give him the pukes, then frame him for your explosion. I can't tell you how sorry I am that Carolyn and I screwed it up so badly for you."

Hearing it all played out, with even greater detail, the whole thing still seemed wildly speculative to Irene. Grand conspiracies with mysterious disappearing witnesses made it all too convenient.

"The guy you had call me with your blackmail threats was named

Wiggins, too, Peter," Clayton said, leaning forward. "What kind of coincidence is that?"

"This is all bullshit," Frankel blustered, and at that moment, from his expression alone, everyone saw just how close Jake's theory had landed to the truth.

"Oh, my God!" Irene breathed. "What have you done?"

Frankel tried to look outraged; like he'd never heard anything so outrageous in his life. But the fear showed through, anyway. "I refuse to listen to any more of this." He stood one more time.

This time when Jake rose to meet him, Frankel was ready, leveraging the edge of the table and using it to shove Jake backward over his chair. "Stay the fuck out of my way," he growled as he prepared to launch a lethal kick to Jake's head.

"Stop it!" Irene commanded. She lunged across the table to intervene, but a stunning backhand sent her staggering backward.

"You incompetent bitch . . ."

Eddie Bartholomew materialized at the doorway, his weapon drawn. "Everybody freeze!" he yelled. "I said no violence, and I meant it! Now, Mr. Frankel, you just back off."

Frankel stood in place, his chest heaving, his face red. "You gonna shoot the next director of the FBI, Eddie? Wouldn't be good for business."

Eddie ignored the bait. "Bullshit. This place'd become a tourist attraction. I can charge double to eat on the spot where you fell."

Frankel laughed. That was a good one, all right. His eyes darted from side to side like a cornered animal, and everyone in the room knew instinctively to stay away from him. "No one will believe your lies," he said, and suddenly his eyelids glistened with tears.

"You okay, Jake?" Eddie asked.

Jake raised himself to a sitting position and nodded, exploring a damaged rib with his fingertip. "Yeah, I'm fine."

"Agent Rivers? Senator Albricht?"

Clayton helped Irene back onto her feet as she rubbed the swollen spot on her cheek.

"I'll live," Irene said. She sounded more embarrassed than injured.

"That's good," Eddie said. "Now, all of you, get out of here."

"Yeah, Frankel," Jake seconded. "Get out of here. *You* try running for a while, you weaselly little shit."

Frankel was speechless. He scanned the faces in the room, then sneered, "This is far from over."

As he turned to make his exit, Frankel raked his gaze from Eddie's eyes down to the muzzle of his gun. "Put that fucking thing down," he said. A final command before the end of his reign.

Eddie hesitated but ultimately complied, letting the muzzle rotate in a slow arc down to his side, until the barrel pointed harmlessly at the floor.

That's when Frankel struck, with amazing speed. Before Eddie could react, his hand was bent at an impossible angle behind his back, and the pistol was free from his grasp. An instant later, Eddie felt the press of steel against the base of his skull, and then his brains were all over the expensive Oriental rug.

Waiting was the single element of police work that Paul Boersky had never gotten used to. In his early days, back in Minneapolis, all he ever seemed to do was wait. And in a part of the world that has only two seasons—shovel and swat—every wait was as physically uncomfortable as it was mentally exhausting.

At least there was purpose to it all back then. Maybe a bad guy was going to move from one point to another, or an as-yet-unidentified suspect was about to take some bait. Here, today, in the chilly streets of Washington, D.C., Paul wasn't at all sure why he even came along on the trip. This was between Irene and the senator—she could not have been any clearer on that point. As for his role, well, he really didn't have one.

Nonetheless, they'd come a long way together over the years, and together, they had a long way to go on this particular case. Whatever transpired, he felt a need to be there with his partner. God knew that no one else would get within fifty feet of her. This screwup was that enormous.

So he waited. For going on a half hour now. He wondered if maybe he shouldn't just peek inside and see what was going on. Thus far, no one else had arrived, and certainly, no one had left. Even with his partially obstructed view of the door he could see that.

He climbed out of the car at 4:37, according to the digital clock on the dash. Years of surveillance assignments had taught him always to mark the time. His back screamed from all the sitting, and a long stretch felt good. The autumn air felt good, too. What he missed most about living in the Deep South was the change of seasons. Sure, the leaves turned in the fall, but without the cold air to go along with it, the colors somehow meant less. Of course, come February, when the rest of the world was buried under a foot of snow, he'd feel damned smug about his southern digs.

He was in the middle of a huge yawn when he heard the first gunshot. His mind processed the sound in an instant, evaluating and rejecting a hundred alternatives. That was no bursting balloon or backfire or firecracker. Jesus Christ, it was coming from inside the building!

He'd drawn his weapon and had flown up the front steps three at a time before he'd even thought about reacting. Once on the stoop, he turned the knob and pushed. Nothing moved. He pounded on the heavy door with his fist.

"Federal officer!" he yelled. "Open up!"

He heard a second shot, and then a third right away.

Holy shit! Why hadn't they informed the Washington office? At least then, they'd have had an official vehicle and a radio channel. *Shit!* He rammed his shoulder into the heavy wood panels, but the door wouldn't budge.

He heard yelling from the inside now. And another shot.

"Shit!" He yelled it aloud this time. Stepping off to the hinge side of the door, he took aim at the lock.

Jake yelled at the sudden explosion of Eddie Bartholomew's head. An instant later he saw the gun in Frankel's hand, and the heat of the man's anger filled the room as he swung the weapon up to finish what he'd started.

Jake's body reacted before his brain could tell him to stop. Even as Irene and the senator dove for cover, he charged at Frankel and hit him with all his driving force, propelling him backward toward Eddie's lectern. Despite the impact, Frankel wouldn't go down. He backpedaled quickly, little staccato steps that kept him from losing his balance, as Jake focused every ounce of his strength on the attacker's gun hand. For just an instant, the muzzle crossed in front of his face, but Frankel missed his opportunity for a sure kill.

Jake shoved his adversary hard into the corner molding of the archway to the dining room, and the impact triggered a grunt. He thought for sure that he heard something break in Frankel's back, but the man still stayed on his feet. The gun discharged just inches from Jake's face; a deafening blast that punched a hole in the plaster ceiling. Half a second later it went off again, disintegrating a crystal globe on the chandelier. Jake winced as grains of burning gunpowder bit into the flesh of his cheeks.

He had both hands on the gun now, struggling to loosen Frankel's grip, and as he reached across the other man's face, he howled in pain as Frankel's teeth burrowed into the flesh of his upper arm. The pain was unspeakable as an incisor found Jake's brachial nerve, but he still hung on. To let go now was to die.

In his peripheral vision, Jake thought he saw Irene dash past. *She's running away!* he thought. Then he knew better. *The gun drawers!*

Irene knew she needed to do something. Jake was losing his fight, but she worried that if she interfered, Frankel might somehow work his hand free. If that happened, they were all dead. If only she had her weapon!

Jesus, that was it! Leaving the senator to fend for himself, she dashed through the dining room and out into the hallway, praying the whole time that Eddie hadn't locked the drawers. There were eight of them altogether, and she pulled on the one she thought housed her black S&W. Sure enough, the drawer opened, and there it was.

Snatching the weapon into both hands, she drew down on the second most powerful man in American law enforcement. "I got him, Jake!" she yelled. "Break away!"

* * *

Frankel was a fucking vampire! Once he got his teeth locked onto Jake's arm, he just wouldn't let go. The pain was exquisite, shooting lightning bolts into Jake's fingertips. As he lost the feeling in his hand, his grip started to slip.

The instant he heard Irene's command to get down, he just let his legs fold, collapsing onto the floor and leaving Frankel suddenly exposed.

Irene saw Jake drop and knew she had her shot. "Don't move, goddammit!" she yelled, and in that instant, the world exploded in gunfire, as Paul blasted the door lock from the outside. Irene whirled instinctively at the sound, breaking her aim on Frankel, then instantly realized her mistake. She dropped to one knee and tried to bring her weapon back around on target, but she was too late.

The first bullet hit her high on her right arm, knocking the air out of her lungs and sending her pistol airborne. The second shot, fired less than a second later, caught her just above her left ear, but she never felt a thing.

Paul looked away as he fired, shielding his eyes from the flying bits of splintered wood and steel. Five slugs pulverized the doorjamb, where the dead bolt joined the keeper, and with a single powerful kick, he sent the solid-core door exploding inward.

All he saw were muzzle flashes as a man in a suit threw an arsenal of lead at him. Paul dropped to the concrete and scrambled for cover as a plate-glass window on the opposite side of Connecticut Avenue shattered and collapsed into itself.

He randomly returned fire, scrambling to find shelter behind the brick wall of the town house. He never aimed a shot; to expose himself would have been suicide. Instead, he exposed only his hand and his weapon as he fired over and over, hoping that the random spray of bullets would keep the shooter at bay.

He felt the slide lock open as the last round exited his weapon, and the instant he withdrew his gun to reload, the brick facade began to pulsate behind his back. The gunman had found his aim, but the bullets couldn't penetrate the masonry shield. Just as he'd been trained through endless hours at the FBI range, he dropped the spent magazine out of his weapon as he fished for a spare from his belt and slapped it in place. The slide jammed the next round home, and he was ready to go again. Total elapsed time: less than five seconds.

Out on the street, the panic had just begun. He heard the heavy impact of colliding vehicles behind him, but he ignored it. As rush-hour commuters dashed for cover, he swung his arm back into harm's way and started pulling the trigger.

Jake never saw Irene fall. He just saw the pistol on the floor, amid a wild, unfocused cacophony of gunfire, and he scrambled for it. He lost track of the number of shots Frankel had fired, but each trigger pull seemed to drive an ice pick into Jake's eardrums. It wasn't until he cleared the archway into the center hall that he heard the return fire coming from the front door. Just random gunplay, really. A hand extended through the open door, spraying bullets through the center of the house as fast as its owner could pull the trigger.

Who the hell is that?

That explained why Frankel hadn't turned back to fire at Jake. He had a far more threatening target to eliminate. Pressing himself as flat against the floor as possible, Jake made his final lunge for Irene's weapon. He brought it around just as Frankel stole a spare magazine from Eddie Bartholomew's corpse and jammed it home.

"Don't do it, Frankel," Jake shrieked, but he couldn't even hear himself.

Frankel didn't hesitate in bringing his weapon to bear.

Neither did Jake. He felt the big S&W buck in his hand before he realized he'd pulled the trigger. Frankel hesitated but didn't fall. Jake's gun bucked again. And again. And one by one, each round found its mark. Belly. Belly. Right arm. Chest. The chest shot dropped him. Frankel sagged to his knees, his face a mask of terror. He knew he was dead, and he knew who'd killed him.

A final shot, this one coming from the cowboy behind the door, ripped Frankel's lower jaw clean off his body. The impact spun him a quarter-turn, then dropped him like a tree onto the carpet.

"*Freeze, goddammit!*" The gun at the door had a voice now, and Jake knew instantly, just from the tone, that it belonged to yet another FBI agent.

Jake froze, just as he was instructed, as the man at the door scampered quickly up the hallway and jammed Jake face-first onto the floor, kicking the pistol free from his hand.

"Jesus Christ, what did you do?" the man panted.

"For one thing," Senator Albricht said, rising from behind his table shield, "he saved my life from that madman on the floor."

Paul looked confused. In all the noise and the flying wood and glass, he'd never gotten a good look at the man who'd been shooting at him. When he did look, recognition was instant. "Oh, my God," he whispered.

"He shot your partner," Jake said. "She needs an ambulance." He struggled under the agent's weight to find a spot to rest his face that wouldn't hurt so much.

Paul looked even more stunned as he fully recognized the cast of characters in the room. "Jake Donovan!" he said.

"Help your friend," Jake said. "I'm not going anywhere."

Clearly, that's what Paul wanted to do, but first, he had a prisoner to take care of. As he reached for his handcuffs, Senator Clayton Albricht placed a hand gently on his shoulder. "Please don't do that," he said gently. "It really isn't necessary."

CHAPTER FIFTY

Travis pulled at his shirt collar, hoping the fabric might stretch and give him some room to move. He hated ties.

"Stop fidgeting," Carolyn whispered. "And sit up straight." She couldn't count the number of times she'd said those words over the years, in that same order, but for some reason, they seemed fresh, unused. The fact that she was able to say them at all was a miracle she'd never again take for granted.

After five weeks of therapy, her neck was better, though not completely. Doctors still weren't sure that she'd ever get full range of motion back, but given the nature of the injury, and progress she'd made so far, there was plenty of reason to hope.

Travis stopped squirming, but he didn't straighten his shoulders. They were his shoulders, after all, and he could keep them slouched if he wanted to. "How come Dad gets to pace around?" he asked.

Jake turned away from the window and its view of Old Town, Alexandria, to face his son. "Because pacing keeps me from exploding," he answered, honestly enough.

Travis leaned heavily on the ancient oak conference table and took a deep, exasperated breath. It caught in his throat and triggered a heavy cough.

"You okay?" both parents asked as one. It was a sound that would forever live in their nightmares.

"Jesus Christ, I'm not allowed to cough anymore?" Ever since Travis had gotten out of the hospital, his folks had been like this, on edge about everything he did; every sound he made. It was like living under a microscope. God only knew what was going to happen next time he caught the flu.

Carolyn closed her eyes and shook her head. For the time being, she'd given up correcting his language. His voice had only recently taken on a husky, smoky quality that was fascinating to listen to, no matter what he had to say. Whether it was the remaining traces of his injury or the onset of adolescence, she wasn't sure, but as long as the words were coming, she couldn't bring herself to interfere.

Jake was the one she worried about. Clearly, they'd won their war, yet Jake still wouldn't allow himself to celebrate. The final details had taken a while to work out, and in the end, he'd had to spend two nights in jail, but then it was officially over.

They were celebrities now, with every talk show host in the country dogging them for interviews. Book publishers, movie producers, and magazine editors fell all over themselves trying to scoop their competition in what was turning out to be the biggest story of the year—at least until the next biggest story came around—and a growing gaggle of celebrity lawyers pandered every day for the opportunity to represent them.

Through it all, Jake had become more and more withdrawn, his outward sense of dread in many ways stronger now than it had ever been while they were on the run. He refused to talk about any of it, but Carolyn knew in her heart that it had something to do with his days alone with Thorne. Something awful had happened, and Jake was either too afraid or too ashamed to discuss it. In their quiet times together, in the hotel rooms provided by the FBI, Carolyn had tried to probe it out of her husband, but he'd have none of it.

In time, she supposed. *All things happen in time.*

When the phone call came two days ago for this morning's meeting at the federal courthouse in Alexandria, she watched her husband panic. After five weeks of interviews and debriefings by Paul Boersky, something about this one call to report in person had left him a wreck. Last night he even talked about not coming in—about going on the run again.

"What for, Jake?" Carolyn had asked. "What are you so worried about?"

He let it drop without answering; stopped talking altogether. Today he'd said barely a word all morning, and as the rest of the family was getting dressed in the hotel, she watched him out the window as he paced the parking lot, staring at the trees and sucking in the November air like it was his last time.

And here he stood at the window, lost in his thoughts again, floating in his mind somewhere out there over the rooftops.

When the door to their conference room opened, Jake jumped a foot. The cockiness he once possessed was all gone, replaced with a kind of timidness that left Carolyn feeling frightened. As her husband smoothed out his suit coat, she strolled around the end of the table to join him.

Paul Boersky led the procession into the room, followed close behind by Senator Albricht; by a woman who looked vaguely familiar but whose face Jake couldn't quite place; and, finally, by Irene Rivers.

The sight of his old nemesis brought a broad smile to Jake's face, even as Carolyn withdrew. "Hello, Agent Rivers," he said. In deference to Irene's heavily bandaged right arm, he extended his left hand as a greeting. "How are you feeling?"

She accepted his grasp with a warm smile. "They tell me it helps when the bullet doesn't penetrate the brain," she deadpanned. "As for the shoulder, we'll have to see."

The group burned up a minute or so with introductions and pleasantries. Neither Carolyn nor Travis had ever met the senator, who in turn introduced the final guest.

"Donovan family, I'd like you to meet Ms. Emma Sanders, attorney general of the United States."

With short, gray hair and a tiny frame, Ms. Sanders stood about five-three and could have been anybody's grandmother, or maybe even the local librarian, but her piercing, humorless emerald-green eyes left no doubt that she was one tough lady. She shook hands politely, then ushered everyone into their seats.

"Do you have any idea why you're here this afternoon?" Ms. Sanders asked.

Jake and Carolyn exchanged glances, then Jake spoke for the family. "No, ma'am, we don't."

"That's good," Sanders said. "That's very good, in fact. With the level of media coverage you're receiving these days, I didn't want anything leaking out before we had a deal."

Jake shot a look to Paul—his primary point of contact these past weeks—who raised a finger, urging him to be patient.

"Excuse me," Senator Albricht interrupted. "Perhaps it would be best if the boy waited out in the hall."

Travis's eyes grew huge as he shot a glance to his mom and dad. "I'm not going anywhere!"

Jake looked to Boersky, who answered his silent question with a nod. "It'll just be for a few minutes," he said.

Jake turned to face his son. "Go ahead, Trav."

"No!"

Jake stood and gently pulled the boy's chair away from the table. "Please," he said. "They wouldn't ask if it wasn't important."

Travis looked to everyone in the room for support but couldn't find any. Clearly, he didn't know what to do next.

"Please," Jake urged again.

"It'll only be a few minutes," Carolyn added.

Haltingly, the boy rose from his chair and allowed himself to be escorted to the big wooden door with smoked glass in the top. Jake opened it and pointed to the wooden bench against the wall. "Just wait for us there."

Travis looked terrified; he knew that something was horribly wrong. "Dad?"

Jake winked at his son and struggled to keep his lip from trembling. "It'll be okay, Trav," he promised. "We'll be out in just a few minutes."

Travis started to say something but then looked as if the words had just dried up. Jake watched the boy drag himself to the bench, then turned back around to face the music for all that he'd done.

"You have some powerful friends in this town, Mr. Donovan," Sanders began as Jake returned to his seat. "These people seem to think that you've gotten a raw deal these past few years."

"You have a gift for understatement, Emma," the senator piped in with a smile.

Ms. Sanders ignored him. "In any case," she went on, "these things can become messy. I know, for example, through conversations with Mr. Boersky and through news reports that you have been approached by a number of parties to vent your spleen, as it were, in very public ways."

Albricht interrupted again. "She's trying to tell you, Jake, that the president's scared to death that you're going to piss in his Wheaties. Get to the point, Emma."

Sanders's glare could have melted an iceberg, but Albricht clearly couldn't have cared less. Across the table, Irene and Paul fought losing battles to hide their discomfort. A sitting attorney general could do amazing damage to a Justice Department career.

Sanders cut to the chase. "I come here today with a one-time-only offer for you." She reached into the oversize purse on her shoulder and withdrew a folded document. "This is a Presidential Pardon, Mr. Donovan, and it's yours, on three conditions. One, that you refrain from any overt effort to seek publicity from this episode in your lives for a period of five years . . ."

"You've got to be kidding!" Carolyn said, but the expression she got in return said otherwise. "Why on earth—"

"Only until after the next election season," Albricht explained.

"Hear her out, Carolyn," Irene said. "This is important."

Ms. Sanders shot a look to Irene that was totally uninterpretable, then continued. "Second, you must agree never to pursue a civil claim against the United States government for any alleged damages incurred . . ."

Carolyn launched from her seat. *"Alleged* damages! Jesus Christ, lady—"

Jake caught the panicked look from Paul and moved quickly to intervene. "Carolyn, please. Let's at least hear the offer before we reject it."

Sanders acknowledged Jake's assistance with a nod. "Lastly, you are never to divulge the elements of this agreement to anyone."

"Now?" Carolyn asked, still hovering above her seat. "Is it time to reject the offer now? It's absurd! We've already been exonerated, for God's sake! Why in the world would I agree to conditions for a pardon I already have?"

Irene answered for the attorney general. "Charges have been dropped only for the original terrorist business in Arkansas."

"But not for our flight? That doesn't make sense."

Irene shook her head, then closed her eyes against the pain it caused. "No, of course not. Because you committed no crime, you can hardly be charged with evading prosecution. The pardon proposed by Ms. Sanders is for any other crimes that may have been committed while you were on the run."

Carolyn still didn't get it. "You want me to give up my right to sue you into outer space, just so we don't get brought up on some bullshit forgery charge?"

It was Clayton's turn now. "That's one example," he said. "But you know, there's any number of other laws you might have broken inadvertently along the way." His eyes narrowed as they focused in on Jake, but his tone remained friendly. "And you never know when some ambitious young prosecutor might stumble on a new piece of evidence and drag you back into the spotlight. With this pardon in your hand, that can't happen. Ever. In fact, even if you'd *killed* someone, you couldn't be prosecuted for it."

The words hit Jake like a fist in the chest, and as he scanned the faces of the people in the room, he saw just how hard Albricht's eyes had become.

"We've known about Nick Thomas's involvement for a couple of weeks now, Jake," Irene said softly. "His prints showed up among hundreds of other prints in the Cadillac. For what it's worth, you might be happy to know that he refused to comment on any of this."

"His wife, on the other hand," Paul finished, "was an entirely different story. Once she started talking, she just wouldn't shut up."

Carolyn had no idea what any of this was about, but as she watched the color drain from Jake's face, she sat back into her seat and squeezed his hand under the table.

Attorney General Sanders closed the loop. "A body was found last week in Shenandoah National Park. Badly decomposed and apparently dug up by predators."

The room fell silent as Jake processed the words. His face hid nothing anymore; it was all right there for everyone to see. Carolyn raised his hand now, still clutched in her own, and kissed it.

"Relax, Jake," Albricht said softly. "No one's going to pursue the body's identity. And no one is ever going to ask you the details of what happened to the mysterious Mr. Wiggins or how you were able to avoid capture for all of these years. Just sign the indemnification papers, and the pardon's yours. This whole mess will be over forever."

Jake looked stunned, and he glanced to Carolyn for advice. She smiled. "This is a no-brainer, honey." She motioned for the document to be slid across the table, then gestured for a pen. Albricht produced a pricey rollerball and handed it to Jake, who lifted the necessary pages to expose the highlighted areas marked with an "X." Signatures on three pages, initials on four. He slid the papers to Carolyn, and then they were done.

Sanders accepted the signed indemnification, then handed over the pardon and rose to leave. "There's a check in there, too," she said. "Three hundred thousand dollars. To compensate you for your trouble." She walked to the door, then stopped. "It's tax-free, by the way." For an instant, a smile flashed across her face, and then it was time to leave. Paul Boersky followed her out, as Clayton helped Irene get out of her chair.

Jake and Carolyn stood as well. "I—I don't know what to say," Jake said.

Irene smiled and shrugged. "You don't have to say anything." She turned her eyes to Carolyn next, who looked to be searching for words herself. "You either, Carolyn. This one was on me. And him." She gestured to Albricht, who smiled his coyest smile.

Clayton extended his hand to Jake. "You saved my life, Jake. And you can't get as far as I have in politics without understanding the importance of returning favors." He turned to Carolyn next and offered his hand. She took it, and Clayton covered it with his left. "I'm afraid that in her haste to leave, Ms. Sanders forgot to say how sorry the government is to have put you through all of this."

Carolyn smiled, surprised by the tears that suddenly formed in her eyes. "Why, thank you, Senator," she said. "That means more than you probably know."

The moment hung awkwardly in the air, no one knowing exactly what to do next. Finally, Irene broke the silence. "Senator Albricht, if you would be so kind as to give me a hand negotiating the steps, I'd be forever grateful."

It was their excuse to leave the room, but Irene paused one more time, at the doorway. "Oh, and Jake? I have an answer for you. Sometimes it really *is* about justice."

It was a pussy way to think, and Travis would never admit it out loud, but he was afraid to be alone anymore. He'd spent too much time being alone, with strangers manhandling him and trying to kill him. He'd thought they were past it all after his dad got out of jail, and they all got back together in the hospital, but now he didn't know what to think.

He recognized the FBI lady and her partner, and he thought he'd seen the old man on the news, but he didn't like the attorney general lady one bit. She had a predator's eyes and a mouth that looked like it didn't get a chance to smile very often.

What shook him most, though, was the look on his dad's face when she walked into the room. He was scared. Really scared; not like the time in the school with Mr. Menefee or in the van or on the hill outside the magazine. This was a kind of scared that didn't have any strength left in it.

They were taking too long. They'd said only a few minutes, and he supposed it hadn't been a whole lot longer than that, but it felt like forever. What could they be talking about that was so secret that they couldn't tell him, too? After all, he was in all of this just as deep as any of them were.

Suddenly, old fears of orphanages and foster homes flooded back into his mind. If they were there to take his parents away again, then they'd have a whole other fight on their hands.

He'd just about decided to storm back into the room when the conference room door opened up, and the sour-faced lady left, with Paul Boersky in tow.

Travis stood and moved quickly to block their path down the hallway, his arms outstretched to either side. The adults had little choice but to stop. "Why don't you people leave us alone?" he demanded.

Paul forced a chuckle, even as he looked embarrassed. "Hey, kiddo," he said. "You need to relax. Everything's going to be just fine."

Travis ignored him, never breaking his gaze from its lock on Emma Sanders's piercing green eyes. As he stared, he saw them soften. "Are you arresting us again?"

The attorney general smiled; not one of the condescending smirks he'd seen so often these past weeks, but a genuine, grandmotherly smile. She shook her head. "No, Travis, we're not here to arrest anyone."

It wasn't what he expected, and the answer left him momentarily speechless. "Oh," he said. He lowered his arms and let them pass on either side. Then he turned to face them again. "You know, they never did anything wrong."

Ms. Sanders stopped and turned. She reached out to touch the boy's face, but when he flinched, she withdrew her hand. For just a few seconds, she looked as if she might argue, but in the end, she just let the smile return. "You're right," she said. "Now, why don't you go on back inside? I think your folks are waiting for you."

Irene and the old senator were just leaving as Travis reentered the room, and then they were alone again, just the three of them. "Is it over?"

Jake looked first to Carolyn and then to his son. When he smiled, his eyes still looked sad. "Yes, Trav, it's finally over. We're free to go home."

Travis scowled. "Do we have one?"

Yes, they did. And it would be wherever the three of them could stand in one place together.

The significance of it all hit Jake first, and it hit him hard. The faces of old friends flooded his mind—all of them long dead; killed in an act of cruelty that by all rights should have taken his own life. The weight of all the lies and all the blood and all the fear suddenly blossomed to huge proportions, and in that moment, he knew he couldn't bear it anymore.

Family first, at all costs. He'd said the words so many times they'd come to lose their meaning. And here before him stood the reasons for all the pain and all the risk-taking. Gone, though, was the danger, and with it disappeared his reason to be strong.

The tears came from nowhere, propelled from his soul by an unspeakable grief. Pain he'd inflicted. Pain he'd endured. Childhood stolen from the heart of his only son.

"I need a hug," he tried to say. The sound was lost in the flood of his emotion.

But no one needed to hear his words. They came to him easily, willingly. Even the tough kid who rejected all gestures of tenderness was there. And they all cried, openly, and free of shame, cleansing the agony of all they'd endured.

Jake prayed that one day God might forgive the sins he'd committed to protect his family, but that could wait. For the time being, he was blessed with all the forgiveness a man could possibly ask for.

They were a family again. The Donovan family. And all that lay ahead of them was the future.